DAUGHTER OF LIGHT

Books by Morgan L. Busse

Follower of the Word series

Daughter of Light, BOOK ONE

Son of Truth, BOOK TWO

Heir of Hope, BOOK THREE

The Soul Chronicles series

Tainted, BOOK ONE

Awakened, BOOK TWO

DAUGHTER OF LIGHT

FOLLOWER OF THE WORD

BOOK ONE

MORGAN L. BUSSE

In darkness there is light!

Morgan L. Busse

an imprint of
GILEAD PUBLISHING

Published by Enclave Publishing, an imprint of Gilead Publishing,
Grand Rapids, Michigan
www.enclavepublishing.com

an Imprint of
GILEAD PUBLISHING

ISBN: 978-1-935929-49-9 (print)
ISBN: 978-1-935929-59-8 (eBook)

Daughter of Light
Copyright © 2012 by Morgan L. Busse

Cover design by Tomisalv Tulikin
Edited by Jeff Gerke

Printed in the United States of America

To God, Who is the Light in my darkness.
And to my husband, Dan, my best friend and greatest ally,
and the first one to encourage me to write.

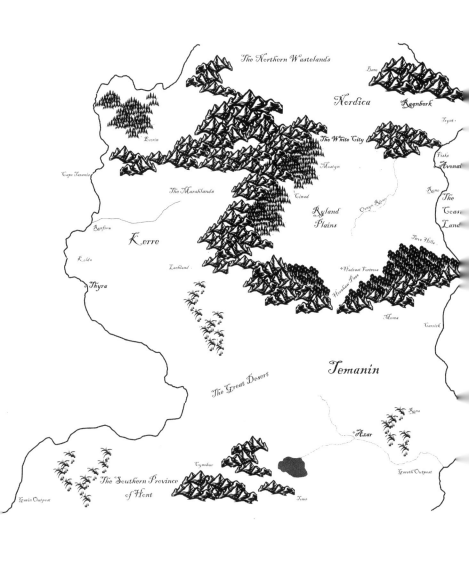

PROLOGUE

Mercia's lungs burned as she ran. She kept one hand clutched tightly to the bundle wvrapped around her middle. Her other hand grasped air as if to pull herself forward.

She could feel them coming. Closer. Closer.

Mercia glanced back. She could see nothing but towering trees, thick as two men and black as night. Naked bushes crowded between the trees. Snow covered the ground. A grey dismal sky hung overhead. White flecks fluttered through the air.

They were not close enough yet for her to see them. But they were coming, their foul presence growing stronger inside of her.

She turned forward and ran harder. The night sky grew darker overhead. More white flakes fell until the air looked like a white haze. Her nose and face froze, and her fingers grew numb. But she pushed herself forward. She couldn't stop now.

A single light flickered between the dark trees. Mercia staggered up against a thick trunk. Frigid air tore through her lungs. She tried to catch her breath. Could it be? Desperate hope flooded her. She squinted through the snowstorm at the single light. Had she finally found someone? Another step closer, and she could make out the dark silhouette of a small cabin. The light shone through a single square window. Above, the barest wisp of smoke made its way from the chimney. Someone had to live there—

The bundle around her middle began to squirm.

Mercia looked down and patted the bundle. "We're almost there," she said. Pain like a dagger tore through her chest as the truth of what she was about to do hit her.

She would be leaving her baby here.

Every maternal feeling she possessed rose up inside her chest, tightening her throat and flooding her eyes with moisture she thought she had already spent on the long journey here. But she had no choice.

Mercia choked back a sob and wiped at her eyes. What a price to pay for arrogance, for deception, for lust. Her daughter did not deserve to pay for the darkness committed by others. But perhaps someday her daughter would atone for them, finish the job . . .

The bundle began to whimper again, and a small fist made its way out of the woolen cloth.

"Shhh, little one." Mercia held a finger near her daughter's fist. Tiny fingers wound their way around hers. "Oh, Word," Mercia said quietly. She gazed down at her daughter. Did He hear her anymore? Care about her anymore? She would know soon enough . . . Soon she would be standing before Him.

A long howl rose up from the trees behind her.

Mercia clutched her daughter and shoved away from the tree. She glanced back. Nothing but trees and snow. She turned and ran toward the light. She should never have paused. She should have gone straight to the house and left her daughter.

Another howl echoed behind her, this time much closer.

"Word," Mercia prayed, her breath deep gasps, "please watch over my daughter, please— Please keep her safe . . ."

More lights appeared in the windows. Mercia pushed her body forward. She reached the cabin and ran around the corner. She found a door on the other side. There was no time to say goodbye— the wolves were almost upon her. She could hear someone shuffling around inside.

Mercia bent down and swept the snow away. Then she placed her daughter down at the threshold of the door. The blanket shifted, revealing a small face with white wisps of hair. Blue eyes stared up at her. Mercia bit back a cry of anguish. She stood and took a step back. A small hand began to reach in the air. She turned and fled toward the trees.

Tears streamed down her face. "Oh, Word, please keep her safe, please keep her safe," Mercia chanted between snatches of air. Long painful throbs raced along her side. She placed a hand on her ribs and kept running as far as she could from the cabin.

If only she had made it to the White City. Perhaps she could've found some of her people there. But she had run out of time. Out of every drop of it. She could only hope her daughter would find a home here, wherever here was.

A dark shape flew out from behind the trees.

Her time had come.

Mercia fell to her knees, gasping in air. Glittering yellow eyes watched her. A black wolf stepped out from the shadows. It stood almost as tall as a horse. Black spiked fur covered its body, and it was covered in snow. With a hard shake, it sent the snow flying. The putrid smell of rotting meat filled the air. The wolf lifted its head and let out a long howl, like the mangled scream of a dying animal.

Three more wolves stepped away from the trees.

Mercia curled into a ball and covered her face. "Word," she cried, "take care of my little one. And let her do what we were unable—"

Fangs like fire tore past her cloak and sunk into her neck. More came, slashing her shoulder, her side, her thighs. She choked back a gurgled scream. A numbing coldness followed the attacks, blocking away the frenzied tearing of her body.

Her powers would not save her this time. There were too many of them. She didn't even try. She had done what she had come to do. The others would never know of her daughter. Their twisted beasts could not sense one so young. She had saved her baby.

Blackness filled her vision. For one moment she regretted her wasted life. Then Mercia reached for the small light ahead of her, grateful that at the end she had turned back.

CHAPTER 1

Nothing changed during war. Weeds grew, the wind came and went, the sun still rose and set each day.

And yet at the same time, everything changed. Loved ones left to fight, rocking chairs remained empty, and only one dish and cup would be set out at dinner.

Rowen let out a sigh and sat back on her knees. Brown earth clung to her dress and fingers. She could feel the hot summer sun beat down on her head. Nearby stood the one-room cabin she had lived in as long as she could remember. Grey stones from the river formed the chimney. Thick dark logs were stacked and packed with mud. Dull yellow straw topped the small home. Vegetables grew beside the cabin in long rows. A fence made from broken branches and twine surrounded the garden, a garden that was sorely in need of her attention.

Nearby, the shadows from Anwin Forest crept closer to her garden. Rowen glanced at the forest. Tall, thick trees crowded out all light, leaving the forest floor in darkness. Dark green moss clung to the trunks. Broad ferns and prickly berry bushes spread between the trees like a blanket of green. Not one bird sang. Only the wind whispered through the trees.

Rowen shuddered and looked away. The war felt like those shadows: creeping toward her life, threatening to take away all she held dear. She focused on a large ugly weed and grabbed it.

Her father was safe, she knew it. She had received a letter from him only last week. She pulled on the weed, but it would not budge. She put both hands around the stem and tugged harder.

The war would end, and he would come home, and everything

would go back to the way it used to be. Sweat trickled down the side of her face. She yanked with all her might. The weed burst from the ground with a spray of dirt.

She dumped the weed on top of the pile next to her and moved on to the next one.

"Attacking the weeds, I see."

Rowen's head shot up. A short, grey-haired man dressed in stained white robes stood by the fence that surrounded her garden. He held a basket beneath one arm. Leafy greens and bright round berries brimmed over the sides. His hair was tied back from his brown wrinkled face.

"Noland," she said. "I wasn't expecting a visit from you."

"Do you need one?"

Rowen shook her head. "No. I'm feeling fine now. Thanks to you."

Noland studied her, then reached into his basket. "I was just in Anwin collecting herbs for my stores. Found some mint growing back that way." He nodded toward the forest. He pulled out a handful of the small green leaves. "Here, try this with hot water."

Rowen stood and walked toward the fence. She hesitantly reached for the mint. Noland had never offered her anything before.

He looked at her with concern. "You're sure you're all right?"

She took the mint and stepped back. "Yes." She touched her face with her free hand. "Just tired."

"No lingering pain? No fever?"

"No."

"Good." Noland straightened. "You gave me quite a scare. Never seen a sickness like it."

"Never felt anything like it."

A look of relief crept across his face.

Her spirits lifted at the sight. Was she finally being accepted into the fold?

"You let me know if anything changes, all right?" he said.

"I will."

His smile broadened. "Well, I should be going. The missus is waiting." Noland raised a hand and shook a finger at her. "And don't work too much on that garden. Make sure you rest." He turned and headed toward the village below.

Rowen watched him until he disappeared down the hill. She leaned across the fence and closed her eyes. The sun felt warm across her face. But not as warm as the glow of acceptance. All she needed was her father to come home untouched by the war and everything would be perfect.

She opened her eyes She looked behind her at the small garden and nodded. She would finish the weeding tomorrow.

Rowen entered the cabin. A long wooden table filled most of the room. Across the table stood the fireplace. A large black kettle hung inside the opening, just above a mound of glowing coals. Dried herbs and garlic braids were draped over the mantle. Sticks were stacked neatly to the left.

Two windows were built into the wooden walls, one to the right and one to the left. The right one faced Anwin Forest. Below the window sat a rocking chair and one small bed covered in a faded patch quilt.

A chest stood in front of the bed. Inside it were a couple personal items: a lock of her mother's brown hair, the smallsword her father had brought back for her during one of his trips to the White City, and a leather glove. Her father believed that a woman should be able to defend herself as well as any man, and so he had taught her how to use the blade. The glove had been a gift along with the sword.

Rowen went around the table and pulled the kettle out from the fireplace. The water had boiled dry. She looked in the nearby bucket. Empty as well. She gave a small sigh and dropped the mint on the table. She would have to go down to the village and retrieve more water.

The left window faced Cinad, the small village that lay just down the hill from her cabin. A low table with a cracked pitcher and bowl sat beneath the window. A single cupboard stood in the corner. Three chipped plates and cups lined its dusty shelves with a tin box on the very top.

Rowen undid the knot behind her and pulled the dirty apron off. She dumped it in the corner, then grabbed the bucket and headed out toward the village.

Cinad was one of many small villages scattered across the Ryland Plains. It wasn't much to look at, just a collection of wood homes thatched with straw. But it was the only home Rowen had ever known.

The smell of smoke clung to the warm summer air. Far away, the faint clang of the blacksmith's hammer echoed across the valley. Children with long sticks ran behind tall thin metal loops they guided down the single dirt road that ran through the village. Beyond the shabby homes and stores lay hills of golden wheat.

Near the end of the village stood the well. It was made of stone and topped with a shingled cone roof. Rowen could see a crowd of women collecting around the well. Her stomach gave a small flip, and she tightened her hold on the bucket. The last thing she wanted was to arrive in the middle of Cinad's gossip time.

Rowen was about to turn back, but she caught sight of her friend Calya. Calya stood to the side, talking with a couple of the younger village woman. Her hair, long and brown, was pulled back in a knot at the nape of her neck. She held a bucket with one hand and a baby on her hip. A little girl with long brown braids stood next to her.

Rowen took a deep breath and let it out with a whoosh. She could brave a visit to the well if Calya was there.

She made her way down the hill and passed the first set of houses. A couple of children between the cabins looked up and watched her. She lifted her chin higher and hurried along. The sound of the blacksmith's hammer grew louder the closer she got to the open workspace.

Inside the dark interior of the blacksmith's hut she saw Cleon bent over the anvil. His father worked the billows. Cleon glanced up. His black curly hair looked wild with the red light from the forge behind it. He stared straight at her.

Rowen fumbled, his look unnerving her. She caught herself and moved on toward the well.

The women ignored her as she approached. Good. Rowen heaved an inward sigh. She could handle that. Let them talk amongst themselves, and she would retrieve water and leave. Then Calya caught sight of her.

"Rowen! Over here!"

Rowen stopped and turned. "Calya," she said. The other women grew quiet. Rowen shoved down the feeling of unease. Calya hurried toward her with her baby. Brighid, her little girl, followed.

Calya looked her up and down. "You look much better." Calya smiled. "I don't like finding people unconscious! When I found you, I thought . . . Well, it terrified me. And Noland wouldn't say anything at first. But I saw the fear in his eyes too." Then she seemed to grow timid. "H-how are you feeling now? Do you remember anything yet? I mean, you were sick for weeks."

Rowen stared down at the empty bucket she held in both hands. She didn't know what to say. She could remember nothing of those last few weeks. "Oh, I'm tired." Rowen looked back up at Calya. "As if everything had been taken out of me."

"Should you be out so soon, then?"

Rowen gave a small laugh and held up her bucket. "And how else would I get water?"

"Someone would have gotten it for you. Everyone pitched in while you were sick. Noland's wife, Sarah, made broth for you, you know. Old Sonja brought over an extra quilt. And I even wrote your father."

Rowen almost dropped her bucket. "You wrote my father?"

"Yes. Although I haven't heard back yet." She shifted the baby on her hip. "The entire village was worried about you, Rowen."

Rowen realized the other women had quietly gathered around and were listening to the conversation. A lump stuck inside her throat. They had cared about her? Hesitantly she looked around. Lenora, the miller's daughter, gave her a small smile. Grace and Tessa merely looked at her, but it was better than the cold stares she usually received from them.

Rowen looked back at Calya. "Thank you. Thank you all."

Calya smiled. "Come now, let's fill your bucket and get you home so you can rest."

Rowen blinked. Calya placed a hand on her shoulder and steered her toward the well. Rowen stumbled forward, her mind still spinning.

"See," Cayla said, "I told you they would come around."

Old feelings of bitterness swirled inside her. Rowen didn't bother to point out how long it had taken for the village to finally accept her—that she had lived here all her life and was now past marrying age, or that they'd come to care for her only when she'd been so ill she'd nearly died. But Calya's kindness and the other women's warm reaction to her quickly dispelled the bitter feeling.

Rowen hooked her bucket to the rope and dropped it down into the well. A splash echoed up the hole. Moments later she hauled the bucket up, placing one hand in front of the other and pulling until the dripping bucket came in view. She secured the rope and unhooked the bucket.

"Would you like me to help you up to the house?" Calya asked.

"No." Rowen turned with bucket in hand. "I think I can handle this." She could feel her strength returning. But it wasn't fully back yet. She would need to lie down once she reached home, after she put the kettle on and washed up.

"Then I'll stop by tomorrow with some dough so you can have a starter for bread."

Rowen hadn't even thought about her food stores. "Thank you." By now, her own starter had probably gone rancid.

Calya said goodbye. Brighid peeked her head out and shyly waved. Even Lenora said farewell in a quiet voice. Grace and Tessa merely nodded.

Rowen gripped the bucket firmly between both hands and began her walk back through the village. Had things really changed? She passed the children again. Instead of hurrying past, she looked at them and gave them a small smile. They stared back. At least they didn't run away like they usually did. One returned to rolling his thin metal hoop and pushing it with his stick. The other children followed, and the group disappeared behind the house.

Rowen walked past the blacksmith. The shop was quiet. She looked over, and she found Cleon watching her. An uneasiness passed over her at the intense look on his face. She gripped the bucket and moved steadily forward.

At the edge of the village, Rowen hurried up the hill to her own cabin. Water slopped and sloshed over the sides of the bucket. But she didn't care. Her mind was elsewhere.

She entered the house and walked around the table toward the kettle. She poured half of the water into the black pot then pushed the pot over the coals. She headed toward the table below the window and filled the pitcher from the bucket. Finally, she put the bucket down and poured water from the pitcher into the bowl.

Rowen dipped her hands into the water. It was tepid, and it turned a muddy brown as the dirt from her garden slowly rinsed from her hands. She reached for the block of soap and worked up a thick lather. She looked out the window as she scrubbed.

She spotted Calya and some other women walking together, carrying their own buckets. In the past, Rowen would have wondered what they were talking about. She would watch them and burn with the desire to be a part of their group. At other times she would feel loneliness and hurt, or be sure they were talking about her. But today was the first time she had been accepted. Perhaps not embraced, exactly, but it was close enough for a start. She was one of them now.

Warmth spread from her heart across her entire body. Rowen smiled. She glanced down to see if her hands were clean—

She stopped and frowned. A patch of white skin caught her eye. Slowly she brought her right hand up to the window. *What is this?* Pale white skin covered her entire palm, spreading out like a large snowflake toward her fingertips. The rest of the skin on her hand was fair and looked normal. Only her palm seemed affected. Puzzled, Rowen dipped her hand back into the water, scrubbed for a moment, then brought her palm back up. The white mark was still there.

Turning her palm from left to right, she studied the strange mark on her hand. Her frown deepened. This was her hand. She knew it well. No paleness or any other discoloration had ever been there before. But wait: Her recent illness had been so strange. Could this be a lingering effect from that?

Rowen looked at her other hand, both sides. No white mark on her left hand. She searched her arms. No white patches. She stepped away from the window and raised her dress. She bent over and twisted from side to side, searching every part of her skin for anything unusual. Her legs looked fine as far as she could see.

Rowen dropped her dress and touched her cheek, wishing she could see her face. She checked her reflection in her wash basin, but it was too soapy to show much. There couldn't be anything there—if something had looked strange, Calya would have mentioned it. Or one of the other women. Or the children. They'd had no problem in the past pointing out what was strange about her.

She raised her hand again. The pale pattern remained on her palm. What in all the Lands could this be? Perhaps she should tell Noland—

A sharp knock sounded at her door.

"Coming." Rowen reached for the white linen that hung on a nearby peg. She dried her hands and dumped the rag on the long table before answering the door.

On the threshold stood a courier dressed in dark blue. The colors of the White City. "Rowen Mar?" the young man said, his voice somber.

Fear swept across her body, leaving her weak and breathless. "Yes?" Her voice cracked through her words. Rowen reached out and gripped the door. It was silly to be afraid. There could be any number of reasons the White City would send a courier to her home. Perhaps it was just a letter from her father. After all, Calya had written to him about her illness. But never had a White City courier brought a simple letter. No, only one reason made sense.

The courier raised his hand and held out a cream colored parchment. "I'm sorry." A look of pity covered his face as he handed her the letter.

Rowen stared at the parchment. No, no. It couldn't be. Her hand moved toward the letter as if detached from the rest of her body. Her fingers clutched the cold parchment. The young man said something else, but Rowen could not hear him over the rush inside her head.

Somewhere in her mind she saw the courier disappear down the path. Rowen backed into the house and sat down on the long bench next to the table. She turned the folded parchment around and found the seal of the White City pressed firmly in blue wax. Her finger shook near the opening. Did she really want to know?

With a quick thrust, she broke the wax and unfolded the piece of parchment.

To Rowen Mar,
We regret to inform you . . .

Rowen let the letter fall to the floor. Her father was dead.

Commander Jedrek Mar's body was brought to the village the next day. Many dignitaries and military men accompanied the coffin. Rowen neither remembered nor cared. To others, he had been a top commander in the Northern Army, a man highly respected and admired. To Rowen, he had been her only family and friend.

Everyone gathered south of the village. Mounds of rocks and flowers stood in straight rows below a lone gnarled tree that had somehow found root away from Anwin Forest. The village burial place. The air felt warm and stifling under the bright summer sun. Bodies pressed close together in a ragged line that led to a new hole in the ground right near the base of the tree.

Rowen stood alone near the hole, with a white flower clutched in her hand. Only once did she look down into it. She caught a brief glimpse of the coffin inside the dark gap, then looked away. It hurt too badly to think of her father inside that wooden box.

Instead, she stared numbly ahead at the fields of wheat. Men from the village began to shovel dirt into the hole. She could hear each dull thud as the dirt hit the coffin. She shattered inside with each sound. But on the outside she stood as still as possible, as if she were frozen in time. She would not cry. Not here, not now.

After the hole was filled, the line of mourners began to walk by, each stopping to place a rock on the growing mound that covered her father's coffin. Some of them then turned to speak to her, but Rowen could hardly hear what they said. It was as if her mind and body had been turned off. She could only watch and hope the day would end soon.

A hand fell across her shoulder. Rowen started at the touch and turned.

Calya looked at her with sorrow etched across her face. "Oh Rowen, I'm so sorry." Rowen worked her mouth to say something, but her voice was gone. "No need to speak," Calya said. "I just want you to know that if there is anything Bardon or I can do," she said, referencing her husband, "please let us know."

Rowen swallowed and nodded. Unfortunately, the only thing she wanted right now was her father back.

Calya gave her shoulder a squeeze. "And that goes for the whole village, you know that. We'll take care of you for as long as you need."

Rowen nodded and turned back toward the growing mound of rocks. Calya stood by her until the last stone was placed on the mound. Then Rowen moved toward the rock mound. She could feel every eye in the village watching her as she laid the flower on the topmost rock.

The village mason moved to her side. Rowen stared down at the mound, hardly believing that beneath it lay her father. He placed a specially carved rock at the head of the mound.

Jedrek Mar, it read. *Loving Husband and Father. Defender of the North.*

Rowen's eyes lingered on the words. Invisible hands began to squeeze her throat. People shuffled around her, some crying quietly, others whispering. Rowen could feel the floodwaters of her own grief welling up inside of her.

Noland came to stand beside her. He said a couple of words to the crowd, then the villagers dispersed. Overhead, the summer sun continued to burn brightly. Rowen stood in the shade of the tree, waiting for the others to leave.

As she turned to go back to her own home, her eye landed on another mound nearby. Small purple and white flowers were sprawled across the rocks. It was her mother's grave. Separated for years by death, Jedrek and Ann Mar were finally together again.

Rowen bit her lip and ran back toward her cabin. And there, in the one room cabin she had shared with her now deceased parents, she let her grief flow over.

Rowen sat beside the long wooden table, slowly sipping hot mint water. Calya bustled around the cabin. Outside she could hear the giggles of Calya's two daughters as they played just below the window.

"I'll have Bardon split some more firewood for you," Calya said, eyeing the low pile of wood near the fireplace. She picked up a couple of sticks and tossed them on the hot coals beneath the kettle.

Rowen watched her friend for a moment. "I'm sorry I'm not much company today. Or for the last three weeks for that matter." She stood and moved toward the bowl to wash out her cup.

"Don't worry." Calya glanced over her shoulder. "I'm just here to help out." She pushed the kettle over the fire.

Rowen finished washing out her cup and placed it in the nearby cupboard. Then she glanced up at the tin box that lay on the top shelf. She had only a few coins left from her father's military stipend. Panic swelled inside her chest. Looking over at Calya, Rowen knew she could never ask her friend for money. Calya already had done enough to help her through this time of grieving.

Rowen closed the cupboard doors. But food and help would not pay for more fabric to mend her worn-out dress or nightgown. She glanced down and fingered the new hole near her waist.

The mark on her palm caught her eye. She glanced over her shoulder. Cayla was mixing something in a large wooden bowl. Keeping her back to Calya, Rowen raised her hand. She really needed to have this checked out. With a sigh, she grabbed her apron from a nearby peg. She would visit Noland later that afternoon, after the weeding was done.

"Rowen?" a masculine voice said.

Rowen's head snapped around at the sound.

Beside the fence stood Cleon. His blacksmith apron was gone, replaced with a faded white shirt that showed how muscular his chest was. The sleeves were rolled back, revealing arms that used a heavy hammer. His face was clean-shaven. Wild black curly hair hung around a round face that ended in a heavy jaw. He looked at her intently with amber eyes.

"Cleon." Her heart sunk. She dropped the weed she had just pulled and stood. She wished Calya were here now. But Calya had left to take her little ones home for a nap.

Cleon leaned over the fence and placed his arms along the top post. The fence creaked under his weight. "Care to take a walk?"

Her heart sank further. Yes, Cleon was definitely here for a reason. And she suspected she knew what it was. Rowen swallowed the bitter taste that suddenly filled her mouth. She already knew her answer. No. But she would need to find a tactful way to tell him. Perhaps a walk would give her time to find the right words to bring him down gently.

"It would be a . . . pleasure," Rowen said, choking on the words inside.

Cleon straightened up and moved toward the gate. The self-assured grin on his face almost made her turn back. Rowen swallowed bitterly again as he opened the gate. "I know just the place," he said, extending his arm toward her. She forced herself to take his arm.

Cleon pulled her close to his side. Rowen narrowed her eyes at his possessiveness, but said nothing. She would let him know where she stood with him soon enough.

Cleon led her away from the house toward a small path that followed the tree line. He spoke little as they walked. Rowen remained silent as well, her mind racing for the right words to say. The path turned and headed into the forest.

"My father's thinking about retiring come next planting." They passed the first line of trees. "Turning the business over to me."

"Oh." A knot began to form in her stomach.

"And I've begun construction on a house down at the south end of Stott's field."

Rowen didn't answer. Cleon didn't seem to notice. Apparently he had thought a lot about the future.

For one moment she tried to imagine a life with Cleon. He had a respectable trade, a rising place of prominence in the village, and wasn't bad to look at. But there was something about him, something unsettling. Something about his eyes . . .

Cleon steered her toward a small clearing amongst the trees. It had been a favorite haunt of the village children long ago, but now with the war and the increase of strangers traveling through the Ryland Plains, families kept their little ones closer to home.

Cleon stopped and turned to face her. "You must know why I've asked you here." He stood so close that Rowen had to look up. She could see each dark curly strand around his face. Her heart began to thud inside her chest. Perhaps coming with Cleon had been a bad idea.

Cleon didn't wait for her to answer. Instead he placed his hands on her shoulders.

"Cleon, wait." Rowen took a step back. He was moving too fast—

Cleon moved in close again. "You must realize that not many men in our village would think of bonding with you." Cleon looked down at her. Rowen could smell the smoke of the smithy on his clothing. "But times have changed. Your father has died—" Rowen scowled at his calloused words— "leaving you all alone. But I can change that."

He placed a rough, thick hand on her cheek. Rowen turned away. Cleon forced her face back. "I want you to bond with me." He moved his head down to kiss her. Rowen tried to twist away. Cleon forced her face still and pressed his lips hard down on hers.

Rowen jerked out of his grasp. "Cleon, no!"

His head followed her movement. "I can take care of you, Rowen. And you know no other man will have you."

"Let go!"

Cleon tightened his grip on her shoulders. Rowen grabbed his wrist and—

Time slowed.

A strange sensation rose from deep within her, racing toward her right arm. It surged out where her palm held his wrist.

Cleon stopped talking. He backed away for a moment, looking at her in puzzlement. "Wha-What are you doing to me?"

"I-I don't know!" Her head pounded. What was happening?

His eyes went wide with fear. "Let go of me!" Cleon pulled at his arm.

Rowen tried, but her hand would not let go. Her vision blurred. Images began to fill her mind, images of Cleon. His father beating him while his mother cowered in the corner . . . Kicking a dog behind the shed until it lay still . . . Dunking a small boy in a stream while others laughed around him. Over and over, pictures from Cleon's life flashed across her eyes. Rowen began to feel dizzy. She became aware of eddies of hatred swirling inside of her. Was it his hatred or hers?

Her vision began to clear. Rowen felt like she was coming up to the surface of a clear lake after being underwater too long. She drank in great draughts of air.

Cleon yanked his hand away. "What did you do to me?" he shouted.

Rowen tried to talk, but her body would not respond. She could only stand there breathing heavily.

"Answer me!"

She glanced up into Cleon's eyes. They were livid with rage. "I don't know," she said, finding her voice. She took a step back. "I saw . . . Cleon, I had no idea . . ."

Cleon snarled and raised his hand as if to hit her. Rowen stared at him in shock. He wouldn't dare—

"Don't ever touch me again, you witch!" He stared at her a moment longer, then lowered his hand. But the look in his eyes told her that if he could have, he would have struck her. "The village will hear of this." He pointed a finger at her. "We will not tolerate witchery."

Before Rowen could reply, Cleon spit on her. She felt the warm liquid dribble down her cheek. He turned and stalked back toward the village. Rowen sank to her knees.

What just happened?

Her hand shook and she wiped the spittle away. Her mind reeled from the feelings and images she had just experienced. What had she done to Cleon?

A glimmer of light caught her eye. Rowen brought her hand away from her face and stared. The mark she had discovered on her palm weeks ago now glowed, lighting up her entire hand.

Her heart thudded faster inside her chest. What was happening to her? Even as she watched, the light began to dim until it faded to a pale white across her palm. But the mark was still there.

Rowen scrambled to her feet and raced down the path. Whatever this was, she had to get rid of it.

She raced underneath the trees, shadows flashing above her. Rowen turned down the path. The roof rose in view. Sharp pain erupted along her side. She pressed a hand against her ribs and ran to the door.

Rowen flung the door open and stood there panting. She squinted in the dark cabin, searching for something she could use to wash the white mark off. There. She headed toward the pitcher and bowl. She poured the water into the bowl and shoved the pitcher aside.

She grabbed the block of soap and began to scrub, alternating between the soap and her fingernails. Soon her hand grew raw, causing the strange white mark to stand out more from the reddened skin. But it would not come off.

Rowen began to shake. What was this thing on her hand? She turned and looked around the room for anything that might take the white skin off. Nothing. In desperation, she turned back to the basin and poured more water in. Perhaps she—

"She's here," a voice called out behind her.

Rowen jerked back. The ceramic bowl went crashing to the floor, scattering water and jagged pieces across the packed dirt. She turned toward the door.

Cleon stood in the doorway, his arms folded across his chest.

Rowen took a step back, bumping into the small table still wet with spilled water.

In three strides Cleon stood before her. Before she could move, he grabbed her by the wrist and dragged her toward the door. "Here's the witch!"

Rowen tried to pull her hand back, but she was no match for Cleon's strength. Bright sunlight filled her vision as Cleon dragged her outside.

"Here's the proof." Cleon held her hand up by the wrist.

Rowen stared at the people gathered. The whole village was there. Even Calya, her baby held tightly in both arms.

But Calya's eyes were not on Rowen's face. No, Calya was staring at the hand Cleon held in the air. Rowen quickly closed it into a fist. But it was too late. Calya glanced back at Rowen with fear and shock.

"She tried to kill me with this." Cleon shook her wrist. "She led me into the forest, then said if I didn't bond with her, she would kill me."

The crowd shifted uncomfortably. Rowen felt like she had been slapped across the face. "What? I never—" Cleon dug his fingers into the underside of her wrist. Rowen gasped in pain. It took everything inside of her not to cry out more.

Cleon took advantage of her silence by sharing his account of their brief time together.

Rowen tried to work through the haze of pain and shock to find a rebuff to his words. Everything was spinning out of control. "No, wait! That's not—"

"No more words, witch!" Cleon gave her a hard shake. Rowen felt her teeth rattle. The crowd began to murmur.

"What do we do?" someone said.

"We cannot let her live!" another cried.

"Burn her," a woman said nearby.

Rowen stopped fighting. A rush filled her mind, drowning out the people shouting around her.

Burn her.

Her knees gave out at the thought. Cleon jerked her back up by the wrist. A painful cry escaped her lips.

"We cannot kill Jedrek's daughter."

The name of her father quieted the crowd. Rowen looked over to find Noland standing nearby.

"He did much for this village and country," Noland said.

Cleon snorted. "Did Jedrek know what his daughter is? After all, she's not his blood."

"He took her into his home, and therefore she is his daughter."

The crowd began to murmur again. Rowen felt lightheaded. What was going to happen to her?

"Let a council of elders decide her fate," someone called out.

"Yes, yes, a council of elders."

More and more voices called for a council. Rowen felt her wrist begin to slip between Cleon's fingers. He tightened his grip.

"Yes, a council of elders should be called." Noland moved to stand beside Cleon and Rowen. "It is the right way to decide what should be done with her."

Now that this had been resolved, the crowd began to disperse. As the people passed her, some looked away and others glanced at her with fear. A woman spit in Rowen's direction, a rock flew over her head, a dog barked nearby.

"Always knew she didn't belong," she overhead someone say.

Suddenly those last few weeks of warmth from the village vanished in an instant. She didn't belong. Rowen swallowed. She had never belonged.

She caught sight of Calya, but her friend avoided her look, turning instead and heading back toward the village. Tears prickled her eyes. "Calya," Rowen whispered. Calya continued down the hill, never once looking back.

"So what do we do with her while we wait for the council?" Cleon said, shaking her hand. Rowen turned to Noland. Perhaps he would have compassion on her?

Instead Noland looked at her with a cold glare. "You are to stay in your house until the council decides your fate. And if you are a witch . . ." he left his threat hanging in the air.

Rowen felt all hope leave her chest. Her eyes grew hot with tears. Stubbornly, she closed them tight. She would not let these two see her cry.

Suddenly Cleon released her hand. "In you go," he said, opening the door. Rowen stumbled in, her hand tingling from Cleon's tight grip.

He slammed the door shut behind her.

Rowen heard the two men's voices slowly fade. With a gasp, she slid to the ground and cried.

CHAPTER
2

Rowen walked down the middle of the village the next day, her hands tied behind her back. Two of the Stotts' boys walked on either side of her with grim faces. The sun felt even hotter today, blazing down on her head. They walked past the first couple of houses, then the blacksmith's. No hammer rang today. Rowen stared straight ahead, refusing to look at the dark interior.

They passed a few more houses before she realized they were heading toward Noland's house. Of course. It made sense. His house was the only one big enough to contain everyone who wished to be a part of the hearing. The thought of seeing so many people made her stomach knot up.

People had gathered outside the two-story house, mainly women and children. Rowen saw a couple of women pull their little ones closer, as if she were some kind of enemy. Calya stood farther away, outside the crowd and in the shadow of the house, her baby wrapped around her middle.

"Calya!" Rowen lurched toward her friend. Calya looked up at the sound of her name. Fear mingled with hope. The Stotts' boys grabbed her arms, but Rowen stood her ground. Calya would come.

Calya looked around, then took a step forward. "Please tell me this isn't true." She drew closer to Rowen. "You didn't do anything to Cleon. He's making it all up, right?"

Rowen opened her mouth, then hesitated. She couldn't lie. Especially not to Calya.

A guarded look came over Calya's face. She began to back away and shielded her baby.

"Wait, Calya. Please!"

"No, Rowen. I thought I had only seen something on your hand. Some blister or stain. But it's true, isn't it? You're a witch."

Rowen wanted to answer, to deny everything. Instead, she found her voice gone and her mind paralyzed. Maybe they were right. Maybe she was a witch. It wasn't as if she could just ask her real parents. Or even her adoptive parents. Who knew what she was?

Calya didn't wait for her answer. She turned and hurried into a nearby house. The door slammed shut behind her. Rowen stared at the door, feeling as though a hole had been punched through her middle.

A hand grabbed her arm. "Get moving!" The older Stotts boy shoved her forward.

Rowen caught herself and numbly began trudging on ahead. *Never belonged.* She felt the words close in around her. She had never belonged.

They arrived at Noland's house. "Watch your step," the younger Stotts boy said. Rowen brought her mind back long enough to carefully step up and enter.

Smothering heat filled the narrow entryway inside the house. Beyond the door stood men and women, their backs pressed up against the white-washed walls and even up the staircase. Dirt and sweat and dung mingled with the scent of mint and roses. They talked in quiet voices that echoed inside the house like a dull buzz.

Rowen followed the Stotts boy down the hall. Sweat poured down her face and neck. Her thin dress stuck uncomfortably to her body. People backed away from her as far as they could. Rowen kept her face down. But she knew they were watching her like carrion birds waiting for an animal to die.

The hallway opened up into one large room. More people stood along the inside wall here. At the far end of the room was a large stone fireplace.

Four men stood before it. The first man was Sylas, owner of the local mill. His light brown hair and thin mustache were combed back perfectly. Next to him was John, head of the Stotts family. Wild tawny hair and beard crowded around his face. Cleon's father towered over the other two men. Kardin was a man built more like a black bear. He stood with arms folded across his chest, his face showing the barest trace of dark stubble. His eyes, an odd amber color, followed her every movement. Noland stood at the far end in faded white robes and his hair pulled back.

Two windows graced the outer wall. Bright sunlight filtered through the dusky glass. The Stotts boys led Rowen to the wall between the windows. They untied her hands, then scurried away as if scalded.

Rowen brought her hands around and clasped them together. She stared at the wooden floor, afraid she would collapse at any moment.

"We are gathered here today," Sylas said, "to determine the validity of the charges against Rowen Mar, daughter of the late Jedrek and Ann Mar. And the charge is . . . witchcraft."

At the word *witchcraft,* the entire room went silent. Rowen squeezed her fingers until they hurt.

"Tell us about Mor," Sylas said.

Rowen looked at Sylas, surprised by the question. Why did they want to know about Mor? He'd died over a year ago—

Oh.

She swallowed and looked back down. "I-I knew Mor a little."

"Did you touch him?"

Her head shot up. "No. Never. We hardly ever spoke to each other." Like everyone else in the village, Mor would have nothing to do with her. She remembered feeling bad when she'd heard of his death. He had been soon to bond with Sylas's other daughter, Grace. Instead he'd been found dead in Anwin without a mark on him.

The four men conversed quietly among each other. Rowen stared down on her hands. She could guess what they were saying. She'd had the opportunity, since she lived right next to Anwin. And someone could say she had cause. Someone could say she had been jealous of Grace. There was no reason for them to believe otherwise.

Would she be tried for every villager who had ever died?

"Tell us what happened the other day with Cleon."

Rowen stared down at her clasped hands. "Cleon asked me to go for a walk. I did. He took me into Anwin. And then . . ." Heat spread across her face. "He tried to kiss me."

A murmur spread across the crowd.

"And?" Sylas said.

"I didn't want him to. I told him to let go. He took hold of me, so I grabbed him with . . . With my hand."

The murmur died down.

"Show us your hand."

This was the part she had feared. For one moment, Rowen imagined running from here instead of answering. She'd rush through the house and past the people and run as far away from here as she could. She pictured herself racing through the trees of Anwin and leaving all of this behind.

"Your hand," a deep masculine voice said.

Rowen looked up and found Kardin staring at her. Her mouth went dry. Cleon looked so much like his father. She slowly unclasped her hands. The room became silent. She lifted her right one up. Every eye followed her movement. There was no running away, no escape from this mark on her hand. She opened her fist.

Several people gasped and stepped back.

"I don't know what it is," Rowen said in defense, her voice cracking. "It showed up weeks ago, right after my illness—"

"You never said anything about a mark when you were sick," Noland said from his place nearby. "And I never saw one."

"I don't believe her," John Stotts said.

Rowen felt the blood drain from her face. She slowly lowered her hand.

"There are stories of people who can kill just with a touch of their hand," John said. "And if you remember, not a mark was found on Mor either."

"But Rowen did not kill Cleon," Sylas pointed out.

Hope rose inside Rowen. Perhaps she had an ally . . .

"No, she used her mark to threaten me."

The flame of hope vanished. Rowen turned and watched. The people made way for Cleon. He walked into the middle of the room and looked over at her. "She threatened to kill me if I did not bond with her." Cleon then turned toward the elders. "When I said no, she touched me with that cursed hand of hers."

Rage shot through Rowen. "What?" she sputtered, unable to keep silent. "I did no such thing—"

"Silence!" John yelled.

"Will I not be allowed to defend m—"

"*Silence!*"

Rowen snapped her mouth shut. Cleon looked at her like a cat with a mouse.

"I did ask her for a walk the other day." Cleon turned to face the crowd. "I had thought about asking her to bond with me. With Jedrek Mar gone, I wanted to take care of her. I took her into Anwin to talk. We stopped in that little field meadow just beyond her cabin. But before I could say anything, she grabbed me and demanded that I bond with her."

Rowen felt like she was going to retch. *She* demanded *him*? Never!

"I was so shocked I didn't know what to do. Then she tried to get into my mind—"

"How?" Sylas said.

Cleon turned toward the elders. "What?"

"How did she try to get into your mind?"

"With that hand of hers." Cleon gestured toward Rowen. "She grabbed me. Next thing I know, I was seeing things."

No, Rowen wanted to shout. *You were seeing yourself.*

"It felt like she was choking me. I couldn't breathe. I finally shook her off and ran. I came right back to the village and told all of you."

The elders turned and began debating again in low tones. Cleon stood in the middle of the room with his arms crossed. He had his back to Rowen and watched the crowd. Men and women turned and talked softly to each other.

Rowen knew she had lost the battle. There would be no more questions. No one believed her. She'd never belonged, whereas

Cleon was one of their own. And even if they did believe Rowen's story, nothing could explain the mark on her hand. Everyone could see it was more than a natural blemish. And something *did* happen to Cleon. Some power had risen inside of her and swept across his mind.

Perhaps she *was* a witch.

Rowen glanced at the elders and wondered what her sentence would be. She had heard stories of people being burned for witchcraft. Never had she imagined her own village would do that. Never had she imagined it might happen to *her*.

They would put her to death. There was no other choice. Witchcraft was not tolerated in the Ryland Plains, and therefore she would need to be cleansed.

A dull ache filled her middle. For a couple weeks she had finally belonged here. Cinad had become her home at last. The Stotts had brought her smoked meat. The Kaspers had given her fruit from their orchard. Many other families had brought grain for the winter. Noland and his wife had stopped by a couple times to chat and drink hot mint water. And Calya . . . Rowen shut her eyes and forced the ache back down. But this would be her home no more, no matter what the elders decided.

Sylas motioned for those gathered to be quiet. A blanket of silence fell across the room. Rowen gripped her arms tightly across her stomach. Hopes and dreams flashed across her mind: bonding with these people, children of her own laughing outside a small wooden home with a garden in back, and growing old with the man she had chosen to share her life with. Instead, she stared at the elders and found herself waiting for the words that would end her life.

"We, the elders of Cinad, in light of recent events, have chosen to pronounce Rowen Mar guilty of witchery."

Rowen felt her knees buckle at Sylas's words.

She was guilty. She couldn't deny it. She hadn't made a potion or uttered an incantation, but there was no escaping the fact that a power lived inside of her. One that had been triggered by the touch of this strange mark on her hand.

The room began to spin. Rowen mentally grabbed what strength she had left and forced herself upright. It took a moment for her body to obey, but her stubbornness won. She would not pass out.

"However," Sylas said, "she is the daughter of one of our most prestigious citizens, a man who gave his heart and his life for both Cinad and the country of the Ryland Plains. With that in view, we have decided against the sentence of execution."

Her mind tried to comprehend what Sylas was saying. They weren't going to kill her? Voices rose and fell around her.

"We have decided that her sentence will be exile. Permanent and irrevocable banishment from Cinad."

The crowd let out a murmur that sounded almost like some of them were disappointed they were not going to get to burn her.

Rowen's thoughts raced. Exile? But where would she go?

Sylas looked at her and continued. "You have two days to pack whatever you can carry and leave this village, never to return. Your home and land will be confiscated and auctioned off, along with whatever else you leave behind. Should you ever return to Cinad, you will be arrested and put to death. Do you understand?"

Rowen nodded, too dazed to speak.

"Good. This hearing is now adjourned."

At once, the house filled with the clamor of voices. She could hear the people discussing her fate. Rowen just stood there stunned. Kardin glared at her. The other three elders ignored her, including Noland.

The two Stotts boys moved past the crowd and walked up to her. "Time to go," the older one said. The younger boy held out a thin piece of rope. Rowen brought her hands back around and felt the rope bite into her wrists as the boy tied her hands together. The older boy grabbed her by the arm and led her past the crowd and back outside.

Everyone stared at her as she was marched through the village. Rowen caught Calya glancing out a window, only to retreat back into the shadows once she realized Rowen was looking back.

Rowen looked away, her eyes swelling with tears. That one gesture from Calya was the last nail placed into the coffin of her life. But she would not show weakness. She took a deep breath and willed away her tears as she passed by the familiar homes and families gathered.

It wasn't until she was pushed inside her home and the door firmly shut behind her that Rowen collapsed onto the dirt floor, heaving with emotions. She knew she should be grateful that her sentence had been exile and not death, but that didn't stop the torrent of fear from rushing through her.

She had spent her entire life in Cinad. She had no skills, save gardening. She could hardly sew, and she knew only enough about cooking to get by. The chest by her bed caught her attention. Rowen looked at the chest. She also knew how to use the smallsword inside. But who needed a gardener who could defend herself?

And where would she go? She had visited Mostyn once, a couple days' ride north. But that was it.

Rowen dragged herself across the room toward her bed. Two days. She had two days to gather what she could and leave. She pulled herself up onto the bed and collapsed. Her body refused to do anything else. The packing would have to wait.

She rolled onto her side and pulled the quilt over her body. The soft scent of lilac drifted up from the quilt. It reminded her of Jedrek and Ann. What would they think of their adopted daughter now? Rowen shivered and closed her eyes. Perhaps it was better they'd never known their daughter was a witch . . .

Rowen woke up at the sound of knocking. She looked at the door then up at the window. The sun had disappeared behind the mountains. Anwin's trees cast long shadows across her cabin. Had she really slept for three hours?

The knock came again. She rolled over and stared at the door. Why would anyone be visiting her? She had two days before they exiled her.

A small movement near the bottom caught her attention. A cream colored envelope made its way beneath the door.

Rowen drew back the quilt and quietly made her way across the cold floor. She picked up the envelope. The seal of the White City was pressed firmly in blue wax along the fold. A lump filled her throat at the sight. What more could the White City have to say to her?

She thrust her finger along the fold and broke the wax. It took a moment for her eyes to clear before she could begin reading the letter.

To Rowen Mar

    I never received your reply. My offer still stands. In view of Jedrek Mar's death, I would like to offer you a position here in the White City, namely, as varor to my daughter, Lady Astrea. The position is yours should you accept and pass the training. However, if you are not interested, please let my courier know. I will wait for your response.

               Lord Gaynor Celestis,
               High Lord of the White City and Ryland Plains.

Rowen read the letter two more times, hardly believing what she was seeing. Could it be? Could she really have a new life apart from this nightmare?

She tore open the door and dashed around the corner. The messenger was halfway down to the path toward the village. "Wait!" she called, waving the letter overhead.

The courier stopped and turned around.

Rowen ran toward the young man. "Yes!" she said with a gasp. She waved the letter in front of him. "My answer is yes."

He eyed her for a moment. Would he retract the offer? Why was he hesitating?

Rowen slowed her breathing, but inside she felt as though she were flying.

"Then I will take your answer back to Lord Gaynor." The courier turned to go.

"Wait! I will be able to start right away. In fact, I can leave in two days."

The courier turned and looked at her with surprise.

"Its just that . . . I have nothing left holding me here." Rowen lowered the letter. "So I can start right away."

The young man frowned. "The captain is currently away from the White City. But I'm sure Lord Gaynor will not object if you show up so soon after receiving the message. I will let him know."

"Thank you," Rowen said.

The messenger nodded then turned and continued back down the path.

Rowen watched him, feeling tears threaten to take her again. How could she have missed the High Lord's offer in that first letter? Then she remembered. She had burned that hateful letter the day after her father's burial, never bothering to read the rest.

How close she had come to shutting the one door that now would save her life.

Rowen turned around and made her way back up to her house. The High Lord of the White City wanted *her,* Rowen, to be the varor to his daughter—to be the bodyguard of Lady Astrea. The offer had been made as a way to take care of her after her father's death. She knew her father had had friends in high places, but the High Lord? She placed a hand on her face, hardly believing.

Rowen stepped inside the house and went directly to the small chest, her mind now pulling together everything she would need for such a position. She lifted the lid and looked inside. The lock of her mother's hair rested on a leather scabbard. Rowen took the hair out and placed it gently on the bed. Then she drew out the scabbard with her smallsword inside.

Heaviness settled across her chest. She remembered the day her father had given her this sword. Her mother had died weeks before. He'd said he wanted Rowen to learn to protect herself. Unfortunately, no sword she knew of could protect a person from ravaging diseases such as the one that had killed her mother.

Rowen placed the sword on the ground beside her and felt for the leather glove. There. She lifted the glove out of the chest and stared at it. Never would she have thought this little bit of leather might save her life.

Rowen slid the sword glove onto her right hand. It was tight, but with a couple of tugs she got it fully fit onto her hand. She flexed her fingers and looked at her hand front and back. The leather covered her palm, but left her fingertips free. It was a great fit. She grabbed her sword and stood.

Rowen took a couple of swings. The memories and her father's instruction came rushing back. She could do this. She took another swing. A small smile tugged on her lips. She could definitely do this. What was it the letter had said? Something about training? She would pass. Her father had taught her well. Rowen sheathed the sword back in the scabbard and laid it on her bed, alongside her mother's hair.

Then she looked at the glove again. It exposed no white mark and allowed no light through. But would it be a strong enough barrier to keep whatever she had done to Cleon from happening again? Her smiled disappeared at the thought.

Rowen closed her hand into a fist. She didn't know. But one thing she did vow: No one would ever know of her mark.

CHAPTER 3

It rained the day Rowen left Cinad. No one said goodbye, and no one watched her go. She chose not to turn back in her saddle as she rode past the last few houses. It would only hurt more. Instead, she thought about the new life she would be starting in the White City.

In her pack she carried a couple of changes of clothing, food, and the lock of her mother's hair. At her side hung her scabbard and smallsword. Everything else she'd simply left behind.

By the time she stopped her horse for the evening, her cloak was soaked. The trees of Anwin provided a little protection from the drizzle. But the rain never let up long enough for her to completely dry.

On the third day after leaving Cinad, Rowen arrived in Mostyn. Tall wooden walls surrounded the old military town. The dirt road led to an archway. One lantern hung on the right side and swung wildly with the wind. Dark skies hung overhead. Rain fell in sheets, leaving large puddles of mud and water along the dirt road. The white-capped Ari Mountains rose behind the town, barely visible through the downpour.

Rowen rode miserably through the archway. She was soaked to the bone and freezing. Rows of stores and homes stood inside the walls. Warm light filled each window. Signs over doorways swayed back and forth.

Rowen moved toward one, shaded her eyes against the rain and squinted upward. Mercantile. No, not what she was looking for. She steered her horse toward the next sign. Blacksmith. The picture of an anvil brought up memories of Cleon and the events from a couple of days ago. The pain from those last few days flared again. She tightened her grip on the reins and moved on.

She passed two more buildings and then found what she was looking for: the local stable. Rowen jumped down from the horse and led her inside. The smell of hay and horse filled the air. Along both walls were rows of stalls. Only one horse was stabled here. It looked up at Rowen, then went back to munching.

A man came walking down the middle of the corrals. "Need a stable tonight, miss?"

"Yes. Just for one night."

"It'll be two coppers."

Rowen unlatched her pack and dug around inside for her coin pouch. She found the pouch and counted the money for the man.

"New to Mostyn?" the man said.

"Yes, sir." Rowen swung the pack up over her shoulder.

"Then the best place to stay is old Jarl's. Clean rooms, good food, and generally good company."

"Where can I find this Jarl's?" Rowen hoped she had enough in her coin pouch to pay. She wasn't sure she could stand one more night under a dripping tree.

"Just down the street. Can't miss it. Largest building in town besides the fort."

Rowen thanked the man and went back out on the street. It was dark now but at least the rain had let up. Large puddles littered the dirt street, barely visible until she stepped in them. By the time she found the large wooden door leading into the inn, she was covered with mud.

Rowen grasped the handle and gave the door a shove. A blast of warm air—filled with the smells of meat, bread, and smoke—hit her face as the door swung open. She took a step inside. The wind caught the door and slammed shut behind her.

Rowen stood there with her dripping cloak and pack, unsure of what to do. The main room was huge. Even bigger than Noland's house. Wood rafters crisscrossed above, and from them hung metal chandeliers with fat, dripping candles. A fire roared in the nearby fireplace. The flames cast a subtle orange light across everything. There were at least twenty to thirty tables, most of them filled with people hunched over wooden plates, stuffing hunks of bread and meat into their mouths. Other patrons held pewter colored mugs topped with froth.

"Hello there," a voice said nearby. Rowen scanned the room for the voice. "Over here," the voice said again. To her left stood a long wooden counter. Behind the counter was a short man with a dirty white apron over his ample middle. His head was bald, and only a tuft of grey hair grew on either side. He held a tattered rag in one hand and a pewter mug in the other. He motioned to her with the rag and placed the mug down. Rowen moved toward the counter.

"Name's Jarl, owner of this establishment," Jarl said. "Looking for a place to stay the night?"

Rowen wiped away the water that still clung to her face. "Yes, sir."

"No need for formality here." Jarl gave her a smile. "Just call me Jarl." He dropped his rag down on the counter and disappeared through a door behind him. Moments later he reappeared with a candle. "Follow me."

Rowen followed him across the room, past the rows of tables toward the back. "Watch your step," Jarl said over his shoulder. He started up a set of narrow stairs. Rowen followed him up. Every stepped creaked and groaned.

Jarl stopped at the top. "It's not much." He opened the first door on the right. "But at least it's clean and dry." Rowen peered past him into the small room. "And it comes with a free meal tonight and one tomorrow."

He was right, she thought as she glanced around the room: It wasn't much. Just a bed in the corner and a nightstand. A small window graced the far wall. At least it was better than the cold hard ground she had slept on the last couple of nights.

Rowen turned toward him. "How much?"

"Five coppers." Jarl placed the candle on the nightstand.

"I'll take it." She pulled out her coin pouch. She had just enough. She counted out the coins and placed them in his outstretched hand.

"When you come back downstairs, I'll send Dara over with your dinner." Jarl turned to leave. "Oh, and one more thing," he said, turning back around. "I'm afraid the ale is extra."

"That won't be a problem." Rowen dropped her pack down near the small nightstand. "I'll just have water."

"Then I'll let Dara know."

After Jarl closed the door, Rowen peeled off her cloak and hung it on the bedpost, but she kept her sword belted around her middle. For one moment she thought about forgoing dinner and going right to bed. But the faint smell of bread drifted beneath her nostrils, making her stomach growl with hunger. She sighed and headed toward the door. The bed would have to wait.

Back downstairs, Rowen surveyed the large room, looking for a place to sit. A few men looked up and stared at her. She ignored them, forcing her eyes to look for an empty table. Animal skins hung along the wall by the fireplace: some deer, a wildcat, and one black bear. She wondered briefly where the bear pelt had come from since there were no bears in Anwin. A couple more heads turned her direction. In the far corner right near the fireplace stood an empty table. Grateful for the find, she hurried toward it before another could claim it.

Rowen sank down on the hard bench. It had been a while since she had ridden. With each ache and pain, her body reminded her just how long. The heat from the fireplace drifted toward her body, soaking through the dampness of her clothing and skin. Rowen closed her eyes, savoring the feeling of warmth as it spread across her body.

A few minutes later a large woman clad in a dark green dress with an apron over it bustled toward her table balancing a steaming bowl of stew and a platter with a round loaf on top. "Here you go, miss." She placed the food in front of Rowen and hurried away.

At the smell, her mouth began to water. Rowen picked up the wooden spoon and began to consume the contents of her bowl in a polite but hurried fashion.

The woman came back with a mug of water. "Are you sure you don't want some ale?" She eyed the water with suspicion.

"No, thank you," Rowen said. The woman shrugged and moved back toward the kitchen. Rowen glanced around, noting the thick pewter mugs others were drinking from, then she took a drink from her own mug, which had only water. She had never cared much for the bitter brew common here in the Ryland Plains.

Halfway through her meal, she began to feel drowsy. Now warm and dry and her stomach nearly filled, her body was ready for sleep. Rowen took a few more bites then pushed back the bowl. The fire continued to warm her back, making her even drowsier. Slowly she stood and stretched. Then she began to make her way through the tables toward the stairs in the back.

"Hey there." A hand reached out and grabbed hold of her wrist.

Immediately Rowen clenched her hand to protect her mark. "Excuse me?" A grizzled, pockmarked face surrounded by wild grey hair looked up at her. The man wore a dark blue uniform. Rowen tried to pull her hand away. "Let go of me, sir."

The man tightened his grip. "Come and sit with us," he said with a slur. "Make a couple soldiers happy."

Glancing around the table she found other men in uniform. "Not tonight," Rowen said, looking back at him. She pulled again.

"Don't you care that we could die in a couple days?"

Rowen saw what the man was trying to do. "I'm sorry, but I have somewhere to be tomorrow." She placed her other hand on the hilt of her sword.

The man stared at the sword, then back up into her face, surprise etched across his face. "Yes, ma'am." He let go of her wrist and turned to his comrades.

Rowen hurried toward the stairs, her heart both relieved and saddened.

She entered her room and shut the door. She walked over to the nightstand. The candle Jarl had left behind still flickered in the dark room. Rowen placed the candle on the floor then pulled the nightstand across the room and shoved it up against the door.

She let out a shaky breath and backed away. It disturbed her that she'd had to resort to pointing out she had a sword to get the man to let go of her. Were all men like this? Is that what the world was like? This new life was proving to be much bigger and darker than the one she'd left behind in Cinad.

Rowen undid the belt that hung around her waist and dropped the sword near her pack. Eyeing the pack a moment longer, she realized her nightgown was most likely drenched as well. She sat down on the bed with a groan. She was too tired to fuss about it tonight.

She pulled her boots off and crawled under the covers still wearing her traveling clothes. The bed felt chilly because of her wet clothing. Rowen leaned down and blew out the candle. She burrowed back under the covers, shivering. Slowly her body began to warm. Exhaustion took over. Her eyelids grew heavy. Raindrops began to pelt the window with sharp quick taps. The last thing she remembered was how nice it was not to be sleeping outside in the rain.

Captain Lore halted his horse and sighed. The rain fell in one long continuous drizzle from dark clouds overhead. He wiped cold water from his face and pulled his hood farther down. Just one more day of riding, and he would be home. The horse shifted beneath him restlessly. "All right, all right, we'll keep going." He gave the horse a gentle kick. The horse started forward eagerly.

Lore kept one hand on the reins and stretched out his back. His stomach rumbled. He placed a hand over his middle and sat forward again. He hadn't eaten since this morning. There were a couple of biscuits left in his bag, but the last thing he wanted was a stale traveler's biscuit or dried meat. Four days of the stuff was enough. He would wait until he reached Mostyn and eat something hot at the inn.

Lore rode on until he could barely see the muddy road in the darkness. The wind came whipping up, slapping across his body and pulling at his cloak. He kept a tight hold on his cloak and pressed forward.

Minutes later, a small light appeared, swinging madly back and forth beside an archway. He sat up straighter and urged the horse forward. He had made it to Mostyn.

Lore rode through the town until he reached the local stable. He jumped down from the horse and led him inside.

A man stood beside one of the stalls with a pitchfork of hay. The man looked up. "One moment," he said and dumped the hay over the gate.

Lore grabbed his belongings from the saddle.

The man placed his pitchfork against the stall and walked over.

"Just one night," Lore said. He handed the man a couple of coins and the reins of his horse.

"Yes, sir." The man took both and led his horse away.

Lore hurried back outside. The wind and rain pulled at him. He dashed across the muddy streets to the inn.

Large brightly lit windows covered the front of the inn. An old sign swung over the door, the words long since faded. Lore passed the windows and reached for the door. Warm air engulfed him as he entered. He shut the door behind him and headed straight for the counter.

At the end of the counter stood a short, portly man. It had been some time since Lore had been to Mostyn. What was the innkeeper's name? Jacen? Jardin? The man turned around. Jarl.

Jarl's face lit up. He made his way down to the end of the counter. "Captain Lore, what a pleasure."

"Good evening, Jarl," Lore said. A bunch of voices rose behind him in raucous laughter. Lore turned. Hazy smoke hung over the large room. A cheery fire burned across the hall in the large fireplace. Everywhere he looked, almost every table was filled. Lore turned back to Jarl. "Pretty busy this evening."

"Aye. The militia is moving out. A lot of unrest at Hershaw Pass. The last Temanin Commander tried to take the pass. Killed a lot of good northern men. We killed a lot of theirs too. Don't know why they think they can take the pass. We've held it for hundreds of years. But it seems the empire isn't ready to quit yet. So more men are needed. Tonight they are enjoying a few last creature comforts before heading out. But I'm sure you know all this."

"Yes. I saw the call go out for the militia." Lore turned and looked over the room again. At least half the tables were filled with men. Most were young and strong looking. There were a couple of older men with salt-and-pepper hair. And one boy who looked barely old enough to grow a beard. All wore the blue uniform. Only some would live through the conflict.

"So what'll it be?" Jarl said.

Lore turned back around. A heavy feeling settled across his chest. "A room, a meal, and a mug of ale."

"Yes, sir." Jarl placed the tattered rag he had in his hand down on the counter. Then he paused as his eyes lit on someone. "Would you mind me asking a favor of you, Captain?"

"Sure, just as long as it does not interfere with my duties."

"See that woman over there?" Jarl pointed toward the far side of the room near the fireplace.

Lore looked over. It took him a moment to spot her, but once he did, she stood out amongst all the other people. She was young and beautiful, out of place compared to the other guests this evening. She had long fair hair pulled into a thick braid that hung over one shoulder. Her skin was smooth with a hint of color on her cheeks. For a moment she looked up, and he caught sight of large eyes beneath dark lashes, unlike the rest of her pale complexion. In all, he had never seen anyone like her.

"Yes," Lore said.

"I don't expect any trouble tonight. But sometimes when the men start drinking, things can get out of hand. And the lady there is traveling alone. So would you mind if I placed you in a room next to hers, just to be safe?"

"Certainly." Lore turned back toward Jarl.

"Good, then let's head up."

Lore settled in the room across from the young woman. Then he headed back downstairs. The young woman was still at the far table, finishing her dinner. Lore noticed many of the men stealing glances in her direction. Some were even bold enough to stare outright, hoping to catch her attention. But she seemed oblivious to all this.

The woman pushed her bowl aside and stood, stretching as she did so. Even in traveling pants and dark shirt, she looked feminine in every way. She stepped over the bench and headed across the room. More heads turned her way. She appeared to have no idea she was attracting so much attention.

As Lore went to sit down, he saw the young woman stop. He waited and watched the exchange between the young woman and the table full of militiamen. His hand stole toward his sword. Then he saw the glint of metal as she briefly moved her hand.

So she was a swordsman, was she? And she wore a sword glove too. Not too common nowadays. The men around the table settled down, and the young woman continued toward the stairs, then disappeared moments later.

Jarl had nothing to worry about, Lore thought. He sat down at a table with two other men. She was probably a mercenary, albeit a young one. It would explain why she carried a sword and traveled alone. If so, she could likely take care of herself.

The noise level in the common room rose. Men began to chat amongst themselves. Lore overheard a couple conversations and knew the men were talking about her. A woman hurried over minutes later with his dinner.

"Thank you," Lore said. He grabbed his spoon and dug into the hot food.

For the next ten minutes, Lore did nothing but consume the meal. Later, his stomach filled, Lore drained his second mug. He didn't feel much like talking. Lore just watched the people around him. The men were becoming more rowdy, having had several drinks already that evening. One broke out in song, which the others picked up immediately. His heart went out to all the young men gathered, knowing that soon they would be facing war.

With this sobering thought in mind, he slowly stood. Lore made his way across the room and headed up the stairs toward his room.

As he prepared for bed, his mind went over the next few days. Arrive in the White City, deliver Avonai's response, and find a varor for Lady Astrea, unless Jedrek Mar's daughter had chosen to accept Lord Gaynor's offer.

Sometimes Lord Gaynor could be so stubborn. Who knew anything about Jedrek's daughter? Far better for a varor to be chosen from one of the daughters of the guardsmen. But in the end, it was Lord Gaynor's decision.

Lore sighed at the thought of training some young woman who probably had no idea how to even handle a sword. Dropping down on the small bed, he pulled the pillow under his head and blew out the candle.

Rowen jerked awake. The rattling noise she had heard in her sleep seemed louder now. She shifted in her bed and glanced at the door, which she had barricaded with the small nightstand. A faint light shone beneath the furniture. The nightstand trembled. A jolt of surprise burned away the last of her fatigue. The rattling noise was the door.

Someone was trying to get in.

Rowen stole away from the bed toward her pack in the corner. If she could just reach her sword—

The door burst opened, sending the nightstand sliding across the wooden floor.

Rowen fell to her knees and scrambled to find her sword, cursing her foolishness for not keeping it near her.

"There you are." It was a man's voice.

Before Rowen could turn, a hand covered her mouth. Another one snaked around her middle, pinning her arms to her sides. The man's fingers muffled her shout for help.

Her assailant laughed, his breath whispering across her cheek. "No one can hear you, sweetie."

Rowen gagged at the rancid smell of his breath. She tried to bite his hand, but his hold across her mouth kept her teeth clenched together.

He stood, hauling her up with him, his arm still tightly wound around her arms and middle. Rowen struggled against his grip and turned her face, trying to break either hold. But the man behind her was too strong.

He let go of her head and forcefully swung her around, gripping her by her forearms. Rowen opened her mouth to scream, but he pushed his mouth down on hers.

Repulsed and terrified, she jerked her head back and screamed, straining against his hold.

The man teetered for a moment, then pulled her back against him. His hand clamped painfully down on her mouth again. "No more of that." He brought his face close to hers.

Rowen stared into black eyes. She frantically searched for a way to escape. She looked down at the wrist clamped across her mouth and realized, as the man began to push her back toward the bed, that his hand was bare.

She could touch him.

For one second Rowen wavered, having sworn she would never touch another with her mark. Then her legs hit the end of the bed. Petrified, Rowen reached for her glove and fumbled it off. Then she reached up and gripped the man's wrist.

Heat burst inside her. It spread across her chest and raced down her arm toward the mark on her hand.

The man stopped and stared at her. "What-what are you doing to me?" He let go of her and tried to move back. "Don't touch me!" He tried to wrench himself free of her grasp.

But Rowen could not remove her hand. Images began to flash through her mind. Heavy, burning emotions passed through her body. She tried to pull away, sick by what she saw, but the heat from her palm continued to enter the man. By now, he was shouting at her and shielding his eyes.

Rowen saw . . . everything.

Then the images began to fade, and her hand dropped.

The man shouted at her and backed away. Rowen could no longer see him. She fell to the floor and retched, the contents of her stomach splattering across the wood. Never had she experienced such darkness. Never had she thought a man could have such thoughts about a woman.

Vaguely she heard others enter her room. Rowen threw herself across the room and grappled for her sword. This time, she found it.

She pulled it out of its sheath, turned around, and held it out in front of her. People scurried around her, startling her every few seconds by their movement. She shook her head in an effort to clear her mind. It took her a moment to realize that the man who had tried to take her was being hauled out of the room by two other men.

"Are you all right?"

Rowen swung her sword toward the voice. A man crouched a couple feet from her, just barely out of reach of her sword. He held a candle in his hand.

"Are you all right?" he said again.

Rowen squinted at him. His face moved in and out of focus.

"She's in shock," she heard him say to someone over his shoulder.

Her mind finally caught up with her. The danger was over. The man who had tried to hurt her was gone. Or was it? What about *this* man? Or the other two still in her room?

"I'm . . . I'm all right," she said. But she kept her sword pointed at the man before her.

The man looked past her sword to her face. "Everything is fine. You're safe now."

Rowen lowered her sword slightly and stared at the man. He looked back. Sandy brown hair hung near green eyes. A tiny white scar followed his clean-shaven jaw. She looked at the hand he offered. His hand was brown from time in the sun with short-clipped nails.

"Trust me."

She wanted to. She dropped her sword a little more.

"Listen to the man," one of the other men said across the room. "You can trust the captain."

Captain? Rowen looked back at the man. He still had his hand extended toward her. He wasn't dressed in uniform. But he reminded her a little of her father.

Rowen took a deep breath and made her decision. She lowered her sword.

"Here, take my hand," he said.

She kept her sword clutched in her right hand and grabbed his hand with her left.

He helped her up off her knees. "I'm afraid your room is a mess. So I want to offer you my room for the night."

Rowen shook her head. "I couldn't take your room. Where would you sleep?"

"I'll sleep in the corridor, next to the door."

"Next to the door?" The cold rush of fear returned.

"I protect people for a living. You have nothing to fear from me."

Rowen looked for the other men, but they had already left. She turned back to the man before her. The others said she could trust him. Could she?

He waited quietly, his warm hand still touching her fingertips.

"All right," she said finally. But she would keep her sword close.

The man led her out of her room and across the hall. His room looked similar to hers except for his clothing that was strewn across the floor, and a large dark cloak that hung on the bedpost. The stranger walked in and began to collect his clothing and gear.

Captain, Rowen thought again. She watched him move around the room. Was he one of the captains in the army?

He finished gathering his stuff and came up to her. "If you need anything, I'll be just outside the door."

Unsure of what to say, Rowen merely nodded. He walked past her and out to the hall. The door clicked softly behind him.

Rowen glanced around the room, still feeling uneasy. The bed stood in the corner with grey wool blankets thrown back and the sheets wrinkled from use. A nightstand stood next to it. The stranger had left his candle lit on the nightstand. Over the bed was a small dark window.

She crossed the room and picked up the candle. She searched the rest of the room and found nothing more but a little dust and a cobweb in one corner. She bent down and looked under the bed. Nothing. No one here but herself.

Rowen placed the candle on the nightstand and her sword next to it. She reached over and pulled one of the wool blankets over the sheets. It felt odd to be sleeping in a bed some stranger had been using only minutes before. She hesitated, then climbed onto the bed. She pulled the top cover over her body and let out a long exhaustive sigh. Perhaps she didn't care.

Sleep, however, eluded her. Rowen stared up at the ceiling. The mental images she had caught while she'd held the man with her hand came trickling back. She watched through his eyes as he gazed at three women gathered at a round stone well . . . He sat on a stool in what looked like an inn and grabbed a young woman passing. He slowly let her hair down. She giggled, but Rowen knew what burned inside his heart . . . He watched a young blond girl play near the open doors of a barn . . .

Rowen twisted around and buried her face into her pillow. She could feel his emotions now, and it sickened her. The images of his deeds kept rolling through her mind. Faster, faster. Woman after woman. Taken, violated. She squeezed her eyes shut. She was going to retch again. *Please, someone, make it stop!*

The images and feelings began to fade away. Rowen slowly opened her eyes and stared at the pillow. She breathed hard, but didn't dare move more. She was afraid the images would trigger again.

She waited a minute longer. Nothing happened. She pushed herself up and stared at the pillow. The images did not return. Her shoulders slumped in relief.

Rowen pushed back her hair from her forehead, and found that she'd been sweating. Her head hurt now. But at least she couldn't see anything. She rolled down onto her side and laid her head on the pillow. She watched the flame dance above the candle. Slowly her heart returned to its normal beat.

Her eye caught a shadow that moved across the thin stream of light below the door. Rowen tensed. She gripped the cover and held still. A shuffling sound came from the other side. She glanced at her sword, prepared to grab it.

Something blocked out most of the light. The shuffling stopped a few seconds later. She thought she heard breathing on the other side of the door.

Rowen reached past the blanket and touched the hilt of her sword. She would not be surprised this time. She would quickly run across the room and fling the door open before whoever was on the other side could do anything—

Wait! Rowen let out her breath. She remembered now. The man whose room she now occupied said he was going to sleep outside the door.

She still watched the door, ready to grab her sword if the man did anything. Seconds turned to minutes. She could barely hear his breathing now. Gradually she relaxed. The man could still be planning something, but fatigue held her mind and body. She could barely keep her eyes open. She would just have to trust him, for now.

Rowen leaned over and blew out the candle. She curled up beneath the covers and watched the door again. He still did not move. Curiosity overtook her fear. Who was he? Why would he offer to sleep outside her door?

Not all men are bad, she reminded herself. Her father had been kind. And Noland, for those couple of weeks after her illness. The stranger had said he protected people for a living. Yes, in a way the military did that.

She closed her eyes. Somewhere along the edges of her mind she could still feel the images she'd seen in that man. But nothing came flashing back now. She curled her fingers over her marked palm and brought her hand up to her chin. She never wanted to be put in that situation again. A situation in which she was tempted to touch someone else.

● ● ●

Lore thanked those who had helped him subdue the drunken man, then he returned upstairs. It was not the first time he had slept on the floor in a hall. His job demanded that he protect those in his charge, even if it brought discomfort to himself. Many times he had guarded Lady Astrea's room that way when she had traveled. But now Lady Astrea was a young woman, and a female varor would be much better than him or any other guard. Her varor could stay in her room with her.

Jarl came up the stairs with a pillow and blanket in hand.

"Captain, thank you so much." He handed Lore the bedding. "With the militia in town, I'm afraid the inn has become more rowdy of late. But we haven't had a problem until tonight. That poor young woman."

"I'm just glad I was nearby to help," Lore said. "By the way, do you know where she's heading?"

"No," Jarl said. "I never asked. But the war has been causing many people to move lately. Seen lots of families come through here on their way to Avonai." Jarl ran a hand through his hair. "Well, I should be off to my own bed. I'll sleep better tonight knowing you're watching over the young woman. Anything else I can bring you?"

Lore shook his head.

"Then goodnight, Captain." Jarl headed back downstairs.

Lore placed the pillow and blanket on the floor and stretched out in front of the door. So what was her story? He shifted so he could see the crack at the bottom of the door. The candle was out, and there was no noise on the other side.

Lore moved back onto his side. There was one thing about this evening that kept niggling at him. He had run into the young woman's room expecting to pull some man off of her. He'd found a man, all right, but he'd been cowering in the corner, shouting something about his eyes and light. Lore had ignored his words at the time, furious to find the man in the young woman's room at all. But now he wondered what the man had been talking about. Perhaps it was only the ale talking.

Lore shifted again. His thoughts went from the man to the

beautiful young woman. How did she do it? Somehow she had subdued her intruder before Lore had gotten there, although the state he had found her in was anything but what he'd expect to see in a victorious heroine. The way she had looked at him, her dark blue eyes wide with fear. No, not victorious at all.

Too bad he would never find out. Lore sighed and pushed his head deeper into the pillow. He had an urgent message to carry back to Lord Gaynor, a message that took priority over helping the young woman any more than he already had.

CHAPTER
4

Caleb Tala stood on the marble balcony just outside his room. He savored the feel of the desert air. It brushed across his body and through his hair like a warm caress. A crescent moon rose to the east. Below his balcony stood the great city of Azar. Countless lights from fires and windows twinkled across the city. It reminded him of a dark piece of velvet with a thousand diamonds upon it.

It was said that Azar was the jewel of the Temanin Empire, and tonight Caleb could believe it. For a moment more he enjoyed the view afforded him by his quarters in the palace. Then he turned back inside.

He had a job to do this evening. Soon he would see if the days he'd spent watching Delshad and planning his mission would pay off.

Caleb entered his room. Along the beige marble floor lay a scarlet rug with intricate blue, white, and yellow patterns. Large potted palms stood on either side of the balcony's archway. Ahead was his bed, a monstrous thing covered in scarlet silk. Pillows with gold tassels were thrown across the silk. White gauze hung from the ceiling and draped over the bed. Changing screens painted with pictures of horses and men dressed in Temanin ancient battle armor stood in the right corner. A dark wooden chest and gold-framed mirror sat next to the screens.

Caleb stopped and studied his reflection in the mirror. Every part of his body was covered in black except for his hands and face. He moved toward the chest and carefully removed a small jagged dagger and a pair of dark gloves. The dagger, he placed in a sheath woven into the inside of his boot. The gloves, he pulled on.

There was hardly any moonlight as Caleb walked back toward

the balcony. But he neither needed nor wanted the pale skylight this evening. The darkness suited his purpose.

Caleb placed his hands on the balcony's rail and leaped over the side. He hit the ground with a soft thud. Silently he made way across the grounds of the palace. Carefully manicured grass and bushes filled the open area. Paths made of tiny stones crisscrossed the garden. A grove of cypress trees grew near the palace wall, a wall made of stones that stood almost three men tall.

He veered toward the wall and followed it until he reached an area where the stones jutted out just barely, then scurried up and over.

Caleb jogged down the low-lit street, using shadows to cover his movements. He passed by two- and three-story sand-colored buildings. Tiny squares of light shone from the windows. Shops were dark with doors barred for the evening. Canvas booths stood empty. Dogs sniffed around the booths, hoping to find something left behind. One looked up as Caleb passed. He ignored the animal and continued on.

He turned a corner and caught sight of a man and woman taking an evening walk. He moved to the side of a nearby booth. Using a breathing exercise, he brought his breath down to a whisper. The couple walked past, never noticing him standing in the shadows. He watched them walk around the corner, then stepped out and continued on.

A half-hour later Caleb reached Delshad's estate. Delshad lived in the wealthier section of Azar. Large stone walls kept the unwanted out and the rich in. A similar wall surrounded Delshad's home. Caleb stood in the shadows. He glanced right, then left. The street was empty. He looked across the street at the wall. A cypress tree hung over one end of the wall, just left of where he stood. Perfect.

One, two, three—He dashed across the street and reached for the top of the wall. His fingers grasped the edge. With one lunge, he brought his legs up and swerved his body around until he was crouching on the narrow ledge. He steadied himself and let his breathing calm. Then quietly he made his way to the tree and hid in its shadows.

The aroma of desert blossoms tickled his nostrils, their scent wafting up from the blooms that covered the bushes below. The bushes circled a small pond. Tiny silver fish darted through the dark water, their scales flashing from the light reflected from the windows along the main house. Lilly pads drifted lazily across the water's surface. Cypress trees surrounded the pond and bushes like tall silent sentinels. Their shadows extended across the entire garden and up to the house.

The house itself stood forty feet away from the wall. Its sand-colored walls were lined with arched windows, seven on the top floor, seven on the bottom. All were dark save for a single window on the top floor. At the end of the house stood a wood awning. Dark green vines wove through the boards. Beige tiles lay along the ground.

Caleb studied the single lit window. A cypress tree grew nearby. One of its branches grew just beneath the window. A shadow passed by the opening. There he was, right on schedule. After a few minutes, Delshad retreated farther into the house.

Caleb jumped from the ledge. He passed the bushes and pond, using the shadows spread across the garden to make his way toward the base of the tree near the house. He stopped at the base and took a second to study the branches, looking for a path up. Then silently he began to climb.

He made his way up the trunk, careful not to shake the branches. When he reached the branch that grew under Delshad's window, Caleb turned and followed the limb. It sank slightly beneath his weight, but still held. He reached the window and stopped.

Inside the room he could see Delshad take a seat at a dark wood desk located at the far end of the room, his back to the window. Two sconces hung above the desk. Both were lit. A large potted palm sat in the corner. Across the sandstone floor was a red and black rug with an intricate swirl pattern. Caleb recognized the pattern. It was one made by the nomad tribes of the Great Desert.

The sweet scent of incense drifted through the window. Outside, the wind rustled through the leaves. Caleb slowly crossed from the branch to the windowsill, careful to keep the branch from shaking.

Once he had all his weight on the windowsill, he brought his foot away from the tree. The branch barely moved.

He silently stepped onto the floor. Delshad never turned. Caleb could hear the soft scratch of quill on parchment. Whatever Delshad was writing, it held all his attention.

Caleb knelt down and drew his dagger from its sheath. The knife glinted in the candlelight. He straightened up and watched Delshad for a moment. Delshad was a short bald man who had served on the Temanin council for years. Caleb had seen him a couple of times, coming and going from the palace, dressed in fine embroidered robes. But tonight Delshad was dressed in a simple white tunic and dark pants. Nothing about him looked threatening. Why Lord Corin wanted him disposed of, Caleb had no idea. It wasn't his place to ask.

Caleb began to make his way across the room, his feet barely whispering on the floor.

Delshad stopped writing. "I knew you would be coming."

Caleb didn't care. Most people could feel death enter their room. He continued toward the older man, tightening his grip on his blade should Delshad decide to run or fight.

Delshad placed his quill down, but he didn't turn. Instead, he continued to stare at the wall ahead. "Before you proceed with my murder, I have a few words for you, Caleb Tala."

This made Caleb stop. How did Delshad know his name? Uneasiness stole over him.

Delshad turned around in his seat and glanced up. "Do you even know why Lord Corin has ordered my death?"

"I do as I am told." A chill ran down Caleb's spine. This was not normal. At this point, his victims were usually begging for mercy or fighting for their lives, not sitting here questioning him. And that look of resignation in Delshad's eyes. As if Delshad had known all along how these last minutes of his life would play out.

"Is that a wise thing to do?" Delshad asked. "Do you really know your cousin?"

Caleb's eyes narrowed. "I know him well enough. And I know

that dissenters need to be silenced." He stepped toward Delshad, the blade tight in his hand. "But there is one thing I would like to know," he said softly, dangerously. "How did you know my name?"

Delshad's eyes grew distant. Caleb knew he should do it now, but he needed to know. Had the old man been tipped off somehow? But then why had he stayed instead of going into hiding? None of this made sense.

"The Word revealed it to me," Delshad said finally, his focus coming back. "Lord Corin is not who you think he is. And you, Caleb, are not who you think you are."

"What does that mean?" Caleb said, even more alarmed now. Corin had said nothing about Delshad being a religious man. It was bad luck to kill those who believed in higher powers. Perhaps because if there *was* such a thing as a god, Caleb certainly didn't want to be on its bad side for killing one of its followers.

"I can tell you nothing more, because I do not know," Delshad said. "You must find that out for yourself."

Caleb scoffed. "No one believes in the Word anymore."

"He doesn't need to be believed in to exist. And He has not forgotten you."

The man's cryptic words were getting on Caleb's nerves. It was time for this to be over. Before Delshad could say anything else, Caleb plunged the dagger into the older man's neck, just above the collarbone.

Delshad gasped, his hands wavering in the air. Caleb pulled the dagger out and stepped back. The older man continued to flail, his life flowing from the wound and staining his white tunic.

Caleb wiped his dagger on one of his gloves. His mission was done.

He turned to go, but Delshad's dark eyes pinned him in place. Caleb watched as the old man tried to speak. Red dribbled from the corner of his lip. "I . . . I forgive you." Delshad's head slumped to the side. His throat continued to spill scarlet fluid.

Hesitantly, Caleb reached over to the man's neck, careful not to touch any of the blood. Delshad was dead.

Satisfied but disturbed, he backed away. Just what had Delshad meant? To be forgiven meant he had done something wrong. And as far as Caleb was concerned, he was merely following orders.

Still, that didn't quench the uneasy feeling that something significant had just happened. As Caleb turned and headed back out the window, he could feel Delshad's words worming their way into the recesses of his mind.

"You are not who you think you are."

It did not take long to reach the palace, but the trip seemed like an eternity to Caleb. All he wanted to do was report the mission a success and then retire to his quarters.

He entered the palace courtyard the same way he had left, making sure that no one knew of his errand that evening. The feeling of unease still lingered as he climbed up into his room. If he had known Delshad had been a Follower of the Word, would he still have assassinated the councilman? *Probably*, Caleb thought. He changed out of his dark clothing into something more fitting a prince of Temanin. His cousin Corin held the ties to his coin pouch and always compensated him well for his missions. This job alone would see him through many months.

If only he could find a way to bury the old man's words still echoing inside his mind.

Caleb placed his dagger carefully back inside the wooden chest. He brushed his hair back and checked his appearance one more time. Satisfied, he left his room.

Golden sconces were lit along the hall. Polished marble glimmered beneath their light. A servant dressed in a short white tunic was on all fours, washing the floor. Caleb didn't so much as slow as he approached the man. The servant scrambled out of his way.

Caleb turned a corner and followed another hall through the palace toward the back rooms. He knew Corin was busy this evening entertaining the court. No doubt to have an alibi in the morning when news of Delshad's death came out. Caleb nodded to himself. It would work to his own advantage as well to be seen by the court.

Caleb passed through the long opulent curtains into the inner court. He paused for a moment and let his eyes wander across the room, taking in its inhabitants. Court musicians played in one corner. Couches and large sitting cushions filled the other three corners. Upon the crimson furniture sat the elite of Azar, sampling wine and food.

Servants dressed in short white tunics carried platters around to those reclining. More colorfully dressed dancers moved amongst the party guests, their graceful bodies flowing to the beat of the music. Red and violet and deep blue silk fluttered with each movement. Gold sparkled from the bangles they wore on their arms and ankles.

Caleb spotted Corin near the back, talking to one of his advisors. He eased into the room. He had no desire for merry-making this evening. All he wanted to do was report and withdraw.

As he took another step inside, a dancer moved toward him, swaying to the sound of the music. Blue silk twirled around her body. Thin gold bracelets jingled along her dark, bare arms.

She stopped before him and gave him a brazen smile. Caleb groaned inside. Usually Ailis's presence made his heart beat faster, but tonight it felt heavy and tired. She placed her long manicured fingers across his chest and looked up into his eyes. "Where were you tonight?" Her voice was low and smooth.

Caleb grabbed her hand. "Not tonight, Ailis."

Her lips tightened, and she pulled her hand back. Caleb ignored her and continued toward his cousin. Ailis would come back to him—she always did. He just wasn't interested right now.

Lord Corin seemed to be in deep discussion. Knowing his cousin would not want to be interrupted, Caleb stopped a few feet away and waited.

Next to Corin sat a woman Caleb did not recognize. Her dark hair fell to her waist like a cascade of black silk. She wore a scarlet gown with slits up the sides, revealing long, elegant legs. She glanced his direction, looked him up and down, then gave him an inviting smile.

Caleb turned his eyes away. Whatever belonged to his cousin was off limits to him.

A moment later, the advisor bowed his head and turned to leave. Caleb moved aside to let the man out, his colorful robes flowing behind him. The woman stood as well, whispering something into Lord Corin's ear.

His cousin smiled and watched her walk away, then turned toward Caleb. "Ah, there you are, Caleb." Corin possessed the dark, handsome features of the Tala men with only a sprinkling of grey near his temples. He was Caleb's senior by ten years.

"Corin," Caleb bowed from the waist.

"Sit, cousin. The party has only just begun." Corin grabbed a jeweled goblet from the low table beside him. Caleb sat down stiffly on the other couch and waited for his cousin to begin. Corin glanced around casually. "So how did it go?"

"Delshad has been taken care of," Caleb said.

"No witnesses? Nothing to link his death back to me?"

"Nothing, my lord."

"Good." Corin took a sip from his goblet.

"May I go now?"

Corin placed his goblet back on the table. "Not quite yet. I have another issue to discuss with you."

Caleb bit down on his impatience. It would not do to anger his cousin. He had seen servants cut down for a mere slip of the tongue. He eyed the loose fitting black robe Corin wore and wondered what his cousin had hidden in there.

Corin looked back at Caleb. "It has to do with the war up north. Things are not going . . . well."

Caleb knew this was an understatement. He thought back to when he had—upon Corin's orders—executed the most recent commander of Temanin's army.

"I have selected Arpiar to become the new commander."

Caleb nodded. He knew of Arpiar. The man had fought for Temanin for over forty years and was known to be a brilliant strategist. "Sounds like a good choice, but what does this news have to do with me?"

"I want to make sure nothing stops us from reaching the north this time. I need someone who will guarantee that Arpiar doesn't get cold feet when the battle turns hot."

Caleb tensed. He didn't like the direction this conversation was going.

"Who I need . . . is you," Corin said.

"Why?" There was no way Corin was going to drag him into that war of his.

"You, my dear cousin, are a man who gets things done, no matter what. That's why you work for me. Now I need that ambition turned toward getting my troops into the north. All you need to do is stay with Commander Arpiar and make sure he accomplishes that. And if he needs a little . . . persuasion . . . you can give him some."

"I don't like it," Caleb said. "My work is singular. I *like* to work alone. No one else."

Corin's eyes glittered feverishly. "I don't care what you *like*, Caleb. You go where *I* send you, and you do the work *I* give you. And if you don't, I know the Keepers are looking for the suspect in a couple of unsolved murders around here. Wouldn't want your name dropped, would you?"

Caleb stared at Corin, his teeth clenched. He wouldn't . . . Would he? Would Corin really give up his own cousin to the Azar Keepers?

Corin laughed and sat back. "But it won't come to that, will it?" He gave Caleb a dark look.

"No," Caleb said through gritted teeth. He was caught. There were only a few people who knew of his covert work, and none of them in the Keepers' order. The Keepers would see him only as a criminal. And the fact that Corin was now using this against him grated Caleb all the more. It wasn't like his cousin to force him into a job. Then again, this wasn't a job he would willingly take.

"Good. I will send papers with you that will let Arpiar know you are to accompany him and why. You should have no problems." Corin took up his goblet again.

"When do I leave?"

"Tomorrow."

Caleb's mood darkened more, but he let none of it show on his face. He stood. "Very well. Do you need anything else?"

Corin took a slow sip. Caleb knew his cousin was doing this just to test his patience. He clenched his hands and waited.

"No," Corin said finally. "That will be all." He waved his hand in a dismissive gesture.

Caleb bowed then exited out a nearby doorway.

He hurried down the hall, snarling at a young servant girl who took too long to get out of his way. He turned the corner and came upon his quarters. Caleb slammed the door shut and walked toward the balcony. The view that had held such appeal for him earlier that evening was, under this cloud of frustration, no longer attractive. He felt his world had been turned upside down, leaving him out of control.

And he did not like it one bit.

CHAPTER 5

The morning sun entered the small window just above the bed and lit up the room. Rowen blinked sluggishly, trying to recall where she was. Then it all came back: the man, the fight, and the other room. She sat up and clutched the blanket to her chest. Her glove was on. She looked around the room. No one else was there. Rowen let out a sigh of relief. She was safe.

Carefully she stood, still clutching the blanket to her body. She grabbed her sword from the nightstand and made her way across the room. She opened the door to the hallway and found her rescuer from last night gone. Only a folded blanket and pillow near the door gave evidence of his presence.

Rowen hurried across the hall. Once inside her own room, she rummaged around for another set of travel clothes and quickly changed. Then she stuffed her belongings into her pack, braided her long hair, and tied it off at the end. Lastly, she belted her sword to her side and headed downstairs.

Jarl was behind the counter cleaning dishes from the previous evening when she entered the large room. Rowen tiptoed across the wooden floor toward the door ahead, hoping to leave quietly.

Jarl looked up. "Oh, it's you." He put down the wooden bowl he had been wiping. Caught, Rowen slowly turned toward Jarl. He was already moving around the long wooden bar. "I'm sorry about last night." He walked up to her with eyes full of remorse. "And so I want to give you back the money for your room."

Rowen shook her head. "That's not necessary—"

"It's the least I can do." Jarl pulled his coin pouch out from beneath his stained apron. He poured out a handful of coins and held them out to her.

"Really, its not—"

"It would make me feel like I've done something to repay you for your trouble. So please, take it."

Rowen reluctantly took the gold.

"I don't know what would've happened if Captain Lore hadn't been here," Jarl said quietly.

Rowen dropped the coins into her own pouch. *Captain*, she thought again, cinching up the pouch. It was nice to know there were some decent men in the military. Unlike the man who had entered her room.

"Would you like some breakfast before you leave?" Jarl said.

"Actually, no," Rowen said. She was anxious to get going. "But I do need directions. I'm heading to the White City."

"Oh, well, that's easy." Jarl tucked his coin pouch back beneath his apron. "Just outside the main gates, go right, toward Anwin Forest. There will be a wide dirt road. It leads directly to the White City. You can't miss it."

Rowen thanked him, picked up her pack, and headed out. At the stable, she retrieved her mount and followed Jarl's directions. As she neared Anwin Forest, she found the road just where Jarl said it would be.

Rowen steered her horse toward the path and entered the forest. It was a clear day, unlike the day before. The sun was shining and she could hear birds singing in the trees.

Rowen took a deep breath. By tonight, she would be in the White City and starting her new life. A small part of her tingled with excitement. The rest of her still grieved over the loss of her village.

Those two emotions battled within her as the day passed. She met one other traveler, a lone merchant wearing his wares across his back, heading south toward the small villages in the valley. He greeted her cordially if not curiously. Rowen merely nodded. Ever since last evening, she had become more cautious around those she did not know.

Evening came and she still had not caught sight of the White City. Doubt began to fill her mind. Had she gone the wrong way?

Rowen squeezed the reins and kept following the same dirt road, now covered with the long shadows cast by the trees overhead.

The path led upward, weaving its way through the forest. A break in the trees appeared where the path crested a hill. Rowen rode toward the break and stopped.

Staring ahead, she felt her breath vanish. In the fading sunlight stood the White City.

She had heard stories of the city made of white stone, but seeing it now with her own eyes, the stories paled in comparison. She rode past the line of trees onto a field of tall grass. Tiny white and yellow wildflowers dotted the green landscape. The field went on for half a league before reaching the city.

Tall impenetrable walls surrounded the city, their white sides turning the color of rose in the dying light. Above the walls she could see towers and battlements, the grey tiled rooftops of shops and homes, and in the far distance, emerging from the mountain itself: Celestis Castle.

The face of Aerie Mountain rose up behind the castle and disappeared in the clouds that swirled around the peak. The city had been formed from the mountain's white stone. Rowen remembered her father once telling her that it had taken the Ryland people over a century to carve the city out of the mountain.

She followed the path that cut through the meadow. The sheer size of the walls became more apparent the closer she drew to the White City. They were at least as tall as the trees of Anwin. She watched tiny figures walking along the top. Blue flags emblazoned with a white eagle flapped in the cool mountain wind.

Ahead, two towering gates stood open, permitting entrance into the city. Large carvings stood out against their wooden surface, but in the fading light she could not make out the symbols.

Rowen rode between the gates. She looked up at the white stone archway high above her. Her breath caught. She scarcely believed that soon she would be calling this place home.

At the entrance began a long cobblestone street lined with lamps lit for the evening. The horses' hooves clopped as the mare stepped onto the street. Rowen looked ahead. She could see that the street curved slowly upward until it reached a second wall and the castle in the distance.

Light spilled out from windows that lined both sides of the street. There were butcher shops with slabs of cured meats and sausage hung on display, clothing shops with beautiful gowns, and even a silversmith. A rolled piece of faded parchment was nailed to the door of an apothecary, advertising that a Rylander could find the cure for almost anything inside.

Rowen rode by a three-story inn with large windows in the front. She could see many people eating and drinking inside its warmly lit interior. There was even a shop that sold toys. She stopped to look inside the toymaker's window and marveled for a moment at the miniature carved horse and dolls with painted faces.

She passed by couples strolling along as she made her way up the street. They nodded her direction, and she greeted them likewise.

Near the castle stood a second wall, this one shorter but made out of the same white stone. A guard dressed in light chainmail covered by a blue tabard with a white eagle stood on either side of the entry.

One of the guards stepped away from the wall. He held up his hand for her to stop. "State your business."

Rowen brought her horse to a stop. "Lord Gaynor is expecting me." She pulled out the letter.

"Lord Gaynor?" the guard said with suspicion. He reached for the letter. The other guard came to stand beside him.

"Yes. I was invited here on behalf of his daughter. I am her new varor." Her words sounded unpolished, and she felt simple compared to the elegance she had observed in the city so far.

"You're Commander Jedrek Mar's daughter?" the second guard said. The first guard continued to read the letter.

"Yes." Rowen turned to look at him.

He turned and whispered something in the first guard's ear.

The first guard rolled up the parchment and handed it back to her. "We were told you would be arriving. Come, I will show you in." He motioned inside the archway. Rowen dismounted and followed, leading the horse behind her.

Just inside the archway, the cobblestone street continued. Ahead stood a tall fountain made of white stone. Water glittered in the torchlight as it splashed down from its uppermost spout. Beyond the fountain was a set of wide stairs leading up to the castle. Large stone pillars were set on either side of two curved doors, just as ornately carved as the gate doors. On either side of the door were lit torches, lighting the darkened area.

"You may leave your horse here," the guard said to Rowen. "I will send someone from the stables to take her."

Rowen nodded and retrieved her pack.

"Here, let me carry that for you." The guard held out his hand.

Rowen hesitated, then handed him the pack. She blushed at his surprised look. She knew it wasn't heavy. But it was all she had.

The guard led her up the stairs and through the double set of doors. Inside, Rowen found herself in a large hall. The air was cool with a hint of smoke in the air. Long tapestries hung from the high ceilings. An iron wrought candelabra hung between the tapestries. Thick dark blue rugs covered the pale stone floor. Silver ornamentals twinkled on a nearby table.

Never had she seen such beautiful furnishings. Everything in her village was functional before beautiful. And since the war, beauty had disappeared altogether.

The guard ignored the finery and continued across the hall, disappearing through a stone archway. Rowen quickly followed.

"Long journey?" the guard asked. He led her down the long corridor.

"Mmm? Oh, yes, took a couple days," Rowen said, distracted by the paintings that hung along the walls. Sconces with tapered candles lit the hallway they followed. The faint hum of voices came through the walls.

"Which village are you from?"

"Cinad," she replied, glancing at another painting, this one with a regal looking woman holding a single white flower in her hand.

"Ah, a farming village. Didn't realize Commander Jedrek was from that area."

Rowen turned back toward the guard, but his face was forward again. They continued to follow the hall, turning twice before reaching a set of doors.

"Here we are." The guard pressed down on the latch and opened the doors. Beyond them was what looked like a common room, similar to one that might be found in an inn. A large stone fireplace stood along the right wall with a couple of chairs surrounding it. In the middle of the room was a long rough wooden table. Doors lined the left wall with stairs leading to a second balcony with more doors.

"This is the Guards Quarter," he said, turning back to Rowen. "Go ahead and take a seat while I inform the captain that you are here." He placed her pack down on the stone floor and left through the same doors through which they had entered.

Rowen stood there for a moment then moved toward the chair nearest the fire and sat down. Dread like a dark, cold fog crept across her heart. What if they decided she wasn't good enough? What if Lady Astrea didn't like her?

What if they discovered her mark?

Rowen looked down and gave her glove a hard tug, making sure every part of her hand was covered and waited. She would know soon enough.

"So the Avonai Council agreed to the meeting?" Lord Gaynor said to Captain Lore.

"Yes," Lore said. He had arrived only an hour ago and had gone directly to Lord Gaynor. He was still wearing his riding cape and traveling clothes.

Lord Gaynor began to pace. "And King Alaric also agreed?"

Lore's face fell. "The king was not present while I was there. Apparently his health has deteriorated more than we knew. He keeps to himself nowadays."

"That's not good," Lord Gaynor said to himself. He opened his mouth to say something more, but there was a knock at the door. "Yes?" Lord Gaynor said, sounding a little exasperated at the interruption.

A guard came to stand in the doorway. "Sorry to interrupt, but Commander Jedrek Mar's daughter is here."

Lore turned toward Lord Gaynor in surprise. "I don't understand. I did not receive word that she had accepted your invitation."

"I did." Lord Gaynor moved around the long table. "I'm sorry, Lore. The message arrived two days ago, and I had planned to tell you after your report. I didn't expect her to arrive for another couple of days."

"I see," Lore said, thinking fast. He turned back toward the guard. "Take her to the Guards Quarter. Tell her I'll be there shortly."

"Yes, sir." The guard closed the door behind him.

"I know you still don't agree with my decision," Lord Gaynor said. "But I did this for a friend. So at least give this young woman a chance."

Lore sighed. "I will give her a chance, but when the time comes for her oath, she will be judged like any other aspiring for the position of varor. I won't be easy on her just because she is Commander Jedrek's daughter. She will need to stand on her own merits."

"I agree," Lord Gaynor said. "But I don't think you'll be disappointed. Jedrek told me much about his daughter. I believe she will do just fine."

"That's still left to be seen," Lore said cautiously. "May I be excused?"

"Yes," Lord Gaynor said. "Go meet the young woman."

Lore bowed and turned. He caught a glimpse of Lord Gaynor pacing, no doubt thinking about the latest news Lore had brought back from Avonai.

Lore headed toward the Guards Quarter, his thoughts on the young woman he was about to meet. He did not relish spending his time on training an amateur when there was work requiring his time elsewhere.

Lore paused just before entering. He straightened his uniform and mentally readied himself for the meeting. Then he opened the door.

There was no one in the common room. No one, that was, except for a figure sitting near the fireplace. Must be her, he thought, and began to cross the room.

The figure turned his direction and stood.

"Welcome," Lore said. "I am Captain—" He choked on his words. It couldn't be. The young woman he had rescued last night stared back at him, shock written across her face. "You? You're Commander Jedrek's daughter?"

"Yes . . . Yes, sir," she replied, her eyes wide with disbelief.

He turned away and ran a hand through his hair. This was not what he was expecting.

"Is something wrong, sir?" she said in a more controlled voice.

Lore turned back. "No, it's just—" With a firm grip, he took a hold of his shock and shoved it toward the back of his mind. It wasn't her fault she had caught him unawares.

He took a deep breath. "Let's try this again, shall we?" Lore looked up and gave her a small smile. "I am Captain Lore Palancar, Captain of the Guard and varor to Lord Gaynor." He bowed in her direction.

She looked at him. "Rowen Mar, daughter of Jedrek Mar."

"Rowen," Lore said. "I would say it's good to meet you, other than we already have."

"Yes, a strange coincidence," Rowen said quietly.

Lore motioned toward the chairs that circled the fireplace. "Please, take a seat." She took the one closest to the fire. "Would you like anything to eat or drink?"

Rowen shook her head. "No, thank you."

Lore sat down, facing her. "First, I would like to say I am sorry about your loss. I knew Jedrek Mar for many years. He was a good man."

Rowen nodded, her face tightening in the firelight. Lore saw her look and moved on. "I would also like to say welcome to the White City. Have you ever been here before?"

"No," Rowen clasped her hands across her lap.

"Perhaps between training sessions you'll have a chance to visit the city. There are many shops along the main street."

"That would be nice."

Lore could still feel tension between them and wondered if it had to do with the previous evening. How to approach that subject . . . ?

"How was your trip?" he asked.

"It was . . . otherwise uneventful."

Lore decided to plunge ahead. "And how are you dealing with last night?"

Rowen turned to look at the fire. Lore studied her silhouette: her smooth pale skin, dark lashes, and the one strand of hair that had come loose from her braid. It fell across her cheek and curled just below her chin. She was certainly a beautiful young woman.

"I am learning to be more prepared for the unexpected," she said.

"Definitely a trait you will need as a varor." Gone was the shocked woman from last night. Instead sat a woman very much in control of herself. No, not controlled, *rigid*. As if she were placing herself behind a solid wall. Interesting. "You never know what you might face when guarding Lady Astrea," Lore continued, "but it seemed to me you handled yourself quite well."

Rowen looked as if she might say something more, then she seemed to change direction. "I still have much to learn."

Yes, definitely hiding behind a wall. Did it have to do with what had happened to her last night? Or maybe she was just the type who stayed cool until she came know to people more. Either way, Lore knew that now was not the time to start scaling that wall. Hopefully Rowen would warm up when they began their training sessions.

Lore realized he had been quiet too long. He nodded toward the sword belted to her waist. "So you already know how to use a sword?"

"Yes, my father taught me."

"Good, I'll test your skills tomorrow to see where you can improve." He was quickly running out of words to say. He could also see exhaustion creeping across her face. Time to wrap up their time.

"Rowen." Lore leaned across his knees. "These next few weeks are going to be tough. Not only will you be pushed to your limits physically, but mentally as well. The position of a varor is not for everyone." He watched her face tighten again. "But I will do everything I can to train you and help you decide if being a varor is for you." And he meant every word he said.

Rowen studied him with those large eyes of hers. "Thank you, sir."

"You're welcome." Lore moved to stand.

Rowen reached out and touched his arm, stopping him. "And . . . thank you for your room last night."

Lore looked at her and smiled. "It was not a problem. I'm glad I could be of service to you." His eyes wandered toward the bag that lay near the long table behind them. "Is that your bag?"

"Yes," Rowen said, glancing at the dark lump on the floor.

"Here, allow me." Lore walked over and picked up the bag. He looked at her, surprised. "Is this everything?" It felt . . . light. At least, lighter than he thought it would be.

"Yes," Rowen said. "I did not pack much."

Lore shrugged and turned toward the staircase. "For now, you will stay in one of the rooms here in the Guards Quarter." He walked toward the staircase. Rowen followed. At the top, he walked along the balcony and opened the last door on the left.

The inside of the room was dark except for pale light streaming in from the window in front of them. A single bed lay against the left wall, a wood chest and small table on the right. On the floor was a braided rug.

Lore placed the bag on the floor beside the bed and went back downstairs. He lit a lamp near the fireplace, then brought it back up.

"There, that's better," he said. He walked in and placed the lamp on the table. Out of the corner of his eye he saw Rowen begin to rub her arms as she looked over the room.

"I'm sorry there's no fireplace. I'll send a servant up with a warming brick for your bed."

She turned toward him. "Thank you. That would be nice."

"First thing tomorrow, meet me in the common room downstairs. And wear something comfortable to move in. You'll be measured for your uniform and training attire in the afternoon. Until then, the shirt and pants you're wearing now will suffice."

Lore moved toward the door, then turned. "If there is anything else you need, don't hesitate to ask." Rowen nodded. It was time for him to go. "Good night, Rowen."

Lore heard the door shut as he headed back downstairs. He still felt dazed by the turn of events. Part of him truly thought Commander Jedrek's daughter would turn down the varor position. To move from a small country village to the White City was a big leap. And most of the Ryland villages took care of their own. But here she was—and the same woman from the Mostyn inn, no less.

Lore recalled Rowen's likeness as he began his trek through the castle toward his own private quarters. She looked nothing like her father. But perhaps she possessed Commander Jedrek's sense of honor and respect. And she'd said her father had trained her. Knowing Commander Jedrek and his skill with the sword, there would probably be very little he would need to teach her.

The next morning Rowen stood in the doorway that separated the guard's common room from the training room. Her mouth hung slightly open. The training room was at least two stories high with a glass dome to let in natural light. Bright blue sky shone through the glass. She kept staring at the ceiling. She had never seen a roof made out of glass before.

Slowly she looked down. White stone encased the room, a room large enough to hold at least three cabins from her village. The floor was made of long wooden boards placed tightly together. A long white line had been painted halfway across the room. The far side of the room had a large circle painted on the wood floor. The side nearest her held no circle.

Along the right wall hung blunt practice swords. Lore stood in front of the weaponry. He appeared to be choosing out their swords. Benches were set around the room. Dull grey rags were tossed on the benches or lay on the floor underneath.

"This should do," Lore said. He turned and held a practice sword in each hand. He crossed the room, his boots echoing against the walls and floor. He stopped and held one out to her.

Rowen reached for the sword and felt her stomach tighten. She had the skills and knew it. But it did not ease the fear that she would somehow fall short of Captain Lore's expectations. She was grateful the training room was empty.

Lore led her to the middle of the first half of the room. "Let's warm up first."

Rowen nodded. She started out slow and jerky. Her fingers were cold and she had a hard time gripping the hilt. A moment later, the sword dropped. She blushed and bent down.

"Relax."

Rowen looked up to find Lore smiling at her.

"There is no need to be nervous," he said. "Take your time with your warm-up. We will begin when you feel ready."

Rowen nodded and grabbed her sword. She straightened up and turned away. She breathed in deeply. This time the exercises came more naturally, more assured. She went through each set her father had taught her until her limbs felt warm and limber.

"Are you ready?"

Rowen stopped. She looked over at Lore. "Yes."

"Good. Let's begin."

They turned and faced each other. Rowen went into position.

"Good," Lore said. "Now keep your sword slightly upward. If you let it drop, you leave yourself open."

Rowen tilted the blade a bit higher but kept the hilt near her body. Unlike the large broadswords used by the military, she used a smallsword. This made it easier to handle. And the purpose of her sword was not to hack at an enemy but to defend and protect.

Lore began to circle her, his sword pointed upward, looking for an opening.

Rowen kept her eyes on him, wary that his superior height gave him an advantage. In her periphery she paid special attention to his sword. When she was younger, she could always sense when her father was going to strike—just by a twitch of his eye or a sudden muscle movement at his neck. She was finding this to be true of Captain Lore, as well.

He lunged, twisting his sword to his right.

Rowen bounced back, dropping the end of her sword a fraction and caught his blade near her hilt.

He brought his blade up again and went for her other side. She parried his attack.

Lore changed his move and went for her other side, moving faster.

She snapped her hands down and blocked the blow.

Each time she blocked, he went for the area she left exposed. Thrust, parry. Thrust, parry, thrust again.

Rowen felt herself drawn into the duel, no longer thinking but acting on instinct. Memories began to flow through her mind of another time and another place, when her father had first taught her to use the sword.

At first it had been a coping mechanism, something for Jedrek to do just after her mother had died. Perhaps he'd felt that, if he could train Rowen to defend herself, she would be more protected in this world where death could come at any moment. Not that a sword could do anything against the ravaging disease that had taken Ann Mar away from them.

But after a few months, it had become a bonding time between them. Through their exercises, Rowen had become stronger, and Jedrek had worked through the death of his beloved Ann. And both had found comfort in their father-daughter relationship.

Rowen swallowed the wave of grief that swept over her and brought her mind back to the duel, moving faster and faster, her hits strong. Soon, she started answering Lore's moves with ones of her own.

Captain Lore made a great opponent. He was fast and creative in his movements. She quickly parried one of his thrusts and blew at a wisp of hair that had come loose from her braid.

He let his guard down.

Rowen struck.

It wasn't hard enough to do any damage, but by the way Lore was now massaging his side, she was afraid that, in her eagerness, she had hurt him.

Rowen brought her sword to her side. "Are you all right?"

Lore glanced up. "Yes. I'll probably bruise, but that's common."

"I didn't mean to hit you so hard."

He laughed and stopped rubbing. "Are you jesting? I *want* you to be so good that you hit me when I let my guard down. Besides, it's nothing compared to when Aren and I spar. Sometimes I think he's out for blood."

Her concern changed to confusion. "Aren?"

Lore laughed again, and Rowen found she liked the sound. "Aren is a guard and one of the varors for Lord Gaynor. You'll meet him soon enough." He sheathed his sword. "That's enough for now." Rowen followed suit. "Come and sit." Lore walked toward one of the benches that surrounded the large training room.

He sat down with his back against the wall. Rowen took a seat nearby. His eyes were half closed in thought. For a moment she studied him. Lore was taller than her, broad shouldered, but not heavyset. His hair was damp from perspiration, and she thought she could detect some grey near his temples.

"You did well today." He opened his eyes and turned toward her. "Your skill with your sword is exceptional. But there is more to being a varor than just being able to fight. A varor uses whatever means necessary to protect his or her charge. And unlike a guard, a varor swears to protect even at the cost of his or her own life." He looked away. "That is something you will need to think about before you choose to become a varor."

Rowen glanced down at her hands. If she wanted this position, she would need to be willing to die for Lady Astrea. Her heart thudded faster at the thought. She stared at the leather glove and swallowed. Better death when saving another than death because of her mark.

"In the next few weeks, I will teach you what it means to be a varor," Lore said. "After that time, if you find you cannot commit, you will be allowed to leave. But if you choose to stay, you will take the vow of a varor and remain here until released by Lady Astrea or . . . for other reasons. Do you understand?"

Lore looked directly into her eyes. For one moment Rowen felt as though he could see right through her. He couldn't, could he? After all, with one touch, she could see inside others. His eyes pinned her in place. Rowen clenched her gloved hand and nodded.

"Good." His face relaxed into a smile. "We will spend the rest of the day going over exercises that will help improve your accuracy and endurance."

Later that day, Lore found himself rubbing his side again as he watched Rowen work through the exercises he had taught her earlier that morning.

"Who's the new guard?" a voice asked nearby. Lore turned to find Aren standing just behind him.

Aren stood a couple of inches shorter than him. He had light blond hair, which was pulled back with a leather cord, revealing the black tattoos that adorned the right side of his face. The black tattoos contrasted with his bright blue eyes. He was dressed in a simple white shirt and dark pants. A smallsword hung at his side.

"Actually, she's not a guard. Rowen is training to be Lady Astrea's new varor."

Aren's eyes went wide and he glanced back at Rowen. "That's Commander Jedrek's *daughter*? She looks nothing like him."

Lore laughed, remembering similar thoughts. "No. But what did you expect? A large bearded woman?"

Aren's face morphed into a mischievous grin, all the more

accentuated by the black tattoos along the right side of his face. "You wouldn't need to fear an entire city of guards falling for a bearded woman. But that one," he nodded in Rowen's direction, "is quite the opposite. She's beautiful."

"And fast and strong," Lore said, massaging his side.

Aren glanced at him. "She got you?" he said in surprise.

"She did."

Aren looked back toward the training circle with renewed interest. "Then I guess I will need to introduce myself. It's not every day the captain is bested by a new recruit."

Lore watched Aren walk toward Rowen, knowing the young man had every intention of doing just that.

Rowen stopped her exercises when Aren began to talk to her. Lore gave his side one last rub and headed out of the Guards Quarter. There was still a lot left to do today. But first, he was going to stop and see a healer about getting something for his side.

CHAPTER
6

Nierne kept one hand along the curled edge of the parchment. With her other hand she dipped a white feather quill into a vial of black ink. At her elbow lay a half rolled scroll, its edges ragged and stained with age. Her eyes darted from the scroll to the parchment beneath her hand. With stained fingertips she copied each word carefully, exactly. Dipping her quill again, she scanned the scroll, then copied the next three words. She did this for another ten minutes before placing her quill on the desk.

Nierne rolled her wrists and glanced out the window. The sun shone brightly across a brilliant azure sky. White puffy clouds chased each other over blue-green waters. Just over the Monastery wall and beyond Thyra's gates, she could see hundreds of ships moored along the docks, their bleached white sails whipping in the wind.

Houses of stone lined the narrow streets leading up from the docks. Women wearing white caps chatted on the street corners. Children ran along the cobblestone street. Dogs yapped at their heels. Squeals and laughter drifted up through the window like the sweet sounds of summer.

The gate creaked below. Nierne leaned over her desk and watched a white-cropped head move through the narrow opening and step out onto the street. She would know that head anywhere. Father Reth.

A basket was tucked beneath one arm, and his brown robes billowed behind him. The children nearby stopped and turned. They ran with smiles on their faces toward Father Reth. Nierne watched as he pulled a dark brown loaf from his basket and handed it to one of the children. The little boy beamed back up at Father Reth, then ran up the street, the loaf clutched securely under his arm.

Father Reth headed north along the street with the children crowding around him until they all disappeared around the corner. Nierne smiled and sat back. She knew where he was going. Every day Father Reth visited the poorer section of Thyra, to give bread to those who had none.

Slowly her smile vanished and her eyes drifted across the city, past the wealthy white-washed homes on the hills, past the deep green parks, past the Senate Hall, a circular white tower that dominated the heart of Thyra, past the fortress of Cragsmoor, toward the section of the city where she knew the lowest of Thyrian society lived.

She could not see the cracked and filthy buildings from here in the Monastery, but she did not need to. She could see them in her mind: two-story houses crushed together, blocking out every bit of sunlight. Bleak grey walls dotted with dingy windows. Sewage flowing along the street and filling the air with stench.

Even after all these years, those images had yet to fade from her memory. Nierne shuddered and picked up her quill. But her mind, now latched onto her past, began dredging up more memories, memories of sitting in a dark corridor, her legs pulled up to her chest, listening to the other side of the wall where her mother conducted business. Blue smoky haze drifting between the rooms and rats scurrying beneath the floorboards.

And the day the plague came.

Nierne felt a tear slip down her cheek. She quickly wiped it away, afraid it would fall on the parchment. She glanced toward the corner where Father Reth had disappeared. If it hadn't have been for him, she would still be in those slums, probably doing the same work her mother had done.

At that thought, she picked up her quill and began to copy the scroll beside her.

Minutes turned into hours. She lost herself in the work, in the precise lettering and the beautiful words. At last Nierne carefully finished the last copied word and began to check her work when a sound caught her attention. She paused, her quill hanging just over the inkwell. She cocked her ear toward the window. It sounded like shouting. Moments later, the sound faded away.

Puzzled, she looked out her window but could see nothing. With a shake of her head, Nierne placed her quill in the inkwell and continued to check her copy.

The shouting came back. She ignored it for a couple of seconds. Screams began to mingle with the shouts. Nierne frowned and lowered the parchment. She leaned toward the window. Below, people were staring toward the center of the city. Nierne leaned further out the window. "What in all the—"

The door burst open.

"Nierne!"

Nierne yanked her head back in. "Crackers, Simon, you scared me!" she said, clutching the front of her robe. "Do you know what is going on?

"No time to explain." Simon glanced back out into the hallway. "Father Cris has called everyone downstairs."

"Why?"

Simon dashed out of her room before answering. Other scribes ran past her doorway, their robes flying behind them. Nierne stood and took a step toward the door, then realized she could not leave the ancient parchment on her desk. She turned around and quickly but carefully grabbed the scroll, rolled it, and placed it back into its tube.

Outside, she could hear panicked shouts and cries filling the streets. The acrid smell of smoke began to drift in through the window.

Nierne popped the top on the tube and left it there on her desk. She hurried out into the hallway. Other inhabitants of the Monastery were rushing toward the stairs. Nierne fell into line behind them.

At the bottom of the staircase she found Father Cris shouting out orders. " . . . has happened . . . need to get the people to safety . . . hurry outside . . ." Nierne caught only snippets of his orders.

She found Simon and squeezed her way toward him. "I don't understand," Nierne whispered to him. "What is going on?"

Simon turned toward her, his eyes wide with fright. "The whole city's gone crazy," he whispered back. "Soldiers are marching the streets, snatching everyone they can."

"Soldiers are arresting people? But why?" The scribes nearest the doors hurried out.

"I don't know," Simon said. "But we're supposed to go and bring everyone we can find back here."

Before Nierne could ask any more questions, everyone was rushing toward the double front doors.

"Come on," Simon said, beckoning with his hand. He turned and followed the others out. Nierne stood by the staircase, fear trickling through her. What in all the Lands was going on? The whole city had gone crazy. But why? She took a deep breath and headed toward the doors.

Nierne crossed the small courtyard that stood between the Monastery and the walls, then stopped just outside the gates. People ran past her in a panicked stampede. Behind them were Thyrian soldiers dressed in yellow and chainmail. The soldiers marched in one long line spread across the street. Nierne watched as one man was caught by the collar of his shirt and dragged back past the line of soldiers. Smoke belched into the sky a couple blocks away, filling the air with its noxious odor. She turned away and coughed on the bitter air.

Nierne rubbed the smoke from her eyes and looked back toward the street. More people were picked off and grabbed by the line of soldiers advancing. Why were Thyrian soldiers doing this? These men and women should be protecting them, not grabbing them.

A woman hurried by, clutching a baby to her chest while trying to hold the hands of two boys. The soldiers were drawing near. With Father Cris' command in mind, Nierne moved. She ran after the woman and picked up one of the boys. The woman looked at her with fear, then relief in her eyes.

"Quick, this way!" Nierne shouted over the bedlam. The woman nodded in understanding—

Then clutched her baby and screamed.

Before Nierne could turn, she felt her hood yanked behind her. She stumbled back. A soldier appeared at her side and tore the boy from her arms.

"My *son!*" the woman screamed. Her hand reached out toward the soldier. Nierne fell to the ground. Hands gripped her shoulders and began dragging her across the street. Nierne struggled against the hold, digging her heals into the cobblestone. She reached up behind her. The grip on her shoulders moved to her hood. The neckline of her robe slipped up across her throat. Adrenaline raced through her body.

Nierne twisted around, trying to free her hood. She gasped in breath. Her throat constricted. Stars danced across her vision. She clawed at her hood—

Her hood loosened. Nierne sucked in great draughts of air. Arms grabbed her by the waist. She kicked back and screamed. She was turned around and tossed into the air—

Whomp. Her elbow and hip hit something hard. She scrambled up onto her knees and hands. She drew in deep breaths, her eyes still seeing flashes of light. Someone cried nearby. The floor lurched beneath her.

Nierne fell back.

"Get off me!" Hands pushed against her from behind. Nierne scurried forward and grabbed the wooden railing in front of her. She pulled herself up. The wagon rumbled beneath her knees. Nierne peered over the railing. She could see the line of soldiers still marching down the street. People were running ahead of them.

Down the side streets were more soldiers and more wagons. Men, women, and children were tossed into the wagons like bags of grain. Strange black smoke wove through the shadows.

Nierne turned and looked ahead. A Thyrian soldier drove the wagon. Two old men, three women, and a very scared little girl shared the wagon with her. Past the driver, she could see a procession of wagons filled with people making their way up the street.

One man leaped two wagons ahead of them. There were shouts of surprise and encouragement. Everyone turned to watch him. The man landed and began to sprint down the street. He had barely past the wagon ahead when a soldier appeared from one of the alleyways. The soldier's sword swung out and caught the man in the middle. The man stumbled and fell. The soldier walked away without a second glance.

Horrified, Nierne stared at the man as her wagon passed him. He struggled to push himself up, then fell flat. Blood pooled around his body and trickled between the cobblestones.

Nierne turned away. Bile filled her throat.

"Why are they doing this?" one of the women asked in a shaky voice.

Nierne shook her head and kept her lips shut.

"I don't know," the older man said. "My son tried to ask and . . ." Nierne looked back at the man. His head dipped forward and his shoulders shook.

More shouts filled the air. Nierne looked over. Another man tried to run. Two soldiers went after him. He fell and was left on the street. A minute later there were more shouts, but Nierne didn't look up this time. She didn't want to watch.

There were no more shouts.

Nierne slid down into the wagon and brought her knees up.

The wagon lurched its way up the street. Somewhere in the fog of her mind were questions. Why? Why were Thyrian soldiers doing this? Why were people being rounded up? Overhead the sky turned crimson red, the smoke from burning buildings coloring the setting sun.

The wagon rumbled beneath a large stone archway. Nierne glanced up in surprise. The towering fortress of Cragsmoor loomed ahead. Why were they being taken to Cragsmoor?

The others in her wagon looked around, surprise and fear etched across their faces.

"Why are they taking us here?" the same woman said.

Nierne shook her head again. But dark thoughts began to fill her mind. Cragsmoor was built for two purposes: to protect and to imprison. Nierne swallowed. She had a feeling they were not coming here for protection.

The wagon came to a halt. Around her other wagons were being unloaded as people were herded inside the fortress like cattle.

"Get out!" a soldier shouted and brandied a long pole. A second later, he used that pole to jab those in the wagon.

"Ouch!" Nierne cried. She rubbed her jabbed side. The others scrambled out.

"Inside, inside!" soldiers shouted, herding the people through the tall curved doorway. Anyone who fell out of line was jabbed by long poles or swords. And if they proved to be too slow . . .

Nierne quickly followed the crowd of people. The air grew hot and stifling inside the fortress. Sweltering bodies pressed together, stumbling forward in the dark. She felt lightheaded. The smell of human fear filled her nostrils. *Oh Word*, Nierne thought, her eyes searching ahead, hoping to see where they were being led, *where are You?*

She stumbled a couple of times. Bodies pressed up alongside her. Some people cried, others shouted questions. Her own voice was trapped behind tight lips.

"In here," a man in uniform shouted. He grabbed Nierne's arm and shoved her through the doorway. Inside was a dark cavernous room. A cold, musty smell hung in the air. The walls and floor were made from grey stone. Two pillars stood in the middle of the room. Three barred windows were built into the far wall.

Nierne stood, staring at the room. No, not room, prison. A prison built to contain many people.

Someone stumbled into her from behind. Nierne fell forward. Shock filled her body. More and more people were crowding into the room around her. Without thinking, she walked toward the far right window. Red sky blazed between the bars set much too high for her to look out.

A door slammed shut behind.

At that sound, many of those around her burst into cries of fear. Others pounded on the door. Nierne turned and slumped down against the cold jagged wall. She could barely see around her. Her hands shook so bad she clasped them together.

"Word, where are You?" Nierne whispered in a shaky voice. She looked around at the people gathered inside the dungeon. No voice answered her, no peace filled her heart. Instead, a steady flow of iciness stole over her, numbing her until she felt nothing at all.

Rain fell in sheets outside the barred window. Slowly a rivulet made its way down from the opening toward the cold stone floor below, where an ever-increasing puddle formed. Nierne shifted her body farther from the puddle, hugging her robes a little closer.

Time had lost its way here. She remembered counting ten days, but she'd lost track after that. A small child whimpered close by. Nierne turned and watched from the corner of her eye as the mother wrapped her arms around the little one. An old woman over in the shadows began to cough loudly, each breath wracking her body.

Nobody spoke anymore. There wasn't much to say. Nierne shifted again, her fingers numb with cold. The rain continued to beat down steadily outside.

A loud creak echoed within the dungeon. The single wooden door slowly turned on its hinges. Nierne stared at the door in surprise. The door never opened here. Food and tepid water was shoved through a small opening, but that was all the contact she and the other prisoners had with the outside world.

Nierne stood, a trickle of hope slowly penetrating her leaden heart. Perhaps this had all been a huge mistake. Perhaps now they were finally being set free.

Two men entered the dungeon, followed by a couple of Thyrian soldiers. One was tall and fair. His hair was pulled back from a face that looked like it had been chiseled from fine marble. The other was shorter but even more beautiful in appearance. Soft black locks surrounded his face. Both wore dark pants and silk shirts, covered by long black cloaks embroidered in silver.

To say the men were handsome would be to say a rose was simply pretty. Nierne found herself enraptured by their beauty. Why would such men be in such a place like this?

"*Shadonae!*" the old man behind her hissed.

Disbelief, then horror filled her mind. Shadonae? Here? Nierne took a step back. How? They were myth—

Her mouth clamped shut and she watched the fair-haired man step forward. He lifted his hand. His cloak slid back to reveal a hand covered in a black glove. Slowly he began to pull at the tips.

At his movement, everyone retreated from him.

Nierne was knocked to the ground. People scrambled like rats to the far corners of the chamber, flattening themselves against the walls. The man continued to pull at his glove, untroubled by the ripple he had caused. Nierne picked herself up and moved toward one of the pillars. Her limbs began to shake.

He couldn't be, she thought, watching him pull his hand free of the black glove. But her body surged with fear anyway. Because if he really were a Shadonae, then what he was about to do—

His eyes began to roam the room, searching for something. Nierne flattened herself against the pillar. His eyes passed over her, then stopped. He lifted his hand and pointed toward an older woman across from her.

The woman's eyes bulged. She began to shriek, the sound echoing across the chamber. The people around her drew away, leaving her to collapse onto the stone floor.

Nierne stared at her, unable to move. The woman held out her hands, begging for help. A soldier stepped forward to retrieve her. "Please!" she cried, pawing the soldier's legs. The soldier ignored her. He grabbed her and hauled her toward the pale-haired man.

The woman fell at his feet. She grabbed his cloak and sobbed. The man bent over and took hold of the woman's arm. The woman became silent, a look of horror flashing across her face. Then a scream erupted from her throat. Her body arched. After a few moments more, she began convulsing.

Someone let out a whimper. Others turned their heads. But Nierne could not look away. Her eyes were riveted on the scene before her. She watched the woman shudder, moans now replacing her screams. But it was her eyes that held Nierne's. Eyes pleading for help. Her eyes slowly dulled, and the last flicker of life faded away.

After a moment more, the man let go of the corpse. No, not man, Nierne thought with horror. She watched the woman's body fall with a heavy thud onto the stone floor.

Shadonae.

With a casualness that belied what had just taken place, he pulled his glove back on and moved toward his companion. The other Shadonae stepped forward and began to look over the crowd. People ducked their heads.

His eyes stopped on Nierne. Stunned, she tried to look away, but with an unseen will he held her gaze. Helplessly she stared into his eyes, desire radiating from those depths. The corner of his mouth turned upward.

Her mouth went dry in raw terror. Nierne backed around the pillar, shaking her head, unable to tear her eyes away from his. The soldier behind him began to move toward her, but the Shadonae stopped him with an upraised hand.

"I will get her myself," he said in soft, low voice. The Shadonae walked slowly toward her, seeming to savor the fear he invoked.

Nierne grew frantic. She tried to shout, but fear held her mouth shut. *Word, save me!* She cried in her mind.

The Shadonae flinched as if burned.

Emboldened, Nierne continued to cry out, desperation lacing her thoughts. *Please, please save me!*

The Shadonae snarled, his eyes now looking past Nierne. His face grew dark with anger. He spoke, his words unintelligible. Nobody moved. Nierne held her breath and carefully glanced behind her. No one stood there. Who was he talking to?

The Shadonae stopped. He flung his cloak behind and turned. The other Shadonae questioned his companion, but Nierne could not hear what they said. A moment later they left through the doorway.

The two soldiers hesitated, as if unsure what to do, then they followed their masters. The door slammed shut behind them.

"Oh, Word," Nierne said, falling to her knees. Part of her burst with relief. Another part remained numb with shock.

Shadonae. They were here, in Thyra. Nierne gasped and looked up. That explained everything.

The woman's body near the door caught her attention: broken, eyes staring at the ceiling, her mouth open in a silent scream. The others inside the dungeon stood as far away from her as they could. Nierne found herself cringing away as well.

Guilt flooded up inside her chest. Nierne turned away from the corpse and covered her face. She pushed her palms into her eyes until stars popped across her vision. But she could not erase the image of the woman's face from her mind.

Nierne, a Follower of the Word, a keeper of His written words, had done nothing to help that woman. Instead, she had let fear paralyze her—until the Shadonae's gaze had fallen on her. Only then had she prayed.

And she had prayed only for herself.

Hours afterward, Thyrian soldiers came and took away the woman's body. But the hopelessness her corpse represented remained.

Nierne lay on the floor in the far corner, her heart heavy. The woman's face kept visiting her mind. She rolled over. Why had the Word saved her and not everyone else? Nierne knew that many were trapped here in Cragsmoor—were they all simply waiting until the Shadonae had need of their service or life? If so, why had the Word stepped in and saved *her*?

She pulled her knees in toward her chest. What about her was even worth saving? Guilt ate at her heart.

She heard something. Nierne lifted her head and turned toward the door, listening. Others were doing the same. There it was again. Soldiers ran past, one shouting orders. His words were muffled, but now everyone was awake. A couple of people stood and moved near the door. Nierne stayed in the back, remembering the last time the door had opened.

The noise outside grew louder. Shouts rang out, and the sound of swords clashing echoed on the other side of the door.

The prisoners began to stand, turning to one another, whispering excitedly.

"Are they coming?"

"They're freeing us!"

"Thank the Word."

Nierne pulled herself up beside one of the stone pillars and watched the door. The fight sounded quite close now.

The door shuddered, and a face appeared in the barred window. "We're getting you out," he shouted. His face dipped below again. The door shuddered one more time.

Everyone began to crowd around the door with eagerness. Nierne took a hesitant step away from the pillar. Was the Word finally going to save them?

The door swung open.

"Quickly, this way," a voice shouted. People began to push their way out.

Nierne felt herself pulled along with the rest, her doubts erasing with every step. They were really doing it. They were finally escaping this nightmare.

She could hear fighting down the hall, but the mass was moving away from it. Fear and excitement gave the people speed. They moved as one along the stone corridor. Ahead, Nierne could see a torch lighting the way.

Someone near the rear hollered, "They're coming!"

Panic erupted, rippling from the back. One woman began to sob hysterically. Nierne was shoved against the wall. It was everyone for themselves. She tried to rejoin the flow but was pushed back again. The third time, her head slammed into the wall. Flashes of light erupted across her vision.

By the time her vision returned, most of the mass of prisoners had already moved on. Nierne turned to follow, but a hand suddenly grabbed hers. Nierne screamed and yanked back.

"Take it!"

That voice . . . "Father Cris?" Nierne stopped pulling and squinted at the shriveled old man who held her hand with an iron-like grip.

Instead of answering her, Father Cris pulled at one of the slender gold chains around his neck. For a moment she thought he was going to give her his pendant, the symbol of his devotion to the Monastery. Instead, he pulled out a key. "This key opens the door to the catacombs below the Monastery." He thrust the cold metal into her hand.

"Why are you—"

"There is no time to talk!" Father Cris shoved Nierne toward the large doorway ahead. "Get these people out of here!" Before Nierne could respond, he had already turned around and was moving farther down the hall.

For one moment she thought about following him, then she realized he had given her the only means to escape this doomed city. Nierne lifted her robe and ran toward the large doorway ahead, her body aching as it readjusted to moving again after weeks of confinement.

She stopped outside the doorway and looked up. Cragsmoor loomed high in the darkening sky. A full moon rose over the city. Over to her right lay the door on the ground. It looked like it had been torn from its hinges.

She stared at the fortress. She never thought she would leave this place. Not long ago, she'd been sure she would die here. Instead, she was free.

"Thank You, Word," Nierne whispered.

She turned and ran toward the gates. As she neared the archway, she glanced ahead. Far down the streets under the moonlight she could see people running. Nierne grasped the key tightly in her hand and ran toward them.

Then the screams began.

Nierne lurched to a stop. She stared ahead in horror. Dark swirls of smoke-like beings darted out from the shadows and swooped down on escapees, attacking them and leaving bodies scattered along the street. She watched as one black smoke cloud wove its way around a woman. The woman screamed, then went silent. Her body dropped to the cobblestones, and the creature moved on.

Nierne held a hand to her neck, her eyes staring at the street, and the wisps of blackness weaving their way along. The Shadonae had brought the Mordra over from the other side? She turned and clutched the stone archway. How could they survive against these shadow-beings? They couldn't even touch them. No one could touch the shadows, let alone kill them.

Nierne felt like she was going to vomit what little she held in her stomach. There was no escape from this nightmare, no escape at all . . .

She felt the hard metal of Father Cris's key press into her palm. She looked down at the key. Perhaps there *was* a way to escape.

Out of the corner of her eye, Nierne saw movement. A wisp of blackness, barely visible in the moonlight, began to weave its way up the street toward Cragsmoor.

She held her breath. It was three blocks away. No one else was near her. She wasn't sure how well the shadow-like thing could see, but didn't want to wait to find out.

Nierne tried to move, only to find that panic had paralyzed her. *Calm down*, she told herself, taking a few deep breaths. Her legs loosened up slightly. The shadow drew closer. It was now or never.

Silently she slipped to the right. She moved from building to building. Far away she heard another scream. Minutes later, another. And another. Each scream pierced her heart.

Why, why, *why*? Nierne cried inside her mind. Why was the Word allowing this? No answer came. She clenched her jaw and pressed on.

After a minute she looked back. The shadow did not appear to be following her. She turned and ran again, expecting to be enveloped by darkness. But it never came.

Slowly Nierne made her way across the city toward the Monastery. The moon moved across the sky, lighting her way. An autumn chill filled the air. She clutched her robes close to her body and ran from building to building.

She stopped to rest inside doorways or behind fences overgrown with weeds. Her time in the fortress had weakened her. But she didn't stay in one place for long. As soon as she could, she pressed on.

Silence hung over the city like a death shroud. Nierne watched for other survivors, but saw no one. The buildings and streets were dark and empty. Perhaps they were being as careful as she was.

As the first rays of dawn began to spread across the eastern sky, she finally reached the Monastery. The stone building loomed ahead, a brooding structure that had stood for countless years as a light of knowledge. Nierne glanced up at the only place she had ever called home. So far it had escaped any damage from the fire and chaos that had been wrought upon so many other buildings in Thyra.

Nierne crept around back and let herself in through the garden gate. Weeds filled the flowerbeds along the narrow path that led up to the back door, something that would never have happened under the watchful eye of Father Karl. Just one more reminder how much everything had changed since that fateful day weeks ago. She opened the back door, and quietly shut it behind her.

The Monastery was silent. No songs, no low whispers of conversation, not even the soft scratch of quills as history and the ancient writings were copied once more to ensure that people never forgot.

But they had, Nierne realized. She walked along the hallway toward the stairs. The deceitful power of the Shadonae had been forgotten, and now the people of Thyra were paying.

She crept up the staircase and walked along the second floor. The wooden floor creaked beneath her feet. She stopped and looked inside the second room. A fine film of dust and dirt lay on her desk. The parchment she had been writing on weeks ago lay on the ground, water-stained and crumpled. Over in the corner sat the tube that held the scroll she had been copying.

A cool, salty breeze drifted through the open window. Nierne crossed the room and carefully peered out. The sun rose across the city. Below, nothing stirred. She looked up and down the street. Nothing. Not even a dog. As far as she could see, the city was empty.

Nierne shivered. She backed away from the window and sat on the floor. She rubbed her arm with one hand and looked at the key Father Cris had given her. What was she supposed to do with this? Father Cris had told her to get the people out of the city. But there seemed to be no one to rescue.

She looked back at the window. Should she wait and watch? But for how long?

Nierne placed the key around her neck and drew her knees up to her chest. She watched the window and listened, hoping to hear something. White clouds drifted across the window. After half an hour, she crawled back to the window and looked out.

The sun shone now brightly over the city. But still nothing moved. Nierne watched for a couple of minutes, then sighed and backed away. She shook her head. She should go find help.

Her eyes widened. Nierne looked up. Of course. There had to be people outside the city, people who had not yet been taken.

Nierne scrambled to her feet and headed out the door. She followed the hall to the stairs and headed down. She crossed the Monastery and stopped by the kitchen in the back. Copper pots hung above a long wooden table. The fire in the fireplace had burned out long ago. Sunlight streamed in through the high windows along the eastern wall. The subtle scent of spoilage hung in the air.

Nierne grimaced and looked for anything still edible. She found two shriveled apples in a basket on the floor. She grabbed the apples and hurried out.

Near the back of the Monastery was a second set of stairs that led down to the underground rooms and catacombs. She followed the stairs down and stopped in front of a tall thick door. Beyond lay the catacombs, the burial place for those honored by Thyra. When she was younger, the catacombs had scared her. Perhaps it was because death had seemed so much closer to the living in such a place.

Nierne placed the long metal rod Father Cris had given her into the small hole near the handle. She heard a soft click as the lock turned. She pushed the heavy door open and entered the catacombs.

The stale air felt warm compared to the cold sea wind flowing through the monastery upstairs. Small slits of light shone down from somewhere above, lighting the dark tunnels. There were large hollowed out sections along the walls, each containing a beautifully carved white box. Her middle gave a slight lurch at the sight. She knew what the boxes contained.

She turned and shut the door. The door closed with a soft thud. She stood there with her hand on the handle for one moment and listened. A deep silence filled the catacombs. Slowly, Nierne turned around.

She made her way along the corridor, passing by tunnels that jutted from the main one. The eerie lights overhead blinked in and out, sending her moving between shadow and light. Childhood fears began to swell inside her. She knew there was nothing to be afraid of in this place. The dead could hold no power over her. Father Reth had told her that. But she still hated this place.

Nierne picked up her pace and hurried through the catacombs. Then she saw the door ahead.

She fumbled with the key and pressed it into the small hole. She turned the lock and gave the door a push. The door swung out with a loud groan.

Fresh, cold air pressed against her face. Nierne breathed in the air and stumbled out of the catacombs. Bright sunlight blinded her eyes. She pushed the door shut and leaned against it. Ahead of her, the bright green hills of Kerre waved in the wind.

She wanted to drop to her knees and rest. But she could not linger here. Behind her stood the walls of Thyra. She might be on the other side of it now, but the enemy could still be close by.

So Nierne turned and locked the door to the catacombs. She placed the key back into her robes and looked around.

She then realized she had no idea where to go.

Nierne glanced to her left. She could see the wide-open sea, the white sails of ships moored nearby dancing in the breeze.

Her heart sank. She had no idea how to sail and suspected that, even if she could, those kinds of ships would require more hands than just hers. So she turned the other way. Green hills stretched as far as the eyes could see until, in the far distance, she could make out the faint tips of the Ari Mountains.

She knew there were some villages near mountains. Perhaps the hand of the Shadonae had not yet reached them. However, the thought of traveling that far on foot and alone overwhelmed her. But what choice did she have? Stay here and hide in the Monastery?

Nierne looked one more time at the city walls. Then she turned and hiked up her soiled robes. She set her face toward the mountains and began to walk. What she would do once she reached her destination, she had no idea. At this point, she was taking it one day at a time. Because that might be all she had.

CHAPTER
7

The next few weeks were a blur for Rowen. She trained hard, her muscles aching every morning when she woke up. But she could also feel her arms strengthening from the exercises.

Slowly she pulled her uniform on, her shoulders protesting every movement. Braiding her hair took even longer.

Pale morning sunlight poured through the window nearby. Rowen took her nightgown and laid it inside the wooden chest that came with her room. On the table a servant had left a fresh pitcher of water and bowl. She quickly splashed her face and dried it with a cloth. Lastly, she belted on her sword and headed out to the common room.

Rowen could hear voices rising from the table just below the balcony. Some of the guards were coming off night duty. Others were grabbing a bite to eat before heading to their posts. She stepped off the stairway and headed toward the back table where a steaming black pot had been brought up from the kitchen. She filled a bowl and sat down stiffly near the end of the table.

"Looks like the captain's been working you hard," a voice next to her said. Aren plopped down on the seat across from her, holding a half-eaten biscuit in one hand. He gave her a grin and took another bite.

Rowen gave him a small smile in return. She had met the Nordic her first day, surprised to find a guard who was not a Rylander. As usual, his hair was pulled back, exposing the black markings across his right cheek. In the culture of Nordica, they were called Marks of Remembrance, each one representing a loved one who had died. On her first day, Rowen had learned Aren's marks were for his father and two older brothers.

"Yeah, a bit sore this morning." Rowen rolled her shoulders.

"If you think that's bad, wait until you start your unarmed training." Aren popped the last bite of bread into his mouth.

"Unarmed?"

He swallowed. "Yeah. The captain believes in training his guards not only in swords but also in hand to hand. After your first day of that, you'll be lucky to roll out of bed."

Hand to hand? Rowen felt her chest tighten. She had not been physically close to anyone since she had touched Cleon and that man in the inn. She paused, her gloved hand clutching her spoon just above her bowl. What if Lore made her remove her glove? Or—she felt faint at the thought, her spoon dropping into her cereal—what if her glove was not enough to stop the power of her mark?

"Rowen, are you all right?"

"What?" Rowen looked back over at Aren.

The grin on Aren's face disappeared. "It's really not that bad, the hand to hand training. Well . . . it is, but the pain only lasts a couple days. We've all gone through it and lived."

"Oh, it's not that. It's—"

"It's the intimate factor, isn't it?" Aren bent his head toward Rowen's. "Training closely with the captain. Don't worry. Captain Lore is a perfect gentleman. You're not the first woman he's taught."

All thoughts concerning her mark vanished. "What?" Rowen felt her face turn bright red. "No, it's not that, not that at all—"

Aren winked at her and laughed so hard that Rowen thought he might choke. A part of her hoped he would. Aren waved his hand as he caught his breath. "The look on your face! You should've seen it."

It took her a moment to calm down, but then a small smile stole across her lips. She wondered if it were possible to stay mad at Aren for long.

"Nah, there's nothing to worry about," Aren said after catching his breath. "You'll be sore, but the captain's the best teacher there is, even compared to a Nordic."

"That's good to know," Rowen said. Never would Aren suspect the true reason for her unease. She let out her breath and picked up her spoon. She ladled up some of the grainy cereal. "Speaking of the captain, where is he?"

"He should be here shortly." Aren stood and gave her another grin. "Time for duty. See you around."

Rowen watched Aren leave and wondered if anything ever got under his skin.

She sighed and took another bite of the warm mush. The other guards laughed down at the other end of the table. No one else ever sat with her. Probably because she tended to move away when they tried. It was just she was afraid of touching others, of accidently triggering that power that lay just beneath the strange mark on her hand.

It was better to be alone and undiscovered than to be found out.

After breakfast, Rowen headed through the double doors at the end of the common room into the training room to begin her less intensive exercises.

Before she knew it, the sun was high in the sky, its light filtering down through the glass dome above. On the other side of the room a couple of the guards had stripped off their shirts and were engaging in some kind of wrestling within the circle drawn on the floor.

Rowen watched them for a moment before beginning her next set. As she moved her arms, a horrible thought entered her head. Surely she would not be learning that kind of combat, would she? She glanced at the guards again.

"Ready to start?"

Rowen nearly jumped from her boots. "Captain!" she said, twisting around.

"Sorry to startle you." Lore took a quick step back from the pointed end of her sword. "I thought you heard me enter the room."

"No, sir," Rowen replied. She realized she was still pointing her sword at him. She quickly sheathed the weapon.

"Actually, you won't be needing that today," Lore said. "Today we will begin your unarmed training. So go ahead and put your sword back in your room while I have a quick word with Geoffrey."

Lore walked toward the other guards while Rowen left the training room. Panic filled her chest. She reached her room and shut the door behind her. Memories of her exile flashed before her eyes. Rowen squeezed them shut. Anguish churned inside her heart. "I can't go through that again," she whispered. "I *won't* go through that again."

Rowen opened her eyes. Her heart hardened under her resolve. She walked toward the chest at the end of her bed. She placed her sword inside and shut the lid. She lifted her hand and stared at the glove. Creases folded in the leather as she closed her hand into a tight fist. No, she thought firmly. Whatever happened, she would not take the glove off. She would just need to find a valid excuse to keep it on.

Lore stood near the door as Rowen entered. "As I said, today we will begin your unarmed training." Thankfully, he didn't mention the glove. He only motioned toward the training circle. "Shall we begin?"

Rowen felt the weight of her mark ease as she followed Lore. They stopped in the middle of the first circle. The other guards had left, leaving her and Lore alone in the training room. The sun had moved overhead, throwing a circle of light against the far wall. The faint scent of sweat hung in the warm air.

"Face me," Lore said. His voice echoed quietly across the training room. Rowen turned so that she stood square with Lore. "First is balance." He had her move her feet until they were slightly apart. "Bend a little." Rowen bent forward. "Now straighten your back." She could feel her weight sitting toward her middle. "Good. Balance is one of the first steps to unarmed training. Without balance, it doesn't matter what you do with the rest of your body, you'll just fall over with the first shove—" Lore pushed her.

Automatically Rowen stepped back, feeling her body distribute her weight between both legs, but the weight still remained around her middle.

"See?" Lore circled her.

"Yes." Rowen brought her body back into the start position.

After a few more shoves, Lore came to stand in front of her again. "You have good balance. Good. Now for the next part." He moved closer to her and began to move her arms into position. Then he grabbed her hand.

For one heartbeat her body went rigid at his touch. It was *that* hand. Rowen waited for the blast of heat to fill her chest, to rush down her arm, to force her to see inside Lore . . .

But nothing happened.

It took another heartbeat for this to register.

Then relief flooded her in one swift whoosh. The glove had worked! Her secret was safe. She could touch another.

"Rowen, are you all right?"

Rowen found Lore looking at her, his hands still on her arm where he had been positioning them. "What?" she said, her mind still on the newfound joy of her discovery.

"You had a strange look on your face. Everything all right?"

"Yes."

Lore took a step back. "Are you sure? I'm not making you feel uncomfortable, am I?"

"No, I'm fine." Rowen broke into a smile. "Go ahead and continue."

Lore stared at her again, as if he were trying to peer beyond what he could see. Rowen looked back. His eyes were such a strange color of green . . .

Lore blinked and gave her a smile. "Then I will continue." He moved beside her and again began to move her arms in place.

They spent the next few hours together. Lore showed her many different moves. It felt invigorating to have so much power in combat without any weapon in her hand. She felt strong and capable. Rowen committed to memory what Lore taught her, all the while sensing something growing inside of her. The newfound knowledge that she could now touch others had released a powerful desire. A desire for connection. For friendship.

That feeling left a wake of pain. Rowen realized how lonely she had been since leaving Cinad. For weeks she had closed up her heart—moving and doing, but not feeling. Sparring with Lore and the guards had allowed her to keep her distance. But now, having to work closely with Lore made Rowen realize how much she craved companionship and touch.

Suddenly she was aware of Lore standing behind her. He said something and moved her arm again. His light touch on her elbow intensified that longing. Rowen moved as he instructed, her heart feeling as though it had crawled out of a dark place into light.

By the time evening crept across the glass dome above, Rowen found every muscle in her body sore. She had fallen down countless times. Lore kept making it past her unrefined defensive moves. But every time she felt the firm grip of his hand as he helped her back up, and every time he touched her glove and nothing happened, her heart sang. Who cared about sore muscles? She could touch again!

"Well," Lore said as he reached down for the hundredth time that day, "we should probably quit for the evening."

Rowen could only nod, barely able to get to her feet even with his help.

He seemed to notice. "I'll have a servant bring a basin of warm water to your room."

"That would be nice." It wouldn't be a bath, quite, but the warm water would feel good on her sore muscles.

Instead of letting her go, he moved his hand to her elbow. "Let's see if we can find some dinner in the common room first."

Rowen nodded, and they walked toward the doors at the end of the training room.

In the common room, only a handful of guards were there. They lingered around the large table. Lore led her to the nearest bench and let go of her elbow. She sat down with a groan.

Without saying a word, he walked to the smaller table, grabbed a plate and mug, and began to fill both. Moments later, he returned and placed both before Rowen. "Here." He smiled when she looked up.

Her heart twisted inside her chest. "Thank you." Then she caught scent of the meat and bread. Her stomach grumbled.

Lore chuckled and turned back toward the smaller table, where he filled his own plate and mug.

By the time he took a seat across from her, Rowen had already torn into the bread and meat, her stomach guiding her movements. She slowed slightly, remembering her manners.

He smiled and tore off a piece of bread, which he popped into his mouth. "Tell me a little about Cinad."

Rowen stopped her mug just before her lips and stared at Lore over its metal rim. Immediately her mind rushed back to her last days there: the sudden turn of her people, their fear, her banishment . . .

She caught Lore studying her again. Rowen tipped the mug and took a drink, dredging up earlier, happier memories. "Cinad is a small village," she began and put her mug down. "About twenty families. Most of them are farmers." She continued to think, her mind moving away from facts to pictures. "I lived at the southern end of the village, near Anwin Forest."

"So Jedrek was a farmer?" Lore said before taking another bite.

"Not really." Rowen's mind went deeper into her past. She remembered the rolling hills of grain to the east, the orchards just north of the village, and the towering trees of Anwin to the west. "He did whatever was needed. He helped during harvest time, traveled to nearby towns to trade the villagers' goods, and carved furniture during the winter."

"I see." Lore picked up his mug. "Was it hard to leave Cinad?"

Rowen's hand tightened around the handle of her own mug. Lore's eyes darted toward her hand as he took a drink.

Rowen forced herself to relax, her face warming. She hoped Lore hadn't noticed. "Yes." She moved her hand back to her plate of food and tore off a piece of bread. She liked Lore, but there were times it felt as though he could see through her words right to her thoughts. It was hard to leave Cinad, but she would never tell him why.

"Would you like to go back to visit?" he asked.

Rowen looked up and found Lore staring at her softly.

"I— That is—" she stumbled, her face warming even more. Yes, she would love to go back to see the people she loved. Or at least to see Calya. But she could never go back. If she did, she would be put to death.

"I'm sorry," Lore said a moment later. "I can see my questions are making you uncomfortable. I only wanted to get to know you more." He turned his attention back to his food.

Rowen stared at Lore, struck by his kindness. She watched him break off another piece of bread and felt her heart grow warm toward the man across from her. He'd known that any other person would have felt homesick by now, especially a small village person like herself, who had lived in the same village, the same house, all her life. Lore had thought of her and had offered her the chance to return. Her heart grew even warmer at that knowledge. Captain Lore was not like any other man she had met.

"Thank you," Rowen said.

Lore looked back up and smiled. "Certainly. If you change your mind and wish to go back for a visit, let me know."

Rowen nodded. But she would never change her mind.

Lore finished his drink, still watching the young woman across from him. Rowen was an enigma, a puzzle he could not seem to figure out. Every time he tried to draw her out, whether by asking about her home or more about herself, her answers seemed . . . dodgy. Like she was hiding something.

But what could she be hiding? He watched her chew, her eyes now looking down at her plate.

Then again, perhaps he was reading too much into Rowen's words and actions. Perhaps she was only shy and took a while to warm up to those she did not know. *But it's been two months now. Surely she is over any kind of shyness by now.*

Lore sighed and tore at his bread. He could tell she missed her village, he had heard the way her voice had turned soft as she'd spoken of Cinad and her father. He glanced at Rowen from the corner of his eye. He could not understand why a young woman like her would leave her village to come here. For the adventure, maybe?

Lore laughed, then put the bit of bread in his mouth. Rowen looked up at the noise. He shook his head slightly, and she went back to eating.

Guard duty was no thrill. He knew that firsthand. It was a life of waiting. Waiting for that one thing to happen that you had trained for, all the while hoping it never did. He chewed slowly. No, if Rowen had come to the White City hoping for adventure, she had come to the wrong place.

He glanced at her again. Could it be that there was nothing back in Cinad for her? Lore swallowed and broke off another piece. This thought had plagued him since she had first arrived. How was a beautiful young woman like her alone? She should have bonded with some young man long ago and been unable to accept Lord Gaynor's offer. Instead, she had come here.

Then Lore had wondered if perhaps Rowen's physical beauty was a façade. Perhaps what lay beneath was a woman no man would ever want to live with. But as he'd gotten to know her more through their sparring and training sessions, Rowen had proved to be gentle and teachable, with a hidden strength inside.

She was beautiful both inside and out.

Lore tore off a piece of meat and began to chew. Perhaps he was trying to see something that wasn't there. Other than her reserve, he could find no reason not to offer Rowen the position of varor. She possessed the skill, the heart, and the mind needed for such a position. And her oath would bind her to the protection of Lady Astrea.

He just wished he could know her more.

CHAPTER 8

Weeks later, Rowen stood by the window, marveling at the first snowfall, watching how it covered the city in a blanket of winter white. Behind her, a large fire crackled and spit as logs were consumed in its blaze. She could feel the heat near the window, causing the snowflakes to melt on contact.

Rowen had arrived in this room shortly after dinner to quietly prepare herself for her oath. The room was empty save for a long dark blue rug that covered the stone floor and a dark bookshelf filled with leather bound books, a small decorative dagger and a gold trimmed vase. Two swords hung above the fireplace.

As the time drew close, her stomach churned with anticipation. It was a serious act to take a vow in the Ryland Plains. Oathbreakers were worse than sorcery.

Rowen turned her head and caught a glimpse of herself reflected in the window. Gone was the simple village girl. In her place, she saw a young woman, her pale hair carefully braided and hanging over one shoulder. Her shirt was a pristine white covered by a dark blue tabard with an eagle embroidered with silver thread. Her cloak was slung over one shoulder, exposing the smallsword she carried with her at all times.

She looked like a varor.

Rowen raised her hand to touch the glass. She could feel the smooth surface beneath her fingertips. The rest of her hand felt only the leather of her glove. It had taken weeks to get used to the fact that she would always need to wear the small piece of leather. Her only reprieve was when she washed her glove. But it was better to wear the glove than the alternative.

An image of a frozen wasteland filled her mind, snow as far as the eye could see without a tree or bush or any living thing. A slow, white death for those with nowhere else to go. That's where she would be right now if it hadn't been for Lord Gaynor's offer.

The thick wooden door behind her swung inward with a groan. Startled, Rowen turned and quickly straightened her uniform. It was time.

Slowly, people entered the room. For one moment, she found herself back in Cinad, in Noland's house, facing the people gathered. People who, with short deliberation, had changed her fate. Rowen blinked and shook the image away. It wasn't like that this time. This time she would be given life, not have it taken away.

Lore entered first. He gave her a reassuring smile then walked toward the fireplace.

Behind Lore came a tall man with long dark hair and goatee. He wore a white silk shirt with a rich blue vest embroidered in silver thread, dark pants, and boots. A simple crown of silver sat upon his head. Rowen felt her heart lurch. He was Gaynor Celestis, High Lord of the White City and the Ryland Plains. She had met him briefly when she had first arrived in the White City.

Next came a young woman, shorter but with equally dark hair and a silver circlet set on her head. Her pale blue gown shimmered in the dark room. She was Lady Astrea, Rowen's future charge. Lady Astrea's dark eyes glanced briefly toward Rowen before she followed her father.

Aren, the Nordic varor, followed the high lord and lady into the room, flashing his trademark smile at Rowen before taking up his position near the door.

Rowen smiled back, then watched the next person enter. He was an older man dressed in the long white robes of healers. His hair was grey and curly with a matching thin grey mustache. The older man glanced at her and smiled before moving toward Lord Gaynor's side.

Justus, Lord Gaynor's third varor, entered the room. He was shorter than Lore, with thinning brown hair and hazel eyes. He wore the same blue tabard as Rowen and Aren. Rowen had found him more reserved than Aren during their brief encounters. He was a quiet man who did his duty.

Justus turned and shut the thick wooden door behind him. At the subtle click, all eyes turned toward her.

"Come here, Rowen Mar." Lord Gaynor's voice was deep and rang with authority.

Rowen walked toward the assembly, her heart beating against her chest. She came to stand in front of Lord Gaynor.

"The oath of a varor is not to be taken lightly," he said. "It is an oath that may require your life someday. But in protecting my daughter, you protect the future of the Ryland Plains, the future of your people. Do you still desire to take this position?"

"I do," Rowen said, her voice firm with conviction.

"So be it." Lord Gaynor backed away.

The older man in healer's robes moved forward. "I am Balint Kedem," he said, "Chief Healer of the White City and Oathmaker. I will be binding you to your oath today. Please kneel."

Rowen knelt before him.

Balint gently placed his hand upon her head. "Rowen, daughter of Jedrek Mar, you vow today to become the varor of Lady Astrea; to be by her side, to protect her from harm, and if it so happens, to give your life for her. Do you bind yourself to this?"

"I do," Rowen said, more softly than before. The solemnity of what she was vowing lay heavily upon her. She was promising to die for Lady Astrea.

"Then I declare this oath bound until such a time that Lady Astrea marries, takes up the mantle of High Lady, or passes away, whichever shall come first."

Rowen suddenly felt something rush through her like wind.

Balint removed his hand. "Now stand Rowen Mar, varor of Lady Astrea Celestis."

• • •

Rowen found herself near the window again as the people made their way out of the room. They had come to witness her oath, congratulate her afterward, and were now going back to their duties.

She watched those gathered make their way toward the door and rubbed the back of her neck, wondering where the wind-like sensation she had felt at the end of her oath had come from. A slight winter breeze escaping from some hidden crack in the wall?

Rowen searched the wall with a sideways glance. Every stone looked solidly in place. She dropped her hand. Perhaps she had only imagined it.

"Rowen."

Rowen turned to face Lore. "Captain."

He stood nearby, dressed casually in a simple white shirt and dark blue leather jerkin. "Now that you have taken your oath, I have something to show you."

"Yes, Captain," she said, straightening up.

She followed Lore out the door and down the hallway. After rounding two corners and descending a set of stairs, she began to wonder where he was leading her. But Lore did not say a word. He only led.

Soon the stone the castle was carved from began to change from alabaster white to a dreary grey. There were fewer doors along this hallway. And the air felt cooler.

"Are we nearing the mountain?" Rowen's voice echoed along the empty passageway.

"Yes." Lore held out a torch he had picked up a couple of corridors back. Near the end of the hall he stopped. "Here we are." He paused before an ordinary door. He pushed down the latch. The door swung open without a sound. Lore entered first with Rowen close behind.

The room was small and bare. No furniture, no fireplace. A couple of cobwebs fluttered in one corner. Lore crossed the room and began to run his hand across the far wall. Rowen walked up beside him, watching his hand move over the jagged surface. It took a moment for her to realize that what he was touching was not a wall but the actual face of the mountain.

"There is a small indent along the surface." Lore held the torch close to the mountainside and searched with both his hand and eyes. Suddenly his finger stopped. "There." He pressed a hidden switch. They both stepped back. The silhouette of a door appeared, outlined by a strange blue light.

Lore moved forward again and pushed the door open. Rowen peered around Lore. She could see a long tunnel disappearing into the mountain, lit with more of that odd blue light.

"This is the Gateway of the Mountain." Lore turned toward Rowen. "It is a secret pathway that leads out of Celestis Castle."

"Where does it end?" Rowen continued to study the tunnel.

"West of here, on the outer edge of Anwin Forest. This hidden passage has served as an escape route from the city for many generations of High Lords and Ladies."

Suddenly Rowen understood why Lore was showing her this. Should the city ever come under siege and Lady Astrea's life be in danger, she would need to lead her to safety. "What are the strange lights?" Rowen asked, studying the blue stones that jutted out of the sides of the tunnel.

"Fre stones from Nordica."

"Fray stones?"

"Yes. It sounds like *fray*, but the Nordics spell it F-R-E."

Rowen raised an eyebrow. "Interesting."

Lore stepped inside the passageway. "They shine indefinitely, making them a wonderful light source for tunnels. The Nordics use them all the time in their deep mining. Are you coming?" he asked, glancing back.

"I did not realize we would be going farther."

"It's important to check your escape routes once in a while." Lore took another step inside. "You do not want to be leading Lady Astrea down here only to find the path blocked by a large boulder. And since it's been a while since I was last here, I thought we would go together." Lore turned and started down the tunnel.

Rowen followed. Stale air filled her nostrils. The light from the torch bounced across the walls. Their footsteps echoed along the tunnel.

As they walked, her thoughts went back again to her initiation, to the end, when the feeling of wind had passed through her. Had it been only her imagination? *And just what is an Oathmaker?* she wondered, remembering the title Balint Kedem bore. "Captain," Rowen said, "what happened at the end of my oath?" Her voice reverberated against the walls.

Lore stopped and turned. "You mean the binding?"

"Binding?" Rowen stopped as well.

"If you mean the rush you felt, it was Balint binding you to your words. He is an Oathmaker. His ability is a gift from the old world."

"Gift?"

"Yes," Lore said. "One of Balint's ancestors was an Eldaran—an Oathmaker, to be specific. Balint possesses the gift of binding, but it's not very strong." Lore turned to go.

But Rowen was not done yet. "What is an Eldaran?"

This time Lore turned more quickly, his face furrowed in a frown. "You have never heard of the Eldarans?"

"No," Rowen said hesitantly.

"Have you ever heard of the Word?"

Her thoughts jumped back to cold evenings when storytellers would visit Cinad. She recalled stories involving some powerful Being called *the Word*. "Only a little," she said. "Something about Him speaking the Lands into existence and dying a long time ago. Honestly, I heard the stories when I was a child, and they didn't make much sense to me."

"Well," Lore said, "what you heard is true. The Word spoke, and the Lands were created. That is why we call Him the Word—everything exists because He speaks."

"So He says something and there it is?" Rowen said, trying to understand.

"Yes. And everything continues to exist because He continues to speak."

"So who are these Eldarans you spoke of?"

"The Eldarans were an ancient race of beings who served the Word."

"They're not human?"

"No," Lore said.

"But you said they live here in the Lands."

"They used to, a long time ago. They left the Celestial Halls to come here to the Lands."

Rowen furrowed her brow. "Why?"

"So that they could serve the Word here. At first, they fought alongside the Word during the Great Battle."

"Great Battle," Rowen said quietly. She had heard of that war, fought thousands of years ago. But she knew only bits and pieces, enough to know that the war had changed the face of the Lands forever.

"Some stayed behind, choosing to serve the Word by living among humans and using their power to help mankind. However, by staying here, they lost their immortality."

"So do any still exist?" Rowen asked. Something deep inside of her began to stir with hope. Perhaps some had survived. Could she possibly be one of the—

"Eldarans? No, I do not believe so," Lore said. "Some people are descended from them, but most who have Eldaran blood do not possess their power. Balint is the only one I know of who has an Eldaran gift. But, like I said, his is not very strong. Too much human blood has thinned out the Eldaran blood."

Rowen's heart sank. For one moment she had hoped that her ability was some kind of ancient power she had inherited from an Eldaran predecessor. But if they no longer existed . . . She sighed and pulled her cloak closer to her body. Her gift—or curse, as she saw it—was much too powerful anyway to have been passed on to her by some distant ancestor and watered down over the centuries.

Perhaps her village was right. Perhaps she *was* some kind of witch . . . or worse.

"Rowen, are you all right?" She glanced up and found Lore

studying her. "If you want, we can talk more about this back at the castle—"

"No." Whatever brief hope she had held about the Eldarans had been dashed.

Lore raised an eyebrow at her quick response.

"I'm sorry," Rowen said, noting his reaction. "It's been a long day."

His eyes softened. "I understand. It has been a long day. Let's finish up our search of the tunnel so you can settle into your new quarters."

Rowen nodded. They resumed their walk through the dark tunnel.

Why can't I just be normal? Rowen wondered bitterly. She followed Lore with her right hand clenched into a tight fist. That movement only reminded her of the glove she wore to cover her palm.

She knew she should be grateful that at least she could touch people now, but suddenly she wanted more. She wanted to go back to the way things were, before the white mark had appeared. Or at least know the reason she was different. When Lore had mentioned the Eldarans . . .

A stinging sensation settled across her eyes, and Rowen bit back tears of disappointment. The Eldarans no longer existed. And even if they did, and if her ability was an Eldaran gift, who would want the "gift" of seeing inside other people, of frightening them so much they turned on you?

Rowen swallowed the lump in her throat. No, that could not be a gift. There was something wrong with her. And whatever it was would forever separate her from those around her.

Like Captain Lore.

Rowen held her candle out and looked around her new quarters.

The room was similar to the one she had left back in the Guards Quarter. A single bed by the right wall, a wooden chest for her belongings, a table with a pitcher and bowl on the top. The ceiling was high and three narrow windows opened up to the courtyard below. A faded blue rug lay on the white stone floor. At the far end of the room, along the left wall, was an open archway that led into Lady Astrea's chambers. Orange light glowed from the lady's room.

Rowen crossed the room and looked out one of the windows. Stars twinkled high in the sky. Down below, everything was dark except for the torches that burned on either side of the gates.

She turned and looked through the archway. At the far end of the room she could see a four-poster bed covered in a midnight-blue coverlet with silver tassels. Similar blue curtains hung around the bed, gathered by a silver cord at each post. The bed was at least three times the size of her own bed. For a moment Rowen wondered what it would be like to sleep in something so big.

She crept closer to the doorway, curious to see more of Lady Astrea's room. The orange glow came from a fireplace that stood against the outside wall. The fireplace was made of white marble, matching beautifully with the white stone of the castle. A blue rug lay in front of the fireplace. Silver candlesticks lined the mantle. Two highback chairs were situated near the fireplace with a low table between them.

The warmth of the room drew Rowen closer until she was standing in the doorway.

"Please, come in," said a low feminine voice.

Rowen started and found Lady Astrea sitting to her left at what looked like a small white desk. She was dressed in a long white nightgown with a deep green wrap draped across her shoulders. A servant girl stood behind her, brushing Lady Astrea's hair, which was long and dark.

"I'm sorry, I did not mean to intrude—"

"Nonsense," Lady Astrea said. "You are my varor and therefore welcome to my room."

"Thank you, milady." Rowen gave her a small bow.

"That will be all, Jaida." Lady Astrea waved her hand dismissively.

"Yes, milady." The young girl bowed and placed the brush on the desk. She turned and left through the main door.

Lady Astrea stood. She pulled her wrap around her body and motioned toward the chairs. "Please, take a seat."

Rowen hesitated, then entered the room.

Lady Astrea crossed the room and sat down in the farthest chair. Rowen took a seat in the other. She clasped her hands together and stared at the fire. She could still feel the residual disappointment from her earlier conversation with Lore.

"You are not what I was expecting."

Rowen's head shot up and around. "Milady?"

Lady Astrea smiled at her. "I met your father, Jedrek, a few times when he visited here. He mentioned a daughter once. I imagined a shy young country girl. When my father told me you had accepted his offer, I was surprised. I wasn't sure a young woman from Cinad would make a good varor. But then I watched you train with Captain Lore."

Rowen shifted uncomfortably. Lady Astrea had been watching her? She'd never seen her.

"I wanted to see what kind of woman would choose to be my protector. I was impressed. Captain Lore highly recommended you when he came to say you were ready to take your vow."

"He did?"

"Oh, yes. He said you were one of the best he has trained."

Rowen felt her cheeks warm at the praise.

"My father values Captain Lore's opinion. And so do I. Captain Lore and his family have served the White City for many generations. He is a man with good judgment, a sincere heart, and wisdom. So when he says something, my father listens."

Rowen thought over Lady Astrea's words. "Yes, he is that. The captain, I mean. Different. Not like other men I have met." Her thoughts jumped to Cleon and the man in the tavern.

"It is because he is a Follower."

"A Follower?"

"A Follower of the Word. I have known others who claim to be

Followers, but Captain Lore is different. He actually takes his devotion seriously."

"I see." That explained why he knew so much about the Word and the Eldarans. But what did Lady Astrea mean by 'Follower'? "Are you a . . . a Follower?"

"No." Lady Astrea turned her attention to the fire. "I believe the Word exists. And that is enough for me. But sometimes . . . watching Captain Lore makes me wonder if there is more to the Word. Perhaps I will find out someday."

CHAPTER 9

Caleb Tala brought his horse to a stop at the top of the hill. The Ari Mountains stood before him like an impenetrable wall of sand-colored stone, as high as the heavens, reaching from east to west as far as the eye could see. No man-made thing, machine or other-wise, could scale those natural walls. A perfect defense for the north, save for the jagged crack that ran longwise across its sheer surface. Hershaw Pass.

Caleb stared at the mountain passageway. He knew the pass had another name, one whispered under the breath of those who had ventured through its narrow walls: the Valley of Shadow and Death. Though only a short distance, those few dark miles had seen more death and blood than anywhere else in the Lands. It was where north met south, where they fought. And soon its floor would run red again.

Gathered below Hershaw Pass were hundreds of siege towers, heavy catapults, and other war machinery. Canvas tents spread out across the rest of the desert like ants on a hill. Wisps from a thou-sand campfires filled the basin with an early morning haze. The sky changed from red to orange to a pale blue. Black banners emblazoned with a scarlet wolf's head hung limply in the muggy morning air.

Caleb shook his head and pulled the reins of his horse toward the right, down a narrow dirt path toward the camp. He didn't under-stand war or why his cousin was so obsessed with this particular one. All he knew was he was here to make sure Commander Arpiar—and his army—made it through the pass.

The commander's tent stood near the outskirt of the camp, its size and grandeur giving it away. The tent had three smaller rooms jetting out from the main. A large black flag waved from the tallest tent post. Guards mingled around the front.

Few knew who Caleb really was. And Commander Arpiar was one of them. Hopefully, that knowledge and subsequent fear would motivate him to finish what the other commanders had not. Caleb hoped so. He had no desire to stay here any longer than necessary. Nor to assassinate any more commanders.

Caleb approached Arpiar's tent. One of the guards headed toward him. "What is your business here?" the man asked.

Caleb held up his right hand.

Squinting against the desert sun, the guard glanced at the large black stone imbedded with the Tala family crest wound around his middle finger. "Lord Tala," the guard said, backing away with a bow. "We had no word that you were coming."

Caleb dropped his hand. "There was no time. I need to see Commander Arpiar right away."

"Yes, sir, this way." Caleb dismounted and the guard motioned to one of the men surrounding the commander's tent. The man came and took Caleb's reins. Another guard held open the tent flap.

Caleb ducked inside. At the far back of the main room stood a table with a man hunched over it, a round lens in his hand.

The man glanced up as Caleb approached. "Caleb Tala." Commander Arpiar slowly rose and placed the lens down. He was a tall, lean man with peppered black hair and mustache. A red sash ran from his right shoulder to his left hip, indicating his position as commander. Caleb noted the curved sword that hung on Arpiar's left side. "To what do I owe the pleasure?" His expression indicated it was anything but.

Instead of answering, Caleb reached inside his cloak. Arpiar stiffened at his movement.

Good, Caleb thought. Commander Arpiar already feared him, or at least what he could do.

Caleb slid his hand across the dagger strapped to his chest then reached for the papers Lord Corin had sent. He withdrew the tightly rolled piece of parchment and handed it over.

Frowning, Commander Arpiar broke the seal and unrolled the parchment.

Caleb clasped his hands behind his back and waited for Arpiar's reply. He did not have to wait long.

Commander Arpiar cursed. "I don't like it." He crumpled up the paper with one hand. "But it seems I don't have a choice." He looked over at Caleb. "Well, you won't have to worry about looking over *my* shoulder. I know what I'm supposed to do."

"Let's hope so." Caleb took a step toward the man. "I'd hate for Lord Corin to have to find a new commander. It would be . . . inconvenient."

Commander Arpiar glared at Caleb, although his face was a shade lighter. He had caught the hint. "I assume you'll need lodgings and a guard detail?" Commander Arpiar said through gritted teeth.

"Lodgings, yes. Guards will not be necessary. I can more than adequately take care of myself."

Commander Arpiar snarled. "I'm sure you can."

Caleb ignored Arpiar and looked over at the map spread across the table. A red X stood just above the small town of Menes, and a jagged line had been drawn through the Ari Mountains. Interesting. What did the commander have planned?

In the end, he really didn't care how Commander Arpiar got across the mountains. Once Temanin held Hershaw Pass, Caleb could return to Azar and back to his way of life.

A fortnight later, as the sun began its ascent and bathed the desert in the pale light of early morning, the Temanin camp geared up for war. Men scurried between tents, checking weapons and armor. Siege towers tottered toward the pass, their stories filled with archers ready to take out the enemy along the high cliffs.

Caleb watched all the activity from his vantage point near the top of the hill where his tent stood. A chilly wind rustled through his clothing, sending a slight shiver down his back.

He had never seen a battle before. Today would be his first taste. And he wasn't sure if he would like it.

Caleb turned and stepped back into his tent. He moved toward a wooden chest that sat in the corner. He opened the box and pulled out his daggers. One, he placed in the sheath across his chest. Two went into the leather casings on either side of his middle. And one small wicked dagger he pushed into the hidden pocket woven inside of his boot. He needed no other weapons. What an average soldier could do with a sword, he could do faster and quicker with his blades and cunning.

However, he had no plans to fight today. Commander Arpiar had needed no persuasion from him since the day he'd arrived. From the shadows Caleb had followed Arpiar, his presence enough of a reminder that, should Arpiar back down and fail to enter the north, a blade would be waiting. But Commander Arpiar had something planned, something to do with that map back in his tent. Caleb had a partial idea of what Arpiar was doing, but nothing concrete. Whatever it was, it had been put into action before Caleb had arrived. Soon, though, he would know.

Today he would accompany Commander Arpiar to the pass. Whatever else Commander Arpiar might be doing, today was the day he would start the battle for Hershaw. And Caleb would be there so that, when the death count began to arrive, he could remind Commander Arpiar that retreat was not an option this time. Even if it cost every Temanin his life.

Caleb threw his cloak over one shoulder and headed out of the tent. Soon Temanin's army would be on the other side of this pass. Whether Commander Arpiar lived to see that would all depend on him.

"Commander Arpiar." The young runner pulled himself inside the commander's tent. "I'm here to report on how the siege towers are faring against the enemy."

"Go on," Commander Arpiar said. Caleb stood nearby, a shadow along the canvas siding. The tent was warm now that the sun had reached its zenith in the sky.

"Two have been burned to the ground, and a third is on fire."

"And the others?"

"The remaining two are still making their way through the pass. But they're only halfway. Captain Falun says we need to turn back and try again with more towers—"

"*I don't care* what Captain Falun says," Commander Arpiar bellowed, cutting the young man off. The runner's eyes widened with fear. "You tell him . . ." Commander Arpiar pointed a crooked finger at the young man's face . . . "that there will be no retreat this time. And if he fails to obey my command, he knows the penalty."

"Y-yes, sir," The young man turned and fled from the tent.

Commander Arpiar sat back into his chair and pinched the bridge of his nose.

Caleb moved out of the shadows. "Very good, Commander."

Commander Arpiar removed his hand and glared in his direction.

Caleb ignored the look. "Don't let your captains dictate this battle."

Commander Arpiar's face twisted in silence. Caleb knew Arpiar wanted to say something but didn't dare. Perhaps his cousin had been right in sending him. Caleb could already see weaknesses in Commander Arpiar's resilience.

"Sir, Captain Falun has lost half his unit."

Commander Arpiar paled slightly. "And how far into the pass is he?"

"Only a quarter."

Commander Arpiar looked down and began to tap the table with his finger. "And Captain Kolin?"

"Not as many, sir, but they are having a hard time following Captain Falun. The . . ." the messenger swallowed as if tasting something bad . . . "the . . . uh . . . bodies . . . are making it difficult."

Caleb took a closer look at the messenger. His face was pale. Most likely, this was the young man's first look at death.

"Let the chief healer know that I want those bodies moved faster," Commander Arpiar said.

"Yes, sir." The messenger bowed and left.

Commander Arpiar glanced at Caleb as if expecting another lecture, but Caleb chose to step outside instead.

The desert sun blasted him once he left the protection of the tent. Caleb shaded his eyes and looked toward the crack in the mountain, where spirals of smoke curled toward the sky, high above the mountain pass. In his mind's eye, he could see the burning towers with dead soldiers piling up along the narrow walls, healers bustling around trying to remove those no longer able to fight. Enough dead that those following behind could hardly wade through the pass.

What did Corin desire so desperately from the northern kingdoms? Land? Slaves? Power? He shook his head. He had no idea, and perhaps he did not care so long as his time here was short. Let Corin run his country, his war, his whatever as he liked. Caleb wanted as little to do with it as possible. He was interested only in his payment when the job was done.

The next day, Caleb stood waiting in the back of the commander's tent. A glass of wine sat untouched on the table in the middle of the tent. Commander Arpiar's round lens and map were also on the table. Arpiar stood by the entrance, watching the activity in the pass.

Caleb rubbed the back of his neck. Another night of no sleep. Maybe it was this place, surrounded by war and blood and death. He needed to get away, get back to Azar. There, he had ways of coping with these dreams—

Movement near the front caught his attention. Another runner. Caleb silently made his way to the front.

" . . . and then the northerners turned and ran. Captain Falun is in pursuit and already through the pass. Captain Kolin is close behind, along with Captain Murik."

Commander Arpiar leaned against the tent and ran a hand across his face. "It worked." He looked back at the runner. "Go tell the other captains who have not yet entered Hershaw Pass to ready their troops. We march now."

"Yes, Commander." The runner gave a quick bow and left.

"What worked?" Caleb said, coming to stand by Arpiar.

Arpiar stared at the pass. "I secretly sent a unit to the town of Menes over to the east. Their mission was to get over the mountains and spring a surprise attack from the rear while we kept the northerners occupied in the pass. It was a long shot. I wasn't sure if they would even find a way over the mountains. I hadn't heard from them in weeks. So when the time came to begin the battle, I took a risk that the other unit would be ready." He let out a long sigh. "And it paid off."

"And if it hadn't?" Caleb asked.

"Then I would have thrown a lot of lives away these last couple of days, just like the commanders before me. And lost. But where they failed, I have succeeded. You will take note of this, I trust."

Caleb turned and watched the pyres burning in the distance. The smell of smoke and burnt flesh drifted on the breeze. The scent made him feel slightly nauseous. He coughed and covered his nose until the breeze passed.

"I'm impressed, Commander Arpiar," Caleb said once he could breathe. "Lord Corin will be pleased."

The grim smile on Arpiar's face morphed into a scowl. "It's not over yet." He looked at Caleb. "This war has cost many Temanins their lives. I'm merely trying to get through it before losing every man under my command. The surprise attack served that purpose." He turned toward Hershaw Pass. "Nothing more."

The Temanin army pushed its way through Hershaw the rest of the day, with everything the empire could shove through it. While the main army poured through the pass, the surprise attack force came from behind. So between the two, Temanin shattered the northern resistance. What had kept the two sides apart for hundreds of years was crushed under the boots of Temanin soldiers in a day.

But that was only one victory. Now Temanin had to keep the pass and gain a foothold in the north. This was where Arpiar would rise or fall. And Caleb was here to make sure he rose.

Temanin soldiers continued to pour into the maw, moving more quickly now that death no longer rained down from the high cliffs above, quite possibly marching toward another death, this one on the battlefield on the other side of the pass. Temanin might hold Hershaw Pass now, but Hadrast Fortress waited for them on the other side.

Caleb stood near Arpiar and his personal company of soldiers. They waited just outside the pass for their turn to enter. The sun began to set to his left, a glowing ball of red. Shadows filled the pass. Caleb swept a hand across his chest and checked his sides. His daggers were ready should they meet anyone inside.

"Such a waste," Caleb heard Commander Arpiar mutter. More Temanin soldiers marched by. "All those men, and for what?"

Caleb took a step closer, and immediately Commander Arpiar went silent. Words like those could be considered seditious. But for once Caleb agreed with Arpiar, so he made no comment. The last few days had given him a new perspective on death. Men were tossed into the pass only to be dragged out later, dead or dying. Healers scurried about, their robes red with blood as they tried to aid their fellow man, only to have the cycle start again with a new batch of soldiers.

For the first time in his life, Caleb felt sickened by it all.

But soon he would be done with this place. He would accompany Commander Arpiar through the pass, ensure Hadrast Fortress was taken, then go back to Azar. And wash away every single memory of this place.

A soldier approached Arpiar. "Sir, we can go now."

"Then let's go." Commander Arpiar proceeded toward the pass, his personal company of soldiers following closely around him. Caleb followed a few steps behind.

Weapons flashed in the dying light. The soldiers ahead of them charged into the dark and smoke-filled pass, ready to join in the battle being fought on the other side. The echo of their boots bounced along the jagged walls, sounding like a thunderous legion.

Commander Arpiar followed the next wave, his company of soldiers pressing close to him, ready to defend their commander if need be. Caleb stayed close, as well. Moments later, they entered the Pass.

It took a moment for Caleb's eyes to adjust to the dark. Then the smell hit him. Burnt flesh and blood filled his nostrils. He choked, the smell overwhelming him. Another couple of steps, and the scent of tar mixed with the scent of human flesh. His stomach lurched, threatening to bring up everything inside. Others around him coughed, and one soldier covered his mouth.

Caleb grabbed a hold of his will and began to breathe through his mouth. The smell slackened. He waited a moment longer until he was certain that he would not lose it in front of the men around him. Then he moved forward.

His eyes grew more accustomed to the smoke and shadows the deeper they went. Around him, soldiers picked their way around the bodies of their more unfortunate comrades. But with the masses behind them pushing them forward, many soldiers found themselves crushing the dead men's bodies beneath their boots.

Caleb swallowed and passed one dead soldier. The man was half burnt, his hands raised in horror. After seeing a couple more bodies, Caleb felt his body begin to prickle with shock. This was nothing like his solo acts of assassination. Those were neat and clean. What he found here was death in its most gruesome form.

Something caught Caleb's foot in the dark, and he tripped. He opened his hands to cushion his fall. When he struck the ground, he felt his hands sink into something wet and sticky. Caleb squinted against the darkness and smoke. He found his hands deep inside the cavity of a dead man's belly, entrails leaking out. Caleb gasped against the urge to vomit. He pushed against the corpse, his hands sinking deeper in as he tried to gain his footing to stand.

Under his frantic attempts to get up, the body jostled. The man's head turned to stare at Caleb, mouth open in an empty scream. Caleb muffled his own shout. He wrenched himself free and jumped to his feet. He backed away from the corpse and began to frantically wipe at the blood that covered his hands. The gag in his throat moved closer toward his lips. Caleb could feel his face paling. He glanced at his hands to see if there was any more blood. He found them still dark with the sticky red substance.

Caleb wiped harder, sickened by the wet feeling. Assassinations were nothing like this. He rarely got blood on himself during a job.

"Sir, you all right?"

Caleb found a soldier staring at him. "Yes," Caleb said, turning off his feelings. He gave his hands one more wipe and walked away from the corpse. Nearby he heard a soldier retching, the sound adding to the moans of those not quite dead. Right then and there, Caleb decided he hated war.

It took almost an hour to make it out of the pass. As they neared the north end of the Pass, the mouth widened until the passage gave way to the open.

Caleb looked up at the sky and breathed in the cool night air, happy to be out of that place. A crescent moon hung in the dark sky, surrounded by tiny bright stars. Thin, naked trees grew to the east. Rolling hills of grass lay to the west. And straight ahead, about a half a league away, beyond the huge bonfires set to light the area, stood Hadrast Fortress.

Hadrast Fortress was a large stone structure barely visible in the dark save for the fires that burned along its top most battlements. A wave of flame came flying from the fortress. Caleb watched the fire arc in the sky then come pelting down onto the battlefield.

He heard the cries of surprise and pain echo across the field. Patches of fire sprung up, but were quickly put out.

More screams and shouts filled the air. Metal clashed with metal.

Caleb wondered how the men fighting could even see each other? Especially since the Temanin soldiers were dressed in black uniforms. Or was it all just massive chaos? He watched the field for a moment then shrugged and turned to find Commander Arpiar. Not his battle.

He passed a couple of Temanin soldiers who were busy cutting down the trees and feeding the fires. Others were assembling the healer's tents. Caleb found Arpiar still standing near one of the tents. His company of soldiers stood around him with swords drawn.

Caleb moved silently around the back of the men. It wasn't until he was almost to Commander Arpiar that one of the soldiers realized he was there. Caleb sidestepped the soldier's swing.

"Tsk, tsk. You should guard your commander more carefully. Good thing I'm on your side."

The soldier scowled at him, but held his sword back this time. Caleb walked by him and joined Arpiar.

"Was that really necessary?" Arpiar whispered angrily.

"It proved a point. Never let your guard down."

"And don't trust assassins."

Caleb gave Arpiar a slight nod and watched the battle.

The fight raged all through the night and into the next day. In the early morning light, Caleb could distinguish the black-clad Temanin soldiers from the blue and green northerners. Dark clouds gathered overhead. He felt a drop on his face and frowned. He hated the rain.

Around noon the northern army retreated back to the fortress, but it was no longer a safe haven for them. The Temanin Army vastly outnumbered them, and it took only a couple of runs with the ram to break down the gates.

As Temanin soldiers scurried into the fortress, Commander Arpiar moved toward the battle, ready to claim victory when the time came. Caleb walked beside him.

"Congratulations, Commander," Caleb said as they drew near the walls. The sound of fighting could be heard echoing from deep inside the fortress. "Looks like you did what no one else before you could—you brought us into the north."

"Yes." Commander Arpiar said the word with little emotion. He looked over at Caleb. "Will you be staying with us once Hadrast is taken?"

"No. My cousin's orders were to make sure you made it through the pass. And you have. Now I only need to wait for his letter stating that I can return to Azar."

"I see." Commander Arpiar turned back toward the walls. "I'm sure you're ready to go home."

"I am." *More than ready.*

A messenger ran up to Arpiar. "Commander, Captain Falun has taken Hadrast Fortress. The few northerners left have been taken captive, and he is ready for you to come."

"Then let him know I will be there shortly."

The messenger bowed and left.

"Well, Caleb, I know you've been corresponding with Lord Corin about my work. You can let his lordship know that the pass and fortress are his." Then in a more quiet tone, Commander Arpiar continued. "But mark my words, Caleb: It will not end here. I saw it with Lord Tarin, and I now see it in his son. This kind of lust for power never dies out, not until every soldier is dead and every land conquered."

"Then why do you fight for him?" Caleb countered.

Commander Arpiar paused. "Because I believe in Temanin. And perhaps I hope that I might save a couple lives by leading these men. Life is precious, not a commodity to be thrown away lightly. Something you might want to think about. Now, if you'll excuse me . . ." Commander Arpiar walked off, leaving Caleb to wonder at his words.

Three days ago those words would have earned Commander Arpiar a warning, or worse. But now, after seeing what he had seen, both in the pass and during the battle, Arpiar's words gave Caleb pause. *Life is precious.* He thought about those words a moment more.

Was it?

CHAPTER
10

"Don't scream."

Nierne did anyway, her voice muffled between clenched fingers.

"I told you not to scream," the man whispered. His hand clamped down harder across her mouth. "You'll alert the shadows."

Nierne swallowed her scream and held her breath.

"Good, now keep quiet."

She looked around frantically. Long shadows filled the forest floor. The wind moaned as it wove its way through the trees. Leaves fluttered into the air. Branches swayed and cracked. Nierne held her breath and stared into the darkness. Could there really be shadows here? This far from Thyra?

"All right," the man whispered. "I'm going to let go of you. Don't do anything rash." His hand slipped away from her face along with the arm he'd held across her chest.

Nierne slowly turned around.

"Are you one of those who escaped from Cragsmoor?" he asked quietly.

She could barely see the man in the dying light. He was slightly taller than her, broad in the chest, with thick arms that now hung at his side. There was a bald spot at the top of his head. He reminded her of Father Karl.

"Yes," she said.

His shoulders relaxed. "So it worked," he said more to himself.

"What worked?"

"The breakout. Although you're one of the few to make it outside the city." He sighed. "We didn't know about the shadows. Glad I found you."

"You're the one who released us?"

"One of them. I wasn't in Cragsmoor itself, just outside the city. I was supposed to guide all of you back here. But the shadows came and captured everyone we had freed. I saw it all happen from my post outside the gate. You're the only one I've found who actually made it. But enough talk. I need to get you back to camp." The man grabbed her hand. "This way."

He led Nierne deep into the forest. Twigs snapped and leaves crunched beneath their feet. Shadows moved around them, making Nierne jump, but the man leading her ignored them.

After walking for a half hour, the man stopped and made some sort of noise with his voice. The sound reminded Nierne of the little birds Father Reth would take her to watch on the beach when she was young. Moments later, a similar call answered.

"That is my signal to let the others know it's me and not a stranger or a Shadonae," he explained quietly as he led her toward the side of a steep hill covered with trees and brush.

At the base, he pushed aside the branches from a thick, short tree. Past the brush was a small opening in the hill. "In here," he said, pulling Nierne in with him.

For a moment they walked in complete darkness. He gave her hand a squeeze as if to reassure her. "Long ago this place was a silver mine," he said, his voice echoing strangely in the narrow tunnel. "Now it's where we live. Those of us who escaped have been holed up here since . . . well . . . since that day." There was a tinge of sadness to his voice, and Nierne suddenly wondered if he had lost family to the Shadonae.

They walked for a couple more minutes before she saw the faint flicker of light ahead and heard the echo of voices.

The tunnel opened up into a large cavern with more tunnels leading off in different directions. Long wooden beams crisscrossed overhead, holding the earthen ceiling above them. In the middle of the room burned a large bonfire with figures gathered around it. As they drew closer, the scent of roasting meat hit Nierne causing her stomach to tighten in hunger.

The figures turned toward them.

"Found one," her escort said, dropping her hand.

Nierne looked around. Only a handful of people looked back.

"You found no one else?" one of the men near the fire said.

"Just her," he replied.

The man who had asked went stone-faced and turned back toward the fire. Apparently he had been hoping to see someone else. Nierne gripped her hands in front of her, suddenly feeling unwanted. These men had risked their lives to rescue family and friends, not some obscure scribe. And yet who had escaped? Her.

Word, why? Nierne rubbed her hands back and forth. Why did she continue to live? What value was she?

"Nierne?"

Her heart did a double beat. It couldn't be . . .

Nierne slowly turned around to find a man standing in one of the tunnels that branched out from the main room. He was older, his white hair cropped closely to his head, a neatly trimmed goatee giving his aged face a look of dignity, brown robes hanging from a timeworn body.

Father Reth.

Nierne stared at him, her voice lost in surprise. Then hope came rushing back. "Father Reth!" She took a wobbly step toward him. Emotions rolled inside of her, brewing up, making her eyes water.

"Nierne!" Father Reth said with a laugh.

In that moment, seeing Father Reth alive, Nierne felt she could believe anything.

He ran to her, arms open wide. She fell into his embrace, laughing and crying. "My child," he whispered, pulling her in close.

Tears trickled down her cheeks. Nierne breathed in his scent, the smell of old parchment and dust, and felt his coarse robe against her cheek. Of all the fathers of the Monastery, Father Reth was the only one who held her heart. He understood her like no one else.

After a moment, he leaned back. He brushed away her curls and looked deeply into her eyes. "After everything that happened, I thought . . ." A deep sadness filled his eyes. Then he gave her a half smile. "Well, I was wrong." He closed his eyes and bowed his head. "Thank the Word you're alive."

Nierne's eyes overflowed. More tears poured down her cheeks. Father Reth drew her next to his chest again, rubbed her back and let her cry.

She realized perhaps there *was* purpose to her living.

At least Father Reth thought so.

Over the next few days more people joined the ragged band of escapees, but nowhere near as many as had been freed from Cragsmoor. No one commented on this, but Nierne could see despair in the eyes of the men gathered inside the cave.

As they sat around the fire that night, eating halfheartedly, someone finally asked the question that had been plaguing Nierne's thoughts since the day of her capture.

"How in all the Lands did this happen?" the man across from her asked. He had just arrived an hour ago, one of those found wandering the forest. "Well?" he said, looking around at the others gathered. A couple of people shifted uncomfortably. "How did two men take over our military and capture an entire city?"

"I can tell you," said a voice from the shadows. All heads turned as a tall, thin man stepped toward the firelight. His face was gaunt and narrow, his eyes protruding and haunted. Oily strands of grey hair hung around his face.

"Senator Regessus," Father Reth whispered to Nierne.

She noted the rich robes the man wore. Only now they were tattered and dirty. He also had arrived an hour ago.

"I was there." Food forgotten, every face was now turned toward Senator Regessus. "They showed up a few months ago, brought to the court by Senator Barron. The moment they stepped inside the court, they held us all." Senator Regessus eyes looked around the room. "Those of you who have seen the Shadonae can testify that they are the most beautiful beings to walk the Lands. Their beauty captured us." His eyes took on a distant look, as if recalling the past.

"And then they spoke. They had so much knowledge to share, such high and lofty ideas. We were all enamored by them. We invited them to our homes, shared meals with them, eager to be counted amongst their closest friends, never once imagining that these beautiful men would turn on us."

Senator Regessus stopped and shuddered. The entire cave was quiet. Nierne heard the fire crackle in the silence.

"Then," Senator Regessus began, his voice cracking slightly, "on *that* day—"

The hair on Nierne's body rose. She knew what day he was referring to.

"We discovered too late what these men really were. We were all gathered in the Assembly Room, waiting to hear from our new friends. Suddenly they ordered the doors shut and locked, which our guards did immediately. We were puzzled, but felt no unease at their order. But we should have." Regessus looked around and took a deep breath.

"Then Valin brought Senator Barron to the center of the room," Regessus continued. "He said 'Today is a new day for Thyra.' Once again, we were puzzled by his words. Then he pulled off the glove he always wore and touched Barron and . . ." Regessus stopped, his jaw working as if he were trying to work the words out of his mouth. "Barron screamed . . ." He worked his jaw again. "He dropped to the floor—convulsing." Regessus closed his eyes. His mouth shut, and he stood there with the fire playing along the sharp angles of his face.

Nierne stared at the senator, her mouth dry. Someone whimpered nearby. Those who had spent time in the dungeons knew what Regessus was describing. They had seen it too.

"It-it was as if the blinders were finally removed from my eyes," Regessus said. "I could see now what stood in the middle of that room. They were not men, but monsters. And we had followed them, allowed them into our homes, our hearts, our lives."

His eyes looked hollow as he turned to stare into the flickering flames. "And now we are paying the price."

"Eldarans don't exist anymore."

"Ah," Father Reth said, "but we would have said the same thing about the Shadonae months ago." He pointed toward the tunnel that led to the outside. "Now we know better."

Cargan continued to scowl, his hairy arms folded across his massive chest. He and Father Reth stood in the middle of one of the rooms that extended from the main mining room. A torch hung from a metal bracket anchored to the rock wall near the doorway. It lit the area near the room's entrance, but left the rest of the area in darkness.

Nierne watched the exchange from the shadows on the other side of the room. She had found a small, private corner, cut off from the rest of the room by a wall of rock and wooden beams. It afforded some privacy from a mine full of men.

She recognized Cargan. He was a city watchman. Or had been, before the Thyra massacre. Now he was the leader of those who had escaped.

"Perhaps Eldarans do exist," Cargan conceded reluctantly. "The problem is that I don't have any extra men to send to the four corners of the Lands to search for them. For each day that passes, those still in Cragsmoor are either killed or mind-possessed. I would rather keep trying to free those people than go on a wild chase that may or may not turn up an Eldaran."

"But in the end, you will lose," Father Reth said softly.

Cargan's scowl deepened. "I don't see how."

"Weapons of steel cannot hurt the Shadonae. You may be able to rescue some of the people still trapped in the city, but the Shadonae will hunt you down, and eventually you will lose. Only an Eldaran has the power to stop the Shadonae."

Cargan stood stiffly, then dropped his arms and sighed. "Then what do you propose we do?"

"We go and search for the Eldarans."

"I already told you. I don't have enough—"

"Then I will go alone," Father Reth said.

Cargan stared at Father Reth, then laughed. "You'll go search for some fable, facing who knows what, all by yourself? You're madder than I thought."

It was Father Reth's turn to scowl. "At least I'd be doing something that has a chance of—"

"I will go with him."

The two men started at the sound of her voice. Nierne stood up. She agreed with Father Reth. The Shadonae possessed a power outside the physical realm, a power no human could ever destroy. But she believed the Eldarans could match that power. If there were any left.

"What are you doing here?" Cargan demanded, stepping forward.

"I was here before you both entered the room," Nierne said.

"And you stayed because . . . ?"

"I did not realize you were having a private conversation until you were well into it."

Cargan studied her for a moment. Nierne shoved down the urge to fidget under his intense gaze. Instead, she stood rigid. She knew the man was suspicious of everything and everyone—and understandably so. After what everyone had gone through in Thyra, most of the refugees here jumped at every shadow.

"Are you sure about this, Nierne?" Father Reth said, coming to stand by her.

Cargan's gaze relaxed. She knew she had been tested and found acceptable.

"I'm not any good here." Nierne turned her gaze to Father Reth. "I can't fight and I don't know anything about the healing arts. I can't even cook." For the last two days all she had done was sit and watch others. Granted, she was still recovering from her imprisonment, but Nierne knew she was just another body for others to care

MORGAN L. BUSSE

for, and that made her feel restless. She wanted to do something to help. To make up for not helping before . . .

Father Reth opened his mouth to speak, but she cut him short with a wave of her hand. "However, I'm young and healthy and can walk wherever we need to go." And knew more about the Eldarans than anyone else in this mine, other than Father Reth. Although unlike him, Nierne believed the Eldaran race had died out long ago. But if there was a chance they still existed, they were Thyra's only hope.

"Well, Father, it looks like you've got yourself an escort," Cargan said, glancing over at Nierne. "And a stubborn one at that." He chuckled.

Father Reth studied her a few moments.

Nierne raised her chin defiantly. There was no way she was going to let him go anywhere without her.

"You're right about that, Cargan." A smile broke across Father Reth's face. "Guess I better take her."

"I have an old friend up in Lachland," Father Reth said the next morning. "If we're lucky, he'll still be there. We can get some supplies from him, then start across the Ari Mountains."

"Ari Mountains?" Nierne said as they headed toward the entrance of the mine.

"Yes. I thought the first place we should travel to is the White City. After all, it is where the Eldarans first came to the Lands. There is an old sanctuary just outside the city. It would seem to be the most logical place for any remaining Eldarans to be."

The two stepped out into the sunlight. Nearby, a bird began to sing. The trees were just beginning to turn color. Red and gold mingled with the green leaves. Bright blue sky poked through the tree branches. Nierne stepped out from beneath the trees and felt the sun's heat spread across her face. It warmed her body, driving away the cold, damp feel of the mines."

A breeze sprang up and played with the curls around her face. More birds joined the first bird in song. A squirrel chattered from the trees. Nierne took a deep breath and let it out with a sigh.

Father Reth came to stand beside her. "Feels good to be out of those mines." Nierne merely nodded, enjoying this moment of peace. "Well," he said finally, "shall we begin?"

"Yes."

Father Reth pulled out a small, round compass from the folds of his robes. "Haven't used one of these in years." He held the compass close to his body and looked down at the glass face. He slowly turned, face still down, watching the small device. He stopped and looked up. "This way."

They walked the rest of the day in silence. To their knowledge, the Shadonae had chosen for the moment to stay within Thyra. However, shadows had been seen patrolling the forest the last few days, so Father Reth insisted on a very quiet journey to Lachland.

It took them a couple of days to cross the country of Kerre, a long and narrow country caught between the sea, the marshes, and the Great Desert to the south. But unlike the surrounding lands, Kerre was lush and beautiful.

It was also known as one of the most civilized countries in the Lands. People came from all over to study in its most prominent city, Thyra. It was said that if pleasure was the god of Temanin, then knowledge was the god of Kerre. But no amount of knowledge could save the people from the Shadonae now. It would require the source of knowledge, the Word Himself.

Nierne thought upon the irony of this as they drew closer to Lachland. The people of Kerre had long ago pushed aside the ancient teachings of the Word for more contemporary ways of thinking. Only the scribes at the Monastery had preserved the scrolls written long ago—written, perhaps, by the Eldarans themselves. And now the salvation of Thyra depended on the God they had denied.

They reached Lachland the afternoon of the third day. It was a small village, out of the way of most commerce. Only a few chose to dwell near the marshes. Tired and hungry, the two of them entered the village. "Ben owns a small mercantile here," Father Reth said. "So watch for one."

They followed the single dirt road that ran through the village. Nierne looked back and forth, studying the buildings that stood on either side. Most were run-down with cracked windows and missing boards. Paint peeled off of white-washed buildings. Dull green moss grew thickly over the wood shingled roofs. Bleak clouds hung overhead, giving the town a tired look.

Nierne wrinkled her nose. A sulfurous smell hung in the muggy air like rotten eggs left in the kitchen.

"It's the marshes nearby," Father Reth said at the look on her face. "The smell is not as bad today as it usually is."

Nierne couldn't imagine what a bad day would smell like.

They continued to walk along the road. The only decent looking place she saw was a tavern. *Probably the only place that gets business here*, Nierne thought. A rough looking man with shaggy brown hair and beard exited the tavern. He stumbled down the stairs and stopped at the bottom. He looked up at Nierne. His look turned into a long stare.

Nierne pulled the hood up from her robe and covered her tangled mess of blood red curls. Even in Thyra, a city that boasted much variety among its citizens, she had always stood out and drew more attention than she liked. She had inherited the unique red color from her mother.

Nierne could feel the man's eyes on her even after she walked by. She hated men staring at her. It made her feel . . . dirty.

"There it is." Father Reth stopped and pointed toward a tall, plain building with a single sign that hung above a narrow door. *Last Chance Mercantile* was written in dark letters, the paint chipping away from the sign. The shop looked as if it had seen better days.

The two entered the dilapidated establishment. It took a moment for Nierne's eyes to adjust to the dark interior. Slowly barrels and crates began to take shape, filled with all sorts of food, seed, and other supplies people living on the edge of civilization would need. Glass jars filled with pickled foods lined the shelves that hung on the walls. Crude farming tools stood in one corner. A couple bolts of ugly grey material lay against the wall of another. Father Reth headed straight toward the back and through an open door. Nierne followed.

In the back was a small room. The white clapboard walls were bare. A worn wooden counter stood in the middle of the room with another door in back. A window along the left wall let in pale light. Cobwebs hung in the corners.

Behind the counter sat a man on a spindly wooden chair. His legs were very long. They sprawled out in front, arms folded across his chest and his head bent forward. His hair was long and white and pulled back at the nape of his neck. A thick, white mustache grew below his crooked nose. The rest of his face looked like worn leather. A dark jerkin covered his stained white shirt and a sword was belted around his middle. A small snore escaped his lips.

Father Reth moved toward the man and laid a hand on his shoulder.

"What the—" The man leaped to his feet, his hand going to the sword. Then his eyes lit upon Father Reth. "Reth?" he sputtered.

"Ben!" Father Reth replied.

Ben took a step toward Father Reth and embraced him. Nierne watched from the doorway. "Reth, I can't believe it. It's been, what, ten years since I last saw you?"

"More like twenty," Father Reth said with a laugh.

"And who is this?" Ben asked, turning to look at Nierne.

"One of the scribes from the Monastery."

"You didn't tell me the Monastery was taking in lovely ladies. I might have signed up."

"Now, now, Ben. Leave her alone." A smile tugged at the corner of Father Reth's mouth. "Besides, I don't think the solitary lifestyle of a scribe would have suited you."

"No, it wouldn't have. Never understood how you could join."

"I was called to it. Nothing to explain."

"Still think you're crazy. Giving up our adventures, gold, *women?*" Ben said the last word with a leer. "For what? Dusty books and parchment?"

"There is more to life than that, Ben."

"Ha! Why, I remember the time when we stumbled into that tavern down in Hont. You know, when we were searching for the necklace of Calbar. And that sandstorm came whipping in. We were holed up there for three days. Not that you minded. You had—what was her name?" Ben waved his hand. "Eh, doesn't matter. You were too drunk to remember." He tapped a finger on his chin. "Think I was too."

Father Reth laughed. Ben joined him. Soon they were nearly doubled over in laughter.

Nierne raised an eyebrow. She knew Father Reth had not always been a father, but to be somehow linked to a story like that made her wonder what he had been like when he was younger.

Father Reth caught his breath. "Yes, yes, but that was a long time ago. Seems your memory is as good as it was then: a bit on the fuzzy side."

"Yeah. Never could keep things straight. Gotten worse since I moved here. So," Ben said, looking back at Nierne, "how did a pretty thing like you end up at the Monastery?"

Nierne felt her cheeks redden.

Father Reth stepped back and placed a hand along her shoulder. "Nierne joined us about fifteen years ago and has been a wonderful addition to our community."

Ben looked at her. "'Nierne,' is it?"

"Yes . . . sir," she replied, not sure how to address the man.

Ben again roared with laughter. "Don't know when's the last time I've been called a 'sir.'"

"Probably never," Father Reth said with a grin. Nierne relaxed under his arm. Father Reth had always seemed less uptight than any of the Monastery Fathers, scribes too. Perhaps his past had something to do with that.

Ben smiled back. Then his face slowly turned somber. "We've all heard about Thyra. Many here have already left, fearing the Shadonae will come here next. How is it you two escaped?"

Nierned looked up at Father Reth. His smile faded. "That, my friend, is a long story."

"Then let's hear it." Ben turned and moved toward the doorway.

He led them out the back door of the mercantile, where there was a small building that the older man evidently used as his living quarters.

Like the store itself, this building was plain and simple. To her right was the fireplace. An old clock sat on the mantle. Logs were neatly stacked in the corner. A braided rug covered the dirt floor. Two wooden chairs sat a couple of feet away from fireplace. Faded yellow curtains framed the window across from her. In the far left corner was a narrow door. The room smelled like smoke and dirty laundry.

"Tell me everything," Ben said, settling down in one of the chairs.

Taking a seat in the other, Father Reth began. Nierne went to stand next to the fireplace. She watched the red coals burning inside. As Father Reth spoke of the Shadonae, the room seemed to go cold. His story was similar to hers: He had been helping others escape when he was caught himself and taken to the fortress. Apparently too old to be of use, the Shadonae had kept him locked up, until a couple of nights ago, when he had escaped, the same night Nierne had.

"So what are your plans now?" Ben sat forward, his elbows propped up on his knees. "I'd offer you a place here, but I'm thinking of leaving myself."

"No, that's all right," Father Reth said with a wave of his hands. "We're traveling to the White City."

"The White City?" Ben sat back. "You're going to try and cross the Ari Mountains? Why?"

"We are searching for the Eldarans."

Ben rose from his chair with a faraway look on his face. He walked toward the fireplace and placed a hand on the mantle. "Eldarans, huh?"

Nierne watched the older man, wondering what he was thinking. At last, Ben turned back around. "Many years ago, an Eldaran stopped in this village, carrying a small baby. She stayed only a night, then left. I have no idea where to. But one thing was for sure—she was scared of something. She was always looking over her shoulder."

Father Reth stood. "You met an Eldaran?" Excitement shone in his eyes. "How do you know she was an Eldaran?"

"Her hand," Ben replied, still looking as if he was gazing into the past. "The mark of the Word was on her hand."

"I knew it!" Father Reth said. "I knew the Word would not leave us without help."

Ben's eyes came back into focus. "You don't know if she's still alive, Reth. And if she is, where she would be now."

"No," Father Reth said. "But it is enough to know that they still exist. Or at least that they did some years ago—within our lifetimes."

The room grew quiet. Nierne turned and looked at the window. Outside, the sun had set, leaving the room dark except for the flickering orange light from the coals.

"I have a map that should help you get over the Ari Mountains," Ben said. "You'll also need supplies." He launched into a list of the provisions they would need to reach the White City.

After a half hour, Ben glanced at the clock on the mantle. "It's getting late, and you'll want a good start in the morning. I have an extra room for you, Nierne," he said. He walked over to the narrow door in the corner and opened it. Inside were stairs. "Just up the stairs." Ben looked both of the travelers over. "And you'll need something more substantial than your monastery robes for traveling. I've got a couple shirts and pants in the store you can try on. Nothing fancy, mind you, but they'll keep you warm and dry."

"We'd be grateful for anything you can give us," Father Reth said.

Ben looked over at him. "Anything for a friend. Just make sure you come back with a good story to tell me when this is all over," he said and winked.

CHAPTER
11

Like wildfire, the news of Hershaw Pass and the fall of Hadrast Fortress swept across the north, leaving a smoke of fear in its wake. Captain Lore could feel the tension even inside the castle. Ever since the day the courier had arrived, panic had rippled through the White City.

Aiden, Lord Gaynor's head messenger, stood in the middle of the meeting room. Lord Gaynor paced back and forth, running his fingers over the backs of the chairs that circled the long dark table at the end of the room. A silver tray with a crystal decanter filled with wine and a goblet sat on the table, untouched. Dark clouds filled the narrow windows that lined the outside wall. Lore stood by the windows and watched Lord Gaynor.

"Send word to all the villages to seek refuge in Mostyn, Garined, and other strongholds," Lord Gaynor said. "And if they can reach Nordica, all the better. Lord Tancred has offered protection to any Rylander who chooses to sojourn to his country." He stood for a moment, his hand resting on the back of one of the chairs.

"Yes, milord. Will that be all?"

"Yes, Aiden. You are dismissed."

Aiden bowed and left the room.

Lore noted the haggard appearance on Lord Gaynor's face. This new development was taking its toll on the high lord. He looked years older than he had a week ago, and it had been only a matter of days since the news had arrived.

"I must send word to Avonai to move up the time of our council," Lord Gaynor said more softly. "The time for waiting is over. Avonai needs to choose if it will ally with us." He turned toward Lore. "Lore, I need you to—"

There was a knock at the door.

"Yes?" Lord Gaynor called out.

A guard appeared in the doorway.

"Sir, Prince Evander of Avonai is here to see you."

"Prince Evander?" A look of surprise flashed across Lord Gaynor's face.

"Yes, sir."

"Show him in at once."

The guard nodded and left.

"Well, this is unexpected." Lord Gaynor turned toward Lore. "Hopefully this means that Avonai is ready to form an alliance." The two men waited the arrival of Avonai's sovereign.

Prince Evander arrived moments later with his varor close behind. "Lord Gaynor," Prince Evander said upon entering the room.

A guard shut the door quietly behind him.

"Prince Evander. Please, take a seat."

Lore watched Prince Evander cross the room. The young man was short and slim. His face was clean-shaven and had a boyish look. He had the same light brown hair that Lore's mother had possessed. And the sea eyes of the coastal people. His cloak was wet, making it seem to be a deeper shade of grey than it probably was. Apparently Prince Evander had come straight here from outside.

His varor followed, a solid looking Avonain. He had the same color of hair and sea eyes as Prince Evander. A scar ran lengthwise over the bridge of his nose and across both cheeks. He gave Lore a slight nod and took his place behind Prince Evander.

The prince took a seat opposite of Lord Gaynor and began without preamble. "I am here about the alliance."

Lord Gaynor gave the prince a small nod. "Please continue."

"I am sure by now that you have received reports concerning my father." Prince Evander paused and glanced at Lord Gaynor.

Lord Gaynor nodded solemnly.

"His mind is . . . unwell," Prince Evander said tactfully. "The council and I have done everything we can to keep the knowledge of his madness from the people for the sake of stability. Unfortunately there have been times my father has passed decrees without our knowledge, making them law. Five days ago, he passed such a decree, one that had to do with the potential alliance between our countries."

Prince Evander stopped. A great weight seemed to sit on his shoulders. Lord Gaynor sat patiently, letting the young man before him take his time.

"My father met with the grand assembly right after Temanin took control of Hadrast Fortress," Prince Evander said. "I happened to be away, meeting with the military commanders down in Roneguard. The rest of the council was never informed of the grand assembly until the moment the assembly began. It was there that my father cited his stipulations for Avonai and the coastal people to join the alliance and the war." A creased formed along the prince's brow. "Lord Gaynor, he will not ally with you unless you enter into a blood alliance between Avonai and the White City—between our house and yours."

Lore felt shocked at this news, but made no move on the outside. Lord Gaynor made no movement either. He merely leaned back, his face unreadable. Prince Evander waited for the high lord's response.

"I'm not surprised," Lord Gaynor finally answered.

Prince Evander looked at Lord Gaynor with a puzzled expression. "Then you are a wiser man than I, Lord Gaynor, for I was completely ambushed by this move."

Lord Gaynor smiled sadly. "For a long time now King Alaric has desired such an alliance between our two peoples. But he also knew that I would never consent to an arranged bonding. I told him that years ago." Lord Gaynor's gaze drifted toward the window in thought.

Prince Evander shifted uncomfortably in his seat. "Then what answer should I take back to Avonai?"

Lord Gaynor looked at the prince. "My statement still stands. I will not bond my daughter to another without her consent. I believe you to be an honorable man, your highness, and potentially a fine match for my daughter. But I will not arrange her bonding."

Prince Evander nodded and stood. "Then I will not take up more of your time." He turned to leave.

"Prince Evander," Lord Gaynor said, "you still do not have an answer to take back to Avonai. This alliance is badly needed if we are to drive Temanin back south."

Prince Evander turned around, a puzzled look on his face. "I'm afraid I don't understand. You just said—"

"That I would not bond my daughter to another without her consent," Lord Gaynor finished. "But we do not know if she will consent or not. So I invite you and your varor to stay as guests here in the White City. And during your stay, I shall let my daughter know of Avonai's request. In a few days, she will give you an answer to take back."

Prince Evander stood unmoving. Slowly he nodded. "I accept your offer of hospitality."

Lord Gaynor rose from his seat. "Good. I will hold a dinner tonight so that you may meet my daughter."

"I would be honored." Prince Evander bowed before Lord Gaynor.

Rowen hurried toward the Guards Quarter, her shift finally done for the day. All day she had followed Lady Astrea around: to her studies, to an afternoon tea, and then time in the library. Not that she was complaining. At least she was able to move around as she followed Lady Astrea—unlike many of the other guards who were stationed around the castle and city. They had to stay rooted in one place until their shift ended.

Rowen pulled open the door and sighed. No other guards were in the common room. She had it all to herself. A fire roared in the fireplace nearby. Even with spring on its way, winter still held a tight grip on the mountain city. She went directly to the fire and sat down in one of the chairs.

She closed her eyes and let the heat from the fire soak through her body. This was much better than going back to her room. She had no fireplace there.

Rowen cracked her eyes open. She had a thought. She looked one more time around the common room. Still empty. Relieved, she began to pull at the tips of her sword glove. Over the months she had grown accustomed to the feel of its leather against her skin, but there was nothing like having her hand free.

She pulled the glove off and dropped it in her lap. The air felt cool and raw to her skin. Rowen flexed her fingers, then on impulse turned her hand over. It had been weeks since she had last studied her palm. Living here in the castle, with her glove to cover her secret, there were moments she even forgot about the mark.

The white skin shone with a soft light, barely visible even in the darkening room. Rowen stared at it, wondering what it was or what caused it to glow. Twice she had almost found the courage to ask Balint, the old healer, about her mark. Lore had said that Balint was part Eldaran. But then, remembering the fear her mark had caused the people in her village, that courage had died away. Besides, Lore said there were no more Eldarans.

Rowen shifted in the chair and placed her hand down on the padded side. Perhaps Cleon was right: Perhaps she was a witch. And if that were true, then it was better for whatever this was to stay hidden.

Suddenly her stomach growled, jolting her from her thoughts. Time go get something—

"Rowen?"

Rowen turned swiftly in the chair. Lore stood behind her.

When did he come in? she thought frantically, keeping her face toward him. Blindly she reached for her glove.

Lore began to walk toward her. "I hoped I'd find you here."

The glove fumbled in her hand.

"I'm afraid something's come up, and I'll need you to escort Lady Astrea tonight." Lore frowned. "Are you all right?"

"Yes." Rowen tugged the glove back on, hoping against hope that

Lore had not seen the mark. How could she have been so foolish to take her glove off here?

He looked unconvinced. "Are you sure? You seem . . . nervous."

"What does Lady Astrea need me for?" The glove was almost on. She just needed one more moment.

Lore looked her over one more time before answering. "We have guests from Avonai here this evening, so there is a special dinner planned tonight. You will need to accompany Lady Astrea."

Suddenly Rowen noticed that Lore was dressed differently. Instead of his usual white shirt and leather jerkin, he was wearing what looked like his formal uniform. Her heart gave a weird tinge and a strange sensation filled her middle. The dark blue of his tabard brought out the blue in his eyes.

Blue? Rowen frowned. Wait, weren't his eyes green?

"I'm sorry about this," Lore said. "If I could have someone else cover for you tonight, I would." He looked at her closely. "You look tired."

He's right, Rowen thought. She had been looking forward to a quick dinner, then bed. Instead, she stood. "It is not a problem, Captain."

"Good, I'll see you there. The dinner starts in a half hour."

Rowen hurried down the hall toward her own quarters. She splashed water across her face and re-braided her hair. She checked her uniform one more time and headed through the adjoining archway into Lady Astrea's room.

Lady Astrea was already dressed in a simple yet elegant white gown. Her hair was pulled up in a dark twist with her silver circlet placed on top. Jaida, her servant girl, was quietly putting her old gown away.

Lady Astrea looked over at Rowen. "Rowen, it is good to see you again." She tried to smile, but her lips quivered instead. "I'm sorry that you will not have the night off. We both must attend a dinner this evening."

Rowen gave her a polite bow. "Milady, I am here to serve you."

Lady Astrea took a deep breath. "Then let us go."

Rowen followed Lady Astrea from the room. Something was going on. But what?

The two walked down the corridor and stairs toward the main dining hall. The double doors were open leading into the room. A guard stood on either side of the doors. Both men bowed to Lady Astrea.

Inside the hall, noblemen and women were seating themselves around a long wooden table, the length of which reached both sides of the room. A white linen runner lay lengthwise across the dark wood. Several silver candelabras were placed strategically along its surface to create an intimate atmosphere of soft lighting. Polished silver and white porcelain plates had been placed in front of each chair.

Lady Astrea turned right and headed toward the end where her father sat. Lord Gaynor stood and pulled out her chair. He whispered quietly after she sat. She nodded mutely. He sat down again, and Rowen took up her position behind Lady Astrea.

Rowen could see new lines creasing Lord Gaynor's face and a slight sag to his usual rigid stature. Aren stood behind Lord Gaynor, his long blond hair pulled back for the evening while his hand rested on the hilt of his sword. Rowen glanced his direction. Aren saw and grinned back.

More people entered the room. Two men walked past her. The shorter one took a seat beside Lord Gaynor. He was of slight built with light brown hair and a pleasing complexion. *Must be the guest from Avonai,* Rowen thought, someone important, if he was allowed to sit at Lord Gaynor's right hand. The taller man stood behind him, his face high enough out of the candlelight that she could not make it out.

"Good evening."

Rowen's hand flew to her sword. "Captain!" She hoped Lore hadn't seen her reach for her sword. Slowly she moved her hand back to her side.

The candlelight softened his face. "Thank you for coming, Rowen. I know it's been a long day."

"It has," she said truthfully.

"I do not expect it to be a long night."

I hope not, she thought.

Lore passed her and walked around Lord Gaynor. He stopped and spoke with Aren, then moved to the empty seat beside the young man from Avonai.

The shuffle of chairs ceased, and the low hum of conversation began. Servants entered the room, bearing silver trays covered with various foods. One servant passed her carrying a basket loaded with warm breads. Hunks of cooked venison and whole cooked game birds on platters were placed between the plates. Wisps of steam floated up from tureens filled with soup. Wine was poured into crystal goblets.

Every smell assailed Rowen, reminding her that she had not eaten since breakfast. Her stomach rumbled quietly in protest. She placed a hand across her middle and hoped no one heard.

Soon the faint tinkle of silverware on porcelain replaced much of the conversation. Rowen subtly shifted her weight from one leg to the other. These were the most trying times of being a varor—standing guard.

To take her mind off of her empty stomach, Rowen began to study the dinner guests around the table. She glanced at Lord Gaynor. He was talking quietly with Lady Astrea. Rowen moved her gaze on to the young man who sat beside him. Who was this special guest? He wore no jewelry except for a single large sapphire ring on his right middle finger. The stone matched his blue silk vest. Was he a nobleman? Or part of Avonai's royal family? She couldn't tell by his looks. He must be someone important, though, to travel with a varor.

Her eyes came to rest on Captain Lore. Tonight he was attending the dinner as Captain of the Guard, not as Lord Gaynor's varor. This was a side of Lore Rowen had never seen before. She was used to finding him in the training room, stripped down to a simple white shirt and dark pants, sparring with the other guards or teaching the new guards some defensive move. Once in a while he would wear his dark leather jerkin and shirt while patrolling the city.

But tonight, with his hair falling on either side of his eyes instead of slicked back with sweat and his shirt spotless, the white of it matching the eagle crest across his tabard, he looked every inch the Captain of the Guard, second in command of the city, and only son of the Palancar family.

As if sensing her gaze, Lore looked up and caught her eye. Rowen felt her face grow warm, and she looked elsewhere. She could feel his eyes lingering on her but found she could not look back. Instead, she continued her study of the other dinner guests. Moments later, his gaze was gone. Rowen looked from the corner of her eye and found him in conversation with the young man from Avonai.

A small part of her sighed with relief. Another part wondered at her strange reaction. After all, she had been in the White City for months now and had never felt uncomfortable with Lore before. Had something changed?

Rowen pondered this as she shifted her weight again and looked over the rest of the guests. She recognized most of them from other royal functions: councilmen and their wives, nobility who dwelt in the city, and merchants with large coin purses.

As if on their own volition, her eyes drifted back toward Lore. He was still in deep discussion with the young man, the latter gesturing with his hands. Lore looked on with interest. Taking advantage of his distraction, Rowen studied Lore more, trying to figure out why tonight was different.

With his hair falling forward, she could barely make out the grey she knew graced his temples. Not that he was old, but he was also not as young as many of the guards. She placed his age to be near his late thirties, perhaps even forty. But time had not begun to diminish his physical prowess. On the contrary, if their sparring matches were any indication, Lore was at the height of his game. Rowen believed he actually went easy on her.

Lore looked up again. That same flush of heat rose to her cheeks. What had gotten into her tonight? Lore flashed her a smile before turning back to the young man beside him. Rowen fought the urge to lift a hand and rub her burning face.

Whatever this was, she hoped it would soon disappear.

Lore took a sip of the golden liquid in his cup. He and Prince Evander reminisced about shared experiences on the coast near Avonai. Apparently the prince had spent his younger summer days in much the same way Lore had: running along the beach, exploring the nearby rock cliffs, checking tidal pools for treasure left behind by the receding waves. Just thinking of those happier times made Lore smile.

He looked up and noticed Rowen staring at him. The pleasant feeling inside him suddenly extended toward her. But instead of smiling back, she shifted her eyes elsewhere. His smile turned to a puzzled frown. He studied her for a moment, noting the slight creases below her eyes and the way she kept shifting. He knew from experience that it meant one thing: She was exhausted.

Lore began to wonder when the last time was that Rowen had been given a couple of days off. Granted, she was the only woman varor—the only female guard, for that matter—so it was difficult to find others to cover for her during those times she went off shift. Difficult or not, he would make sure she had some time off. Lore took another sip. He would fill in for her after Prince Evander's visit.

"So your mother was from Fiske?" Prince Evander said, interrupting Lore's thoughts.

"Yes."

"But you only spent your summers on the coast."

"Yes. It was difficult for my father to leave his position here for extended periods of time. So my mother and I would go during the summer."

"Wasn't that hard? To be away from the sea, and then to come back."

"Yes. It still is. Every time I visit Avonai." Lore stared at his cup, remembering his visit a few months ago. His Avonain blood had connected him to the sea, causing him to feel the storm that had moved in. Most Avonains were used to the feeling, since they lived by the sea and felt it every day. But he rarely visited the coast. The storm felt like fire was running through his veins. "The sea still overwhelms me. I have not yet learned how to disconnect myself from it."

"Do you ever feel the sea, way out here in the White City?"

"No, not usually," Lore said. "Thankfully. I can't imagine trying to do my job while the ocean wreaked havoc on my emotions. On the other hand, more exposure would probably have built up a tolerance in me."

Prince Evander asked him questions, using his hands to emphasize his words. Lore replied, enjoying his talk with the young man. As he got to know him, Lore felt more and more confident that, if Lady Astrea were to choose to accept the bonding, it would not be a bad thing. Of course, one night of conversation with a man was certainly not going to reveal everything about him. But Prince Evander proved to have a good head on his shoulders, a humble attitude, and a love for his country and people.

Lore felt like he was being watched. He looked up and found Rowen staring at him again, this time with a thoughtful expression on her face. He gave her another smile. In the dim light, he could see her face color. Was she . . . blushing? Embarrassed? Immediately her eyes moved away, staring intently down toward the end of the table.

Curious now, Lore picked up his goblet and took a sip of the sparkling liquid inside. He studied her over its silver-tipped rim. After months of knowing her, Rowen remained a mystery. He had been able to establish a relationship with her up to a point, but there was an invisible wall around her, and no one, not even Lady Astrea, seemed to be able to get past it. Rowen held everyone at arm's length.

Which made Lore wonder why. Did Rowen feel such a strong sense of professionalism that she was unwilling to forge any relationship with anyone beyond that of a fellow guard? Or had something happened in her past that had caused her to shun others, not in a hateful way, but in a protective way?

Did a wounded soul hide behind the beautiful face?

Lore placed his goblet down and felt a gentle stirring inside his heart. Having followed the Word for years, he knew immediately what it was. And he knew that he had somehow touched on the issue surrounding Rowen.

Word, he thought, *please show me how to reach her . . . if I can.*

CHAPTER 12

Rowen stood at the edge of the castle gardens, watching Lady Astrea and the young man from last night walk along one of the paths.

It had rained the night before, leaving the air smelling fresh and new. The sun shone with a white brilliance. She could feel the heat and water combine, making her clothes sticky. Raindrops clung to the mountain roses that lined the pathways, and in the morning light, they sparkled like tiny diamonds. Ahead, the garden ended abruptly at the face of the mountain. The sheer grey rock wall went up higher than the castle, ending past the lazy wisps of fog that clung to the mountaintop.

The young man's varor stood on the opposite side of the garden, in the shadow cast by the mountain wall. His arms were folded across his chest, his face unreadable in the dark.

Out of the corner of her eye, Rowen saw Lore exit the castle and walk toward her. He was dressed in his usual way: white shirt and jerkin, dark pants, and boots. At the sight of him, the strange tickling sensation from last night returned.

Lore smiled. "Good morning, Rowen."

"Morning, Captain."

"Sleep well?"

"Yes." She felt herself begin to relax, and the tickling sensation slowly disappeared.

Lore motioned to the couple in the garden. "I did not have a chance to tell you who our guest was last night. He is Prince Evander."

"Prince?"

"Yes, of Avonai and the coastal region."

The prince of Avonai, Rowen thought, studying the young man more. "So he is the reason for our dinner last night." Rowen turned to look at Lore. "Why is he here?"

"To negotiate an alliance between Avonai and the White City."

"I see." That made sense. She knew that for the last year the Ryland Plains had been negotiating with the neighboring northern countries to unite against Temanin. Nordica had agreed and sent troops, but Avonai—Prince Evander's realm—had chosen to stay neutral. But now, with Temanin in the north and the Ryland Plains troops stretched thin from the losses at Hershaw Pass, the north needed Avonai to join the fight.

"I will need you to accompany Lady Astrea the entire time Prince Evander is here, not just during your shift." Lore watched the couple. "Not that I don't trust Prince Evander or his varor, but when we have guests here in the White City, I like to have the royal family watched closely the entire time."

"I understand." Rowen turned her attention back toward Lady Astrea.

The two young rulers had stopped at a nearby bench. Prince Evander brushed away some of the water, then motioned for Lady Astrea to sit. The young woman did, a faint pinkness to her usual white cheeks.

"When Prince Evander's visit is done," Lore said, "I've arranged for you to have a couple days off. You've been working hard, and after the prince's visit, you'll need some time to rest."

Lore's words surprised Rowen. True, she had spent many long days the last few months following Lady Astrea around. But that was her job. "Who will take my place?"

"I will. Before you came, Aren, Justus, and I would take turns watching Lady Astrea when her governess was needed elsewhere. We can do it again."

Rowen opened her mouth to protest. Lore's face grew stubborn, one eyebrow raised and lips pursed together.

"Yes, Captain," she said instead. Perhaps Lore was right. Anyway, she'd seen Lore's stubbornness with other guards, and she knew that there was no getting around it. Besides, she really could use the break. Perhaps she would explore the city. Since arriving in the White City, she'd had little time to visit the city itself. Rowen's mood brightened at the thought.

"I will see you tonight." Lore turned and headed back toward the castle.

Rowen's eyes followed him, the tickling sensation in her middle returning.

Later that afternoon, Rowen and Lady Astrea meandered through the field just outside the city. After spending all morning with Prince Evander, Lady Astrea had said she wanted some time to think.

The walls of the White City provided a pale background to the colorful field in full bloom. White daisies, yellow buttercups, and tiny bluebells bobbed on the warm breeze. Long grass waved back and forth. Rowen could smell the wet rich earth and subtle flower scent. Overhead, the sky was a brilliant blue except for a few white puffy clouds.

Other people were enjoying the warm spring afternoon, as well. Rowen spotted a couple far across the field, walking near the walls, which had grown hazy with the distance between them. Next to the gates were four little girls, twirling amongst the flowers. She smiled.

Her glance slowly moved toward Anwin Forest half a league to the west. Its tall, dark trees bordered the field. She could see no ray of sunshine past the treeline. Only shadows. The forest was a stark contrast to the bright and cheerful field. Rowen reached over and felt for her sword. Its cool metal hilt reassured her. Perhaps they should head back to the city. Anwin was giving her the chills.

"Rowen, I do not know what to do."

Rowen turned around. Lady Astrea wore a simple green dress with a golden cord around her middle. Her hair was pulled back into a braid and wrapped around her head like a dark crown.

"Do about what, milady?"

She bent down and picked a single white daisy. "Of course—you're wondering what I'm talking about." Lady Astrea stood back up and laughed softly. "Seems I'm starting to talk nonsense." She studied the white flower in her hand.

Rowen frowned. She heard the slight tremble in Lady Astrea's voice. There was something going on, something between Lady Astrea and Prince Evander. But what? Might it have something to do with the alliance Lore spoke of?

Lady Astrea dropped the flower and covered her face. Rowen heard her sob.

"My lady, what is wrong?" Rowen hurried to Lady Astrea and placed a hand on her shoulder. "Are you not feeling well?"

Lady Astrea turned her face away and wiped her eyes.

"We can head back to the castle if you like . . ." Rowen felt at a loss at what to say. She had never seen Lady Astrea cry before.

Lady Astrea wiped her cheeks again. "No, I'm well. It's just that—" She looked at Rowen as if debating with herself. "Avonai will not join the alliance unless I bond with Prince Evander." Her lip began to tremble again.

Rowen stared at Lady Astrea. "What? That can't be . . . It's not right . . . I . . ." Rowen stuttered to a silence. What should she say? Never had such a thing been done in the Ryland Plains. Other countries were known to force a bonding between their royal members, but the Ryland Plains had always been above such barbarism. Until now, apparently.

"It's still my choice," Lady Astrea said. "When my father told me about King Alaric's proposition, he emphasized that I did not have to go through with it. In fact, I think he secretly hopes I won't. But Rowen . . ." her voice quivered a moment . . . "it's the only choice I have. Without Avonai's support, we cannot hope to drive back Temanin."

So that's why Lady Astrea had been with Prince Evander all morning. He was negotiating the part of the alliance that required the hand of the Lady of the White City.

Rowen felt her heart move toward the young woman before her.

She couldn't even begin to imagine making such a choice. And the pressure . . .

Lady Astrea studied her fingers. Rowen could see the silver trail left by the tears Lady Astrea had been unable to keep back. "I'm sorry." Lady Astrea wiped her eyes again. "I just needed to tell someone and you're always so—"

A long piercing howl filled the meadow.

Rowen dropped her hand to her hilt. She swerved her head toward the tree line a half league away.

The howl echoed for a moment, then faded. A chill raced down her back. Something was watching them.

Rowen took a step away from the forest, straining her eyes against the shadows. She could see nothing. "My Lady," Rowen said quietly feeling the sudden need to get to safety, "I think you should . . ."

A dark creature moved past the trees and onto the field. It was as large as a horse but looked more like a wolf. Its body was covered in spiky black fur. Eerie yellow eyes darted back and forth, searching for something. The smell of rotting meat filled the air, even across the distance. Rowen stared at the creature, horrified. It lifted its head and howled again.

Rowen staggered back, pushing down the urge to cover her ears. The creature's unearthly howl made her insides shatter. She had heard of the black wolves of Anwin in stories told to scare little children. Never had she thought they were real.

Another wolf stepped out from the trees.

Rowen's hand tightened over the hilt of her sword. She had to do something quickly. According to the stories, the wolves could not see, at least not the physical world. She didn't know what that meant, but she hoped it could work to their advantage.

"Lady Astrea," Rowen called softly. She kept her eyes on the two black wolves. Lady Astrea did not reply. Rowen chanced a quick glance to her left and found Lady Astrea paralyzed, her mouth open and eyes wide. Rowen turned back to the wolves. Their large shaggy heads were bent to the ground, sniffing. Slowly Rowen sidled toward Lady Astrea. Hopefully they wouldn't see—

One glanced up and looked straight at the women.

No time left.

The wolf charged.

"Lady Astrea, run!" Rowen placed herself between Lady Astrea and the wolf. Astrea stood frozen. "Astrea, run *now!*"

Lady Astrea turned and ran.

This is it. Rowen drew her sword. Her whole body shook with fear. No escape for her. She needed to give Lady Astrea enough time to reach the city gates. Her body urged her to run. *Stay, I need to stay.*

The wolf slowed as it approached her, its yellow eyes darting between Rowen and Lady Astrea fleeing behind her. Suddenly its ears pricked up with interest, and it sniffed the air as if catching a tantalizing scent. The wolf looked directly at Rowen and began to sprint toward her in a frenzied dash. It covered the distance with astonishing speed.

The wolf leaped high in the air.

Rowen barely had time to swing her sword. She swung with all her might and caught the wolf across the shoulder. The blade slid through muscle and tendon, catching on the tip of the bone.

The wolf yelped. It landed awkwardly. When it got up, it was favoring the injured leg.

Rowen staggered back as well, thrown off balance by the blow. She breathed heavily and brought her sword back into a defensive posture.

She felt sick. It was one thing to spar back in the White City, and it was another thing to draw blood. Her hand continued to shake.

The wolf hauled itself up and snarled at her.

Rowen took a step back.

The wolf began to circle her, a slight limp to its walk.

Rowen kept her blade pointed at it. Where was the other wolf? A chill ran down her spine. Had it caught Lady Astrea? She couldn't turn to look. She had to finish this wolf first, or it would finish her.

A sudden twitch in the animal's back made Rowen lift her sword. The wolf snarled and leaped toward her. Rowen swung the weapon.

This time she caught the wolf across the chest.

The tip slipped across black fur. She tried to drive it into its chest, but she did not have the strength behind her blow to penetrate. Instead of piercing its heart, her blade simply followed the wolf down.

The wolf backed away again, watching her with its yellow eyes.

Rowen held her sword and panted, sweltering under the springtime sun, drenched from the adrenaline racing through her. She lifted the sword again and shifted into a defensive position. The wolf just watched her. Why wasn't it—

A massive weight slammed into her from the back. The ground greeted her, knocking her breath away.

Her shoulder burst into a flame of agony. She screamed and tried to roll away from the pain, but slavering jaws above her clamped down again and tore into the flesh of her shoulder.

Her vision clouded. A deathly coldness began to seep in from her shoulder down along her arm.

Rowen gathered what coherency she had left and swung her other arm, elbow first, into the wolf on top of her.

The dark creature grunted and staggered off her, giving her a chance to roll.

She went to put weight on her left side. Her arm buckled beneath her.

Rowen dropped back to the ground, her vision alternating between color and black. She struggled to clear her mind, only to find the two wolves advancing on her.

She clawed at the dirt and grass and tried to pull herself up. The darkness called to her, beckoning her to follow it. She fell back down.

No, Rowen thought weakly, unable to lift her head. But she couldn't fight it any longer. The coldness from her arm spread down her body. Darkness closed her eyes and carried her away.

• • •

Lore walked along the city wall, visiting with the guards who stood on top and checking the battlements that lined the wall. With the threat of the Temanin Army now a reality, Lord Gaynor wanted the White City prepared. Even now, Temanin scouts could be watching them.

He came to the main gates and stopped near the guardhouse. The two guards on duty nodded toward Lore. He nodded back in greeting.

Lore leaned over the battlement and glanced at the fields of flowers that grew outside the city. A couple was walking just below the wall. Four little girls sat near the open gates, weaving flowers together. After being stuck inside the city all winter, Lore couldn't think of a better way to spend the warm spring day.

A sudden movement of color to his right caught his attention. Far off, it looked like a woman running, her green dress billowing out around her. Her dark hair triggered something inside his mind. Straining his eyes more, his heart suddenly stopped. Lady Astrea.

"Kalfar, Donar, with me!" Lore shouted. He ran toward the stairway that led to the gates below. The two guards followed.

Down the steps he flew, two at a time. Then taking a sharp left, Lore ran under the stone archway and out onto the field.

Lady Astrea began to shout as she ran toward him. A sick feeling began to roll inside his gut. Where was Rowen?

"Wolves," Lady Astrea shouted, close to hysterics. "Black wolves. And Rowen—" She stumbled forward and cried, covering her face.

Lore pointed to Lady Astrea. "Kalfar, take her to the castle. Donar, get those people inside the gate."

Without waiting to see his orders carried out, Lore took off across the field, searching for Rowen. He ran and ran, sweeping his eyes back and forth, but he could see no figure amongst the tall grass. His stomach clenched in fear. Where was she? Was he too late? *No, Word. Please, no.*

He saw two dark shapes far across the field, almost at the tree line. Black wolves.

With renewed strength, Lore pushed his body and raced across the grass. He could feel rage and fear building up inside him. He would not let those vile creatures kill an innocent person.

Lore spotted a body amongst the grass. He drew his sword and yelled. He had to reach that body.

One of the wolves turned toward him and snarled. Lore ignored the wolf and ran harder.

The wolves took a couple of steps back from the body.

Lore reached the body—it was Rowen—and placed himself between her and the wolves. He dropped into postion and raised his sword. "Come on!" he shouted, his adrenaline high.

One of the wolves backed away.

Lore focused on the one closest to him. "Do it," he whispered. He was a tightly wound coil ready to spring. Just one move, and he would be on them.

The wolf answered his challenge. It snarled and leaped at Lore.

Lore shifted his weight to his back leg and swung. Jaws snapped at him, sending spittle flying. His sword caught the wolf just below the head.

The wolf landed on the ground, Lore's sword still in its neck. It howled, followed by a strangled scream. The hair on Lore's neck rose. He jabbed deeper, wanting the evil thing dead.

It shuddered and lurched to the side. Lore kept his sword buried inside its neck. The wolf glared at him and screamed again. It snapped its jaws, but could not reach Lore's hand.

"No more!" Lore shouted. "No. More."

Its eyes dimmed. Lore felt the wolf begin to fall. He slid his sword out. The wolf dropped to the ground and lay still.

Lore dropped back into position and faced the other wolf. It regarded him with yellow eyes. He stared at it, willing it to come fight him.

Instead, it turned and ran.

Lore watched the wolf run toward the protection of the forest. Where had the wolves come from? His father had hunted the black wolves down years ago. So what were they doing back?

No matter. Lore sheathed his sword. The wolf would not live

long. Tomorrow he would send out search parties and destroy that last wretched creature.

He turned toward Rowen. Slowly he knelt down, hissing at the gaping wound in her shoulder, blood flowing freely. Lore tore the bottom of his shirt and ripped off a long piece of cloth. He carefully placed the cloth against her shoulder, holding pressure on the wound for a few seconds.

But time was against him, and he knew it. He needed to get Rowen back to the castle and to Balint. Only the chief healer could save her from the poison he knew was flowing through her veins. Poison from the wolf's bite.

Please, Word. Lore picked up Rowen and held her close to his body. *Please save her.*

He tore across the field. Ahead, he could see a crowd forming around the city gates. *Not now,* he thought. *I need to get Rowen to the castle.* Lore spotted Donar near the edge of the crowd. He was trying to herd the people back inside.

"Donar!" Lore shouted. Donar turned. "Go get Balint! Tell him—" Lore panted. "Tell him Rowen was bitten by a black wolf."

Donar's eyes went wide. He nodded and ran inside the gates. The crowd began to shout questions at Lore.

Lore ignored them. "Move it!" he cried. The people scattered. "Stay inside the gates." He ran under the archway. Ahead, more guards were running down the street toward the gates. "Get the people inside and shut the gates! Black wolves in the forest."

His boots hit the cobblestone. Lore ran past the guards and toward the castle. Fatigue danced around the edges of his being. He shoved his exhaustion aside. He let his mind dwell on one thing—fear, fear that he would be too late. Energy surged within him.

Lore raced through the second set of gates toward the castle ahead. Rowen's eyes fluttered. Lore saw and slowed down.

Her hand flailed weakly against his chest. "Lore?" she said feebly.

"Yes, Rowen, I'm here."

Her eyes shut, and she went limp in his arms.

Lore clutched Rowen tighter and ran past the fountain and up the stairs to the front doors. The doors were wide open. He ran inside the castle, praying over and over. He knew the Word could heal Rowen. But he also knew that there were times when people died, no matter how hard one prayed. Perhaps Rowen's time had come to an end.

Lore choked at the thought.

"Captain!" Donar came running into the entrance hall. "I alerted Healer Balint about Rowen."

Lore gave Donar a curt nod and ran by, barely able to breathe. He sucked in air and felt his arm and shoulder muscles screaming under his load. He ran down the dark hall, the sconces flickering by. Ahead, he could see the doors that led to the Healers Quarter.

One of the doors slammed open. Balint came rushing out, his white robes flying behind him. His grey hair looked wild around his head. The old man saw Lore and skidded to a stop. "Donar told me about the wolf bite. Quick, place her on one of the beds."

Lore found one more ounce of strength and stumbled through the doorway. Four beds covered in pristine white sheets lined the right wall. A long wooden table filled the middle of the room, covered in books, vials, and herbs. Long, narrow windows reached toward the high ceiling above. Bookcases were wedged between the doors on the left.

"There, put her there." Balint pointed to the nearest bed.

Lore staggered forward and all but dropped Rowen on the bed. He stepped back to let Balint through, suddenly weighed down by fear and exhaustion.

Rowen was barely breathing now, her lips having lost their soft pink hue. Now they were pale, a shade darker than her skin.

Balint stood next to Lore. "Now leave. I do not need distractions."

Lore nodded. His eyes darted toward her still form one more time before turning and stumbling out of the room, shutting the door behind him.

Lore took a few steps down the hall, only to fall against the wall and slide to the floor. He leaned against the wall and slowly drew his knees up. He placed his arms over their tops and stared at the wall.

Something wet began to run down his face. Lore lifted his hand and found his cheek damp. He brought his hand away and studied in surprise the moisture that clung to his fingers. He could not remember the last time he had cried.

Lore stared at his wet fingertips and realized something: He did not want Rowen to die. Not in the general sense that a good man never wishes the passing of life. Nor even in the way a commander never wants to lose a soldier under his command. No, it went much deeper than that, and he knew it. The truth stood before him as clear as daylight.

He did not want Rowen to die because . . . he loved her.

The moment Donar told him Rowen had been bitten, Balint had rushed about his room, gathering anything he thought could help. He'd grabbed books from the shelves and tossed them onto the table. Next, he'd searched his collection of herbs and vials. When he'd heard boots echoing in the hallway, he had dumped his supplies on the table and hurried out.

He'd directed Captain Lore to place Rowen on one of the beds, and then he'd sent him out.

Now Balint stood looking down at his patient, and fear coursed through him. The last time he had dealt with the poisonous bite of the black wolf, he had been too late, leaving Lord Gaynor a widower and Lady Astrea motherless.

He placed a hand on Rowen's neck. He remembered her. Not long ago he had bound Rowen to her oath. She seemed like a nice young woman. What a tragedy that she—

He felt a faint pulse beneath her skin. She was still alive!

Balint carefully pulled back her shirt. There was too much blood to see where the wounds were. He ran to one of the adjoining rooms and grabbed a bowl of water and a clean cloth. He hurried back and began swabbing her shoulder. After a moment, he pulled back the cloth and looked. He could find no wound on her shoulder. So he swabbed some more, searching for the puncture marks. Still nothing. His fear turned to confusion.

Balint dipped the rag again and continued to clean the skin. Under the blood, all he could find was smooth skin with a couple of long but thin scars. There was no sign of the wolf's bite.

He stared at the skin, puzzled. The scars were in such a fashion that it looked as though Rowen had been bit—but weeks ago, not minutes ago. How could that be?

An incredible thought occurred to him. "Impossible," he muttered. But there was no other explanation. Balint moved around the bed toward Rowen's right side. He picked up her hand and tugged the sword glove off. He turned her palm side up.

Shocked, Balint stumbled away. Her hand fell back onto the bed. There, on her palm, was a large white mark, a mark Balint knew only too well.

"Dear Word," he whispered in amazement, his eyes still riveted to the mark across her hand.

The young woman was an Eldaran.

CHAPTER 13

Damp grey mist swirled across the mountain, weaving its way between boulders and stunted, scraggy trees. Tufts of brown grass shot up wherever it could find soil. Rocks covered everything else. The sky held the same sad grey color, blending the landscape into a wet, colorless painting.

Nierne pulled her cloak tight in an effort to keep the chilly mist out. But it still found its way in, spreading its frosty fingers across her skin. It clung to her hair, her face, her fingertips. She stumbled up the path and wondered which was worse, the mountains or the marshes they had just crossed?

The marshes, she decided, blowing on her hands. At least there were no biting insects here at this altitude, no mud up to her knees. And she could actually breathe through her nose up here, unlike in the marshes, where everything had smelled of rot and sewage. Nierne breathed in deeply as if to confirm that. Sweet, chilly air. Her eyes watered at the cold.

Father Reth trudged on ahead, a mound of green under the cloak he wore. Nierne fell back into line behind him. To take her mind off the chill, she dredged up memories of warm summer days she spent in Thyra. She remembered the way the sun felt as its rays seeped through her robes in the prayer garden, the smell of Father Karl's roses, the sound of laughter as children played on the other side of the wall—

"Ouch!" Nierne pulled back, her forehead smarting. She glared at a low hanging branch and rubbed the injured area.

"I'm sorry." Father Reth looked back, "I thought you saw the branch."

"I'm fine. It just smarts a bit." Nierne gave her head one final rub before gripping her cloak again.

They continued up the mountain in silence. The trees began to thin and the mist grew thicker. Nierne stayed near Father Reth, wary of losing him in the blanket of grey.

"We're almost there," Father Reth said, breaking the silence.

"Almost where?"

"The summit."

A burst of energy filled her at the thought. Nierne climbed faster, eager to reach the peak. It seemed Father Reth felt the same way. The two soaked travelers moved quickly up the mountainside.

"There are some old ruins just a short way down on the other side," Father Reth said, his breathing quicker now. "At least there were years ago when I last crossed these mountains. If they're still there, and if I can find something dry to light, perhaps we can have a fire tonight."

Nierne smiled at the thought of a fire. A warm, dry, crackling fire. And maybe something warm to eat for a change. Dried meats and fruits went only so far in filling the belly.

By late afternoon, they reached the top. The sun struggled through the mist that swirled around the mountaintop.

Father Reth stopped and looked around. "It's been many years," he said, more to himself.

"Many years?" Nierne looked at Father Reth.

"About forty years, to be precise." Father Reth turned and smiled. "When I last stood on this spot."

Nierne looked around. The summit was even barer than the terrain they'd passed on the climb up here. Small twisted bushes and more rocks. She could see nothing beyond, the mist and low hanging clouds obscuring everything.

Father Reth took a few steps off the path. "If it were a clear day, you would be able to see Anwin Forest to the east." He pointed into the mist.

Nierne looked out into the grey shroud. Even though they would be entering Anwin soon, she wished she could see the forest now.

"And on either side of us are two of the highest peaks in the Ari Mountains, other than Mount Aerie, the mountain from which the White City is carved. But you can't see the two peaks now, the fog is too thick." Nierne looked up and around. "This summit is really just a pass between the two."

Nierne turned back to Father Reth. "How is it you know so much about where we're going?" She knew very little of Father Reth's past, other than he hadn't always been a father. But watching him first with Ben, and now for the last few weeks leading them along the trail with familiarity, she wanted to know.

Father Reth threw back his head and laughed. "I was wondering when you were going to ask." Nierne frowned at his reaction, and he smiled back. "I'm glad to see your spark of curiosity did not die in Thyra, although it's taken some time for it to return."

Nierne felt her face redden. "I wasn't sure— That is, it's your past. And you always say the past is in the past and to live your life you need to move on . . ." She fumbled to stop, feeling foolish.

"I have nothing to hide."

Nierne looked up.

Father Reth smiled and motioned for Nierne to follow him. "Let's keep walking, and I'll tell you." The two of them began to walk, the path descending downward now. "When I was a young man, I was a . . ." He paused for a moment. "Well, let's just say I was a treasure hunter."

"Treasure hunter?" Nierne mulled the term over in her mind.

"A plunderer, if you will. I would find ruins and search them for artifacts, scrolls, jewelry—basically anything that could be sold. The money was good, I was able to see much of the Lands, and I was not responsible to anyone but myself. Or so I thought. That's how I met Ben. We traveled together and split the profits on whatever we found. Then something happened."

Father Reth walked quietly for a few moments. Nierne continued by his side, silently waiting for him to continue. This explained why, at the Monastery, Father Reth always knew so much about the places mentioned in the old scrolls and writings. He had probably been there.

"Ben and I decided to explore the eastern part of the world," Father Reth began. "We had heard of old Eldaran and Shadonae ruins that had not been touched by humans in hundreds of years. So we crossed these mountains, just the two of us. It wasn't as unheard of as it is now. In fact, long ago, the White City and Thyra had runners who would take messages between the two cities several times a month. The ruins just ahead were one of the outposts used by those runners. But I'm straying from my story . . .

"We discovered an old sanctuary just outside the White City. Actually, 'abandoned' is probably a more appropriate term. It was an Eldaran Sanctuary, built next to the waterfalls where the Eldarans had first entered the Lands. Ben and I poked around inside. There wasn't much there, except one thing: along one wall, from floor to ceiling, were pictures made of colored glass. Not something we could take, of course. But to look at . . ."

There was such awe in his voice that Nierne turned and looked at Father Reth.

His expression was faraway. "It was so beautiful, Nierne. How the people of the White City could have forgotten such a place . . ." He shook his head and looked down. "I guess that is what happens when people become too familiar with sacred things. They become commonplace and forgotten.

"Anyway, while we were in there, there was a groundquake. The ceiling came crashing down. Ben was unhurt, but a part of the roof hit me. Next thing I know, I'm waking up in a healing ward inside the city. It was there that I met Balint, a young healer at the time, and a Follower of the Word."

"Balint shared with me about the Word." Father Reth laughed suddenly and shook his head. "All I knew of the Word at that point was that anything about Him sold for lots of gold." Father Reth stepped over a fallen tree that lay across the path, then turned back to give Nierne a hand.

"Since I had a broken leg," Father Reth began again once they were walking down the path, "I ended up staying in the White City for a couple weeks. As I lay there, with Balint talking to me every day, I felt a burden of darkness inside me, a burden I had not felt before.

"Oh, I knew the darkness was there," Father Reth said, waving his hand. "But in the past, I had always shoved aside my guilty conscience. But sitting there in that small healing room, day in and day out, with nothing to do, I had a lot of time to think. My life stood before me, bleak and exposed. I couldn't escape the truth Balint was sharing with me. And suddenly I wanted to be free of the darkness.

"You know the rest of the story: I sought the Word and He freed me. And from that moment on, I knew I wanted to use the knowledge I had gained on my travels for a greater good than just my coinpurse. Ben didn't understand. He continued his travels. But I went back to Thyra and joined the Monastery."

"Why the Monastery?" Nierne asked. "You could have found other ways to share your knowledge. You could have written scrolls, given lectures, taught at one of the academies . . ."

"I guess it's because I wanted to see the truth that had been shared with me preserved for others," Father Reth said quietly. "At the Monastery, I could do that. And many of the scribes have benefited from my travel experiences."

Nierne thought for a moment. "Did you ever want to bond?" As part of the Monastery oath, every person entering that life had to choose to never bond with anyone—in order to be free to serve the Monastery until death.

"No," Father Reth said. "I'd had my chance a couple of times while wandering the Lands. By the time I arrived in Thyra, I had thought over my options and knew that bonding would never be for me."

"Why?"

Father Reth turned toward Nierne. "Having second thoughts about your own oath?"

"No."

"That was a quick answer." Father Reth studied her for a moment. "You do know that you are free to leave the Monastery before taking your oath. You might find you want another life. You can serve the Word in many ways without being a scribe."

"I enjoy my work as a scribe."

"Are you sure it isn't more?" Father Reth said softly.

Nierne's mouth tightened.

Father Reth sighed and looked forward again.

Nierne knew what he was thinking. A small part of her whispered that he was right. Nierne slammed that thought down just as it rose up. She wasn't hiding in the Monastery. She really did enjoy her life there. She felt deep satisfaction in her work and loved reading about history and places and people. And the quiet life suited her. So why did the thought of living another life frighten her so much?

She knew why.

"Perhaps this trip will benefit you more than you know," Father Reth said. "You will have an opportunity to see life outside the Monastery. Open your heart and your mind. And Nierne . . ." he said, his expression filled with compassion . . . "don't be afraid."

Nierne sat by the fire and thought on Father Reth's words later that night. They had found the old stone outpost. It was still cold inside the small building, but at least it was dry. The fire spat and crackled as it ate the leaves and small twigs Father Reth had found scattered around inside.

Nierne sighed, wrapping her arms around her legs. Father Reth was right: There was more to the Monastery than just her love of her work. Ever since she had been left at its gates years ago, it had become her security, her haven. A tower where she hid from the rest of the world.

It was Father Reth who had helped her adjust to her new life all those years ago, which was probably why he understood her fear to leave. Outside those walls she had been forced to grow up much too fast for a young girl.

Nierne tightened her grip on her knees as she remembered long nights sitting in the hallway while her mother did business on the other side of a thin wall. Of course, that was before the sickness had come—

"Look what I caught for us." Father Reth walked into the small room and held up something.

"What is it?" Nierne squinted in the darkness.

"A rabbit," Father Reth said, digging around in his pile of sticks.

Nierne looked at the lump again. It seemed that Father Reth had already skinned it. She felt her stomach turn at the thought.

Minutes later, he had a makeshift spit set up over the fire, the rabbit securely fastened to it. It took longer for the smell to permeate the small room. One sniff and Nierne felt her stomach stop rolling and begin to growl. She couldn't imagine trying to kill an animal to eat, but she was grateful that Father Reth knew how and that there would be something other than "dried" to eat tonight.

Father Reth sat nearby, peering down at the map Ben had provided. "We still have a ways to go."

"A couple of weeks?" Nierne asked.

Father Reth looked up thoughtfully. "Probably three to four." He carefully rolled up the map.

Nierne turned back toward the fire. "Do you think we'll actually find Eldarans in the White City?" She knew it was question they both were asking themselves.

Father Reth turned the spit a couple of times. "Well, if they still exist, I think there would at least be some knowledge of them there. As far as actually finding one, I don't know."

At least he was honest. Nierne watched him as he continued to turn the spit, making sure the rabbit cooked evenly.

Later that night, after licking greasy fingers and placing a few more dry sticks on the fire, they both crawled into their bedrolls. Outside, Nierne could hear the wind blowing.

"Sounds like a storm is coming," Father Reth said as he pulled up the top part of his bedroll. "Glad we have this old outpost to sleep in."

Nierne murmured something in reply followed by a large yawn.

She couldn't remember when she had felt this warm or comfortable. She rolled onto her side and curled into a tight ball.

"Nierne!"

Nierne felt someone shaking her. "Wha- What?" she said, her mind still drugged with sleep.

"Nierne, we need to get out of here," Father Reth whispered, his voice tinged with fear.

"Father Reth?" Nierne sat up and tried to clear her mind. There was a high pitch noise filling the room. It took her a moment to realize it was the storm outside. The wind sounded like banshees screaming.

"We need to get out of here."

"Why?" she asked, slipping out of her bedroll. But Father Reth was already gathering their things, throwing them into the packs as fast as he could. Nierne scurried to her feet and picked up her bedding, stuffing the bedroll into her pack with one hand.

"Quick, follow me." Father Reth headed toward the doorway.

Nierne followed. Outside, the air whipped around her head and pulled at her clothing. With her free hand, she pulled her red curls away from her face.

The sky was still dark. A half moon hung overhead, shedding its pale light on the rocky terrain. She could see tall dark trees half a league down the mountain. They bent and swayed in the violent torrent. Orange light lined the eastern horizon.

Wait. Nierne tried to think. The wind screamed in her ears. Her hair tore from her hands and flew into her eyes. She grabbed the hair and pulled it back. Then it hit her.

This was no storm.

"Nierne, this way."

She could barely hear Father Reth over the wind. He motioned wildly with his hands. She hurried to his side. He grabbed her hand and began to run down the steep mountainside. Nierne tried to watch for rotting logs and bushes in the pale moonlight. The wind howled in her ears. She used her free hand to cover one ear.

A couple of times she saw Father Reth glance back. She looked back once and saw nothing. She tried to ask what he was looking for, but the wind made her words impossible to hear.

The third time, he stopped. Gripping her shoulder, he pulled her close. "Nierne, you've got to run!" he shouted.

"Run? Run from what?" she shouted back. "And what about you?"

"No time!" He shoved his pack into her hands.

Nierne felt the hair on her arms rise. A shiver ran down her back. No, it couldn't be—

"They found us. I don't know how, but the shadows found us." Father Reth kept his hand on her shoulder. He steered her toward the east. Faint light had replaced the orange sky along the horizon.

"Find them, Nierne. Find the Eldarans. And bring them back to Thyra." Father Reth pulled her tightly into an embrace. "I always saw you as the daughter I never had," he said, his words flying away on the wind.

Fear filled her heart. "No wait! Father—"

He kissed her cheek. "May the Word watch over you." He shoved her forward. "Run!"

"But—"

He pointed east. *"Run!"*

Nierne turned. She half ran, half stumbled down the steep mountain slope. Her hair flew around her face. The wind wrapped her cloak around her legs. She struggled to pull the cloak free. She tripped over a log and barely caught herself. Her knapsack slammed into her back. Her breath came in hard, labored pants.

Dear Word, help us!

Nierne couldn't stand it anymore. She had to know what was happening to Father Reth. She staggered to a stop and looked back.

Halfway up the mountainside stood Father Reth, his back toward her. Coming down to greet him was a large billowing cloud of black.

It twisted and writhed like a hundred snakes made of smoke slithering down the mountain.

"No!" Nierne screamed.

Father Reth raised his arms. The black cloud split into smaller swirls. Tiny beads of red light shone from the shadows. They converged on Father Reth, churning around him, swallowing him. He disappeared from her sight.

Nierne scrambled few steps up the mountain. Tears blurred her eyes. No, this couldn't be happening. Father Reth . . .

The shadows began to join again into a cohesive black mass.

Fear dowsed her grief.

Nierne turned and ran. The wind howled. It seemed to grab her knapsack and pull. She ran harder. The sun rose before her. She could see the forest below, the trees covered in golden morning light.

The shrieking grew louder around her. Her lungs burned, and her side throbbed. She didn't dare look back.

Suddenly the ground began to shake. Nierne screamed. She was thrown to the side. Her legs caught on a rotted log. The weight of her pack hurled her forward. She fell face first . . .

Crack.

Intense pain bloomed across her cheek. Nierne lay in the dark, stunned. Her body vibrated with the groundquake. She tried to grip the rock beneath her. *Slam.* Her head hit the rock again. Stars danced across her eyes. *Slam.* She felt like a pebble bouncing across the back of a wagon.

Nierne wrapped her arms around her head and curled up into a ball. She closed her eyes and shook with the ground.

Slowly the vibrations lessened. A moment later, they stopped.

Nierne lay still. The only sound she could hear was her breathing. The air smelled like damp soil. Cautiously, she turned her head and glanced up. Dirt, roots, and rocks made a wall around her. The sky was a pale blue. Tree branches and grass grew at the top of the ravine she had fallen into.

Slowly Nierne lifted her body, regretting the action instantly as bile filled her throat. Her head throbbed, and she could feel the side of her face tingling. Flashes of light filled her vision, but were quickly replaced with darkness.

Nierne fell back across the rock. The darkness expanded, drawing her in. She fought it. Taking a few gulps of air, she again raised her head, this time more slowly.

Her head still hurt, but it seemed her stomach would let her be. Nierne moved up to a sitting position. She held her head in her hands and waited for her mind to clear.

She took a deep breath. A moment later, she stood. She blinked and looked around for a way out of the ravine. A long thick root stuck out of the ground a couple of feet away.

Nierne grabbed the root and hauled herself up. Her foot found an indent in the dirt side. She looked up and grabbed another root, heaved, and placed her foot where her hand had been moments before. After a few more roots, she hauled herself over the ravine's edge, panting.

She lay on the ground, catching her breath and realized she had left Father Reth's pack below. She groaned. It would have to stay there. There was no way she was going back down for it.

Nierne slowly stood. She brushed the dirt off of her pants and shirt. She began to adjust her own pack and stopped. She lifted her eyes and stared at the mountainside.

Trees were splintered, uprooted or halfway buried in the ground. Some with their roots up in the air, others submerged so far that only the tips could be seen. Farther up the mountain, everything lay flat or mixed with boulders. It reminded Nierne of when Father Karl would turn the dirt over for his garden. Only on a massive scale.

The outpost was gone, the pass was gone. It even seemed that the mountains were gone—

Wait. Nierne stared at up the mountain. Where there should have been two mountaintops, there was one. One massive wall of a mountain. And the pass that she and Father Reth had crossed the day before—that's what was gone. It was as if the two mountaintops had been pushed together so tightly that they had become one.

Nierne just stood there, her mouth open. A shiver swept across her spine. What kind of power could move mountains? She knew. She had read about that kind of power. Only One could, with just His voice. The Word.

She took a step forward, then stopped. Where were the shadows?

Nierne clutched her cloak close to her body and looked around. Nothing moved, not even a blade of grass. She took a few more steps up the mountainside. Had everything . . . ? No, it couldn't be. Nierne stepped around a splintered trunk, her insides wound tightly inside her. The thought flashed across her mind again. Had everything been . . . buried?

Nierne jumped back and looked down. The ground beneath her boots was solid. She looked up at the ruined face of the mountain. Nothing left. It really did seem as if a large hand had shoved the two mountains together into one, burying and upturning trees and rocks and anything else in its way. Including the pass. And including . . .

Nierne began to run up the mountainside. "Father Reth!" she called out, quietly at first, then louder. "Father Reth!"

She ran everywhere, looking under fallen logs, checking every boulder. But there was so much debris, and the green cloaks she and Father Reth had been wearing would make it even harder to find him.

The sun slowly made its way across the sky and still she continued to look, though the feeling of despair was rapidly filling her heart. "Father Reth!" Nierne called out again, this time weakly as she sank to her knees.

"Oh, no," she whispered. She covered her face with her dirt-stained hands and sobbed. Deep down, she knew the truth. Father Reth had been buried as well. He had stayed there to keep the shadows focused on him so that she could escape.

A swell of emotions ripped through her: grief, anguish . . . and rage. Nierne brought her hands away from her face and clenched them tight. How could He? How could the Word have done that? How could He have buried Father Reth, one of His own Followers? And Father Reth—

The truth hit her as hard as the rock she had fallen upon. He had known. The moment Father Reth had told her to run, he knew he would go down with the shadows, in order to save her. And he had embraced that.

"What am I supposed to do now?" Nierne cried, looking upward. "I have no idea where to go or what to do."

Find the Eldarans. Bring them back to Thyra.

Father Reth's words echoed inside her mind. But how could she find the Eldarans? It was Father Reth who was supposed to lead them to the White City. It was Father Reth who was supposed to find the Eldarans. She had come along for support, not to become the leader. And now she was alone.

You are not alone, a voice whispered.

Nierne recoiled from the voice. She was still too overcome with grief and anger, her heart too raw, to acknowledge the small voice trying to speak inside.

Instead, she picked up her pack and, with shaky legs and weepy eyes, began her descent of the mountain.

One thing Nierne knew: If she did find the Eldarans, they would not be coming back to Thyra this way. The path between Thyra and the White City had been shut forever.

CHAPTER
14

Rowen slowly sat up, blinking her eyes as she tried to get her bearings. Where was she? How long had she been out? An hour, a day? Her sense of time felt warped.

She brought a hand to her head, trying to shake off the last bits of fatigue that still clung to her mind and body. Her eyes fell to her lap, where a white sheet was draped across her legs.

Puzzled, Rowen looked around. There were three other beds besides hers covered with the same pristine white sheets. Against the wall were rows of shelves filled with leather-bound books. Nearby stood one long table covered with herbs, vials of dark liquids, and more books. Her eyes traveled to the end of the room, where tall, narrow windows were dark with night.

"Good, you're finally awake."

Rowen jumped at the sound. She looked to her left and found an old man dressed in white robes walking toward her. His hair was grey and curly with a matching grey mustache. She recognized him from the night she'd taken her oath. Balint, the chief healer.

"I was beginning to fear you would not wake up," Balint continued. "You've been asleep for almost twelve hours."

Twelve hours?

He smiled at her and took a seat in the chair that sat next to her bed. "How are you feeling?"

"Exhausted." Rowen felt she could sleep forever.

"That is to be expected after healing from that kind of wound," Balint said. He folded his hands neatly in his lap.

Suddenly she remembered the wolves and the pain—and her charge. "Lady Astrea! How is she? Did she—"

"Fine. She's fine," Balint said. "A bit frightened, of course, but no injuries."

Rowen sighed and lay back against the pillows. She felt along her shoulder. She frowned and felt some more. There was no bandage, no cloth. She felt again. No wound? She looked at Balint. "How did you heal me? Am I dreaming?"

"No, my dear. This is no dream." His smile faltered a little. "It wasn't me who healed you . . ."

Rowen slowly brought her hand back down. "I don't understand. Was it one of your—" She caught a glimpse of her mark as her hand moved below her eyes.

Her glove was gone!

Rowen shoved her hand below the sheet that lay across her lap. Her face grew hot. Had Balint taken off her glove? Had he seen her mark? She looked at Balint, who was now studying her curiously.

"Why do you hide your hand?" There was no fear in his eyes, no accusations. Just curiosity.

Rowen felt her mouth go dry. There was no use denying it. He knew. "I- I . . ."

"Are you afraid?"

Rowen looked down. How could it have come to this? She had been so careful, wearing the glove every day. Why did she have to be different and heal herself? Of course, a small part of her argued, if she were normal, she would probably be dead right now.

I'll be dead soon enough, she reasoned back.

The chief healer of the White City knew her secret, and soon everyone else would. And when word got out, it would be just like it was back in Cinad—the fear, the hatred, and, shortly after, the banishment, if she was lucky. More likely, she would receive a quick execution for her deception.

"Let me see your mark," Balint said.

Rowen jerked back up, shoving her hand deeper into the sheet. "Why? Haven't you had enough time to look at it while I was unconscious?" The question came out sharper than she meant.

Instead of answering, Balint held out his hand, palm up. Rowen's eyes were drawn to the faint mark across his wrinkled palm. He had a mark too! His mark was similar, yet different. It was smaller and faded so that only a faint trace of it could be seen.

"It is the mark of the Word," Balint said softly.

Rowen stared at his palm, hardly able to believe her eyes. He reached over with his other hand and gently wrapped his long slender fingers around her wrist. Rowen tensed.

"You have nothing to fear, Rowen. At least, not from me," he said.

She looked up into his eyes. They were kind and gentle. Taking a deep breath, she nodded and let Balint slowly pull her hand out from the sheet. He turned it over and brought his hand next to hers. The white mark on her palm was much larger than his, and it glowed with a faint light.

"We are both marked," he said quietly. "But I've never seen the mark so pronounced on anyone." He studied their palms.

Rowen began to piece together what he was saying. If they shared the mark, then she wasn't a witch, right? Unless Balint were a witch, as well. But if she wasn't a witch, what was she? "I don't understand."

"My dear, you have this mark because of what you are."

She almost didn't want to ask. "W-what am I?"

Balint lifted his eyes from their hands to her face. "You are an Eldaran."

A what? Wait . . . an Eldaran? Not a witch? Eldaran had to be better than witch, right? But it also meant she wasn't . . . human. And it didn't explain the awful ability she had with her touch . . . Did it?

"An Eldaran?" Rowen looked at Balint. "Are— Are you sure?"

"Yes. You have the mark. And . . ." he glanced back down at their palms . . . "as much as I would like to say I healed you from the wolf's poison, it is you who healed yourself. I had nothing to do with it. In fact, when Captain Lore brought you in, you were already healed."

"I was?"

"Yes. Quite healed. All my best poultices lay useless beside the bed. There was no need of them." He looked at her more closely. "How much do you know of the Eldarans?"

"Not much." She recalled her conversation a few months ago with Lore, the night she took her varor's oath. "Captain Lore told me a little. But all I remember is they had some kind of power . . ." She knew hardly anything.

"So you know nothing of why they came here to the Lands or the gifts they possess?" Balint said.

"No." After her own bitter conclusion that she was not Eldaran, Rowen had never questioned Lore about them again. And deep down inside, she was not entirely convinced she was one. The way Balint talked, it would seem people would be attracted to these beings. So why had her village reacted to her with such fear and hate?

"After the Great Battle," Balint said, "some of the beings who had come to the Lands with the Word, well, they chose to stay. They came to be known as the Eldarans, the ancient ones. And while they took on the limitations of man, such as mortality and a weaker body, they also maintained some of their ethereal gifts. This was so they could continue to watch over and protect mankind should the Shadonae ever return."

"The Shadonae?" Rowen asked.

"The dark ones who opposed the Word and sought to destroy mankind. During the Great Battle, the Word tore down their strongholds and bound their leader. The rest of the Shadonae fled. But they still posed a threat after the Word left. So a few of His servants stayed."

"Where are the Eldarans now?"

Balint hesitated, his face thoughtful. "Well, I had believed they had died out," he finally said. "We live in a different time now, an era that no longer requires the Guardians of the Word. I have my small gift only because one of my ancestors was Eldaran." Then he looked at Rowen. "But seeing you now makes me think otherwise. Your mark has not begun to fade and you still possess the gift of healing. So perhaps I am wrong. Perhaps there are still Eldarans dwelling here in the Lands."

Rowen suddenly felt self-conscious under Balint's stare. "If I am an Eldaran, what can I do?"

"Well, one you have discovered already," he said. "Eldarans have the ability to heal from almost any wound or disease. It is a carryover from their ethereal bodies. An Eldaran can also use that gift to heal others."

Rowen looked at Balint in disbelief. "I can heal people?"

"Yes. However, it comes at a price . . ."

But Balint's words were only a distant echo in her mind. Rowen's thoughts were on all the loved ones she had lost over the years. Their faces flashed before her eyes: her mother, her father, villagers whom she had loved and who passed away long before the mark . . . all the people who had ever cared about her. And all that time, she could have saved them?

Rowen thought on this and grew bitter inside. For so long she had felt alone and forsaken, everything stripped from her. To find out now she could have prevented it . . .

"So I could have saved my parents?" Rowen said, resentment lacing her words.

"Perhaps. Even with Eldarans around, people still died. And every healing comes at a price," Balint said, watching her closely. "Besides, I do not think you were strong enough to save your parents. When did you say the mark appeared?"

She thought back. "Just before I learned my father had died."

Balint shook his head. "Eldarans do not receive their mark until they are fully adult. So you would have been too young to save your mother. As for your father, he had already passed away by the time you knew. And, like I said, the gift comes with a price. You cannot just touch people and wish they were better. That only happens in stories. The only way you can heal someone is to take on that person's injury or disease."

Rowen frowned "What do you mean?"

"Well, we already know you can heal yourself. The wolf bite proved that." Rowen nodded, so Balint continued. "So in order to heal another person, you need to absorb their hurt—to take their wounds onto your body—and then you'd need to heal yourself of their wounds or illness."

Rowen sat back. The resentment she had been feeling earlier drained away under this new knowledge "So I will have to experience a person's pain in order to heal them?"

"Yes."

She lifted her hand and studied the mark on her palm. It seemed everything this mark did brought pain and suffering. "Why would the Word give such terrible gifts?" she asked without looking up. "If the Eldarans had stayed to serve the Word by helping people, why would He make it painful for them to do their service?"

Balint did not answer. Rowen found him staring out the windows. She waited until he turned back toward her. "I believe," Balint said, "it is because that is what *He* does for *us*. Nothing worthwhile in life is free."

"What do you mean the Word does that for us? He heals us?"

"In a manner of speaking. During the Great Battle, it was not combat that overcame the Shadonae but the sacrifice the Word made on behalf of man. The Word willingly took on the darkness inside the human heart."

She shook her head. "I don't understand."

"You see," Balint leaned toward Rowen, "it was darkness that enslaved man to the Shadonae. The Shadonae could not survive in the light of the Word's sacrifice. Many of the Shadonae were destroyed or captured on that day. Only a few escaped."

"But if the Word created everything," Rowen said slowly, remembering one of the stories she had heard about the Word, "then why did he make man with darkness inside?" She knew about the darkness. She had seen it in others.

"Oh, the Word did not make man with darkness," Balint said. "He made man with the ability to choose. And man chose to invite the darkness in."

"Then why doesn't the Word just speak and make everything right?"

"Because . . . nothing worthwhile in life is free," Balint said. "When it costs something, that item becomes much dearer. Yes, the Word could have saved all of mankind by just His words, but instead He chose to heal mankind a different way, by taking on the hurt and darkness Himself. And in doing so, we realize just how dear we are to Him."

Rowen grew quiet. She had never heard this before.

"Real love is displayed when a choice has to be made. It would be easy to heal everyone who was sick if it didn't cost you anything. But what if it meant excruciating pain? Then you would have to make a choice: Do I love enough to take on that pain, or do I take the easy route and keep this gift to myself?"

Rowen sat back. If what he was saying was true, then to heal anyone would be a true act of sacrifice, because it would cost her something. Deep down, she wasn't sure she could do it. Not even for her parents. "How did the other Eldarans do it?" She looked at Balint. "How did they find the courage to make that choice?"

Balint sighed. "I'm not sure. But from what I have read in some of the ancient scrolls here in the White City, it seems the Eldarans drew their strength from the Word. And His example of self-sacrifice inspired them to do likewise."

He leaned closer toward Rowen. "You must understand, Rowen, the Word never created the Eldarans to use their power apart from His strength. It would be too great a burden. In fact, some gifts are so great and terrible that, without the Word's help, they would overpower the possessor." Balint paused. "Rowen," he said quietly, "has anything else happened to you since the mark first appeared on your hand?"

Rowen looked down, her heart suddenly heavy inside.

Pulling his chair closer to her bed, Balint took her unmarked hand and held it between his own. "Tell me about it."

She didn't know where to start. All the images and feelings of her past began to resurface. The anger, hate, and lust she had experienced at the touch of another. "I can . . . I can see things when I touch people. And feel their thoughts."

Rowen saw a flicker of worry cross Balint's face. "Explain."

She drew in a deep breath and subconsciously clenched her right fist as if to protect the mark. She saw his eyes dart toward her gesture with another flicker of worry. Rowen let out her breath and began.

As she stumbled through her story, she felt her heart tear anew. It had been months since she had thought back on her village. But the grief and pain were as real now as on the day when she had been banished.

They hated her. The people she had grown up with, they hated her. And Calya . . . Rowen's voice hitched as she thought about her old friend. She missed her. She missed their conversations, missed the sound of Calya's little ones playing nearby, missed her friend's friendly advice. And Rowen had done nothing wrong other than bear this awful mark.

Rowen finished her story, crying as she held her face in her hands. She would give anything to be free of this mark.

"You are a Truthsayer," Balint said quietly.

Rowen wiped her eyes. "I'm a . . . a what?"

He looked at her with a sad smile. "A Truthsayer. You have the gift of revealing what lies deep within another person. That day you touched Cleon, you revealed the hatred buried inside of him."

Sudden uncontrollable rage filled her. "And that's a gift? To see the hatred and darkness inside people? Do you realize I can never touch another person? That all I will ever know is loneliness?"

Rowen knew Balint did not deserve her torrent of anger and rage. Who she really hated right now was the Word. He had given her this mark and the burden that came with it. All she had ever wanted was a normal life. She wanted to bond, have children, live in a small home just like Calya did. Just like every other woman in the Lands. But it seemed the Word had another future for her. One she would never have chosen for herself.

Balint shook his head. "That is not necessarily true. When there is a need to *heal,* that is what your touch will do. When there is a need for truth to be revealed, *that* is what your touch will do. And you only reveal the truth to a person who is blind to it or hiding it."

"But why? Why is such a gift needed?"

"Because if a person does not realize the darkness inside of him, he can never be healed by the Word," Balint said. "Your touch makes people see what is already there inside their heart. You show them, and then they need to make a choice. Do they seek healing from the One who can heal them, or do they bury the darkness again, where it can fester and grow like an infected wound? And that is a decision you cannot make for them. You can only present the choice."

Rowen looked down, her thoughts and emotions churning. More than anything she wanted to rip the mark off her hand and the truth it revealed. "Is there any way to get rid of the mark?

"Get rid of it?"

"Yes. Like what if my hand was cut off or something?" She inwardly shivered at the thought. Would she really go that far to get rid of her mark?

"Well, I'm not sure." Balint rubbed his chin. "You see, the power is inside of you, not inside the mark. However, the mark is the conduit of that power. If you lost your hand, I don't know if another mark would show up or if you would simply lose the ability to touch others. I have not read about such a thing."

Balint reached over and gave her hand a squeeze. "Rowen, I believe the Word has gifted you for a future we do not yet see. Truthsayers were rare, even in the day when Eldarans walked the Lands. To be one now, in this age . . . there has to be a reason. The Word will give you the strength to use your power. Trust in Him, Rowen. He will not leave you to carry this burden alone."

Rowen looked up with hatred. She wanted to shout at Balint, to tell him he had no idea what it was like. But Balint did not deserve that. He had only told her the truth. Suddenly the irony hit her; she was mad because someone else had told *her* the truth.

Balint let go of her hand and stood. "I will leave you now so you can rest."

Rowen nodded and looked down at her clenched hand. Out of the corner of her eye she saw him quietly open the double set of doors and walk out. Then she shoved the offending limb beneath the sheets. Her heart beat with strong, angry thuds.

She hated the Word. She hated Him and any future He had planned for her.

CHAPTER 15

"How is she?" Lore said. He stood in the doorway to the Healers Quarter the next morning.

Balint glanced up from the long table where he was working. He placed a small glass vial down and walked toward Lore. "Sleeping right now," Balint said in a low voice. "But she will recover."

For the first time since yesterday, Lore relaxed. He had spent all night tossing and turning. One moment, he feared Rowen would die. The next, he was shocked at his revelation.

He loved her.

Lore knew he wasn't the first man in his position to be attracted to a woman under his command. But how to handle it? Then he would remember there was a good chance Rowen wouldn't recover, thus restarting the cycle.

"That's good to hear." Lore glanced over at the one occupied bed. A long white sheet covered her body. He moved closer until he stood an arm's length away. He could see the steady rise and fall of her chest. Her hands, one still covered by her glove, clutched the white sheet in two tight fists. Her face looked pale and pinched. "How did you do it?"

Balint came to stand beside him. He was quiet for a moment before answering. "It wasn't me. There is still no cure for the black wolf's bite."

"Then how—"

"The Word healed her."

Lore could hear the hesitancy in his answer. He glanced over to find Balint looking down at Rowen with a look of pity. How strange.

Balint should be delighted that Rowen would live. Lore narrowed his eyes. There was something Balint wasn't telling him.

"How long do you think it will take for her to recover?"

That same period of silence ensued before Balint answered. "Physically, she is almost healed. But her mind . . ."

"Her mind?" Lore said, subtly pushing the question.

"More happened to her than just the physical attack."

Yes, there was definitely something going on.

"And that would be . . . ?"

Balint turned to look at him. "Captain, if you care for this young woman, you will give her the room she needs to recover."

Lore felt like he had been slapped in the face. "I'm sorry. I didn't mean to push. I just need to know if Rowen will be able to do her duties and when."

The protective look across Balint's face morphed into understanding. "I've known you for many years, Lore," he said, dropping all formalities. "You care about the men and women under your command as if they were your family. The best way you can help Rowen is to give her space and time to work out what happened yesterday."

There it was, that same dodge. But this time Lore chose not to push. "I understand," he said. "When should I let her come back to duty?"

Balint thought for a moment. "Give her a couple days at least to finish recovering physically. As far as her mental state . . . don't push her. If Rowen chooses to open up to you, then listen. If not, well, hopefully when she is ready she will find someone to talk to."

His heart twisted at Balint's words. What made Balint so concerned for Rowen? What had happened besides the wolf attack? Lore looked back down at where she slept. "I will do as you say," he said, fighting the urge to reach out and touch her face. He would not press her, but deep down he hoped she would open up to him. She should not fight alone whatever this was.

Lore straightened back up. "I need to get back to my duties. Keep me informed."

"Yes, Captain."

Lore escorted himself out.

The next few days he restrained from going to the Healers Quarter. He wanted to honor what Balint had said and let Rowen recover at her own pace without him or anyone else looking over her shoulder. The other guards asked how she was doing, and Lore told them the truth: Rowen would live, but she still needed time away. He forbade anyone to visit her, and he followed that command himself.

Apart from Rowen, there were other matters weighing heavily on his mind. The hunting parties had successfully found the other black wolf and brought the pelt back to the castle. But that didn't mean there weren't more. He debated whether to send more parties out and shut the city gates or to assume the wolves were gone. The fact that there had been only two rather than a pack seemed to indicate perhaps it was an isolated event.

Lore rubbed the back of his neck and headed toward the training room. Then there was the Temanin Empire to think about. Now that Temanin had broken through the pass and was moving through the north, it was only a matter of time before the empire headed toward the White City. At Lord Gaynor's command, Lore had scoured the city for more recruits. Now he needed to train them.

He walked into the large training room. Dark clouds filled the glass dome above. Torches were lit and hung from the metal brackets in the walls.

"Captain." Aren came and stood beside Lore. "You training these recruits?"

Lore looked over the room. There were at least fifteen men and two women. And they all looked so young. Lore ran a hand through his hair. Was he really getting that old? Suddenly he felt conscious of his grey hair and the few wrinkles near the corners of his eyes.

A couple heads turned his direction. "As a matter of fact, I am," Lore said "Care to join?"

"An opportunity to show off my skills?" Aren said with a grin.

Lore let a small smile cross his lips. "Then follow me."

• • •

Lore spent the morning teaching the basics. Most of the new recruits caught on fast, allowing him to progress further than he had anticipated.

Lore wiped his forehead. "Time for a break," he said, motioning for everyone to stop. "Feel free to spend your time in the Guards Quarter or out in the courtyard. In one hour we'll resume training."

The recruits began to wander toward the double doors. Lore reached for one of the small rags sitting on a nearby bench.

Aren edged up next to him. "Captain."

"Yes?" Lore took the rag and wiped his forehead. Aren nodded toward the doorway. "Rowen is here."

"*What?*" Lore turned and stared.

Rowen stood rigidly in the doorway. She was in uniform, her long pale hair braided and hanging over one shoulder, her blue cloak clasped around her neck. A couple of the recruits looked her over.

"Aren," Lore said, "clear out the training room. Rowen and I need to talk."

"Yes, Captain."

Aren followed the crowd out, stopping once to say something to Rowen. Moments later, the training room was empty. Rowen continued to stand in the doorway.

Lore walked toward her, noting her stubborn stance. Then he glanced at her eyes. Shocked, he faltered. Her eyes were dull and lifeless, the sparkle he remembered, gone.

"Captain," she said, tilting her chin upward.

"Rowen." Lore stepped closer. "What are you doing here?" Her eyes looked up into his, giving him full view of the pain radiating within.

"Returning to duty, Captain," Rowen said.

Unwilling to embarrass her in front of the guards in the other room, Lore placed his hand on her arm and steered her into the training room. Then he turned to look at her. The stubbornness present moments ago melted away into hesitancy. Her eyes flickered as he studied her.

"You've just recovered from what should have been a fatal wound."

Rowen stiffened. "I'm feeling fine," she said, "and I'd rather—"

Without thinking Lore placed a finger on her lips, shocking her into silence. "No, Rowen," he said. "We are leaving for Avonai in five days, and I need you to be at your best for the trip. Until then, you are to rest."

"Avonai?" Rowen said in a puzzled voice, her lips moving against his finger.

Lore withdrew his hand as if scorched, his heart suddenly thudding loudly in his chest. "Yes," he said, grateful his voice sounded normal. "Avonai has agreed to join the northern alliance."

"So Lady Astrea agreed to the bonding?"

So Rowen knew about that too. "Yes," Lore said.

Rowen's face turned downcast.

"So I'm asking that you rest until the trip."

Her shoulders slumped even farther. "Yes, sir." She turned to go. "Rowen?"

Rowen turned back to look at him. "I'm here . . . if you need someone to talk to."

She gave him a sad smile. "Yes, sir." Then she walked away.

For one moment Lore almost followed her, then thought better of it as he remembered Balint's words. *Please help her, Word,* he thought as he watched Rowen leave. *Whatever is killing the life inside of her, please help her.*

Rowen turned right and continued down the long hallway. Disappointment swelled inside her chest. Had she really expected Lore to let her come back? *Yes,* a small part of her answered. After spending three days in the Healers Quarter with nothing to do but reflect on what Balint had shared with her, she was ready to return to duty. Yet Lore had said no.

Rest he had said. Rowen laughed bitterly. That was the last thing she wanted to do. So instead she headed toward the front doors.

She passed two guards. They glanced briefly her way. Rowen ignored them as she opened one of the doors. Rain poured down in thick sheets from dark clouds, pounding the portico and stairs in a deafening staccato. The sight of it drew her in. The sky looked the same way she felt.

A reckless spirit came over her. Rowen pulled her hood over her head and walked out into the torrent. The rain hammered her head and shoulders as she hurried down the stairs and past the water fountain toward the first gate.

No one stopped her as she walked beneath the first archway. The stone overhead shielded her momentarily from the rain. Then she stepped back out into the rain and continued down the long main street.

Water rushed between the cobblestones, pooling beside the stone buildings. Cheery lights shone from homes and shops, a contrast to the dark outside. The streets were empty, devoid of life. No one in their right mind would be out in a storm like this, even though it was midday.

Halfway through the city, she turned down one of the side streets. The rain stung her face and the wind tried to whip back her hood. Rowen held her cloak tightly beneath her chin and made her way toward the city wall. Ahead she could see the dark silhouette of a door. The reckless feeling inside of her grew. She knew the gate opened up on the western side of Anwin Forest, a small entrance for those who needed lumber from the forest. She bent her head down and hurried toward the door.

As Rowen approached the gate, she felt a twinge of caution. She knew the black wolves had been tracked down and killed. Balint had told her so. However, there could still be some in the forest. Would she risk it?

The rain pounded her face. She raised a hand to wipe away the water, and she felt the rough texture of leather against her cheek. Anger roared to life inside her chest. Suddenly she knew: She didn't care. She wanted to run away. Run somewhere, anywhere. Anywhere but here.

Rowen edged alongside one of the buildings. She placed a hand above her eyes to keep the rain out and glanced up. She could see figures moving in and out of the guardhouse near the main gates. If she were careful, none of the guards would see her leave.

She hurried along the wall toward the gate. Tugging on the gate, she found it unlocked. She pulled the door open, slipped out, and carefully pulled the door shut behind her.

Rowen blinked against the rain. She could barely see the trees. She put one foot in front of the other, the water battering her body. But the storm overhead was nothing compared to the way she felt inside: the utter grief and despair over Balint's revelation. She was an Eldaran, a Truthsayer.

And all she had ever wanted to be was human.

Instead, she found herself hiding behind a glove, terrified of touching another person, terrified of seeing the darkness that hid inside the heart of another.

The rain continued its steady downpour as she drew near Anwin. Tall trees branched out overhead, catching the rain between their spindly fingers. Rowen stopped beneath the foliage. She took a moment to catch her breath. Then she plunged into the forest, keeping the city wall to her back and the side of the mountain to her right. The trees grew thicker the farther she went, their trunks broadening with the years they had spent in the forest. The rain, where it was able to find its way between the branches, had reduced to a steady drizzle.

Rowen walked through the wet underbrush, her thoughts wandering bitterly now toward her parents. Her real parents. In the past, she had been only somewhat curious about them. But her thoughts had never lingered long on their absence. She had never known them, after all. And the loving attention of Ann and Jedrek kept her more than content. But now she wondered who they were, what had happened to them, and why they had left her on the Mar's doorstep over twenty years ago.

Why weren't they here when her mark had appeared? Why weren't they here to explain to her who she was? Instead, they had left her to stumble through the dark misunderstandings of others, to be hurt and wounded simply because she had been ignorant of her abilities, her *gift*.

So where were they now?

Rowen wiped away angry tears, then stopped. She stared ahead at a small meadow. Lush green grass grew, dotted with tiny white flowers. A mist gently floated along one side of the field. An old stone ruin stood on the other. Nearby, she spied a deer and her fawn grazing quietly, neither noticing her presence.

There was such a peaceful lull to the tiny meadow that for one moment she forgot her heartache. She lowered her hand and began to walk across the meadow. Her movement startled the deer. With lightning speed, the mother and fawn bounded back into the trees.

The grass clung to her boots and pants. Tiny white petals broke off and scattered at her footstep. Halfway across the meadow, the mist shifted. Falling from the high mountain cliffs above were dozens of waterfalls. Rowen stopped, the sight catching in her throat.

At the bottom lay a pool of water that caught the cascades. White mist drifted up and around the waters. A moment later, the mist covered the falls again, leaving a wall of white. Rowen stared at the white haze, then over at the white stone ruin. A shiver ran down her spine.

What was this place?

Hesitantly, she took a step toward the ruin, then another, feeling as though she were walking on hallowed ground. She could see long cracks along its white surface. Dark green ivy climbed its walls. A doorway stood in the front with charred remains of two doors on either side.

Rowen carefully made her way up the broken set of stairs to the door. She could not remember anyone mentioning a stone ruin outside the city. And that seemed strange, for when she reached the top of the stairs, she could see carvings etched into the wood doors where fire and ivy had not reached. The same carvings she had seen on the gates that hung on either side of the White City's entrance.

Rowen bent closer to the wood and looked at the carvings. She had no idea what the symbols meant, and now she wished she had asked someone about the symbols back on the city's gates. She straightened up, still staring at the doors. Could the White City and this decrepit building be somehow linked?

A sudden desire to see inside filled her. She carefully stepped passed the burnt doors and looked inside. Small bits of light filtered down from somewhere above.

It *looked* safe enough.

She craned her neck to look a bit more. Overhead, thunder boomed and the rain started up again. A shiver rushed across her body. Freezing, Rowen went inside the ruin.

Damp, musty air filled her nostrils. Her eyes slowly adjusted to the dark interior. Rain fell through a partially collapsed roof overhead. Huge chunks of masonry littered the stone floor. Dirt and windswept debris crowded the corners. Spider webs shimmered along cracked columns whose job had once been to hold up the ceiling.

Rowen cautiously made her way across the floor. Ahead, a collapsed wall cut off her view of the rest of the room. She sidestepped another chunk of masonry. What was this place? An abandoned academy? Religious abbey? Or perhaps a military outpost dating back to the foundation of the White City?

Rowen looked around and made her way across the room. She could find nothing that explained what the old ruin had once been: no broken furniture, no scattered scrolls, not even a scrap of cloth. Just crumbling walls and a caved in ceiling.

She turned to go, but a flash of color caught her eye. Rowen turned back. A small archway stood half hidden behind a large slab of rock. She should really be getting back . . .

Color flashed again.

Just one more minute.

Rowen walked around the slab. The archway was clear of webs and debris. Odd, she thought. The color flashed again. She followed the colors through the archway. Rainbows danced across the white stone floor. Puzzled, Rowen raised her eyes . . . and everything inside her stopped.

From floor to ceiling stood a wall made entirely of colored glass.

The ruin stood silent around her as if it were holding its breath. Rowen took a step, then another. A stray sunbeam suddenly shone from behind the glass, illuminating the entire room. The hairs on the back of her neck rose.

What is this place?

Moving closer, she realized the colored glass was broken up into multiple panels by thin dark metal rods. And within each panel was a picture.

Rowen moved toward the nearest panel. It was a picture of a young woman kneeling near a man in uniform. The detail of the glass was such that she could see the pain etched across the man's face and a look of peace on the woman's. Dark red glass covered the man's chest. Blood.

The young woman held her hand above the man's wound. Rowen stared at the woman's hand and froze.

On the woman's hand was an oddly shaped white mark.

Shaken, Rowen quickly moved toward the next frame. In this one she found an old woman. By her bedside were two people. Both had their hands raised just above the woman's body. Taking a step closer, she peered at their hands and found the same marks across their palms.

A chill ran down her back. These people . . . It couldn't be. Rowen moved on toward the next frame.

This one was different from the other two, the image much darker. The picture consisted of a young man standing near a creature she had never seen before. The glass that made up the creature's body was a swirl of blacks and greys, as if to portray the creature as an incorporeal being. Its narrow eyes glowed with flame-colored glass, and a protrusion of sharp fangs extended out from its upper lip.

Rowen turned back toward the young man. There was neither fear nor surprise on his face. Instead, he looked confident and determined. Her eyes traveled down the black lines toward his hand. But instead of a mark on his palm, he held a sword—a strange pale yellow sword that seemed to fade in and out of the glass.

Rowen looked again into the man's face. Who was he? And why was he different than the others?

On and on went the portraits, each containing people with a white mark upon their palm. As she studied the pictures, Rowen felt a twisting inside her heart. She knew there was no mistaking who these people were.

Stopping halfway through the panels, she raised her own hand and, finger-by-finger, pulled off her sword glove. Rowen held up her hand, mark upwards. It pulsed softly with faint light. She glanced between the pictures and her hand. Their marks were identical.

There was no mistake. These people were Eldarans.

Suddenly Rowen clenched her hand and drew it back. Anger crept across her face and chest. She looked up at the pictures again, pictures filled with the peaceful faces of Eldarans.

And abruptly the darkness inside her caught fire.

She hated them. She hated their serene and loving looks. They looked as if they had never experienced hate or loneliness or fear, all the emotions that seemed to fill her. How could they look like that if they had really seen inside any human heart?

Rowen fell to her knees. The rage inside her burning so brightly that it felt like it would rip from her chest. How could she be related to these people? Their worlds were nothing alike.

"*I hate you!*" she shouted. Her words echoed throughout the ruin, bouncing across the stone. None of the pictures changed. The Eldarans continued on in their peaceful duties. The fading echo sobered her, but that did not stop her heart from crying out.

Rowen felt more alone than ever. She bowed her head in defeat. Raging against the glass pictures did not change anything. The mark on her hand was permanent, a sign that she would forever be different from those around her.

The ray of sunshine disappeared. Colors faded. Rain began to fall through the broken ceiling above, gently hitting her body.

"I never wanted this," Rowen whispered.

Only silence answered her. The rage that had burned inside her heart moments ago left abruptly, leaving her cold and dead inside. The rain fell harder until the stone floor was washed in its torrent. Rowen vaguely sensed the chill that began to sweep across her body. Her clothes became drenched again in the downpour.

But she didn't care.

From the corner of her eye she noticed a dull grey mist begin to spread across the stone floor. It drifted toward her, obscuring everything as it moved along. Soon the outer walls disappeared as the mist consumed them, steadily drawing near.

A subtle alarm sounded inside her mind. Rowen shook off her emotional stupor and looked up. The grey haze spread quickly. The mist reached her and began to swirl around her body.

Rowen scrambled to her feet. She turned away from the wall of colored glass and ran back toward the doorway. But it was too late. The mist rose with such speed that it instantly enveloped her body in its moist embrace.

Terror clawed at her chest. She placed out her hands and tried to find her way by touch, but she found nothing to lead her. There were no stone slabs, no wall. Everything was gone.

The mist began to change color. What had been a dull grey peeled back into warm white. Rowen hid her eyes for a moment, the light within the mist suddenly intensifying.

As the light faded, she cracked open her eyes. A shadow approached her from within the mist. Terrified, Rowen reached for her sword, only to find it gone. She glanced down to find everything gone except for her drenched shirt and pants.

She looked up. The shadow drew closer. Rowen began to back away. She held out her marked hand as if it were a weapon.

A man stepped out from the mist.

Fear dropped her to the ground. Rowen lay there shaking. Although the man's silhouette was ordinary in appearance—not monstrous or brawny or unusual in any way—her sixth sense screamed that he was anything but.

He stopped just beyond her sight. "Rowen, look at me."

Rowen felt her mouth grow dry, her breath coming in quick succession. But she obeyed and lifted her eyes.

The Man before her was ageless. He was dressed in a brilliant white robe tied with a golden cord. There were no other adornments: no crown, no scepter, no gems, nothing to signify His rank or who He was. Instead, Rowen could see scars covering every part of His visible body. Some were thin and white. Others were grotesque, distorting His skin in unnatural ways.

She lifted her eyes to His face. He gazed down at her, His face soft, His eyes dark and fathomless. And there were more scars. Her eyes were drawn toward a particularly cruel one that ran the length of the right side of His face. She wanted to ask who He was but felt unable to utter a word.

"I am that was, that is, and that is to come," He said, as if reading her thoughts. "I am known as the Word."

Rowen's eyes dropped, and her body went rigid. Suddenly she felt exposed. She felt like He could see everything inside of her, like she could with others. Except, unlike her, He did not need to touch her.

"You have nothing to fear from me, Daughter of Light," the Word said softly.

Rowen licked her lips and stared at the swirling mist, but found no words to say. Daughter of Light?

"These scars," He said and motioned above her, "are for the people of the Lands. They are the blood price I paid to free them."

She swallowed. "F-free us from what?" Rowen raised her eyes but did not dare look Him in the face.

"You have seen it already," the Word said quietly. "The darkness that lies within the heart. Every man, woman, and child is born with it. It cannot be seen with the eyes. But it can be felt."

Rowen felt a subtle stirring in her chest even as He spoke. The rage she carried began to surface again, baring its fangs at the Man who stood before her.

As if sensing the black beast, the Word stopped. Rowen glanced up and found Him looking at her, a serious expression on His scarred face. "I can heal the darkness inside of you."

At His words, a war erupted inside her. She wanted to say yes, to be free of the fear and anger she carried around. But it did not want to let go of her. She could feel it clinging to her, digging its long talons deeper into her heart. And, perhaps, a part of her didn't want to let it go either. The battle grew fierce, causing her to hunch over and hold her arms over her chest in pain.

The Word crouched and held a hand out to Rowen. "Let me take your pain and your anger, Rowen. All it takes is one touch."

She stared at the hand He offered. There was no mark upon it. Rather, His entire hand glowed as He reached for her. Suddenly, the wish to be free rose up inside her, just as strong as the hate that had held her moments ago.

"Yes," she whispered.

As if sensing its doom, the darkness inside her ignited, encompassing her entire being in its black blaze. It did not want to die. Rowen gasped at the intensity and almost shouted *No*. The Word placed His hand upon her head.

Then . . . it was done. The deep twisting rage she had felt moments ago was gone.

Rowen blinked. Something had changed inside of her. She could feel it. It was like she had been freed from a dark place and was now seeing light for the first time.

She touched her face and ran her fingers down her neck, following the edge of her tunic. She held her hands there. She almost expected her outside to feel as different as her inside did.

The hatred was gone.

But instead of feeling empty, Rowen felt full of life. She wanted to laugh and dance. All the broken pieces inside of her had been fused back together, every crack filled. "I'm free," she whispered, savoring the sudden sense of joy.

The Word stood. His light had dimmed. Rowen looked up and saw a fresh cut just below His eye. Blood trickled down His chin, leaving a scarlet trail across His face.

"No!" Rowen scrambled to her feet. But even as she moved, the cut began to heal over, leaving a short white scar just below His eye. She watched in amazement. "You . . . you healed me."

The Word looked at her with such love that she could feel the intensity of it from where she stood. How could she have ever hated Him?

"Dear one, you may be able to heal others of their physical ailments, but only I can heal the heart."

Rowen placed her hand across her chest, feeling her heartbeat beneath her shirt. And deeper still, beyond where she could feel with her hand, her heart felt . . . whole.

"Thank You," she said, awed.

The Word placed a hand on her shoulder. "There is much for you to do, Daughter of Light." He was serious now with a hint of sadness. "And so it is time for you to return to the Lands. But do not fear. In the moment of your greatest weakness, you will fully know My power."

The Word began to back away. Rowen took a step forward. She wanted to follow Him. She still had so many questions. What did He mean? What was she to do? And what did He see that made Him look so sad?

But before she could move, He vanished into the swirling mist. Then the mist changed from white to a dreary grey. The mist dissipated, leaving her in the middle of the stone ruin. Rain fell gently on her body.

Rowen stared at the colored glass. Had it been a dream?

No. She bent down and picked her glove up from the floor. She had left the castle an angry and bitter woman. And then, with one touch, the Word had healed her. Her heart had changed. She felt . . . new.

With startling realization, Rowen knew this change was permanent. She could still feel the echo of darkness inside, but it no longer controlled her. She was free. And something new had moved into her heart: a peace and joy that had not been there before.

Rowen cast one more look back at the stained glass wall before turning and heading out of the stone ruin. She understood the pictures now. The Word had touched those Eldarans too. And changed their hearts forever.

CHAPTER 16

Caleb eased into a deeper sleep, his mind slowly releasing its grip on the real world. In his mind's eye, there was nothing but darkness around him. The darkness slowly twisted until its shadows resembled tall gnarled trees, their branches reaching high into the heavens. Tiny lights flickered between the dark branches. He stood in a clearing below, arms crossed, feet spread apart.

His dream always began this way. And, like always, he felt driven to walk toward the trees.

Caleb dropped his arms and slowly walked toward the trees. With his hands he brushed his sides, searching for his daggers, only to remember a heartbeat later that here, in this place, they did not exist. He clenched his hands in frustration. But that did not stop him from continuing toward the forest ahead.

Soon a path appeared. Caleb stepped onto the hardened dirt and followed it through the trees. Dark shapes gradually emerged between the tree trunks, just a shade darker than the shadows that covered the forest floor. At the same moment a memory tried to surface. It felt like a clanging bell inside his head, telling him to run from this place. But an invisible force beckoned him toward the shadows. And its call was stronger than the alarms sounding in his head.

Caleb left the path after a couple steps and moved toward the dark shapes between the trees. The tiny lights that floated along the branches above widened, allowing more light to filter down over the figures below. In that light, the shapes finally revealed their true form.

They were bodies, hundreds of them, standing motionless amongst the trees.

Caleb walked toward the nearest one. He stopped and stared at the body. The body opened its eyes. With a jolt of recognition, he found himself staring at Delshad.

With a cry, Caleb stumbled back, tripped, and fell to the ground. Delshad moved forward, no expression on the old man's face. In his outstretched hand he held a wicked looking dagger. Caleb only had time to realize the blade was his when Delshad stood over him.

"I forgive you," Delshad whispered. Then he plunged the knife into Caleb's chest.

With a loud gasp, Caleb sat up in his bed, his hand clutching at his bare chest, sure he would find the hilt of his blade protruding from his heart. But there was nothing there. He made another sweep to make sure, then he sighed.

It had been only a dream.

He'd had nightmares about his victims for years, but they seemed to be reoccurring more often of late. The last few nights he even feared going to sleep.

Caleb ran a hand through his dark hair, now damp with perspiration. From across the room he could see the first few rays of dawn through a small square window. Might as well get up and start the day.

Caleb threw on a black tunic and pants. He strode out of the room and headed toward the courtyard below, ready for some physical exercise to clear his mind of this most recent nightmare.

"Message for Lord Tala."

Caleb looked up at the mention of his name. He had long ago removed his shirt, and he now stood panting, savoring the feel of sweat trickle down his back and chest. A soldier pointed his direction.

Finally, a message from his cousin. Caleb watched the courier walk across the courtyard. He had been stuck at Hadrast Fortress ever since Commander Arpiar had taken over, waiting for Lord Corin to say he could return home. This had to be it.

"Lord Tala?" the courier said once he reached Caleb.

"Yes." Caleb stood to his full height. The courier reached into the pouch that hung at his side. Out came a long cream colored parchment with a red seal on one side. The courier handed it to Caleb.

"You are excused," Caleb said, waving the young man away. The courier bowed, then left. Caleb grabbed his shirt and headed toward his room, anxious to read the note. He was more than ready to leave the north behind.

Caleb took a seat in his room and slowly read the parchment once, then twice. After the second time, he crumpled it and threw it across the room. The last lingering images of his nightmare were banished as his mind grappled with the words he had just read.

Lord Corin wanted him to stay.

Caleb worked his jaw as he thought on his cousin's words again. Corin wanted him to continue his role as an "advisor" to Commander Arpiar. And this time, his dear cousin wanted to move against the White City.

Unable to sit any longer, Caleb stood and paced the room. Although not a tactician, even he knew that the best place to hit was Avonai, not the White City. The coastal city had chosen to remain neutral, believing that by doing so, it could remain separate from the war. But Temanin did not see countries as neutral. They were either for or against the empire. And since there was no formal alliance between Temanin and Avonai, the city was fair game.

Avonai was the best choice. By taking the coastal city, Temanin would gain another foothold in the north and demoralize the northern troops.

But Avonai would not be neutral for long. Caleb came to a stop beside the window and looked out. He had heard from the Temanin spies that a treaty would soon be signed creating an alliance between Nordica, the White City, and Avonai. And when that happened, the northern military would be a force to be reckoned with.

Caleb cursed and turned from the window. What did Corin think he was doing, interfering in matters he had no knowledge of? And worse yet, keeping Caleb right in the middle of this war when all he wanted to do was go home and back to what he did best. He was no good here. He was an assassin, not a military man—

Wait. Caleb stopped. Treaty signing in Avonai. Attack the White City. Pieces began to fall into place. What better way to weaken a stronghold than to take out its leader? And the leader of the White City would be in Avonai in a couple of days.

A predatory smile crossed Caleb's face. Now this was something he *could* do. In fact, this job fit him perfectly. He and a few spies could slip into Avonai and take out Lord Gaynor. During that time, Commander Arpiar could prepare an attack on the White City.

In a more perfect world, Avonai would then be hit after the assassination. But Corin's word was law, so neither he nor Commander Arpiar had any choice. Still, Lord Gaynor's death would give Temanin an advantage.

Caleb felt his body surge with adrenaline. He left his room and hurried for the stairs. He turned at the bottom of the stairs and headed toward the outer wall where he knew he would find Commander Arpiar. Around him Temanin soldiers sparred, waiting for the next battle in which to apply their skills.

Caleb caught sight of Commander Arpiar along the southern battlement. He took the steps two at a time. He reached the top and headed for the older man.

As he drew near, Commander Arpiar turned and frowned. "What brings you here?"

Caleb rarely visited anyone, choosing to remain alone. He had seen no point in integrating himself among the rest of the troops. "I just received word from Lord Corin."

"Yes," Commander Arpiar said, his face darkening. "So did I. Lord Corin wishes to move on the White City."

"Yes." Caleb chose not to add that he had been ordered to stay with the commander as well. Besides, he had a feeling Commander Arpiar already knew, judging by the way the older man stared at him. "But I have an idea." Then Caleb spent the next few minutes laying out his plan and watched Commander Arpiar's face grow from hostile to thoughtful.

"It could work," Commander Arpiar said after Caleb finished. "And you definitely possess the skills to pull off such a feat. But why do this? Why put yourself in harm's way when you could just stay back and wait for this war to be over?"

Good question, Caleb thought. He knew Commander Arpiar pegged him as a selfish man. So why *would* he put himself in a dangerous position?

"Simple. Because by eliminating Lord Gaynor, there is a chance we could end this war quickly."

" And ending this war serves you . . . ?"

"I will be able to return to Azar."

"I see."

Caleb did not want Commander Arpiar to get any illusions that he was offering his assassin skills to benefit the Temanin Army. Commander Arpiar was right: He *was* a selfish man. He was doing this so he could leave this military life and get back to his other life, the one he had been forced to leave behind in Azar.

"So when would you leave?" Commander Arpiar said.

"As soon as possible," Caleb said. "Although we know the treaty will be signed soon, the spies were not sure of the exact time. It could even be happening as we speak."

"Then I will send some of Temanin's best your way. About how many do you need?"

Caleb paused to consider. "About four to five. Not too many. I do not want to attract attention."

"Sounds good. I'll have them sent to your tent within the hour for briefing."

Caleb nodded and walked away, his mind already going over what he would need to pull this off. And pull this off he would. He had never failed at a mission before, and he would not start now.

Avonai. The capital city of the eastern coast and the people of the sea. Caleb lay on his belly from a nearby hilltop to the south, his body hidden by the thick brush and trees that grew along the coast. The sky was dark. Nearby, the moon had just begun to rise over the ocean. He could hear the dull roar of the waves. Cold salty air flowed up from the sea.

Caleb pulled out his eyeglass and studied the city. Tall, thick walls surrounded Avonai. There were four gates along the walls. He could see two Avonain guards at each gate. Inside the walls, Avonai sparkled with the reflection of countless lamps and windows. The streets jutted out from the main one like spokes on a wheel. The castle stood on the far side of the city, overlooking the sea.

He slowly swung his eyeglass around. Outside the walls lay the port, a crisscross of wooden walkways, ships, and rundown pubs. Crates were stacked along the walls and boardwalks. A few people wandered the walkways, but most of the port lay empty.

Feeling his muscles beginning to cramp, Caleb stood and slowly stretched. He had seen all he could from here. It was time to gather information from one of the taverns below.

Beside him, were five other men dressed in dark clothing.

"Time to move out." Caleb stuffed his eyeglass into his pack. "We'll split up, three to a group and check out the pubs below. Find out what you can, then meet back here later tonight. Let no one see you coming or going from this hill. We're supposed to be sailors just in from a stint at sea. Understand?"

"Yes, sir," they replied.

"Good. I'll take Raul and Daleth with me." Two men stepped forward at the mention of their names. He turned toward them. "Let's go."

Carefully they made their way down the hill, through the thick brush, onto the walkway.

Lamps hung from poles every couple of feet, creating pools of light across the boardwalk. Rats scurried under the crates as they approached. The smell of salt and rancid fish hung in the air. Water lapped gently beneath the walkways. The few people out that night ignored the Temanins, their heads bent as they hurried along with their business. Caleb ignored them as well and headed down the nearest pier. At the end was a dilapidated pub. He and his men would start there.

A large grimy window graced the front of the tavern. Above it swung a solitary sign. Caleb glanced up. In faded letters it read *The Seagull*. Looked good enough for him.

Caleb pressed down on the rusty latch and pushed forward. The door swung inward with a loud groan. The inside of the tavern reminded him of a den of filth. Smoke filled the inside, mixed with the scent of unwashed bodies and sour ale. Wrought-iron chandeliers hung from a stained ceiling. Crumbling bricks lined the walls. A bar counter stood to his left with a portly man behind it. Pewter mugs hung from a low hanging rafter above the counter.

Caleb took a step inside and felt something crunch beneath his boot. He looked down in disgust, but could see nothing on the dark wood floor. He shook his boot and made his way across the tavern.

Round tables filled the rest of the small, cramped room. Most of them were occupied with men from every corner of the Lands—tall dark Honts from the south, Nordics with tattoos across every visible patch of skin, and a couple of Thyrians who looked worn and tired. He noted a couple of Avonain soldiers in the far right corner, and he selected a table farthest from them.

Caleb smiled. He had chosen well. No one would notice a couple of foreign sailors here, since they all were strangers. Not even those Avonain soldiers. He pulled off his dark cloak, revealing the usual pale white shirt and dark pants of the common sailor. A gold chain hung across his chest with a matching gold hoop in his left ear. He placed his cloak over the back of his chair and sat down. Raul and Daleth sat down in the other two chairs.

A heavyset Avonain approached, his strange blue-green eyes glittering under a mop of dirty blond hair. "What can I get for you?" the man asked in a reedy voice.

"Whatever you're serving tonight," Caleb replied.

"Let's see your gold first," the Avonain demanded.

Caleb shrugged and dug out his coin purse. He flashed a handful of gold coins. The man's eyes glittered even more than the coins. "And a couple mugs of ale as well."

The man hurried away without a word. Caleb put away the gold. He took note of the man's greed, his experience telling him the Avonain could be bought.

From the corner of his eye, he could see that Raul and Daleth were already taking in the room and judging its occupants. Good, they weren't inexperienced after all.

A short time later the Avonain returned with steaming bowls of fish stew and dark crusty bread. Caleb took one sniff of the stew and felt his stomach turn. The ale was even worse. But he wasn't here for the food or drink. Drunken men had loose tongues and even looser pockets.

Caleb picked at the stew and kept his ears open for any tidbit of news. Nearby he heard the Thyrians muttering amongst themselves.

"Never seen such a thing," one of the sailors muttered.

"Everyone rounded up and taken up to Cragsmoor."

"Glad we got away when we did."

He found the conversation interesting. Apparently something had happened in Thyra. But Thyra was not his mission at present, so he tucked the sailors' words away to dissect later.

After a couple of minutes, the Thyrians stood and left. Caleb pushed the bowl of stew away and took a sip of the ale. He spit the ale back into his mug and wiped his mouth. How could anyone drink this swill?

"Don't like the ale?" Raul asked before taking a huge swig from his own mug.

"No." Caleb pushed the mug next to the bowl of stew and glanced around. It was late now and many of the men had consumed more than their share of the pungent brew. Daleth got up and sauntered over toward the bar and began to talk with one of the sailors from Hont.

Caleb heard raised voices to his left.

"King Alaric has no right to send us to war."

"King Alaric can do whatever he wishes."

Caleb slowly turned and watched the four Avonain guards in the corner. The one closest to Caleb was a skinny young man who looked barely older than twenty. The two guards on either side of him were middle-aged, one short with a receding hairline, the other with a face that reminded Caleb of the pet monkeys some of the nobility kept in Azar. The farthest guard was an old man with a droopy grey mustache.

"King Alaric is only doing it so his son can bond with Lady Astrea. He isn't concerned about the war," the young guard said.

"Who cares?" The old guard took a sip from his mug. He wiped the froth from his mouth, missing the bit that clung to his mustache. "We won't be called to fight. That's what peons are for. They sure aren't good for anything else."

The other two guards laughed.

"You mean you don't care if good men die?"

The old guard pursed his lips thoughtfully. "No, not really. You see, Tristan, we're not talking about good men. We're not talking about men at all. Those fishers just take up space and make the city filthy. Seems better to put them to use to me. Have them fight the war for us."

"But they're human—"

"They're fishers!"

Interesting, Caleb thought. Looked like a fight was simmering amongst the guards. Perhaps he could use it to his advantage. He kept a covert gaze on the table, watching for an opportunity to present itself.

"You don't actually *like* fishers, do you, Tristan?" the monkey-faced guard said.

Tristan muttered something that Caleb couldn't hear.

The old guard sat back and laughed. "No way! Boys, we have here a fisher lover. Tell me, Tristan: Was your mother a fisher? Is that why you defend them? What was she like?"

"I bet she was easy," the other guard said. "They all are."

Tristan sat rigidly in his chair. "Don't say that about my mother."

"How about a sister? You have a sister? She a fisher too?" The three guards laughed.

Caleb watched Tristan's hands ball up on the table.

"I know what I'd do if I got a hold of a little fisher—"

"Not another word."

The three men stared at Tristan. The Nordics at the next table broke out in song. The older guard smiled and said something.

Tristan stood up and kicked his chair back. He leaned toward the other guards, hands firmly planted on the thick wooden table. "Don't ever call my family that again."

The Nordics sang louder. Caleb strained to hear what the old guard said.

Tristan's face turned purple. "That's it," he shouted. He swung his fist and caught the old guard in the nose. Immediately blood spurted from the wound. The Nordics stuttered in their song. They turned to watch.

A look of rage and surprise spread across the old guard's face. He clutched his bloody nose and stood. He glared at Tristan "You'll pay for that." The other two guards stood alongside him.

Suddenly, as if realizing what he had done, Tristan began to back away from the table. His face drained of color.

"You'll never work in Avonai again!" The old guard advanced around the table toward Tristan. Blood dripped down his chin. "Did you hear me?" He swung his fist back and caught Tristan in the stomach. Tristan bent over and clutched his midsection, groaning in pain.

Caleb saw his opportunity. In three strides he was next to Tristan. "Are you all right?"

Before Tristan could reply, the old guard was in Caleb's face. "Get out of the way, sailor!" He raised his fist. "This isn't your fight."

Behind him, Caleb could hear the barkeeper yelling something about nobody fighting.

Caleb chose to ignore both of them.

With lightning reflexes Caleb reached out and grabbed the bloody guard, holding the man at arm's length.

The old guard struggled against Caleb's grip. "Do you know who you're dealing with?" the guard yelled.

Mentally Caleb thought the same thing, but instead he replied, "No."

"I am second in command of the city guard." The old guard tried to twist out of Caleb's hold. Caleb tightened his grip. The guard switched tactics and reached for his sword.

Caleb suddenly hauled the guard toward himself, lifting the man off the ground. "I wouldn't do that, if I were you," Caleb said in a low, dangerous voice. He watched the old guard's eyes dart toward his companions, only to discover the other two were being held by Raul and Daleth.

"No fighting!" The barkeeper came panting to Caleb's side.

Slowly Caleb lowered the old guard but kept a firm hold on his shirt. "A good leader never attacks his subordinates," Caleb said coldly. He released the man.

The old guard stumbled back. He brushed off his shirt and wiped his face, smearing more blood across his cheeks and mustache. "Come on, men," he said to his companions. "Let's go."

Caleb gave a small nod, and the two Temanins released their hold.

The guards headed toward the door. Caleb turned to assist Tristan. Out of the corner of his eye, he saw the old guard spin back around.

Instantly Caleb had a dagger in hand, ready to throw if the old guard did anything.

The old guard didn't notice. "If I find you in Avonai, sailor," he said, looking directly at Caleb, "I will have you arrested so fast your head will spin." Then with a final glare, he and the other two guards left.

Caleb pushed the dagger back into the small sheath that hung at his side. He held out a hand toward Tristan.

Tristan took the hand and straightened up. "Thanks, sailor," he said with a sheepish look.

"Let me get you a drink. I'm sure you could use one."

"Yes, I could." Tristan followed Caleb to the counter. Caleb shook his head slightly toward his companions. He wanted to handle the young man himself. Nodding, Raul and Daleth each turned and moved toward different tables.

The barkeeper watched Caleb with a wary eye and filled two more mugs of ale. Caleb poured a handful of gold out onto the counter. The barkeeper's expression brightened.

"So you're against the alliance," Caleb said, more as a statement than a question.

Tristan reached for one of the mugs. "What? Oh, that—right." His expression darkened. "By signing that treaty, King Alaric is sending us to war."

"What do you care?" Caleb ran a finger around the rim of his own mug, "You're a guard. You won't be sent in to fight."

"No, but my younger brother will." Tristan lifted his mug. "Because, after all, we're just fishers, right? Who cares about us?"

Caleb watched Tristan drain his mug. He knew that, if he played Tristan right, he would be able to attain all the information he needed for his mission. Caleb felt a slight twinge of guilt for using the young man, but he quickly smothered it. He had no time to deal with these base feelings of morality when he had a job to do.

So Caleb ordered more drinks and began questioning Tristan, using every bit of sympathy and companionship he possessed to draw the man out. By the end of the night, Caleb had all he needed and more to accomplish his mission.

CHAPTER 17

Captain Lore heaved a sigh of relief as the tall walls of Avonai came into view. Though not expecting an attack on their traveling party, he had feared one nevertheless. There was something about this trip that had him on edge, a sixth sense that something was going to go wrong. But here they were, after a week of travel, approaching the city, and still no sign of Temanin. They had made it.

The sand colored city stood out amongst the evergreen trees and fields that surrounded it. Not as magnificent as the White City, but just as ancient, the city of Avonai had stood centuries on the edge of the Illyr Sea, greeting any seafaring traveler to the land of the north.

Overhead, the call of gulls greeted his ears, and already Lore could hear the dull roar of crashing waves. His heart began to stir, surrounded by these reminders of the sea. It was said that salt water ran in the veins of Avonains, and perhaps it did. The coastal people were as connected to the sea as one could be without dwelling within its depths. Lore felt the pull of the ocean and the Avonain blood in his body stirred. He was home.

Lore took a deep breath of the cool salty air. He felt his eyes begin to change, taking on the mood of the sea. Today it was calm. He shuddered slightly under the change. Being so close to the sea caused the change to be more powerful. Lore took another breath as the ocean's mood swept over him, then he urged his horse forward until he came up next to Lord Gaynor.

Lord Gaynor looked solemn as he gazed at the large city ahead. He turned toward Lore. "Have I done the right thing?" he said in a low voice. Conflicting emotions danced across the older man's face.

Lore paused for a moment, choosing his words carefully. The

last residual effects of the change passed. "You didn't force Lady Astrea into this agreement. You gave her a choice, and this is what she chose."

"I know, I know, but what kind of life will this be? Will she find love in this bonding?"

In that moment, Lore caught a glimpse not of a high lord, but of a father concerned for his daughter. It was a side of Lord Gaynor that few ever saw, and Lore felt privileged to be given a glance of the high lord's human side.

"Prince Evander is an honorable man," Lore said. "And your daughter is a lovely and kindhearted woman. They will find love if they choose to look for it."

Lord Gaynor stared at Lore for a moment. "You are very wise, Lore. Much like your father was. I'm not sure if I've ever told you this, but I am honored to have you serve as my captain."

"Thank you, milord."

Lord Gaynor turned his gaze back toward the city.

Lore sighed and he pulled his horse back, letting Lord Gaynor ride ahead of him. There were so many burdens on the shoulders of the people around him, what with this war, the treaty, and life. He could feel his own burdens weighing heavily on his heart. His eyes slid toward Rowen. At least there was one burden that had been lifted.

Rowen was smiling at the moment, her horse close to Lady Astrea's. The two were talking about something. Then Rowen reached over and placed her hand on Lady Astrea's arm.

Rowen had changed.

Lore had first noticed it the day after he had ordered Rowen away from the training room. When she had left, the look on her face had made him feel he had just thrust his sword into her heart. But the next day he had found her sitting quietly in the library, curled up in a chair near one of the windows. They had talked briefly. And when he had looked into her eyes, he'd realized the look of death was gone. There were still deep stirrings within those blue eyes, but the pain he had seen earlier had disappeared.

However, duty had called him back before he could ask her about it. When Lore left, he had felt a small measure of peace steal over his heart. He never wanted to see that dark look in Rowen's eyes again.

Lore turned his attention back toward Avonai. Walls the color of sand encircled the city. Ahead of them was the western entrance. Broad wooden doors were wide open. Deep sea green banners with a ship and anchor fluttered in the breeze. Long narrow buildings, beige with white shutters, lined the main street inside the entrance. A large crowd of people dressed in dark clothing stood just inside the gate.

Lore frowned. Was Avonai expecting them?

He got his answer a moment later when horns began to blow.

"What in the Lands?" he heard Lord Gaynor exclaim. Bright color streamers filled the air and the people began to cheer.

Rowen looked back at Lore with a puzzled expression. Lore motioned to Justus to take his place beside Lord Gaynor, then he urged his horse forward toward the two women ahead.

Rowen leaned toward Lore and cupped her mouth. "I thought our visit was supposed to be a secret."

"It was. But apparently word got out."

"So what do we do now?" she asked.

"Stay near Lady Astrea. Let no one near her. And keep your eyes open."

"Yes, Captain," Rowen placed her hand on the hilt of her sword.

Lore let his horse fall back until he was next to Lord Gaynor again. The high lord's face was pale, whether from fear or anger, he didn't know. Probably anger. But Lord Gaynor kept his head high as they rode through the gates and down the main street toward the castle ahead.

Caleb Tala stood with the crowd that eagerly awaited the party from the White City. His clothes were dark colored and ragged, much like the men around him. A hat covered his dark hair and shaded his eyes.

Across the street, people lined up in front of storefronts and houses. The only splash of color in the city was the deep sea-green banners that some had hung outside their windows and blue kerchiefs a couple women waved in the air. All the greens, greys, and blues made him wish for Temanin.

Soon, Caleb reminded himself. And this job would make that day come faster.

He congratulated himself on obtaining not only the time of Lord Gaynor's visit, but the exact room he would be staying in at the castle, thanks to young Tristan a few nights ago. Now he stood, waiting to catch a glimpse of the man he would soon kill.

The people crowded around him, bumping him. Caleb inched his way toward the side of a nearby building. Crowds always made him nervous, probably because he knew how easy it was in a crowd to slip up behind someone, plunge a dagger in just the right spot, then back away before anyone knew what had happened. Not that anyone was looking for him in this mass of people. But just the same, he felt better having his back up against the protective surface of stone.

Caleb glanced over the heads around him and watched the entourage approach the castle. All of them were wearing traveling garb, nothing ostentatious that would give hint that they were royalty from the White City. But word had leaked who they were, and, honestly, it did not take a trained eye to see that the people approaching the castle were not common.

The man in the middle of the entourage caught his eye: Lord Gaynor.

A small smile crept across Caleb's face. Lord Gaynor rode stiffly through the crowd with two men beside him and one behind him. His varors. But they were no match for Caleb. He had slipped past tighter security than that—

A warm haze brushed across his mind.

Caleb went rigid. He backed up against the wall and reached for his dagger. His eyes darted from Lord Gaynor to the crowd. Everyone stood around him, cheering. The feeling grew stronger, like a warm wind flowing through his mind. A seed of panic took root inside his chest. He gripped his dagger. The world began to spin around him, colors and people fading in and out.

Caleb let go of the dagger and reached for the wall instead. His fingers felt cold stone, but he could not see it. All he could see was a sandy mass swirling in front of him. He could hear someone speaking to him, but the words were garbled, as if he were listening underwater.

Then everything went black.

Caleb tried to speak but found his mouth would not move. He could hear nothing, save the rapid beat of his heart. He strained against the darkness, hoping to see something. A small speck of light appeared in the distance.

His mind scrambled to find an explanation for this strange phenomenon. The light slowly moved toward him. It grew and expanded until suddenly Caleb realized that the light he saw was . . . a woman.

Paralyzed, Caleb watched the woman approach him. Slowly she lifted her hand and reached toward him. Bright light radiated from her palm.

Show him the truth.

Caleb could hear the words echoing in the darkness and through his mind. The woman's hand drew near his cheek. He shivered. Even his nightmares never left him feeling this terrified. Caleb tried to back away, to shout, to do *anything,* but he could not move, not even his head. The woman's hand reached for his face, as if to give him a lover's caress. Closer, closer . . . .

Then he found himself staring at a beige stone wall. Caleb blinked.

"Are you all right?" a voice said next to him. Caleb turned to find an old man staring at him. "Perhaps you need to see a healer—"

"I'm fine." Caleb took a step back. People were mingling around him, some staring at him, others going about their business.

"But you were—"

"I said I'm fine!" Caleb glared at the old man.

The old man shook his head. "If you say so . . ."

"Yes."

The man shook his head again. "People these days . . ." The old man shuffled away.

Fighting the urge to turn and run, Caleb clamped down on his feelings and began to walk back through the dwindling crowd toward the gate that led to the port.

What in all the Lands was going on with him? How could he be having nightmares in broad daylight? Caleb sidestepped a crate full of fish, and hurried through the gate. A sea of grey flowed gently between wooden walkways. What was wrong with him? And who was that woman?

Show him the truth.

What truth? He knew who he was, *what* he was. An assassin. With a mission tomorrow that would require his full attention. Caleb stopped and took a deep breath. He closed his eyes and mentally shoved the disturbing vision deep into the dark recesses of his mind. Dwelling on the dream would only hinder him.

Satisfied it would stay back, Caleb opened his eyes. Determination filled his heart and soul. Time to report back to his men and perform this operation.

Rowen gripped her head. *Show him the truth.* The words echoed inside her mind until they shouted above every other thought. *Show him the truth.* Then they faded into a whisper, finally drifting away on the salty air.

"Rowen!"

Rowen snapped her eyes open. She found herself in her saddle, her hands still gripping the reins. A massive fortress-looking castle stood before her, the color of fresh milled wheat. Along the wall facing her was a double set of doors. Windows lined the second story. Sandstone walls surrounded the perimeter. Packed dirt covered the ground.

"Rowen!" said the voice again.

Rowen turned and found Lady Astrea bringing her horse up beside hers. "Are you all right? I called to you, but you kept riding."

Rowen shook her head as if to clear it. She could not remember how she had gotten here, or where here was. "I—I think so."

"Lady Astrea." Both women turned. Lore stood behind them. "Please excuse us for a moment. I need to speak with Rowen."

"Yes, Captain," Lady Astrea steered her horse away.

Rowen grabbed her saddle and swung her leg around to dismount. A pair of hands grasped her by the middle and helped her down from her horse.

"What happened?" Lore said, removing his hands. Rowen turned around. She could see creases of worry across his forehead.

"I blacked out for a moment." And more, but she wasn't ready to tell Lore that. She was still trying to work it out herself.

He stared at her, searching her face.

Heat filled her cheeks. Lore thought something was wrong with her, Rowen realized, staring up into his grey eyes. Wait . . . *grey* eyes? Weren't his eyes green?

"Rowen, I need you to tell me the truth. Can you handle your duties as Lady Astrea's varor during this trip or not?"

Rowen took a moment to assess her mind and body. She felt normal again. No visions, no words, no blackout. Just fatigue. "Yes." She looked back up into his face. "I'm fine now."

Lore sighed and rubbed the back of his neck. "Well, then, you're free to return to Lady Astrea. But the moment you feel . . . anything . . . you need to let me know."

"Yes, Captain."

Lore looked like he was going to say more. Instead he motioned toward Lady Astrea. "You are free to go."

"Yes, Captain." Rowen grabbed her pack from her horse and quickly moved toward Lady Astrea, who stood waiting beside the double doors. She hoped that whatever had caused her to black out would not happen again.

• • •

Lore watched Rowen cross the courtyard, wondering if he had made the right decision. There had been a moment when he'd almost demanded that Rowen see a healer, but he instantly realized it would not be Captain Lore requesting this, but the man Lore. And that had stayed his tongue.

He watched the two women enter the castle. His feelings for Rowen were starting to affect his decisions as her captain. That worried him. Never had a woman distracted him so much.

Lore grabbed his pack and headed inside the castle. Three halls diverged from the main hall. He went right, following the sand colored walls. Intersecting circles were carved into white molding that followed the ceiling. Marble floors flecked with rose and gold veins twinkled beneath silver candelabras. A hint of rose hung in the air.

Rowen was off limits, Lore reminded himself. She was under his command as Lady Astrea's varor. And, as far as he knew, she was not a Follower of the Word. A bonding between them would be in body and heart only, but never in spirit.

Lore shifted his pack across his shoulders. A partial bonding would eventually tear them apart. He had seen it happen before. Besides—he ran a hand through his hair—would Rowen want a man like him? A man fifteen years her senior or more?

Lore dropped his hand and sighed. As much as his heart desired Rowen, there were things far worse than loving a woman from afar.

But his heart twisted in hope just the same.

CHAPTER
18

Lore stood in front of Lord Gaynor's guest quarters in Avonai the following day. Guard duty was not one of his usual jobs, but Lord Gaynor needed time alone to prepare for that evening, and, having just dismissed Aren and Justus, Lore found himself the only varor on duty.

He rolled his shoulders, then his neck, hearing his joints pop as he did so. He shifted his legs. Anyone who thought the job of Captain of the Guard was glamorous never had to stand and guard a door for any length of time. It made him appreciate all the more the guards who did this on a daily basis back at Celestis Castle.

He studied the circles carved into the white molding along the ceiling. Each circle interconnected and looked almost at if it were a seamless, curving, neverending line. Then he looked down at the marble floor and wondered how such rock formed, with gold- and rose-colored veins. He knew the special marble was found only in Nordica and had been brought here over a hundred years ago.

Lore looked at the beige wall, then glanced out the window. The sky looked subdued. Grey clouds were scattered across a dull blue sky. No changes today. The sea seemed content to stay calm.

Footsteps sounded down the hall. Lore reached for the hilt of his sword. A courier dressed in dark blue hurried down the hall. A courier from the White City. Lore frowned. What could possibly bring a courier here during this crucial treaty signing?

"Captain Lore," the courier said upon reaching him.

"Aiden," Lore replied, recognizing the young man.

Aiden still wore his riding cloak, and mud was splattered across his boots and pants. "I need to speak with Lord Gaynor."

Lore didn't like the somber look on Aiden's face. And the fact the young man hadn't even taken the time to make himself presentable meant the message was urgent. "I will let Lord Gaynor know you are here." Lore turned and opened the door.

Inside, Lore found Lord Gaynor standing at the far end of the room, gazing out a large window that overlooked the sea. A fire burned in the hearth nearby. Two matching chairs covered in a light blue brocade sat in a semicircle around the fireplace. A low table stood between them.

"Lord Gaynor." Lore took a step inside.

Lord Gaynor turned around. "What is it, Lore?"

"Aiden has come from the White City."

Lord Gaynor frowned. "Send him in."

Lore nodded and turned back toward the door. Moments later he followed Aiden back in.

"Lord Gaynor," Aiden said with a bow. "Commander Kelyn sent me here with all haste to tell you that the Temanin army is mobilizing. A spy was caught a few days ago, and from him we learned that the expected assault will fall upon . . ." Aiden paused and swallowed . . . "the White City."

Lord Gaynor's face blanched. He moved toward one of the chairs and grasped the back. "So Temanin is finally making its move on the White City." He sighed. "And I'm stuck here in Avonai."

The room remained silent. Lord Gaynor stared into the fire. Then he pulled himself to his full height and turned toward the men. "Aiden, I'm afraid I must ask you to ride back right away. Tell Commander Kelyn we are returning. We will leave tonight, after we sign the treaty."

"Yes, milord." Aiden gave a hasty bow, then left.

Lore moved toward the door and shut it with a quiet click. Lord Gaynor stared at the fire. Lore crossed the room and stood by his side. "So it has begun," Lore said, breaking the silence between them.

"Yes. I never thought I'd live to see the day." The fire crackled and spit as a log collapsed within the bright blaze. "Lore," Lord Gaynor said a moment later.

"Yes, milord?"

"I know you are a man of the Word. I've never been one myself, but I guess times like these can change anyone. And so I'm asking you to . . . to pray for our city."

"Milord," Lore said quietly, "I already am."

Lore stood at one of the side doors inside the audience chamber and watched the dignitaries and nobility gather to watch the treaty signing between Avonai and the White City.

The chamber was large enough to accommodate over a hundred people. Men and women crowded inside, standing between the two stout pillars that held the high ceiling up. Their voices echoed across the room, bouncing off walls covered in blue and green tapestries. He could hear the excitement in the air.

A platform stood at the front of the room with a table set in the middle. On top lay a white linen cloth and piece of parchment upon which the terms of the treaty had been written out in black ink. Behind the platform were five windows, each reaching from floor to ceiling. They gave a panoramic view of the Illyr Sea. The sky looked like the inside of a conch shell: a mixture of grey and blue and pinks. A wispy fog lay across the sea. The evening star twinkled just above the horizon.

Lore turned his attention back onto the crowd. He knew it would be even more chaotic if the people knew of the impending attack on the White City. Lord Gaynor's choice to keep the attack silent had been a prudent one.

After a couple of minutes, the doors on his right and left opened up. Lord Gaynor entered on his right just as King Alaric entered from the left. Both men were dressed in their city's colors: Lord Gaynor in the dark blues of the White City and King Alaric in deep sea green. King Alaric held the arm of what looked like his manservant.

Lore did a double take at King Alaric. The ruler looked twice as old as the last time Lore had seen him. His hair had gone from long grey locks to a wispy white. Had his madness done this too him? Pity filled his heart, pity for King Alaric, for his son Prince Evander, and for the people who did not know of their ruler's ailment.

Prince Evander followed his father. He was dressed in the same deep sea green, and he wore his crown on his head. Two varors came to stand behind him. Lady Astrea entered from the other side of the room. Her dark hair hung loose around her shoulders, and her silver circlet was set on top. Rowen and Aren followed her in. Both of them stood behind Lady Astrea.

Lore's eyes lingered on Rowen. Her pale hair was pulled back in a long braid that hung over her shoulder. Her tabard made her eyes look deep blue. She began to scan the room and caught sight of him. She gave him a small smile and then went back to scanning.

Lord Gaynor stepped onto the platform. King Alaric followed, assisted by his manservant. The room hushed. Both men made their way to the table. Lord Gaynor reached for the parchment, but King Alaric reeled forward and snatched the paper up.

The crowd shifted uncomfortably. Lore felt his own face grow warm at King Alaric's actions. Lord Gaynor stepped graciously back and clasped his hands together.

King Alaric began to read it aloud. His voice was high and shrill. His face looked eager, almost hungry. Lore looked at Prince Evander. The prince stood stiffly, his eyes on his father. He wondered how the prince was feeling.

Lore turned away and listened with half an ear, his eyes darting across the crowd, watching for any danger.

It was a simple treaty, short and to the point. King Alaric finished, then placed the parchment down. "Anyone opposing the treaty, speak now."

No one spoke.

"Then let it be done."

Lord Gaynor stepped forward. Both men signed the treaty and placed their signet rings in the cooling wax. A small murmur rose from the crowd, but quickly hushed as Lady Astrea and Prince Evander approached the table.

MORGAN L. BUSSE

"As part of the treaty," King Alaric said, that same eager, hungry look on his face, "our two families have chosen to align by bonding."

Lore watched Lord Gaynor pale slightly, the only indication that the high lord was distressed. Lady Astrea stood beside her father, a faint blush creeping along her cheeks.

King Alaric spoke excitedly about the bonding that would take place later between the two young people, the shrill in his voice even higher now. Lore winced and went back to watching the crowd. He began to feel on edge. Those premonitions of doom he had first felt when traveling to Avonai were coming back tenfold. He had the urge to clear the building and conduct the rest of the ceremony in a more secure location.

Something was wrong. He could feel it. Perhaps it was only the news they had just received an hour before. Or perhaps he just felt uncomfortable with the whole ceremony. He could tell Lord Gaynor was. But whatever the reason, his vigilance refused to stand down.

The couple before him removed their crowns. Lady Astrea lifted from her head the silver circlet that was the symbol of her status as lady of the White City, then handed it to her betrothed. Prince Evander did the same with his crown. The exchange was a symbol of the joining of the two countries, and each would keep the other's crown until the day of their bonding.

Lord Gaynor stepped forward and spoke over the couple, and then it was over.

The room filled with noise. The crowd discussed both the treaty and the future bonding of Prince Evander and Lady Astrea.

Lore moved along the wall and up the platform to Lord Gaynor's side. Lord Gaynor whispered to his daughter. Lady Astrea nodded, then turned back to Prince Evander. Rowen and Lady Astrea had already been alerted to the change in travel plans. Lord Gaynor would be leaving within the hour for the White City. And Lady Astrea would stay here in Avonai, for her own protection.

"Come, Lore, let us finish up and head out," Lord Gaynor said, moving toward the side door. Justus, Lord Gaynor's other varor, joined them as they left the audience chamber. Aren would stay behind and help Rowen guard Lady Astrea.

They followed the side hall toward the guest quarters. Lore rubbed the back of his neck. He could feel his body already protesting the thought of a long night's ride. And at the edge of his senses, he could feel a storm brewing out at sea, not close enough to mess with his emotions, but enough to warn him it was coming.

Once they reached Lord Gaynor's rooms, Justus walked in first and performed a quick sweep of the sitting room. Lore went to join him when Lord Gaynor stopped him just outside the doorway.

"Lore, a moment, please."

Lore turned back, puzzled. "Of course, milord."

"Watching my daughter tonight and signing that treaty made me realize how much has happened over the last few years. We are at war now, fighting for our lives. And Astrea—" a soft smile spread across Lord Gaynor's face— "my little star, has grown up." Then he frowned. "And having to learn the sacrifices of being a leader." Lord Gaynor grew quiet.

Lore waited.

"Anyway, all that is to say," Lord Gaynor looked back at Lore, "that you have been a constant in my life ever since your father passed away sixteen years ago. I can count on you, Lore, unlike any other man I know. You are a man of integrity and trust. I don't know what we're going to face when we return to the White City. Or what's going to happen. But I wanted to let you know that I appreciate your service to my family and me. No ruler could ask for a better captain. Thank you, Lore."

Lore nodded, deeply touched. "It has ever been my pleasure to serve you, milord."

"Now we should get going."

"Yes, milord. Let me finish checking your room."

Lore entered the guest quarters. He passed by the nearest door and saw Justus checking the bedroom. He moved across the sitting room, giving the room another look. The fire in the fireplace had burned down to glowing embers. The chairs and table were untouched. Out of the corner of his eye, he saw Lord Gaynor enter the room. Lore headed toward the balcony. He pushed open the glass doors and stepped outside.

Darkness filled the night sky. Stars twinkled high above. A pale moon peeked just above the sea, barely shedding light on the balcony. Lore searched around, but found nothing.

He took a moment and leaned over the balcony's edge. Waves lapped the rocks and sand below, their crests white in the moonlight. Toward the north, he could feel the storm gathering. Lore rubbed his chest, feeling his blood already moving with the tempest. It was a big one. Hopefully they would stay ahead of it.

He dropped his hand and turned. A shadow moved out of the corner of his eye—

Excruciating pain filled his middle. He felt something twist just above his hip. Lore gasped and caught himself on the outer wall. A man stepped around him.

Lore slid to the balcony, barely able to breathe. He reached with his hand and felt his side. Warm, sticky blood flowed freely from his wound, just below his jerkin. Lore sucked in a painful breath and looked up. He saw the back of the assassin. Then metal flashed as something sailed toward Lord Gaynor, who was standing near the fireplace.

No! Lore choked. Another wave of agony tore through his body. His eyes misted over. Blinking, he saw Lord Gaynor step back, the dagger quivering from his throat. The high lord clawed at his neck, tugging weakly at the blade.

Justus came racing out from the far room. Lord Gaynor collapsed onto the floor and lay still.

Justus drew his sword and engaged the assassin. The assassin pulled another knife from the sheath at his side.

All Lore could do was watch. The attacker was dressed all in black with dark hair and olive-toned skin. One word slammed into Lore's mind: Temanin.

Justus swung his sword. The assassin evaded the blow with lightning agility. Lore had never seen a person move like that. Each move fluidic and fast. Like a dancer. A deadly dancer.

Lore dragged himself across the floor. The movement jolted his side. He cringed, feeling as though his insides were falling out. He reached the glass doors and pulled himself up with one arm. His other arm cradled his bleeding side.

Inside, the assassin stumbled over the small table that lay between the two chairs, giving Justus a chance to strike. Justus swung his sword in a tight, controlled arc.

The assassin was too quick. He rolled to the side just as Justus's blade came down. The table cracked under Justus's blade.

The assassin came up from a tucked roll nearby.

Lore saw the glint of metal before it went flying. With sickening knowledge, he knew the assassin had struck again.

Justus twisted away, the edge of the assassin's blade quivering just above his collarbone, then fell to the floor with a thud.

In that moment, something snapped inside Lore. He knew he was injured, could feel the pain radiating throughout his entire body. But the sensation dimmed under a new kind of hurt: grief. With a roar of anguish, Lore drew his sword and rushed toward the assassin.

The assassin looked up in surprise.

Lore swung his sword with all his might at the assassin, all skill and finesse gone. His hands were now guided by rage and guilt.

The assassin scrambled to the side and shoved a chair in Lore's direction.

Lore sidestepped the obstacle and kept advancing toward the man. For the first time in his life he felt such rage that he could kill a man with no remorse and had every intention to this evening.

With another swing of his sword, Lore grazed the assassin across the chest.

The man grunted in pain and dove to the side and rolled a couple feet. Lore followed him.

The assassin hurled himself across the table in a feat of acrobatics, his legs arcing over his head as his hands touched down on the table. The table groaned beneath the man's weight.

Lore began to go around the table when he felt his strength finally leave him. He could no longer keep up the fight.

Sensing that as well, the assassin sprinted past Lore, dodging his final swing, and escaped out the balcony doors.

Lore tried to turn, but fell to the floor instead. He had lost too much blood. And now the murderer of his lord had escaped.

Lore lay where he had fallen, each breath a painful reminder that he was still alive. Ahead of him he could see Lord Gaynor, a pool of blood beneath his head and a look of shock still etched across his face. Lore closed his eyes to the vision, but it continued to dance behind his eyelids, taunting him of his failure.

Lore grunted and slowly twisted his body, trying to get away from the view. He fell back onto the floor with another groan.

Oh, Word, why? He cried out in his mind. *Why did you let this happen?*

The silence around him gave him no answer. Lore lay his head down on the floor, the feeling of guilt overwhelming him. It was his fault. He should have seen the assassin hiding in the shadows.

Lore closed his eyes. He could feel his body slowly slipping toward unconsciousness. Perhaps he would die. He welcomed that thought. Then he could atone for his failure.

Just as the darkness closed in, Lore heard a voice call his name. Opening one eye, he saw Aren rush toward him.

"Captain, you're alive!"

Lore tried to say something, but found his mouth would not work. Ignoring the gesture, Aren pulled him to his feet.

Fresh waves of pain rushed through his body. Lore cried out, clutching his side with his free hand.

"We've got to get you out of here, Captain." Aren gently placed Lore's arm over his shoulder and started toward the door.

Lore merely nodded his head, the darkness coming back.

Caleb sucked in another painful gasp and scrambled down the rope that hung from the balcony. That was too close. A few more inches and he would have been lying up there alongside Lord Gaynor.

He jumped from the rope and landed on the white sand. The beach was clear, except for the massive boulders scattered across the shore. Dark waves lapped the sand a couple feet away. The moon lit up the beach with pale light.

Caleb glanced down. His shirt was torn and a long gash spread across his chest. Luckily it was only a flesh wound, but it hurt like a hot poker pressed against his skin.

He grabbed the pack he had stowed between two large boulders near the base of the cliffs and took off at a run toward the port side of Avonai. He stayed near the water's edge so the incoming waves could wash away his footprints.

Other than this minor setback, the mission had been a success. He wondered how the others had fared. Had his men been able to get King Alaric?

Caleb dodged another scattering of rocks along the beach, each of them big enough to look as if a giant had tossed them up from the sea. Ahead, he could see the twinkle of lights from the waterfront. Slowing down, he took more careful steps. No use being caught now. There was still much to be done.

He used the shadows to conceal his movement and made his way to the docks. Caleb ducked behind a couple of large wooden crates and changed out of his black clothes and into his sailor's outfit. He stuffed the dark clothing back into his pack, then sauntered out onto the wooden walkway, looking like a newly landed seadog.

No one paid any attention to him. It seemed that no one really paid attention to anyone here on the pier. Making his way across the waterfront, Caleb kept his pace slow and even, throwing in a few awkward steps now and then to give the appearance of being slightly inebriated. Once he reached the other side of the waterfront, he did a quick glance either way then slipped through the bushes back up the hill. The moon lit his path.

Caleb reached the top and bypassed where his team had made camp and went farther in, toward a small field where their horses waited, hidden from view by the abundance of ferns and brush that grew along the coast. He grabbed the gear stored away under the brush and began saddling the horses. As soon as the other men arrived, they would leave.

Caleb cinched the last pack on. Satisfied, he quietly made his way back toward the short cliff to watch. An uneasy feeling began to settle in his middle. The other men should have been here by now. He dropped to his belly and looked over the edge. There was something going on down on the pier.

Suddenly someone scrambled up beside him. "Lord Tala?" Daleth whispered.

"Right here," Caleb said, his voice barely audible.

"We've been followed."

Avonain guards scurried across the boardwalk. Caleb thought he saw one of his men being dragged away toward the city. Two guards were talking to a woman near the crates. She pointed up the hill toward where he and Daleth lay hidden. About five guards started making their way through the thick brush and up the hill.

Caleb cursed under his breath. Time to go.

"What should we do?" Daleth whispered.

"We leave." Caleb began to back away from the cliff.

Daleth looked at him and balked. "We're leaving the others behind?"

"They knew the risks." Caleb stood. "If you want to live, follow me."

Daleth hesitated. Caleb left him behind, ducking beneath tree branches and dodging the low-lying brush. If Daleth wanted to stay behind and die with his friends, so be it. As for himself, Caleb desired to live another day.

He reached the field and went for the closest horse. He grabbed the saddle and heaved himself up. The wound across his chest shifted. He winced and gritted his teeth. Caleb glanced back toward the hill to find Daleth racing toward one of the other mounts.

"Come on," Caleb said angrily. Daleth scrambled over the brush. He turned and grabbed the reins. Every moment that ticked by brought the Avonain guards closer.

Daleth leaped onto the horse and brought it about. Unwilling to wait any longer, Caleb gave his horse a kick and went galloping into the trees. Shouts filled the air behind him.

Suddenly a scream sounded behind him. Caleb turned. Daleth toppled off his horse with long thin rod sticking through his body. Caleb urged his horse to go faster, his heart thudding to the beat of the horse's hooves.

Shadows whipped by overhead. He tried to see into the dark forest. An arrow flew by, filling his mouth with the bitter taste of fear.

Caleb pressed his body down close to the horse. He could still hear the Avonain guards shouting behind him, but the sound grew dim as he raced beneath trees and moonlight. An arrow grazed his upper arm. Caleb clenched his teeth and rode on.

Minutes later, all he could hear was the pounding of his own horse's hooves across dirt, moss, and leaves. Caleb twisted his head and looked back. Nothing but shadows. He let out his breath in one long sigh. He had escaped.

Caleb rode hard for a couple more minutes, then slowed his horse and let it pick its way between the trees. The dark forest swayed and moaned with the wind. Pale patches of moonlight poked through the branches. The air grew chillier by the minute.

Caleb reached around to his pack and felt inside for a blanket. He pulled it out and wrapped it around his body. He watched the branches move and felt unease spread across his body.

Only he had escaped.

Not my fault, Caleb countered.

But deep inside, he knew the truth. The next time he slept, Daleth and the other men he had left behind would visit him in his dreams.

There, they would haunt him.

And make sure he never forgot that he'd considered his life above their own.

CHAPTER 19

Pound, pound.

Rowen turned to Lady Astrea. "Are you expecting someone?"

Lady Astrea sat in one of the two chairs near the fireplace in her guest room, a book in her hand. A large, ornate bed with green curtains stood against the other wall with a white wardrobe next to it. She looked up. "No."

"You didn't ring for a servant? Are you expecting a message?"

"No."

Rowen placed her hand on her sword and approached the door. "Who is it?" she called out.

"Aren," came the muffled reply.

It *sounded* like Aren. But Rowen wasn't going to take any chances. She drew her sword. "Get back," she said to Lady Astrea, motioning behind her.

Lady Astrea stood and moved to the far side of the bed.

The door rattled again. Rowen unlocked the door and opened it a crack.

Aren stood in the hallway, a worried look across his face.

"Aren," Rowen said, opening the door wider, "I thought you were going to—"

"We need to get Lady Astrea out of here!"

Rowen stepped back and let Aren in. "What do you mean? What's going on?"

"I'll tell you on the way out." There was a frantic look on his face. "We need to go now."

Another figure stepped into the doorway. Rowen spun around and focused her blade on the man. "Who are you and what are you doing—"

"Traver?" Aren said behind her. "What are you doing here?"

"Assassins have infiltrated the castle," Traver said. "Dressed as our guards. Prince Evander sent me to see Lady Astrea safely away from the city."

"*What?*" Rowen took a step back, but kept her blade trained on the tall Avonain. He started to move through the doorway. "Not one more step," she said.

A hand settled across her arm. "It's all right, Rowen," Aren said. "Traver is on our side."

"You sure?" Rowen quickly glanced at Aren.

"Yes."

Rowen hesitated, then lowered her blade.

Traver walked in. "My lady," he said, looking past Rowen, "Prince Evander sent me to escort you away from Avonai—"

"I know." Lady Astrea came to stand beside Rowen. "I heard you."

"Then you know the danger you are in and that we need to leave immediately."

"Yes. But what about my father?"

"I'm heading to his room right now," Aren said. "I'll make sure Lord Gaynor and the others make it out."

"We're heading out the back way." Traver looked at Aren. "There is a small exit inside the storeroom I showed you. We'll watch for you on the beach."

Aren nodded and left.

Lady Astrea snatched her cloak from the wardrobe. There was no time to change. Rowen did the same with her own cloak. Her stomach coiling inside her. She had saved Lady Astrea once. Could she do it again?

Lady Astrea stepped up beside Traver. "Lead the way."

Traver nodded.

"I'll take the rear," Rowen said. She saw her pack slumped in the corner and grabbed it too.

Traver turned and walked out the door, Lady Astrea and Rowen following.

Cheery candles flickered in silver sconces, a direct contrast to the deathly quiet that filled the empty hallway. Their boots slapped the marble floor, breaking up the silence. Rowen stayed close to Lady Astrea. Traver led them down the corridor and a set of stairs.

As they turned a corner, Traver halted. Rowen heard Lady Astrea suck in her breath. Peering around the two, she saw bodies littering the hall, their blood pooling across the marble floor. Rowen clenched her sword and felt sick. How could someone do this? These men had families, children, *wives* who were now bereft of a loved one. And for what? War. A war she did not understand.

"Wait here." Traver carefully made his way through the bodies to the other side.

Rowen moved to place herself in front of Lady Astrea, her hand ready with her sword.

Traver disappeared around the corner. They waited. Moments later, he reappeared. "The rest of the way is clear," he said.

Rowen led Lady Astrea around the bodies, careful to keep her head high and gaze away from their lifeless eyes. Once they reached Traver, they hurried on.

At the bottom of a second set of stairs, Traver stopped and pulled out a set of keys. He chose one and placed it in the keyhole in the door to their right. The door unlocked with a soft click.

"Quick, this way." Traver held the door open. Rowen followed Lady Astrea into what looked like a storage room filled with barrels and crates. Traver grabbed one of the torches that hung in the hallway and handed it to Rowen. The door shut behind them with a muffled thud. In the dim light, Traver began to move the stack of crates nearby.

Lady Astrea stood in the middle of the room, her arms wrapped around her midsection. Rowen stood next to the door.

"There," Traver said. He picked up the last crate. Rowen could now see a dark gap in the wall where the crates had stood moments before. "This tunnel will lead us out near the sea's edge. From there, we will head toward Fiske, a small village north of here and find horses."

Traver took the torch from Rowen and headed in, followed by Lady Astrea and Rowen. They hurried along the dark passage. The earthy smell of dirt filled her nostrils, and her feet sunk slightly in the moist soil. Roots stuck out from the dirt wall. She could hear the dull roar of the sea ahead of her. After following the damp passage for over a minute, Traver stopped.

He opened a large wooden door. An earsplitting creak filled the tight space. Rowen winced at the sound, sure that everyone in Avonai could hear it. Traver stepped outside and held up long strands of dune grass growing overhead. Lady Astrea ducked beneath the grass. Rowen followed.

Outside, a blast of cold, salty air hit them. Rowen pulled her cloak tightly around her and moved to Lady Astrea's side. Traver put out the torch and rearranged the dune grass to once again conceal the door.

A full moon rose swiftly over the sea, lighting up the beach with pale light. Large black boulders the size of two-story houses stood along the shoreline and out in the sea. Tidal pools and dark clumps of sea vegetation lay scattered across the white sand. Behind them, Rowen could see the walls of Avonai and the castle perched on a high cliff.

"We'll wait for Aren and Lord Gaynor over there." Traver pointed toward an outcropping of rocks as tall as the city's walls. "The rocks will keep us out of view should anyone be keeping watch from the balconies above."

Lady Astrea nodded and clutched her cloak tightly to her body. The three of them hurried toward the rocks. Once there, Traver immediately took up a position where he could see the door. Lady Astrea moved farther in toward the back of the rock enclosure. Rowen followed.

They stood there shivering in the wet night air. Rowen closed her eyes. And, for the first time in her life, prayed.

• • •

"Here comes someone," Traver said quietly.

Lady Astrea leaned forward, eagerly looking toward the opening between the rocks. Rowen remained where she was, her sword ready if she should need it.

"It looks like . . . Aren," Traver said a moment later. "And he's helping someone." Traver stepped out from behind the rocks.

Rowen stepped toward the opening and looked out. It took only one glance to realize something was wrong. There should be four people: Lord Gaynor and his three varors. Where were the other two?

"Where's my father?" Lady Astrea whispered.

Suddenly Rowen realized she was right: It was not Lord Gaynor whom Aren was assisting—it was Lore.

Fear punched her in the stomach. Rowen stumbled away from the rocks and followed Lady Astrea across the beach. What had happened? Had the assassins— *No!* Rowen shook her head in an effort to clear away the shock. She needed to be focused. Here. Now.

Lady Astrea staggered toward the men, her voice beginning to rise. "Where's my *father?*"

Aren collapsed nearby, letting Lore's body fall across the sand.

"Lady Astrea!" Traver glanced back. "You need to calm down—"

"Where is he, Aren? *Where is my father?*"

Aren looked up at Lady Astrea. Rowen came to stand beside her. The usual twinkle in his eyes was gone. Instead dull eyes stared back. "He is dead, milady."

"No, No!" Lady Astrea screamed, staggering toward the concealed door beneath the dune grass. Traver grabbed a hold of her and held her. *"We need to go back and get him!"* she cried, fighting Traver's hold.

Lore moaned and began to thrash across the sand. Aren pinned him down and tried to calm him.

Lady Astrea's cry cut short. She turned back and stared down at Lore.

Rowen just stood there, frozen. Everything inside her had stopped—her breath, her mind, her heart. In the moonlight she could see a dark stain spreading rapidly beneath Lore and soaking into the sand. His leather jerkin lifted. Blood was smeared across his entire midsection.

Aren swore. He ripped off a long length of cloth from his shirt and immediately applied it to Lore's side. "You can't die on me, Captain," she heard him say through clenched teeth. "You can't die!"

Lore groaned, his head moving back and forth, eyes fluttering beneath their lids. Then he began to thrash again.

Rowen tried to move to help, but her body would not listen.

Traver let go of Lady Astrea and fell to his knees on the other side of Aren, pinning Lore down so Aren could wrap Lore's wound.

"We're losing him," Aren cried. He turned the bloody wad over and reapplied it. "He's losing too much blood!"

"No," Lady Astrea whispered, staring at Lore in shock.

Traver sighed. "There's nothing we can do for him." He looked up at Aren. "We need to let him go and get Lady Astrea away from here."

Aren's face twisted with fear and sorrow. "I won't leave him here to die."

Rowen watched the scene, paralyzed.

Balint's words drifted up from the back of her mind. *You can heal another.*

Lore stopped thrashing, his head slumping to the side. Aren swore and tore more of his shirt. Lady Astrea cried softly nearby.

You can heal him.

Rowen felt the warmth begin to fill her chest, swirling inside of her. Time slowed. With her eyes on Lore, she reached for her glove. Her hand trembled as it touched the leather fringe. Then she stopped.

It will cost you.

A stab of fear tore through the warmth. It would hurt—hurt unlike anything she had ever felt before. And if she did this, her secret would be out. There would be no going back. Everything she had done to keep her mark hidden will have been for nothing. And those around her might turn on her, like her village had. But if she didn't . . .

Rowen vacillated for one heartbeat, her body motionless as her mind worked feverishly. Lore groaned, his face unusually pale in the moonlight.

Suddenly she knew her answer.

The worn leather glove fell onto the white sand below.

Immediately the world came roaring back. Rowen fell to her knees beside Aren. The warmth inside her had already moved to her hand where it waited, the energy tingling within her palm.

Rowen reached across Lore's body and pulled Aren's hand away along with the bloody rag he had been holding down. He fought her, but her strength was too great.

"What are you doing, Rowen?" she heard Aren shout, but it was as if hearing through water. All her senses were centered on her palm.

Rowen held Aren back with her left hand and reached over with her right, her palm now pulsing with warm power. She heard a couple of gasps and knew they could see her palm glowing in the darkness. No time to think about that now.

She searched for the tear in Lore's shirt, then finding it, placed her hand inside where she could touch his skin. She felt the warm, slick feel of his blood. She searched further with her fingers until she found the gash in his side. It was so deep that Rowen almost retched.

She took a deep breath to clear the nausea. *Word, be with me.* With that, she pressed her palm on the wound.

The warmth flowed from her palm like a dam let loose. It surged down her arm and through her palm, eagerly entering Lore. She could almost feel the tendrils of warmth search his body, finding the place of pain. Then the energy slackened. The last of the warmth left her palm.

One heartbeat later, she felt a burning coldness enter her hand.

Rowen breathed harder. It was coming. The coldness rose steadily up her arm and down her side. She braced herself. But no amount of anticipation prepared her for the real thing.

Wave after wave of agony rushed over her body. Lore's wound was deep, and she could feel it penetrate her side, tearing muscle and rupturing organs. She tried to bite down a scream, but it escaped her lips.

"Oh, Word, help me—" Rowen wanted to let go, would do anything to let go. She panted, then tensed as another cold wave moved up her arm. "Can't give up, can't give up," she whispered, shutting her eyes. She pressed her hand firmly against Lore's side and braced for the next wave.

It slammed into her, knocking her breath right out of her chest. Rowen could hear shouting above her, but her senses were now dim under the constant barrage of pain. Darkness stretched across her eyes. She could not hold on much longer.

Please, Word, she prayed weakly, *let me finish.*

A feeling of peace rushed over her. She doubled over with pain again. Her hand slipped away from Lore's side. But somewhere inside she knew she had done enough. He would live.

Rowen collapsed across his body, unable to hold the darkness back any longer.

Lore felt warmth enter his body, filling him, chasing away the cold and darkness he had clung to moments before. And the light . . . It was the most beautiful thing he had ever seen. He wanted to reach out and touch it but found he could not lift his hand.

The light began to fade away.

No, Lore cried, trying to grasp it, to keep it inside of him. But like the waves of the sea, the warmth and light receded from his body, leaving him suddenly bare. Lore tried to take a breath, but there was something heavy across his chest. Voices were arguing above him. He cracked open his eyes—

And found a body lying across his chest.

"Ugh." He tried to move. The body above him shifted slightly. That hair, it looked so familiar—

Someone lifted the body off of him. Coughing again, Lore sat up, rubbing his chest. Then he tensed. His hand stole toward his right side, fingers feeling for where the assassin had buried his blade. There was still blood, but no pain. And underneath . . . smooth skin.

"Captain Lore, are you all right?" Lore turned and found a strange man looking at him. Wait . . . he recognized him—

"Traver," the man said, "my name is Traver, Prince Evander's varor."

"What h-happened?"

"She's bleeding heavily," Aren shouted nearby. "I can't stop it! I don't understand. She wasn't injured at all. Or did we not see it?"

Lore felt like his world was spinning. Traver hurdled past him. Lore gripped his head and shook it. What in all the Lands was going on?

Aren swore. "Not her. Please, not Rowen . . ."

Lore's head jerked up. Rowen? He twisted around. Traver and Aren crouched around a body. Rowen. Lying on the sand.

What in all the Lands? Lore turned and scrambled toward her body. "What happened?" he cried. "Why is she like this? Wha—"

"She healed you."

"What?" Lore found Lady Astrea kneeling next to him.

Her eyes were swollen with tears still seeping from the corners.

"How— Never mind." There was no time for questions. Lore ripped off his leather jerkin and threw it to the side. He looked down and found half of his shirt stained with blood. He grabbed hold of the left side and tore a long strip off. "Hold that rag in place," he told Aren.

Lore began to wrap the long piece of cloth around Rowen's middle. *Oh, Word, I can't do this*, he panted. He tied off the end of the cloth, hoping it would staunch the wound until he could get her to a healer. *Not after Lord Gaynor. I can't handle another death.*

"Captain, wait," Aren said. "You're in no shape to—"

But Lore was already gathering Rowen into his arms. He needed to get her to a healer, now! He stood, clutching Rowen close to his body. He turned and looked around. Boulders, sea, sand. Where was he? He looked behind and saw the high walls and castle of Avonai. There. He started across the beach.

A hand grabbed his arm. "Captain," Aren said, "we can't take her back to Avonai."

"Why not?" Time was running out, he had to do something.

"There are assassins all over the palace. And we have no idea if there are more throughout the city."

There was more than one assassin? Lore stopped, his mind churning.

"We need to go north," Traver said. "There is a healer—"

"Fiske is too far away," Lore said, his mind now taking charge over his emotions. "How did this happen? How did Rowen get hurt?" He needed to know how bad the situation was.

"She healed you," Lady Astrea said again.

"How? No one can . . ." Wait. A chill ran down his spine. She couldn't be—

"She's an Eldaran," Aren answered. "It's the only explanation."

"But that's impossible," Lore said with a shake his head. "They don't exist anymore. Perhaps you did not see her injured—"

"We watched her heal you. I wouldn't have believed it if I hadn't seen it myself. Her hand *glowed*."

Lore stood there, holding the one woman he loved in the world, and watching her slowly die in his arms. To find out she had sacrificed herself for him . . . that she was an Eldaran. A Daughter of Light.

If that were true . . . then Rowen had a chance to live. If she were truly an Eldaran, she could heal herself. Suddenly Balint's words after the wolf attack came back. The Word healed her, Balint had said. The old healer was right. The gift of healing the Word had given to every Eldaran had healed her. So in a sense, the Word *had* healed her.

And now she could heal herself again. All she needed was time. If he could just find a place for her to rest.

Voices echoed across the beach.

Traver looked across the sand. "We have to go now."

"But what about Rowen?" Lady Astrea asked.

"We need to get you safely back to the White City, milady, now that . . . I mean, we can't—"

"I'll take her." Everyone turned to look at Lore. "If we drag

Rowen to Fiske or the White City, she will bleed out. But if we let her rest, she might be able to heal herself." Lore swallowed. He knew exactly how close she was to death at the moment. "So I will take Rowen to a safe place. That is, if you will allow me temporary leave, Lady Astrea. You are, after all, now the ruler of the Ryland Plains."

Lady Astrea looked puzzled for a moment. Then her face fell. Lore knew she now understood that she was in charge.

Lady Astrea straightened her shoulders and lifted her chin just slightly. "Permission granted, Captain Lore."

So like her father, Lore suddenly realized. And the gut-wrenching sense of guilt ripped through him again. Lore swallowed and turned to Aren. "You are Lady Astrea's varor now. Guard her with your life."

"You know I will, Captain." Aren held out a pack. "This is Rowen's."

Lore took the pack.

"Good luck. And . . ." Aren hesitated. "And return Rowen to us. Yourself too." Aren glanced once more at Rowen, then moved to where Traver and Lady Astrea were waiting.

The three of them turned and moved toward a narrow gap between two large rocks. Moments later, they were gone.

Lore knew where they were heading. There was a small trail nearby that led up to the trees that grew along the edge of the coast. A few miles north, and they would arrive in Fiske. But that was not where *he* was going.

Lore readjusted his grip on Rowen and moved in the opposite direction. There was a cave near here, an old childhood haunt that he had played in summers ago when his mother would bring him here to the coast to visit her people.

Now perhaps it would keep them safe, at least until Rowen healed.

CHAPTER
20

Lore made his way across the sand, then cut across to where the dune grass grew thicker. He could feel the storm moving in, the sea's tumultuous waves tugging at his emotions. He was in for a rough night.

Rowen moaned once in his arms, shaking her head. Then her head fell back against his chest. Lore gripped her tighter, pushing his legs to move faster.

The farther he went, the heavier she became, along with the added weight of her pack on his back. At least this time, he wasn't having to run while carrying her. And the physical labor kept his mind from revisiting the events of earlier that evening.

Lore trudged on ahead until the dune grass gave way to a large rocky hill beyond. Bushes and moss were scattered across the mound with a single gnarled tree at the top. Lore moved toward two overgrown bushes he recognized. He held Rowen tightly to his body and swept back the branches to reveal a small dark entrance. He let out a sigh of relief. There had been no collapse, and he had correctly remembered the location. The cave was still there.

He carefully placed Rowen down outside the cave entrance and began to rummage through her pack for a flint stone to light a torch. He found the small stone and searched for a long piece of driftwood. He spotted one nearby and, after tearing more of his shirt away to wrap around its end, he lit the torch.

Lore glanced at Rowen. She lay still on the ground, pale in the moonlight. A sudden chill rose up from the sea, and he felt another one of the sea's moods sweep over him.

The storm was closer now. Lore glanced out over the water. The sea looked like white froth in the moonlight. He could hear the waves crashing across the shore. Lightning flashed in the distance. A gust of wind slammed into the hill, shaking the bushes and bending the tree.

Moving quickly, Lore entered the small cavern. In his mind he was instantly taken back to when he used to come here as a boy. Ahead was a small room with a high ceiling. The ground was uneven with rocks and sand spread across its floor. Two boulders the size of tables stood against the far wall. Not much else was in here. It would do as temporary shelter.

He wedged his torch between the two boulders and went back out to retrieve Rowen. He gently lifted her up again and moved her inside. A loud clap of thunder echoed across the cave. The storm was moving in more quickly than he had anticipated. He found a flat spot amongst the jagged ground and carefully placed her down. Then he went back out for the pack.

At least we made it to the cave, Lore thought, grabbing the pack and a couple of pieces of driftwood. He hurried back inside. The wind howled through the opening. Lore dropped the driftwood near one of the walls and moved toward Rowen. Another chill raced through the cave, causing him to shiver. With only a half ripped shirt on, there wasn't enough on him to ward off the cool air.

With shaky hands, he opened Rowen's pack. Inside he found two thin blankets, one extra set of clothes, a water skin, and dried food wrapped in cheesecloth. Lore took the clothes and rolled them into a bundle. He placed the bundle under Rowen's head. She groaned and tilted her head to the side.

Lore moved to place the blanket over her and stopped. He hadn't checked her wound recently. Placing the blanket down, Lore moved to her other side and carefully unwrapped the long piece of cloth he had tied around her midsection. He lifted the bloody wad of cloth away and found blood caked along her side. He reached over and grabbed the water skin. He moistened his finger with a drop of water and wiped away the scarlet fluid. Underneath, he found nothing. Rowen had already healed herself.

Lore stared at the spot in amazement, his finger running over the narrow scar that lay lengthwise across her side. He had grown up hearing stories of the Eldarans, how they had fought alongside the Word during the Great Battle. Then afterward, some had chosen to stay in the Lands. They had traded their ethereal bodies for flesh in order to continue their protection of mankind. But they had been stories, history, not something he had ever expected to see in his lifetime.

His eyes followed the curve of her side, his hand at the narrow part of her waist. Such beautiful, flawless skin—

Lore yanked back his hand and covered her side up with her shirt. He had no business going there, not when Rowen was unconscious, and not when she did not belong to him. He grabbed one of the blankets and tucked it around her body instead.

As he placed the last edge of the blanket around her neck, he looked down at her face. That Rowen was an Eldaran was astonishing. But there was more to it than that. Not even an Eldaran would necessarily take on such a mortal wound as his. Why had she done it? Why had she healed him? He had been both ready and eager to die.

"Why, Rowen?" Lore whispered.

His memories flashed back to the fallen bodies of Lord Gaynor and Justus. Guilt wrapped itself around his heart, choking out any other feelings. He had failed them.

Lore stood and moved across the cave. He could feel his blood starting to stir. Another peal of thunder echoed across the cave. Outside, the rain began to fall.

He grabbed the driftwood and placed it in the center of the small room. He looked around and found bits of windblown debris lodged under the rocks or piled up in the corners. He stuffed the kindling under the driftwood. After striking the flint twice, a spark fell. The tiny flame spread across the dead grass and leaves.

Lore moved back to Rowen's side and stared at the fire. It made its way up and around the driftwood, casting shadows across the jagged stone walls.

The rain fell harder. But he knew the full storm wasn't here, not yet. He rubbed his arms. He did not look forward to when it arrived.

Dark thoughts slowly entered his mind, thoughts of death and despair. For a moment Lore wished he had died. But then he would glance down at the woman who had almost given her life to save his. That reminder brought shame to him, and he ventured to those thoughts no more.

But the guilt remained. For what she had done for him. For how he had failed Lord Gaynor. And he could not run away from it. Lore ran a shaky hand through his hair, wishing there was some way he could rid himself of the feeling. And it did not help that as the storm approached, it intensified his emotions.

"Word, why did you . . . ?" Lore stared at his hands. Why? Why . . . ? His head dropped. He could not finish the thought.

Eventually he laid down an arm's length away from Rowen. He was beyond exhaustion, but his mind would not let him go. He had experienced many dark moments in his life, but this was by far the darkest. It seemed dawn would never come again. Even words of prayer ceased to enter his mind.

Lightning lit up the cave, followed by a clap of thunder. Lore stared at Rowen. He reached over and pulled the blanket slightly aside, exposing her left hand. Gently he touched her fingertips.

Lore relaxed at her touch. He kept his hand next to hers and watched the fire burn. Then slowly he closed his eyes and gave in to his exhaustion.

Lore woke up with a shudder. The storm outside was in full rage, churning the air and pelting the outside with hail. His own heart raced in tempo with the wind. Pulling the blanket tightly around his neck, he felt his fingers trembling. His blood boiled with the agitation of the sea.

This is bad, Lore thought. Another shudder passed through his body. Sleep now driven from his mind, he sat up and began to rub his aching arms. His sea blood sped through his body. As a boy, his mother would do this, singing softly as she rubbed away the storm.

Now he fought his sea blood alone.

The fire quietly burned in the middle of the room. Lore turned and studied Rowen in the dark. She lay unconscious, her chest barely rising and falling. Her eyes were tightly shut.

Lore pulled one hand away and reached over and touched her cheek. It was cold, colder than it should be. He frowned. He felt along her cheek and along her jaw. Her skin was frigid to the touch. *Was this a normal part of Eldaran healing?* Lore felt her neck and hands. Both were chilled. He had no idea.

Concerned, Lore tore his blanket away and draped it over her body. The chill in the cave air barely touched his skin, his blood now hot from the storm raging through his body.

He pulled Rowen up to a sitting position and hugged her to himself. He kept her covered by both blankets. Her head lulled across his chest. Lore placed his legs on either side of her and began to rub her arms.

"Come on, Rowen," Lore said quietly, his hands tingling with the friction. "Whatever this is, pull through." Another flash of lightning brightened the cave, followed by a resounding boom. Lore shuddered under the effects. His body hurt, and fatigue ate away at what little energy he had.

After the tremor passed, he touched her face. Her skin still felt like ice beneath his fingers. Fear gripped his heart. Lore rubbed her arms again, willing his warmth to seep through to her. "Come on, Rowen. Fight this!"

Moments later, another shudder rippled through his body, this time so strongly that Lore hunched over and stopped. "Word, help me," he whispered. Never had a storm hurt this bad, and just when he needed his mind and strength to help Rowen. "Help me, I can't do this alone."

Lore pulled himself back up. His throat felt tight, and his body ached. He began rubbing her arms again. He fought against the next shudder. Sweat broke out across his forehead and body. He did everything he could to help her, warm her.

Only, nothing seemed to be working. A few minutes later, Lore felt for the pulse in her neck and found a weak throb.

Lore wrapped his arms around Rowen and buried his head in her hair. "Why did you do this?" he whispered. It seemed her power wasn't enough to heal them both.

Outside, the rain fell, its harsh patter echoing across the cave. Thunder boomed every few seconds. The fire had burned down to a pile of glowing embers.

That was it. He could do no more.

Lore slumped against the cave wall and closed his eyes. *Word, she's Yours now. I've done everything I can.* Then Lore laughed, but it came out more like a choke. Here he was, handing Rowen over to the Word, when in fact she had been in the Word's hands the entire time. He closed his eyes, too tired to move.

Rowen shifted slightly and moaned.

Lore's eyes snapped open. "Rowen?" She moaned again. Her voice gave him one last ounce of strength. Lore pushed himself up, fighting the fatigue that weighed down his arms.

"Rowen?" he said again, readjusting his hold on her until he could see her face. Her eyes were still closed, but not as tightly as they had been minutes ago. He felt her cheek, warm now to the touch. He reached for her left hand. It felt warm, the iciness from minutes ago gone. Relief flooded his weary body. "Thank You, Word." Lore gripped Rowen tightly to his chest. "Thank You."

He pulled the blankets back over her shoulders. He went to move her but found all his strength gone. Lore fell back against the cave wall, Rowen with him. He would move her, eventually. But for now this would have to do. He had no more strength left to move.

The world was dark and cold. Rowen shook, feeling the coldness envelop her body, starving out any warmth left within her. She almost wished for the searing pain from minutes before—it was easier to bear than this impenetrable coldness. Or had it been hours ago?

Rowen tried to shake her head in order to clear it but found she could not move. The only thing she could do was shiver.

Now and then the coldness was punctuated by brief moments of warmth. She clung to these, wishing she could pull the warmth into her very being, but they warmed her only on the outside. When the warmth left, Rowen would begin to shake again and her mind filled with darkness.

After hours or days—she didn't know which—she finally saw something. It was hazy, without any clear lines, but it looked warm. So she struggled toward it. The red haze continued to spread across her vision.

Rowen opened her eyes.

The world came into sharp focus. The red she had seen was a fire burning cheerfully a few feet away. For a moment she watched the flames leap and dance in the air, the dark background causing them to burn more brightly.

Rowen closed her eyes. Even looking around for just a moment exhausted her. Slowly she opened them again. Her eyes roved beyond the fire, where she spied a dark figure sitting just beyond the fire's light. It was hunched over, but in the dark she could not make out much of its shape. Was it a friend or foe?

Either way, Rowen felt compelled to get its attention, to let someone know that she was still alive. She opened her mouth to speak, but instead a raspy cough left her throat.

The figure turned. "Rowen?" the figure said, the tone a mixture of surprise and relief.

The figure knew her—that was a good sign. Rowen tried to speak again, but her mouth and throat would not work. The figure moved toward her. She still could not see who it was, but the voice sounded familiar.

"Oh, thank the Word, you're finally awake!"

Suddenly she was looking into Lore's face. "Captain?" she said, rasping.

"Yes, I'm here." She felt him take her hand. "How are you feeling?"

She tried to lick her lips. "Thirsty," she said weakly.

"I have a full water skin here," he said, reaching behind him. Then, placing one arm behind her head, he lifted her up to the skin.

The water tasted heavenly on her parched tongue. "Thank you," she said, her voice more normal now. Lore laid her gently back down. "Where are we?" she asked, glancing up at the jagged stone ceiling. It looked like it had been carved out of sandstone. Only the stone wasn't smoothed down. It looked instead as if it had been left in its natural state.

"A cave just north of Avonai."

A cave. That explained the rough ceiling. "Where is everyone else?

"Hopefully near the White City by now."

She turned her eyes back toward Lore.

"We had no time to take you to Fiske," he said. "Someone had to stay behind and take care of you. And since I grew up around here, I knew a safe place to take you."

"You grew up around here? Wait, you're—you're Avonain?"

"Yes."

"As in one of the coastal people?"

Lore chuckled. "Yes."

Rowen looked back up at the ceiling. She had known Lore for months now, but had never realized . . . Wait: his eyes. That explained why his eyes changed. Why they changed from green to blue to grey. By looking into his eyes, she was really seeing the ever-changing surface of the ocean. Living in Cinad, she had never met an Avonain before, but she had heard about their connection to the sea.

A gust of wind tore through the cave, shoving its icy fingers beneath her blanket. Rowen clutched the woolen cloth to her neck. The fire flickered for a moment, then resumed its burn. Her eyes darted back toward Lore.

He was shaking. She eyed him more carefully as he placed another piece of driftwood on the fire. The trembling was more noticeable around his hands. Was he cold, or was the storm outside doing this to him? Belatedly, she noticed that his shirt was torn and part of it was missing. Hardly clothing for a cold storm like this. What had he done to his shirt? And where was his jerkin—

Rowen sat straight up. The cave went spinning around and dark spots popped across her vision.

"Whoa, should you be doing that?" She felt Lore's hands across her back.

Her vision came back into focus. "I'm-I'm fine." Rowen brushed her head with her fingertips.

"You sure?"

"Yes, yes. But what about you? Are *you* all right?"

Lore dropped his hands and gave her a funny look.

Rowen looked at him with concern. "You. You almost died. And your hands, they're shaking. Are you—are you all right?" Had she been able to heal him?

Lore lifted one hand and looked at it. It trembled in the firelight. "Yes. I'm fine. From the knife wound, that is. As far as my hands shaking, it's the storm outside." He put his hand back down and jerked his head toward a small opening in the cave wall. "It does this to me."

Rowen looked toward the opening, then around the cave. It was small, about half the size of the training room back home. The walls and ceiling were made of rough sandstone. The fire's light danced across the pockmarked surface. Two boulders stood against the far wall. Her pack lay open near a stack of wood. Both of her blankets were spread across her lap.

"You can feel the storm?" she said, looking back at Lore.

Lore smiled. "Yes. Most Avonains develop a tolerance for the sea's moods, but since I've lived most of my life in the White City and not near the sea, my tolerance is very low. Storms like this can wreak havoc on me."

"I'm sorry." Rowen pulled one of the blankets off her lap. "Here, take this. I don't need two blankets. You look like you could use one."

Lore took the blanket and placed it next to him.

"I had no idea, about the storm, that is. Does it . . . hurt?"

"It did." Lore took a stick and stoked the fire. "But I'm better now, now that the storm has lessened." He pushed the wood around a minute longer, then tossed the stick in. "How about you?" He turned to look at her. "How are you doing?"

"I'm feeling . . . better," she said, wondering if Lore meant more by his question. He hadn't brought up the fact that she had healed him. Or maybe he didn't know? Suddenly her stomach rumbled loudly.

"And hungry too, by the sound of it." Lore gave her a quick smile and reached for the pack that lay near the fire. He rummaged through it and found a small hard biscuit. "Sorry," he said, holding it out to her. "It's not much. In the morning I'll try and catch something."

She waved off his comment and tore into the biscuit. The small round contained dried fruits and nuts. She chewed greedily on the hard biscuit.

Lore laughed. Rowen glanced up, puzzled. His features relaxed into a gentle smile. "It's good to see you better."

She felt more than heard his relief. "I guess I really am hungry, to be eating this." Rowen held up the last bit of her biscuit. She studied for a moment. "Always thought they were nasty."

Lore laughed again. It echoed off the cave walls. It was a nice sound, she decided. "I always thought so too," he said.

She finished the round and brushed the crumbs away.

Lore turned toward the fire. He drew his knees up and placed his arms casually over their tops. In the low light, Rowen could make out a couple days of growth on his face, giving him a more rugged appearance. It looked nothing like his usual neatly kept self.

Rowen turned her gaze toward the fire as well. She felt her heart begin to pound inside her chest. It was time to tell Lore the truth. And even though she was sure he already knew or at least had guessed, it did not make it any easier.

She wiped her clammy hands across the blanket and took a deep breath. "Captain," Rowen began, her heart hammering so loud she could hear it inside her head. She watched him turn toward her from the corner of her eye, but she lacked the courage to look back.

"Yes?" he asked, his voice light.

"I- I've been keeping something from you all these months." She felt like she was going to retch, but she pressed on. "I am not who you think I am. I am not . . . actually . . . human. I am—"

"Eldaran," Lore said quietly.

Rowen took another deep breath and nodded. "Yes." She waited for him to say more, but nothing came, so she continued. "I did not know until a couple days before we left for Avonai."

"*What?*" Lore turned and looked at her. "I don't understand. That was only a few weeks ago—"

"Yes." Her hands trembled, and her courage ebbed away. She needed to say everything now. "I never told you what happened to me in my village, before coming to the White City. Balint knows, only because I told him after he revealed what I was." Rowen swallowed, feeling the bitter words form in her mouth. "I was . . . exiled."

Silence filled the space between them. "For what?" Lore finally said.

"Witchcraft."

Oh, Word, this is hard.

Lore said nothing, his face toward the fire. Did he feel betrayed by her words? She had never outright lied to him, but neither had she been totally honest. Could he understand why? Would he let her explain?

"Why did your village think you were a witch?" he asked.

Painful memories resurfaced. Sharing her past with Lore would be like opening her chest and telling him to stab where he pleased. And deep down she knew that, if he rejected her after she told him, it would be a stab straight to the heart. But she had no choice. She was a Truthsayer, and nothing would change that. It was time Lore knew.

"You must understand," Rowen began, her voice trembling, "that neither I nor my village knew of the Word. We had heard stories from traveling bards, but that's all they were . . . stories. And we knew nothing of the Eldarans. So when my mark appeared, I only thought it was a lingering effect from a recent illness. It wasn't until I touched someone that I came to realize . . ."

Rowen choked, remembering Cleon's hatred. Her hands were shaking so hard that she had to clasp them together. Swallowing the lump inside her throat, she whispered, "I can see the darkness inside people. And apparently they see it too, when I touch them. It terrified the man I touched—terrified him so much that he accused me of witchcraft. And everyone believed him."

Rowen closed her eyes and took a deep breath to steady herself. "At the time, I had no idea what I had done. Nothing like it had ever happened to me. All I could do was stand there as my village . . ." She swallowed again, her eyes squeezed shut as she remembered the faces of those standing inside that room. Her throat grew tight, but she had to get the words out "As my village c-condemned me."

Rowen clamped her mouth shut. She could not go on. Inside, her emotions pounded against her body like dammed up water pressing for release. She clenched her hands, refusing to let any of her feelings loose. She would not show weakness, she would not be vulnerable.

She felt a hand cover hers.

Rowen jerked away as if burned by fire.

"Rowen," Lore said, his hand following her movement. "I'm sorry. I had no idea."

Rowen licked her lips, her throat dry from the rapid changes of emotions inside her. "I know." Her voice cracked, and she stared ahead. "But now you understand why I hid my mark beneath my glove. I never knew when I might touch someone and trigger that . . . power. And I truly thought I was a witch, or worse. I hid my mark so I would not harm others." Rowen lifted her head and looked Lore straight in the eye. "I never meant to deceive you. Only to protect you."

He stared back. And in that moment Rowen knew they stood on an edge. Lore would either accept her or fear her, like Cleon had.

Instead of answering, Lore placed his other hand over his first one, both of them covering her own. "You have nothing to fear from me, Rowen Mar," he said finally, looking directly into her eyes. "I understand what you are. I know something of the Eldarans, and even among them in their prime, the power you are describing was rare." Then he turned and gazed at the fire. "To see the darkness in others . . ." Lore shook his head. "It's bad enough to see that darkness acted out, but to see it in the heart . . . I can't imagine."

"Then . . . then you've heard of Truthsayers?"

"Yes," he answered, his voice full of emotion.

Her heart began to beat faster. "And you're not afraid of me?"

"Of your power . . . yes," he said. Rowen's heart dipped. "But I have nothing to hide. The Word healed the darkness inside of me a long time ago. Only an echo of that darkness remains. All you would find in me is . . ." then Lore stopped as if he were about to reveal something he wasn't ready to disclose.

"You do not need to worry. I will not touch you." Rowen removed her hand from beneath his, careful to keep her mark away, and lifted it up. Her palm glowed with a faint light. "But it would be good to find my glove. Or another one. I lost mine on the beach." She could see Lore staring at her upturned hand from the corner of her eye.

"Forgive me," Lore said a moment later. "I've never seen the mark of the Word this close before. And I didn't think it was right to stare at your hand while you were unconscious. The only time I've seen the mark is on Balint and his isn't . . ."

"As bright," Rowen finished for him, "or as pronounced?"

"No."

Rowen moved her hand back and forth, feeling the familiar sense of camaraderie that had existed between her and Lore fall back into place, only this time stronger. Lore knew her secret now. And he wasn't afraid. That thought sent a surge of elation through her.

"Balint doesn't understand why my mark is this way either," Rowen said. "Perhaps my parents were full-blooded Eldarans."

"Jedrek was an Eldaran?" Lore said, surprised.

Rowen turned toward Lore. "No, I mean my real parents." Judging from Lore's puzzled expression, he didn't know. "Jedrek and Ann were not my real parents. I was left with them a long time ago, long before I can remember. I never knew my real parents."

Lore leaned back. "I see." He watched the fire for a moment. "Having your parents around to explain your mark would have been helpful. As an Avonain, I cannot imagine growing up without my mother to help me with my sea blood."

Rowen nodded and lowered her hand. She turned back toward the fire. The flames had flickered down to glowing embers.

Lore reached around and brought out more driftwood, which he placed on the fire. He sat back. "Rowen," he said quietly, "I want to thank you . . . for healing me." Rowen opened her mouth in protest, but Lore held up a hand. "By healing me, you went through great pain. I know—I saw it. And by healing me, you exposed your secret. Even if you wanted to go back to wearing your glove, I do not think you can. You gave everything for me. So . . . thank you."

Rowen sat staring at Lore, remembering how he'd looked on the sand with blood pooling around him and the gash in his side. No, there had been no choice. "I couldn't let you die, Captain."

"Yes, you could have, if you had wanted to remain hidden."

"No." Rowen shook her head. "As much as I would have liked to keep my mark a secret, I do not think I could have. Eventually the truth would have come out, just as it always does." She gave Lore a half smile. "I'm just glad I was able to do something good when the time came."

Later that night, Lore lay staring up at the jagged ceiling, his back against the cave floor, his hands folded beneath his head. His mind felt full from turning over everything he had learned in the last few hours. Rowen was an Eldaran. No, more than that. Rowen was an Eldaran Truthsayer.

He turned his head and looked at the sleeping figure a few feet away from him. Everything about her made sense now: her glove, her distant attitude with others, the guarded expression she wore whenever he'd questioned her about her past. No wonder she never wanted to speak about Cinad. To be banished from her home . . .

His heart twisted inside of him at the thought. And not only banished, but to bear the burden of such a terrifying power. To see the darkness in others.

Lore shifted onto his side, his face toward the dying fire. The embers cast a red light across Rowen's face. Her long hair was slowly coming loose from the braid she usually wore, the stray hairs curling around her face. Peace radiated from her body.

Lore breathed in deeply, then let it out with a sigh. He loved Rowen more than ever. But what did he do with that? He could feel his heart bonding with her, the tie growing stronger each day. And now that he knew the truth about her, it was as if that bond had intensified tenfold. He wanted to be with her, to help bear the burden she carried.

But could he? Lore sighed and shifted onto his back. So many things were calling him. Lady Astrea would need him greatly in the next few weeks as she took over her father's position.

A sharp jab of pain tore through his heart. A position she would need to fill because he had failed.

Lore rolled onto his back and stared at the sandstone ceiling. Could he have done anything different? Over and over he ran the events of that night through his mind, dissecting each piece. The assassin in Lord Gaynor's room had been a Temanin. Lore was almost positive on that account. And if he were a Temanin, then it followed that he was most likely working for the Temanin Empire.

So why that night? Why *after* the treaty signing? Why not before, to prevent it? Just how did the assassin know what time and which room?

And why hadn't he seen the assassin on the balcony?

Lore hated that question the most, because he had no answer. He had checked the balcony, even leaned over the edge. But the assassin had somehow slipped by and stabbed him. And then had moved on to kill Lord Gaynor and Justus.

Rowen stirred and rolled onto her side. Lore looked at her again. A part of him wondered how he could even think of love when his one duty in life lay cold on the marble floor with a knife through his throat.

Lore pulled the blanket up over his body. No matter how much he wished, he could not go back in time and undo what had happened. But he *could* do his best to make sure it never happened again. He would protect Lady Astrea. And if he ever met that assassin again, it would be the assassin on the ground dead.

CHAPTER 21

Caleb Tala drew his map out again, checking it against his compass. He had been on the run for two days now. If he guessed correctly where the Temanin army was, he still had a couple more days' ride before he would reach them.

Scattered clouds rushed overhead, sprinkling their life-giving moisture before sprinting toward the mountains. A couple of droplets fell across the parchment, making the ink run. Caleb cursed and rolled the map back up.

He hated this land: the cold air, the abundance of trees one had to constantly navigate, and all the rain. Especially the rain.

Caleb quickly stowed the map away and pulled his hood up over his head, cringing as the gash across his chest shifted. He had checked it this morning and found it red and swollen. If only he had access to some herbs or medicine . . . He slowly brought his hand back down. All the more reason to find the Temanin army: His wound needed a healer's touch.

The clouds plagued him the rest of the day as if intent on driving him back south where he belonged. Growling inward, Caleb continued toward the northwest where he knew the Temanin army was slowly lumbering its way toward the White City.

The next day, the sun rose and drove away the last few clouds. The trees finally thinned, exposing vast rolling hills covered in long grass.

Caleb felt dizzy and his head throbbed with unusual heat. He steered his horse toward the open plain. His body ached and felt hot to the touch. He knew little of the healing arts, but it felt like the infection had spread from his chest wound.

Looking across the tall grass, he hoped he would make better time now that he was no longer dodging trees and tall shrubs. His body was beginning to shut down, and he had no idea what he would do if he passed out here in the middle of nowhere.

About midday he spotted a caravan slowly making its way across the grass. Caleb took out his spyglass. It took him a moment to clear his mind and look through the lens. He counted and realized there were about forty people ranging in size and age along with a couple of wagons and horses. Probably refugees trying to make it to Avonai and the coast.

Caleb put the spyglass away and thought for a moment. He could circumvent their route and avoid meeting the group. However, he had spotted a woman healer amongst their group, the telltale white robes standing out from the mixture of bodies.

He rubbed his heat-filled eyes and wondered if he would be coherent enough to make up a story on the spot and convince the people to help him. On the other hand, he wasn't sure he could make it any farther in his condition. He needed help.

He guided his horse toward the caravan and began to formulate a story, praying to whatever gods there were that they would be gracious to him this once and not let his cover slip.

A couple of people began to shout as he drew near. Caleb looked up, thankful he already looked the part for his story: that of a lone survivor of a Temanin attack. He felt awful, and he was pretty sure he looked awful as well.

"Dear Word, what happened to you?" an older man cried out as he ran to Caleb's side.

"A..a . . . attacked," Caleb said, barely able to hang onto his saddle.

"Tania, we've got another one," the man yelled over his shoulder. Caleb glanced up to find the woman healer making her way toward him.

Slowly, painfully, he dismounted.

"Easy there, fella," the man said, taking the reins from Caleb's hand. "Tania here is one of the best healers around. Trained under

Balint Kedem himself. She'll get you patched up." His eyes roamed Caleb's body. "Looks like those southern swine got you good."

Caleb fought down the sudden spark of anger at being called swine, reminding himself he was suppose to be a fellow northerner.

Tania arrived breathless. "They got you too, did they?" She lifted his shirt and viewed the wound for herself. "Bring him to the wagon," she said to the men around her. She turned back toward the camp.

Someone moved in to assist Caleb. Another led his horse away.

His plan was working, Caleb thought feebly, feeling the fever burn through his head. The person assisting him led him to one of the few wagons and helped him in.

Inside was a narrow bed with hardly enough room for anything else. A single candle burned nearby for light. And in the back sat Tania rummaging through a large black bag.

"Lay him down there," she said, looking over her shoulder and pointing toward the bed.

His body sank into the thick quilt that covered the boards that lay underneath. Caleb couldn't help the sigh of relief that escaped his lips. It wasn't what he was used to, but it was better than the backside of a horse or the ground. The man who had assisted him left, letting the thick curtain fall in place.

"Where did you say you were from?" Tania turned back around with a bowl and pestle in hand. Gently she began to crush whatever was inside.

Caleb wracked his mind, drawing up a memory of the map now stowed in his pack. "Tieve," he replied, picking a village he remembered from the map, hoping against hope this group wasn't from there.

"Tieve?" Tania poured water into bowl, then stirred the mix. "I heard about Tieve. Can't believe you escaped."

Caleb stiffened slightly. Could she see through his story?

"You were one of the lucky ones," she continued.

"Yes," Caleb said, eyeing her now. "I was."

"Leave anyone behind?" She continued to stir her concoction.

"Yes," he replied flatly.

She glanced up. "I'm sorry," she said, the feeling mirrored in her eyes. "I lost family too." The wagon grew quiet as she finished mixing. "Now I need you to drink this up," Tania said a minute later. She moved a hand beneath his neck to assist him. "It'll knock you out for a while, but you'll be fine afterward."

"Knock me out?" Caleb gripped the boards that held the quilt in.

"Relax, it won't hurt you. Just a little something to keep you from feeling anything. And it will let me see to your wounds."

Before Caleb could protest further, she shoved the bowl beneath his lips and tilted upward. For one moment he considered spitting it out, but he realized such an action could blow his cover. So he took a big draught . . . and gagged.

"Swallow it," Tania said in a sweet yet forceful voice.

Caleb complied, quickly downing the bitter liquid.

"Good. It'll take a few minutes for the stuff to work, so just lie still and relax." She began to hum and turned back toward the black bag.

It took only a minute before his vision began to blur. The candle that hung above him became two, then one, then a mesh of both. Caleb blinked his eyes, his lids heavy. The song the healer hummed echoed in the distance.

Then everything went black.

Days later, Rowen and Lore found themselves on the banks of the Onyx River near a dilapidated shed. The river ran black from the sediment it brought down from the mountains of Nordica. A small barge floated along the river's current, tied to an old wooden dock. Insects buzzed along the shore and the water whooshed past, dodging rocks and weaving its way south.

On either side of the river, the grass plains turned golden beneath the summer sun. The sky was bright blue with a scattering of clouds. Tall, jagged mountains filled the far horizon.

Lore searched the river's edge. "He should be around here."

266

Rowen stood next to Lore, holding the reins of the horses they had acquired shortly after leaving the cave. She could feel Lore's urgency as he searched for the barge keeper. "Could he already be gone?" Rowen asked, looking down the river the other way.

"Could be," Lore said tightly, glancing north again. "If Temanin has already reached—"

"Greetings, folks!" Up from the bank came an old hunched back man, his clothes hanging off of him like rags on a clothesline. Rowen recognized him immediately as the barge keeper. He had ferried them across the river over a week ago when they traveled to Avonai. He approached and his eyes grew bigger. "Captain Lore—and madam—" the old man nodded at Rowen. "What are you doing here?"

"Bart, it's good to see you." Lore smiled with relief. He walked over to Bart and clapped him across the shoulders. Rowen winced. The man seemed barely able to hold his own weight up, let alone Lore's exuberant greeting.

"It's good to see you too, Captain." Bart's face turned more serious. "But what are you doing here?"

"It's a long story. And I'm afraid there's no time to tell it now. We need to get to the White City."

"I'd say," Bart said as he led them down to the barge. "Mostyn's under attack."

"Mostyn is under attack?" Lore said, his voice turning serious. "This is not good."

"What do you mean?" Rowen asked.

Lore turned. "You remember Mostyn, right? It was the town we first met in, at the inn?"

Rowen slowly nodded. She remembered.

"Mostyn is the first line of defense for the White City. An army the size of Temanin could not enter Anwin Forest except by passing Mostyn. Mostyn protects the path that leads up to the White City." Lore turned back to Bart. "When did the attack begin?"

"Most likely yesterday afternoon." Bart walked over to the river and began to untie the barge. "The courier who told me was dispatched just before the Temanin Army arrived. I was ordered to keep a watch over the river banks." Bart motioned for Rowen and Lore to board the barge. "I was also ordered to not allow anyone to cross, but seeing how you're the captain, I'll make an exception."

"Thank you, Bart."

The old man nodded. Rowen and Lore led their horses onto the barge. The barge shook slightly under the weight. Once they were setteled, Bart pushed the barge away from the bank with his long pole.

Rowen's horse whinnied anxiously and took a step back.

"It's all right, girl," Rowen said, brushing the horse's neck. The horse settled down, and Lore moved toward Rowen's side. "I had no idea the Temanin Army would move so quickly," he said in a hushed voice. "We'll need to find another way to the city."

"Do you know another route?" Rowen looked up into Lore's face. His eyes had changed color again—now they were a deep blue.

"I do, but it's not as easy as following the road. We'll have to cut across the forest." He glanced at their horses. "Hopefully the path isn't too overgrown."

Twenty minutes later they were off again.

That night, Rowen and Lore sat around a small campfire. The tall ancient trees of Anwin surrounded them. Stars twinkled high above in a dark blue sky. A stream gushed nearby. The air was still and warm.

Rowen watched the fire. Smoke gently drifted upward in long, pale wisps. Fish bones from dinner were strewn around the fire. Lore sat on the ground across from her. She had found an old tree stump to sit on. "Do you think Mostyn has been taken by now?" she said, looking across the fire.

Lore took a moment to answer. "Mostyn has enough resources to stop Temanin for a couple days," he said slowly. "But it will probably fall. It was built to give the White City enough time to gear up for an attack, should one ever happen. The last time the White City was attacked, it was during the Nordic Wars."

Rowen frowned. The fire popped and consumed sap still on the logs. "But that was over four hundred years ago."

"I know." Lore poked the fire with a stick, sending sparks up into the night sky. "Except those wars were led by the Shadonae. At least this time we're fighting just men."

"Shadonae?" Rowen said. The word conjured visions of tall pale men in black robes.

Lore glanced over at her. "Powerful twisted beings who wished to destroy everything the Word made."

Rowen pulled her blanket closer. "Do they still exist?"

"I don't know." Lore dropped his stick into the fire and watched it burn. "There isn't much written about them. I would have said no a couple days ago, but then again, I did not believe Eldarans existed anymore, at least not full blooded Eldarans."

Rowen felt her face redden. Lore's words were just another reminder that she was different. "So because I exist, these . . . Shadonae may also exist?" she said, studying the tree stump she sat on.

"Perhaps. But perhaps not. Anyway," Lore waved his hand as if to erase the last few minutes of conversation, "there is no reason to speculate about that possibility now. There's enough trouble with the Temanin army advancing on the White City."

Rowen lifted her head. "You're right."

But later that night, her thoughts wandered back to the Shadonae. *Powerful, twisted beings* Lore had called them. Beings who almost wiped out the north with the Nordic Wars. Beings who should no longer exist.

Like her.

Rowen shivered and shifted over to her side.

They rode most of the next day through Anwin Forest. The trees shaded them from the bright summer sun.

Lore brought his horse next to Rowen's. "The White City is just around this mountain. So we'll probably reach the gates near sunset."

"What about the Temanin Army?" Rowen asked.

"Hopefully Mostyn has kept them occupied. But if Temanin is already at the White City, I'm afraid we'll have to turn back."

"Turn back? To where?"

"Back to the river. With the treaty now in place, both Avonai and Nordica should be sending troops to help the White City. The courier Bart met up with the other day was probably carrying the message. When their troops arrive at the river, we'll join them."

"But what about the city guards?" Rowen asked. "Who will lead them if you're not there?"

"Aren," Lore said. "He's more than competent, despite his youth and less than serious outlook on life. Deep inside that man there is a strong leader. His humor is a mask, a façade to hide the hurt he's been through."

Rowen looked over at Lore questioningly.

"I'm afraid that's his story to tell," Lore said, glancing at her.

"I understand."

"I know you do," Lore said quietly.

Caleb Tala woke up with a start, cold sweat pouring off his body. He looked around, frantically trying to figure out where he was. Everything was dark. He felt around and found a blanket across his lap. The walls next to him were made of canvas. He felt his chest and found that his shirt had been removed. What the—

Then it all came back: his wound, the group of refugees, and the healer.

Caleb shivered and grabbed the blanket and pulled it over his exposed body. His nightmare had returned, this time more vivid than ever. He had found himself in the middle of Hershaw Pass with dead bodies all around him. And the blood . . .

He shivered again, remembering the sickening feel of blood all over his hands. And no matter how much he tried to wipe the sticky fluid off, it had clung to him, slowly crawling up his arm.

He remembered yelling and dashing, only to run into someone

deep within the pass. The body had turned, and Caleb had found himself staring into Lord Gaynor's eyes. The high lord had laughed and held a dagger poised to thrust deep into Caleb's body . . .

Caleb lay back down, his heart slowly returning to its steady beat. Outside the wagon he could hear a cricket chirping. So it had to be nighttime. Caleb listened to the tiny bug's trill and lifted his hand, feeling for his wound. There were ridges across the skin where the healer had sown the wound shut. It was still tender to the touch, but no longer infected, and his body no longer ached. Caleb brought his hand away. Whatever medicine she had given to him, it had worked.

Suddenly the cricket stopped. Caleb tensed, his ears alert for any sound. He could hear movement outside.

"Tania!" a voice called out.

"Shhh!" The sound came from the right, just outside. Caleb thought he could hear another person approaching.

"What do you want?" a feminine voice said moments later.

"I want to talk to you about the man you helped today."

"Yeah? What about him?" she said quietly.

"Me and a couple others don't think he's telling the truth."

"I already know that," she said.

"And we . . . What? You know?" he sputtered.

"Shhh!" she said again.

"Can he hear us?" he said in a strained voice.

"Don't think so," Tania said. "He should still be out. But just in case . . ."

Wanting to hear more, Caleb stole away from the bed toward the canvas flaps. He parted them slightly and found the outside almost as dark as inside the wagon. A few fires burned a short distance away. Other wagons surrounded the fires. A half moon hung in the dark sky, over hills of grass. A lone tree stood to the left, apart from the fires and wagons. A couple of horses grazed beneath it.

Caleb looked to his right. Two figures stood near the wagon he was in. The man held a torch. Tania stood a short distance away. He waited to see if he could still hear them. He could, barely.

" . . . a Temanin," Caleb heard the male voice say.

"Boyd, just because someone has dark hair and dark eyes doesn't make them a Temanin," Tania said. "Take Corra's daughter. We both know that child is a Rylander through and through, yet looking at her you'd think she had been born to a Temanin."

"But Tania—"

"But I think you're right," Tania interrupted. "His story doesn't add up. He said he was from Tieve, yet Tieve was attacked weeks ago. His wounds were recent. So either he's lying, or he received those wounds some other way than during the attack on Tieve."

"He's a Temanin," Boyd said. "I feel it in my gut."

"Either way, he was hurt and I was bound to help him," Tania said. "But now my job's done. If you want to take charge of him, be my guest. But . . . no killing." Caleb watched her wave a finger at Boyd. "I didn't patch him up for you to cut him open again. You make sure he's a Temanin before doing anything, you hear?"

"I'll guard the wagon tonight," Boyd said. "We can question him tomorrow."

"That sounds like a good plan, Boyd. I'll let the others know."

Time to go. Caleb pulled his hidden dagger out from his right boot. There was no time to retrieve his shirt. He doubted he would be able to find it anyway in the dark wagon.

He watched Boyd approach the wagon and suddenly felt a feeling of apprehension wash over him. Visions from his nightmare still lingered in the back of his mind. Caleb glanced at his dagger. He couldn't believe it: He was second-guessing himself. For the first time in his life, he had doubts about taking the life of another.

Panicked by the sudden rise of conscience within him, Caleb scrambled mentally to figure out what to do. Boyd drew closer. Should he kill him or not? He readjusted his grip on the dagger, noting the slight shake of his hand. Sliding the dagger back into its sheath, Caleb made his decision. He knew other ways to incapacitate a person . . .

Boyd stopped beside the wagon, near the opening. He was close enough that Caleb could hear Boyd's breathing. Foolish man. He should have checked the inside of the wagon first.

Caleb reached out and grabbed Boyd by the throat and dragged him inside the wagon. They tussled in the small space. Caleb squeezed with all his might. Boyd let go of his torch and fought back. But it was too late.

Moments later, Caleb let go. Boyd fell to the floor, unconscious. However, the torch had fallen into the black bag, and something inside had caught fire during their fight. Now the fire was spreading.

Snarling, Caleb threw back the canvas flaps and leaped from the wagon. He turned toward the tree with the horses beneath it. Caleb sprinted through the long grass and reached the horses. He found his own a moment later. He began to untie the reins. Shouts filled the air behind him.

"Come on," he muttered angrily, working on the knot still wound around the tree branch. He glanced back and saw people running toward him.

Cursing again, he bent down and retrieved his dagger from his boot, then cut the reins. Behind him, flames reached for the sky. The wagon and its contents were fed to the inferno.

So much for not killing the man, Caleb thought darkly. He leaped up into the saddle and urged his horse forward. Then he raced off into the night, not sure what direction he was going, only that he needed to get away.

Lore came through the trees, a frown on his face. Just beyond the trees lay the field that bordered the walls of the White City. To their right, the face of the mountain, a sheer wall of stone reaching to the cloud covered peak above. The sun was a ball of red ahead of them, slowly sinking into the west. Purples and blues spread across the sky.

"There are men on the far side of the forest." Lore took his reins from Rowen. "South. From the direction of Mostyn."

"Temanins?" Rowen asked.

Lore leaped up into his saddle. "I could not tell from where I was standing, but probably. Looked like they were watching the gates from within the tree line. Probably the first wave."

"So do we turn back?"

Lore was quiet for a moment, his eyes turned toward the far end of the field. "I am willing to ride to the gate. They probably won't try to stop me, because they'd reveal their position. But they might." He turned and looked at her. "What about you?"

Rowen readjusted her grip on her reins. She knew Lore would stay back for her. But the White City needed him. And she knew her place was there as well. "I am willing to ride."

He nodded solemnly. "Then may the Word watch over us."

Yes, thought Rowen. She urged her horse forward. After a minute, they came to the tree line. Ahead she could see the field . . . and the White City.

It stood like a glorious edifice in the dying light. Tall, proud walls. Homes and shops and Celestis Castle, all chiseled out of the mountain. Blue banners with the symbol of the eagle waving in the wind. The city had turned a light pink from the sun's last rays.

Home.

Lore brought his horse up beside hers. "Are you ready?"

Rowen took a deep breath. "Yes."

You go first. I'll follow."

She nodded. She dug her heels into her mare. The horse leaped forward, and she was racing across the field. To her left, she saw movement among the shadows.

A long thin projectile whizzed by her head. Looked like the Temanin's weren't concerned about blowing their cover.

"Keep going!" Lore yelled behind her.

Rowen pressed her body closer to the horse. She drew in deep breaths. Her heart pounded inside her ears. She may be able to heal, but one arrow to the heart and she doubted even she could survive that.

The gates drew closer.

Come on, she thought, willing her mount to move faster. She dared not look back for Lore. Fires flickered across the wall. Fifty meters . . . Twenty meters . . . "Open the gate!" Rowen shouted, straightening up. Her horse danced beside the wooden barrier.

"Rowen?" shouted a voice above.

"Yes!" She glanced up but unable to see who had called down. "Hurry!"

The gates groaned and swung inward. She nudged her mount closer. A moment later, the gates were far enough apart. Rowen went in.

She moved her horse away from the gate, then turned to watch for Lore.

The city was dark inside. Torches hung from the metal brackets on either side of the gates. Farther up the street, candles shown through windows. Men came running toward the gate. She could hear muffled thuds hit the wood.

"They're shooting at us," she heard someone shout.

Lore came bursting through. "Close the gates!" But his words were not needed. The gates were already slamming shut.

Rowen brought her horse to his side. "You've been hit," she said, noting the tear along his sleeve.

Lore looked over at the graze and touched it. "Only my arm."

Rowen brought her gloved hand up.

"No," Lore said, pulling himself away. "It's a minor wound. I can handle it."

Before she could answer, Donar ran toward them.

"Captain, Rowen, where have you been? No one would say a word when Lady Astrea arrived days ago. Other than . . ." Donar swallowed.

Apparently, the city knew of Lord Gaynor's death.

More men came running. Others continued to shout overhead.

One man in particular caught Rowen's attention. Lore continued to speak to Donar.

"Captain Lore," the man said. Rowen recognized the man's uniform. It was the same one her father had worn the day he'd ridden off to war.

"Commander Kelyn." Lore dismounted. Both men bowed to each other.

Rowen watched from the top of her horse.

"We have much to talk about." Commander Kelyn looked up toward Rowen. "Is this Commander Jedrek's daughter?"

"Yes." Lore turned to look at her. "Rowen, this is Commander Kelyn of the Northern Army. Commander Kelyn, Rowen Mar, varor to Lady Astrea."

"It is a pleasure to meet you." Commander Kelyn gave her a polite bow. "Your father was a great man."

"Thank you, sir," Rowen said, not sure if she should dismount and bow.

"I'm glad to see that both you and Captain Lore made it back to the city, and in good health, no less. We had heard you both had been wounded . . ." She could see Commander Kelyn's eyes searching for her wounds, and she suddenly felt exposed. What if he realized she was no longer injured?

"Commander Kelyn," Lore said, intervening. "Please excuse us, it's been a long trip. Give me a half hour to cleanup and report to Lady Astrea, then I'll meet you in the council room."

"Very good, Captain." Commander Kelyn glanced briefly at Rowen. "In one half hour."

Lore bowed again, then mounted his horse.

"Thank you for covering for me," Rowen said once they were away from the main gate and the throng of soldiers and guards. Ahead stood the second set of walls that surrounded the castle and the archway that led into the inner courtyard.

"Of course," Lore said. "But we might have a problem. I'm not sure how your healing was explained, but clearly Commander Kelyn suspects something. He's a smart man, much like your father. Two and two are not adding up to him. Which brings up the point," Lore turned to look at her. "What are you going to do?"

"I'm not sure." It was one thing to have Lore know her secret, because he wasn't afraid of her. But what about others? Like Aren? Or any of the other guards . . . people whom she now called family?

They passed beneath the second archway and found a stablehand ready to take their horses. Rowen dismounted and handed over her reins.

The courtyard was empty. Torches had been lit on either side of the castle's double doors, providing ample light across the white staircase. The water fountain splashed nearby in the darkness. She began to climb the stairs, still pondering Lore's question.

"Wait."

Rowen stopped midway up and looked back.

"You may not like what I have to say." Lore caught up to her. "But in a few minutes you will likely be questioned by Lady Astrea and perhaps her council as well."

"Why?" Rowen asked before she could stop herself. Her insides gave a hard twist at the thought.

"Because Lady Astrea will want to know what happened on the beach. She will want to know who and what you really are."

Rowen wrapped her arms around her middle and turned away. Lady Astrea wanted an inquiry. And what would she decide once she knew Rowen really *was* an Eldaran?

"However—" Lore came around to face Rowen—"Lady Astrea may give you a choice: to continue to live as you have the last few months, hiding your mark under a glove and hoping nothing happens. Or, to reveal what you are, with no repercussions. She has the power now as High Lady to protect you from those who might be afraid of your . . . abilities."

"But what if *she* is afraid?"

Lore nodded. "She might be. But she owes you her life. Besides, from watching both of you together and her witnessing how you healed me, I believe Lady Astrea understands that you would use your power to help others. Not to terrorize or threaten."

"Never," Rowen murmured.

"So which do you want? Hide who you are, or embrace who you are?" Lore searched her face. "And more importantly, how you think the Word would have you live?"

Rowen looked away from Lore. She watched the torches flicker in their brackets next to the castle doors. The human part of her wanted to retreat back behind a glove and go on with life. But her Eldaran part said it was time to fully become who she was, that it was time to follow the Word in the way *He* had made her: by exposing the darkness in others.

"Isn't it better to tell the truth?" Lore said, his words breaking through her thoughts.

Rowen took a deep breath. "Yes." She looked back toward Lore. Her insides coiled with fear, but she knew her time of hiding was over. "I can't hide forever. And your right, that's not how the Word would have me live. But," she took another shaky breath, "it doesn't mean I won't be rejected again."

Lore faded away. Rowen saw her life spread out before her, a long narrow road barely visible in the darkness, lined by dark jagged cliffs and even darker crevices. But at the end of that road blazed a light so radiant it stood in sharp contrast to the lonely black road that represnted her life below. Her heart gasped at the sight. She desired the light at the end, but the path to it terrified her.

"You won't be alone."

Rowen was brought abruptly back to the present.

"Even if people do turn on you," she heard Lore say, "there is at least one person who won't . . ."

Rowen turned and looked up into Lore's eyes.

"Me," he said softly. "And the Word will never leave you either." He reached up and pushed back a strand of hair that had come loose behind her ear. "And for that reason alone, there is nothing to fear."

I won't be alone. Rowen mentally looked down that dark road again and suddenly saw small flickers of light nestled within the darkness. The Word would be with her. And others . . . others like Lore.

Lore glanced at the the main doors. "We should head in now. But think about what I said."

Rowen nodded and followed Lore up the rest of the stairs.

She already had.

CHAPTER 22

Nierne stumbled toward the sound of water, her water skin firmly gripped in hand. The sun shone through Anwin Forest with the heat of a summer afternoon. Wild berry bushes grabbed at her with prickly branches, blocking her way to the stream.

She plowed through the bushes, ignoring the stinging welts their long thorns left across her face and arms. Overhead, a couple of blackbirds laughed at her attempt to reach the water.

Nierne stopped. She panted and glared up at them. Caw, caw. She had half a mind to break off a branch and throw it at them. Instead, she gritted her teeth and plunged back into the thicket. Branches cracked and snapped beneath her boots. She clawed away at the barbed limbs, the sound of water driving her through the thorny nest—

Suddenly her foot hooked across a branch. Nierne shot her hands out to break her fall. "Oh, crackers— *Ouch!*" Her hand slid across a sharp rock. She straightened up and held out her hand. A large gash greeted her eyes, and her hand began to throb.

"Crackers," she said again with a groan. She didn't need this. Glancing up, she could see the stream just beyond the berry bushes. Carefully she tucked her hand close to her body and stood. She lowered her shoulder and plowed through the last few branches.

Nierne panted for a moment, a small smile of victory on her lips. It was a small stream, but it would do. Water rushed across jagged rocks and mossy logs. She dropped her pack and waterskin, knelt down beside the stream, and dipped her cut hand into the icy mountain water.

She washed out the gash. The wound stung, making her eyes

water. She lifted her hand back to her face and studied the cut. It was long but thankfully shallow. She dipped her hand one more time, then opened her pack and drew out a small bottle.

Uncorking the top, she tipped the bottle downward and watched three dark drops of ointment fall on the wound. Satisfied, Nierne placed the bottle back and pulled out a long stocking. It was not wrapping cloth, but it was clean, and she could tie it around her hand.

Nierne used her teeth and free hand to carefully bandage her wound. *There*, she thought, turning her hand over once to inspect her handiwork.

She grabbed her canteen and filled it, drank, and refilled it again. As she brought her hand across her mouth to wipe away the excess liquid, she caught a glimmer of her face in the slow moving water.

Bending closer, Nierne stared at her reflection, stunned. Looking back at her was a face gaunt and thin. She touched her cheek with her bandaged hand, noting the dark circles under her eyes and the chapped lips. Her hair was a wild mess of red around her face.

Nierne sat back in disbelief. She hardly recognized the woman who stared up at her from the water's reflection. Gone was the young scribe with ink-stained hands and tidy complexion. In her place now knelt a woman who had seen too much in a short span of time. That thought conjured up an image of Father Reth. Nierne squeezed her eyes shut, but she could not close off her heart. Even now, weeks after he had died, she still felt the sudden stab of grief.

She quickly wiped her eyes and stood. With her uncut hand, she pushed back the wild red curls from her face and grabbed her pack. She followed the stream until a game trail broke through the berry thicket. Following the narrow path, she stepped back onto the mountain path she had been following since Lachland.

Dark greens and deep browns of the forest surrounded her. Ivy and moss covered trees as thick as two men and taller than any building she had ever seen. Ferns spread out across the forest floor. The air smelled damp and earthy. Here, back on the path, the sun barely made it through the thick ceiling of tree branches.

Hours later, what little sunlight there was began to disappear, signaling the end of another day. As it grew darker, depression welled up inside Nierne. Another day gone, and she still had not reached the White City.

Perhaps she was lost. Perhaps the map was wrong. After all, it looked quite old. Nierne pulled out the tattered piece of parchment, squinting at the black markings in the dying light.

No, she was still on the right path. It was the *only* path. Her finger followed a thin line that looked like it could be the stream she had drunk from earlier that day. According to the map, she was only one or two days' walk from the city, maybe even closer.

That gave her hope. Nierne rolled up the parchment and stuck it back in her pack. Perhaps if she just kept walking for a bit longer, she might be able to see it over the next hill.

Energized by the idea, she hurried along the path. Visions of civilization filled her mind, pushing out the dark forest before her. A cozy room, hot fresh food, and a bed. Nierne sighed at the thought of a bed, a bed off the ground with a feather tick mattress. And a large quilt to keep warm.

The sun set behind her. Still Nierne pressed on. She was so close now, if the map was to be believed. And she had nothing else to believe. Her hand stole to the small pendant that hung around her neck, but she still refused to acknowledge anything to do with the Word.

One by one, the stars began to creep out and the last glorious rays of day vanished. Nierne squinted into the dark, already accustomed to the noises of night. Nothing natural scared her now, not after her experience with the shadows.

But it was growing harder to see. And the depression from earlier slowly seeped back. She would have to stop soon. The light patter of her feet turned to a slow drudge. The sadness deepened.

Nierne sighed and finally stopped. With the stars overhead and only a crescent moon for light, there would be no more traveling tonight. Her throat tightened with disappointment. Heavyhearted, she heaved the pack off her back and reached in, feeling with her fingers for the last bits of food.

Only small crumbs met her fingertips. Tears of frustration stung her eyes. She began to wonder if this trip had been a huge mistake. Maybe they were never meant to leave Thyra. Or maybe it was Nierne herself who was the mistake.

She withdrew her empty hand from the knapsack. Despair and hunger gnawed on her insides. Nierne placed the pack on the ground, and she wrapped her arms around her body. Black thoughts filled her mind. Perhaps Father Reth had saved the wrong person. Perhaps he should have saved himself.

"It's all my fault," Nierne whispered. This time a tear ran down her cheek. She wiped it away. Deep inside, she wanted to cry out to the Word, but she still felt betrayed by Him. He had let Father Reth die.

A light twinkled faintly between the trees.

Nierne blinked away her tears. She rubbed her eyes and stared hard into the trees. Only darkness and shadows—

A light twinkled again. She dropped her hands and took a step forward. Hope cautiously moved inside her heart. Could it be? She took a couple more steps.

More lights flickered between the trees, so faintly that for a moment Nierne thought she was imagining them. *Maybe I am*, she thought. She turned and picked up her pack. There was only one way to find out.

Carefully Nierne made her way through the dark, using the faint lights ahead as her compass. Yes, they were definitely lights. Could it be a village just outside the city? The map did not indicate there was one, but then again, it was old. Perhaps the population had outgrown the city's walls?

No, that's not it, thought Nierne. The lights were not contained, like they would be if they were shining out of windows. They looked more like . . . campfires.

Thousands of them.

She stopped. Why would there be so many campfires? Alarmed, Nierne grabbed her cloak out of her pack and clasped it on. She pulled the hood over her head, careful to tuck her hair inside. Hopefully the dark green cloak would keep her hidden. It was certainly big enough. Then she crept toward the fires.

Tall ferns and bushes masked her approach. She saw dark figures walking amongst the fires and what looked like tents. It couldn't be. But that was the only explanation.

It was a large army.

Nierne stopped, her heart sinking into a dark pit inside her chest. She could hear the buzz of voices coming from the campfires. What would an army be doing out here? Was the White City under attack? Or maybe it was the White City's army leaving on campaign against another kingdom.

Dark flags fluttered above the tents. Nierne raised her head higher and strained against the darkness. Who were these people? She watched the flags until one flapped open. A large wolf's head filled the banner.

Nierne let out a quiet gasp and ducked. The Temanin Empire? Here in the northlands?

Time to leave. Nierne turned around. White City or no White City, she couldn't just walk on through a Temanin war camp. She had read accounts of the brutality of the Temanin Empire and did not want to experience it firsthand.

She carefully pushed back the ferns and brush. She would just head back up the path, find somewhere safe to spend the night, and figure out her plan tomorrow—

A sharp jab caught her in the back. Nierne flinch and turned around. From beneath her hood she saw two men nearby, both with swords pointed toward her.

"Not so fast, spy." The taller one motioned toward the shorter man. "Tie her up."

Nierne twisted around and shot forward. She'd taken barely two steps before a hand locked around her arm, pulling her back.

"Don't you dare think about running," a gruff voice said.

Her other arm was wrenched back. She could feel the sharp point of a blade against her side while rope was tied around her wrists.

"Now get moving!" Fingers dug into her shoulder propelling her forward toward the camp ahead. "And if you try anything . . ." Nierne felt the blade dig deeper into her side. She bit down the cry of pain scrambling up her throat.

"Where do we take her?" said another voice.

"To Lord Tala," the gruff voice said behind her.

"Won't take much to crack this one," the deeper voice said. Nierne felt another jab to her side. "Hardly anything underneath the cloak." A low guttural laugh followed.

Nierne kept her head down, her hood still covering her hair and part of her face. Her thoughts scrambled frantically inside her mind. One moment she was counting tents to keep her bearing, the next she was remembering the stories she had read of Temanin lords.

Dear Word. She was going to die. *Think, Nierne, think.* Nierne concentrated instead on the tents she passed. Six. Seven.

"Did you hear what Lord Tala did in Avonai?" the gruff voice said after they passed a rowdy group of men.

"Yeah. Do you believe it?"

Eight.

"I do. Saw what he did to that one spy a couple days ago. He's ruthless."

Nierne tried to lick her lips but found her throat dry. Were they saying this just to scare her? Maybe. Then again, maybe not.

The man dug his talon-like fingers deep into her shoulder and steered her toward the right. Pain radiated up and down her arm. Nierne fought the urge to buckle beneath his grip. Instead, she kept her face down and counted tents.

Nine. Ten. Eleven.

Suddenly his hand clamped down. "Stop here."

Nierne tilted her head up so she could see past her hood. Ahead stood a large tent, its opening flanked by two robust, dark-skinned men. She'd never seen anyone from the Province of Hont, but these men clearly matched the descriptions she'd read.

"Here to see Lord Tala," the gruff voice said behind her. "Tell him we've caught another spy."

One of the guards moved inside the flap.

Nierne's insides froze.

The guard emerged moments later. "Lord Tala says to bring him in."

Fingers dug again into her shoulder and directed her toward the tent's opening. As they passed through the flap, Nierne was thrown to the floor. Unable to catch herself, she fell hard on her knees, her pack slamming against her back.

"So you've found another spy?" a smooth masculine voice said.

Nierne looked up. A man walked toward her, dressed all in black. His dark hair was swept back from piercing black eyes, strong face, and well-built chest beneath an open black shirt. Handsome and yet terrifying. The man reminded her of the Shadonae. She dipped her head. His boots stopped just before her face.

"Yes," the gruff voice said, "just inside the forest."

"Those fools," Lord Tala said harshly above her. "You would think they would have learned by now. Very well, leave him with me."

"Yes, sir." From the corner of her eye, Nierne saw a man bow and leave.

"Now to deal with you." A hand reached out and tore back her hood.

There was a moment of silence.

"A *woman!*"

Nierne cringed at the anger in his voice and looked away, afraid to see those dark eyes looking at her.

"Do your people really think I would treat a *woman* spy any differently than a *man?*" Lord Tala hauled her to her feet by the neckline of her cloak.

Nierne tried to find words to refute his accusation, but instead found herself coughing.

"Look at me!" He grabbed her chin between his fingers and yanked her head up. His dark eyes penetrated her own. "What were you sent here to do?"

"I- I'm not—" Nierne began coughing again.

He stepped back, a look of disgust on his face.

"I'm not a spy!" she cried, finally finding her voice.

He stared at her for a moment, then laughed. It was a cold laugh, lifting the corners of his mouth but never reaching his dark eyes. "Of course you're not." He reached for the dagger that hung at his side.

Nierne's eyes followed his hand and stared at the blade. Her mouth went dry.

"We'll try this again," Lord Tala said softly, dangerously. "What were you sent here to do? Check our numbers? Sabotage our equipment?" Suddenly she hated those dark eyes that stared back at her, merciless and black. "TELL ME!"

Nierne jumped. "I-I'm just a scribe from Thyra." She could barely breathe out the words.

"A scribe?" he said, a sudden wariness in his voice. "Why would a scribe be traveling to the White City? I thought your kind were solitary, living behind walls, reading useless old manuscripts." His eyes grew hard again. "How do I know you're not lying?"

"I . . ." Nierne wracked her mind. How could she prove she was who she said she was? "My necklace," Nierne said and looked down. "It was given to me at my initiation. Only those of the Monastery may wear them." She swept her head back and forth, but the necklace was not in its usual spot. "It must have slipped beneath my cloak." She looked back up. "If you were to untie my hands . . ."

Lord Tala studied her as if viewing something distasteful. Then he reached over and undid the clasp of her cloak. It fell in a heap around her worn boots. Shame filled her. Nierne realized how dirty she was: sweat-stained shirt, pants stiff from weeks of travel. And surely that wasn't her smell, was it?

"Well, you're starting to convince me that perhaps you *have* traveled a long way . . . or at least that you haven't bathed in weeks."

Her cheeks burned at the man's harsh words. How dare he—

"At least that's what I'd do to convince someone I was a traveler from . . . where did you say? Thyra?" He reached over and, with a fingertip, lifted the small pendant that was clasped around her neck.

Nierne stiffened at his touch and swallowed the lump she found in her throat. His head bent closer, studying what she suspected were the markings on her pendant. She looked away, her body rigid.

"Interesting craftsmanship," Lord Tala said finally, letting her pendant drop back onto her chest. He took a step back and looked at her. "I'm not an unreasonable man. Some of your story rings true. And to try you as a spy would be . . . unjust." Nierne found his words ironic. "So until I can decide whether you are who you say you are, you will remain in my tent, tied up, and under surveillance. But if you are lying to me . . ." he touched his dagger again, his face cold and unflinching.

Nierne swallowed and nodded.

"Since you will be staying with me," Lord Tala continued, "I'm afraid I must insist that you bathe. I will also have some new clothing found to replace your . . . current attire." He stepped carefully around her and walked toward the tent's flap. Nierne followed him with her eyes.

"Oh, and one more thing." He glanced back. "There are two guards just outside my tent, not to mention the entire Temanin Army. Any attempt to escape would be suicide." There was a wicked gleam in his eye. Then he turned and left.

Nierne lay on a brightly colored rug, her hair wet from her washing, the shirt on her much too big, and her hands retied. A couple of scarlet cushions hemmed with golden thread and tassels at the end sat nearby. Wisps of dark smoke floated up from a clay jar that sat on the low-lying table between the cushions. The air smelled faintly of sweetness and spice.

Near the back of the tent she could see a desk with a lamp on top, a jar of ink, and scrolls of papers. A wooden chest stood in one corner and a bed covered in dark red silk stood in the other. Lord Tala lived in wealth, even here on the battlefield.

Hopelessness moved in, holding her heart in its iron fist, squeezing until every beat hurt.

Where was the Word? She stared at one of the large pillows that lay beside her. *I will be with you always.* A promise to anyone who followed the Word. But where was He when the Shadonae had taken over Thyra? Where was the Word when Father Reth had tried to save her from the shadows? And where was He now, as she lay tied up?

Nierne sniffed and curled her body up into a tight ball. Her hands were tied behind her back, leaving her in an awkward position. Her feet lay on top of each other, fettered together with thick cords.

A rustle nearby made her tense. Nierne watched the tent flaps move through half-closed eyes. Lord Tala entered the tent. He looked at her for a moment, then moved toward the back.

She heard the quiet creak of wood. Glancing toward the sound, she found him sitting at the desk dipping a tall quill into the jar of ink. How long had it been since she had sat at a similar desk, scratching away across long rolls of parchment?

Nierne closed her eyes. That part of her life seemed so far removed from her now that her memories were more like dreams. And her reality a nightmare.

Curling tighter, she willed herself to sleep.

Caleb sighed and laid his quill down beside the parchment. He hated these weekly reports his cousin insisted he send. Corin was obsessed with this campaign.

For one brief moment he wondered why his cousin did not just lead the troops himself. After all, it wasn't that unheard of. Their ancestors had led many armies to victory.

Caleb tapped his finger on the smooth grain of the desk, studying the black signet ring on his middle finger. At least there was one thing he could look forward to: going home. And Corin had better keep his promise this time. He was tired of war.

A small groan interrupted his musings. Caleb turned toward his sitting area and studied the small body that lay between the pillows. He still had not decided what to do with the young woman the patrol had caught.

Caleb stood and sauntered toward her. Deep down he knew she wasn't a spy. Sure, if the White City had really wanted to fool him, this was what they would send: a dirty, scruffy woman with weather-worn clothing and a half empty pack. But faking a Thyrian accent would be difficult. And that necklace she wore . . .

He knelt down and watched her. Sastisfied that she was deep in sleep, he let his eyes rove across her body. She looked different now with all that grime gone. Smelled better too. The woman was small, with curves that showed even with the baggy shirt and pants. Not like the women from Temanin who were tall and lean.

His eyes came back to her face. Her hair mesmerized him. Caleb had never seen hair like hers, blood red and curly, falling just below her chin. He reached out and touched one of the curls. Her hair felt soft between his fingers.

He looked back toward her face, noting the sprinkling of tiny red spots across her nose and cheeks that matched that same blood red color, a startling contrast to her pale skin.

His curiousity about her grew. He saw the thin gold chain around her neck and wanted another look at that pendant.

Caleb extended his finger and carefully pulled the chain until the pendant emerged from the oversized shirt. He held the pendant between his thumb and finger.

Only once before had he seen similar markings: in a book he had browsed while visiting a distant cousin. He could not recall what the book had been about or why he had picked it up, but he did remember the markings. For some reason, they had intrigued him.

Caleb held the pendant a little higher, noting the three smooth ovals near the bottom, one longer than the other two. Engraved above one of the smaller ovals were three slash marks, and engraved above the other was a long curved line, like a snake rearing its head.

They were the symbols for the Word.

He let the pendant drop and turned his attention back toward the young woman. He believed that she really was a scribe from the famous Monastery in Thyra. But what was a scribe doing here? And a woman one, at that?

Why would a pretty young woman like her join such a rigid institution? He could never live that way. He enjoyed life too much.

Caleb stood and stretched, extending his arms above his head. He looked at her one more time. What had brought her here, away from the Monastery? Thyra was a long ways away. And where were her companions? Surely she hadn't traveled over the mountains alone, had she? He shook his head and moved toward the back of his tent.

Caleb stripped off his shirt and tossed it over the wooden chest. A familiar sense of dread began to pour through him. Maybe tonight his nightmares would stay away. He pulled back the scarlet covers. No, they would come. They always came, each one worse than the last.

He lay down on the silk sheets and stared at the canvas ceiling above. She would be back tonight: the woman with the glowing hand. She would be there, standing in the midst of those who haunted his mind, beckoning him with that hand of hers, promising to show him the truth.

But I don't want the truth. Caleb turned over. He just wanted one peaceful night's sleep. Maybe he should have gone to the chief healer today. He almost did. Until the thought of explaining his dreams kept him away. And fear that whatever the healer gave him would interfere with his mind or body.

Not that the dreams weren't already doing that.

When the dreams had begun, he would wake the next morning with a strong desire to find her. But this morning had been different. This morning he'd found himself heading out of the tent before he could stop himself. The urge to find her had driven his subconscious mind. And that had scared him.

Who was she? Caleb shifted again. He wasn't sure he wanted to know. And he sure as sands didn't want her messing with his mind anymore.

Caleb leaned over and blew out the lamp. He settled back down between the sheets. Deep inside he wondered, if he stayed here much longer, one day he would finally give in. Would he just walk out of this tent and go wherever the dream led him?

He knew the answer. Just as he also knew that whatever truth this woman showed him would probably change his life.

And that terrified him most of all.

CHAPTER 23

Rowen stopped in front of the double set of doors. On the other side was the main audience chamber and Lady Astrea. Perhaps even the council, as well. All here to decide her fate.

"Don't be afraid." She closed her eyes. "You do not have to be afraid." Rowen took a deep breath, filling her nostrils and lungs. She held the air there for a moment and let it out. But it did not help the paralyzing fear sweeping across her body. What she really wanted to do was turn and run.

"Not anymore." She tugged at the new leather glove Lore had procured for her, since her old one had gotten lost somewhere along the beach near Avonai. It felt stiff compared to her old glove, but at least it covered her mark.

Rowen straightened her tabard and checked the sword that hung at her side. Then she reached over and pressed down on one of the door handles. It was time.

The door opened with ease. A guard stood on either side of the door. They both nodded at Rowen. She stepped inside and quietly shut the door behind her.

The chamber felt cold and overwhelming. Everything inside had been carved from white stone: the floor, the ceiling, and the walls. White stone pillars ran along either side of the chamber. The ceiling was at least two stories high, arching to a point that ran down the middle of the room. The room itself looked big enough to hold over a hundred people. The only other color in the chamber was from a long blue runner that ran from the doors directly to the platform two hundred feet ahead on which sat a white throne carved from the wall behind.

Long narrow windows lined the left side of the room. Beams of sunlight shone through the windows, across the white floor and blue runner. Silence hung inside the room like a cold winter morning after a new fallen snow.

Rowen looked around again. Where was Lady Astrea?

She proceeded along the runner, passing between the pillars toward the throne. It wasn't until she passed the second to last set of pillars that she saw Lady Astrea. She stood to the left, near the last window.

Rowen stopped and stared. Lady Astrea had changed seemingly overnight. Instead of the young woman Rowen had followed around the castle, a young ruler stood in her place. Lady Astrea stood in front of the window, the sun streaming down across her face and body. Her face looked pale and drawn, even in the sunlight. She wore a long white gown that flowed behind her. A white mantle trimmed in white fur hung from her shoulders. Her hair was pulled up in loose curls. A silver crown sat on her head.

Behind Lady Astrea, in the corner of the chamber, Rowen spotted Aren. He stood rigid, his arms folded across his chest. He wore his formal uniform, and his hair was pulled back. The shadows cast his face in sharp relief. That, combined with his tattoos, made Aren look like a true Nordic, a barbarian from the north, and not the fun-loving man Rowen knew.

Had everyone changed while she was gone?

Lady Astrea turned. "Rowen, you're here."

Rowen bowed. "Yes, milady." Dread came rushing back.

Lady Astrea moved away from the window toward the throne.

Aren looked at Rowen and gave her a small smile.

Rowen tried to return it, but her lips would not move. She straightened and headed toward the platform.

Lady Astrea sat on the white throne, her dress sweeping around her like fluid silk. Her hands came to rest on either arm of the throne. Aren stood discreetly to the left.

Rowen stopped at the bottom of the platform. *At least the council isn't here,* she thought. That gave her a little courage.

"Rowen."

Rowen looked up.

Lady Astrea folded her hands across her lap. "How long have you known you were an Eldaran?"

Straight to the point. "Since the wolf attack, milady."

"How long have you had the mark?"

Rowen swallowed. "Since my father's death."

Lady Astrea nodded. "I have been investigating you, Rowen."

Rowen felt her blood rush to her head. So she knew about the charges of witchcraft and her exile . . .

"Do not worry. I have not contacted your village. I have only talked to Balint. He told me your story. I do not think it would help anyone for me to talk to the elders of Cinad. This is a delicate issue, and for good reason. For hundreds of years there has been a ban against the use of magic or supernatural power. It was an edict drawn up by my great-great grandfather. Due to the Nordic Wars."

Rowen bowed her head. "Milady, I did not know."

"Most people do not. The edict was passed a long time ago, as a way to ensure another Nordic War never occurred. It was a proclamation written out of fear. And there are powers that we *should* fear." Lady Astrea sighed. "By our laws, you should be put to death."

Rowen stiffened, and her breath caught in her throat. Here it was, all over again, like in Cinad. Only this time, it would not be exile. *Lore, you were wrong.*

"I have thought through my choices," Lady Astrea said. "I must think of what is best for my people. I could have you burned at the stake or banished. That is what my forefathers would have done."

Rowen stared at the bottom hem of Lady Astrea's dress, still as a stone. Now came the declaration of her death.

"But one thing I learned from my father is that not all power is evil. This is why Balint was allowed to use his power. Because of my father's mercy and understanding. And because we knew his power was of Eldaran descent."

Shock raced through Rowen. She raised her head slightly. Her lips trembled. Did she dare to think that Lady Astrea would show her mercy? Or perhaps the "mercy" would be exile again. She was afraid to look at Lady Astrea. But she needed to know. Rowen looked up.

Lady Astrea gave her a half smile. "I have watched you, Rowen, over the last year. You are kind and gentle to those around you. You have been a loyal varor and twice have placed yourself in danger to save others—not least, to save me. Those are not the traits of a person who would use her power to conquer others. Those are the traits of a true Eldaran of old."

Rowen swallowed, and tears filled the corners of her eyes. No one besides her father had ever said anything like this to her before.

But a sobering thought pierced through her moment of joy: Did Lady Astrea know what she really was?

"I understand why you hide your mark. Balint told me what your true power is."

"Then . . . you know?" Rowen said, her voice cracking.

"Yes. From what I know and what Balint told me, it is the most powerful and most feared of all the Eldaran gifts. But I have never seen you use it on others, at least not willingly. And what little I know of the Word, I do know He would not give a gift like this if there weren't some reason. I believe you will use it only when needed. Therefore," Lady Astrea looked Rowen straight in the eye, "today and henceforth, I choose to extend my protection over you, Rowen. As long as you use your power for the good of others."

Relief rushed through Rowen, leaving her legs shaky. No banishment. No death. Instead, Lady Astrea herself would shield her. Rowen didn't know what to say. If she opened her mouth, she knew she would start crying. So she looked at Lady Astrea and gave her a tight nod. *Thank You, Word.*

"However," Lady Astrea continued, "I'm not sure if the people of the Ryland Plains are prepared for an announcement of this magnitude. Especially during war. At some point, I will need to make known who you are. But I believe it prudent to wait, for now."

Rowen nodded again. She agreed.

There was a pause. Lady Astrea grew somber. "Rowen, I must say something, because I know many others will be thinking the same thing." She took a deep breath and let it out slowly. "The fact that you exist . . . It frightens me."

The joy inside Rowen dimmed. She saw Aren frown from the corner of her eye.

Lady Astrea leaned across her lap with clasped hands. "What darkness has come into the Lands that the Word has seen fit to cause Eldarans to rise again? It's not that I wish you didn't live. Not at all. But is it just a coincidence that an Eldaran survives with almost all her powers intact? Or are you, like Balint, just a descendent of an almost dead race?"

Rowen looked down. It was the same question that had haunted her ever since Lore had talked about the Shadonae. Suddenly the world seemed larger and scarier than it ever had when she'd been a simple woman living in Cinad. And it was a large and frightening world with her right in the middle of it.

"I hope it is the latter," Lady Astrea said quietly.

Rowen swallowed and found her voice. She looked up at Lady Astrea. "I do, as well, milady."

Lore entered the war room the next day. The room was dark, save for the wrought-iron chandelier that hung low over a long wooden table. There were no windows in the room. Just four bare walls and a narrow table shoved against one side with a decanter and four glasses. Fat candles dripping with wax lit up the area around the table but left the rest of the room in shadows.

A heavy musty smell hung in the air. Muffled voices carried across the room. Scrolls and maps were spread across the table. Two men stood at the end of the table. They both looked up at Lore's entrance.

"Captain Lore." Commander Kelyn came around the table, his chainmail jingling beneath his dark blue tabard. His dark hair was combed back and his face carefully shaved. He gave Lore a quick bow.

"Commander Kelyn," Lore said, returning his bow.

The other man approached him.

Commander Kelyn extended a hand toward the man. "Captain Lore, this is Commander Eirik of the Nordic forces."

Commander Eirik bowed. "Pleasure to meet you, sir." His thick golden hair hung to his shoulders and a full beard covered the lower half of his face. A single black tattoo crisscrossed his left cheek. He wore the dark green tabard of Nordica with the symbol of the bear over his chainmail.

Lore bowed. "And the same to you, Commander Eirik."

"We were looking over the maps and discussing defense while we waited for you and Lady Astrea. Would you care for a drink?" Commander Kelyn gestured toward the table along the wall with the decanter and glasses.

Lore could barely see it in the dark. "No, thank you."

The door opened behind him. Lady Astrea entered. Her white apparel lit up the room like a pale moth on a dark night. Lore backed away to let her in. Aren followed, shutting the door once they were inside.

"Milady," both commanders said, bowing deeply. Lore followed suit.

"Gentlemen," she said in her low, feminine voice. "Let us begin."

Commander Kelyn led the way back to the end of the table where a large map of the White City lay amongst the scrolls and other maps. He brushed the other parchments to the side.

"So what do we know?" Lady Astrea said.

"Not much," Commander Kelyn said. "The Temanin Army continues to stay hidden within the trees of Anwin. We have searched the treeline with spyglasses from every corner of the outer wall."

He ran a finger along the line that represented the outer wall. It was half a square, extending from the sheer face of the mountain the White City was carved from, to the southwest corner, along the wall where the main gate was located, to the southeast corner and back to the mountain again.

"But we can see nothing. Whatever the Temanin army is planning or building, they are doing it deep in the forest."

"What about our spies? Have they reported anything?" Lady Astrea said.

Commander Kelyn sighed. "We have sent out spies, but only one has returned. He reported that the Temanins are chopping down trees. That was about all he could see."

"For what purpose?"

"Most likely siege weapons: catapults, ladders, battering rams. With Anwin Forest right here, the Temanin Army has more than enough wood to build anything they want. And from the battle at Mostyn, we know that they already have many of these weapons. No doubt they built them while they were stationed at Hadrast Fortress after they crossed Hershaw Pass. My Lady, I believe it's just a matter of time before they attack the White City."

Lady Astrea looked down at the map, her face grave. "How much time do you think we have?"

Commander Kelyn shook his head. "I do not know. We have enough supplies to hunker down and wait until our allies arrive. But if the Temanin Army is efficient and quick, we may only have days before the attack begins."

"And then what?"

"Fight and hold out until Avonai and Nordica answer our call."

Lady Astrea turned to Commander Eirik. "How long will it take for Lord Tancred to muster more troops and help us?"

Commander Eirik stroked his beard and looked down at the map. "A couple days to gather more men. So not long. It's the march down here from Nordica that will take time. Most of the men will be on foot." He grimaced. "At least a month."

Lady Astrea sighed. "Captain Lore, do you know how long it will take Avonai?" She turned and looked at him.

Lore was struck again by the similarity between Lady Astrea and her father. The same dark hair and pale skin, the same rigid stance, the same worry creases across her forehead. "I do not know," Lore said slowly. "King Alaric and Prince Evander were aware of the impending attack, but with the assassinations—" Lore saw Lady Astrea's lips tighten into one red line—"I'm not sure how quickly they have mobilized the Avonain troops."

Lore watched Lady Astrea quietly compose herself. He had a feeling he was the only one in the room who could see how much she was hiding. She wore the same mask of confidence her father always had. But Lore had seen the man beneath the mask, and he could see a small glimpse of the daughter too. She was worried, grieving . . . and afraid.

She looked back at Lore. "If they did mobilize, how long would it take Avonai to reach us?" Her voice never cracked.

"Five days. Four, if they rode hard. But that is only the cavalry. It will take the rest of the Avonai forces at least ten days to march here."

Lady Astrea nodded and looked back at the map. Commander Kelyn stood near the edge of the table, his arms folded across his chest. "So, gentlemen, what do we do while we wait for reinforcements?" she asked.

Both commanders looked at Lore.

"Go ahead, Captain Lore." Comander Kelyn backed away from the table. "We will do what we can to help, but this is your city. Its defense is yours to command. How can we carry out your plan?"

His turn now. Lore stepped toward the table. "Here is what—" he paused and glanced at Lady Astrea. "Here is what your father and I planned."

She gave him a small nod to continue.

If only he had . . . No. No time for regret. Live in the present.

"First, we need to bring every civilian into the castle," Lore said, forcing his thoughts back. "The people will be best protected here. While we are doing that, we need to station archers along here—" He ran his finger along the southern wall and the main gate. "They will shoot any Temanins who start across the field from the trees."

"What about shooting flaming arrows into the trees to start a fire in the Temanin camp?" Commander Eirik said.

"I've thought about that possibility. Problem is, there is no way to contain the fire. Anwin Forest is dry this time of year. The fires might burn the Temanin camp. But they also might grow out of control and spread, burning not only Anwin Forest, but the plains as well, destroying much of the Ryland Plains." Lore shook his head. "It's an idea, but not one I want to use, at least not yet.

"So archers along the southern wall. I also want archers stationed at both the smaller east and west gates. We will have hot tar ready for rams and soldiers along the battlements to push back any ladders—and fight anyone who makes it over the wall."

"And if they use catapults?"

"We will answer with our own catapults. Without fire at first. With fire, if we must."

"What about using the cavalry?" Commander Eirik said. "Sally out the western or eastern gates and destroy their catapults."

Lore rubbed his chin. "It's an idea. But if the Temanins have the city surrounded and all three gates guarded, then a mission like that would probably be suicide. The moment we left the city, they would shoot us. But I will consider it, depending on where we find the Temanins stationed or where they move their siege weapons."

Commander Kelyn tapped the table with a finger. "What if the Temanins decide to set fire to our own walls and gates?"

Lore looked over at him. "I'm confident they will. Your men can bring barrels of water to the walls and soaked animal skins to place on the gates."

"And what if they make it past the first wall?" Everyone turned to look at Lady Astrea. "What will happen if they breach our outer defenses?"

Lore sighed and looked down at the map. The mountain protected the northern side of the White City and Celestis Castle. There was no force that could scale that cliff, so no surprise attack would come from there. A thick outer wall surrounded the White City. Lore was counting on that to protect them. But if something did happen . . .

"We would need to retreat. Those along the battlements would be instructed to hold back the Temanins as they conduct a fighting withdrawal to the inner gates." Lore traced the line that represented the second wall that surrounded the castle and courtyard. "We will close the second gates before the Temanins reach the inner wall. Inside, we will hold out until Avonai and Nordica arrive."

The room became silent. Lore had a feeling he knew what the others were thinking: What if the second wall is breached? He prayed that did not happen. They could maybe hold out in the castle, but if the second wall fell, there would be no time to lead the people through the underground tunnel.

And even if they were able to begin such an escape, someone in the Temanin Army was bound to notice a crowd of people emerging in Anwin Forest. The tunnel was meant only for the high lord or lady and a few guards, no more.

"Thank you, Captain Lore." Lady Astrea stepped forward and placed her hand on the map. "This is it, gentlemen." She slowly turned her head and looked each man in the eye. The light from the candles above illuminated her fair skin and white gown, making her look ethereal. "We must hold on our own until help arrives. We must hold, for the sake of our people. And, Word willing, we will live to see the end of this war."

If only Lord Gaynor could see his daughter, Lore thought. He would be so proud.

CHAPTER 24

The next morning, Rowen leaned against one of the sidewalls inside the guards' training room. Men and women crowded the room and spilled out into the common room beyond. Almost everyone wore a dark blue tabard. Voices echoed back and forth between the stone walls. Chainmail chingled, leather creaked, boots clapped on the wooden floor. Heat filled the room like embers in a fireplace.

The warmth did not help the fatigue that ate away at her body and mind. The last two nights she had hardly slept. Over and over, her mind kept coming back to the dream that had haunted her ever since she had arrived back.

Show him the truth.

Rowen shook her head, feeling as though the words were rattling inside her skull. What did they mean? And who was the "him" the dream was about? She remembered vaguely having the same dream weeks ago in Avonai, but she'd thought it had been a onetime event, something she had brushed away as not worth mentioning.

But now . . . now she wondered if there had been something more to the vision.

Sweat began to trickle down the side of her face. How much longer did they have to stand here? She wiped her face and looked up. Blue sky dotted with wispy clouds filled the glass dome high above. Such a beautiful day. Sometimes it seemed hard to believe the skies could go peacefully on when down below war killed and destroyed.

The crowd shifted around her. She could see Lore making his way to the front of the training room. Finally. A couple of men pressed closer to her.

One bumped into her.

"Pardon me, I didn't mean to— Rowen?"

"Hi, Donar."

The gate guard was a short, thickset man with a face that still held on to a babyish grin. Sweat beaded his balding head, making his thinning brown hair stick to his scalp. He wore a belt across his blue tabard and his smallsword hung at his side. "What are you doing here? I thought you would be with Lady Astrea today."

"Aren is serving as her varor. I'm here to help out where I can." She remembered the guardsman's wife had recently had a child. "How are your wife and little one?"

Donar beamed. "Good. The babe is healthy and very strong. And Matilda . . ." His smile faded.

A shadow passed over Rowen's heart. "Your wife, she's fine, right?"

"Oh, yes. Doing quite well. It's just that with the Temanin Army outside the gates and me being a guard and all . . ." his voice trailed off.

"I understand." Poor Matilda. Rowen knew the fear of having a loved one serve during war. And the grief when war took that loved one away.

"I've had Matilda and little Hanna transferred to the castle. At least here I know they will be safe."

I hope so, Rowen thought.

Lore began to speak, so Donar turned back around.

"Lady Astrea, Commander Kelyn, Commander Eirik, and I met last night," Lore said. "We have decided what needs to be done before Temanin attacks, and we have an excellent defense plan. Now we do not know when the battle will start, but we do know it will start soon. And so the first thing we need to do is move every person within the city into the castle. The castle is set back far enough that anything a catapult can launch should not reach us . . ."

Rowen looked over at her fellow guards. Some of them were stone-faced, having been trained to look at trouble head on. But one or two of the younger ones and most of the new recruits looked anxious. She felt a bit nervous too. Who knew what the next few days would bring?

She turned her attention back to Lore. He wore a dark blue tabard like everyone else did, but instead of his leather jerkin, he wore chainmail. Rowen frowned. Why would he be wearing chainmail . . . ? Her breath left her lungs.

Lore would be at the front line.

Of course. She turned and rubbed her forehead, feeling faint. Lore was Captain of the Guard. His place would be first to ensure Lady Astrea's safety, then the city's safety. That's why he had met with the other commanders. He was in charge of protecting all of them.

Rowen looked up again. Lore stood straight and tall as he gave instructions. His eyes slowly moved across the room, looking over the crowd. His voice held passion. He assured those gathered that their families would be protected here in the castle and that Avonai and Nordica were on their way. His confidence seemed to seep into those around her. Heads tilted up, shoulders straightened, and hands stopped fidgeting and dropped to their sides.

"I will divide you into groups and tell you where to go," Lore said. "I want every civilian brought to the castle by nightfall."

"Yes, sir," the crowd answered.

Lore disappeared amongst the guards. Rowen remained next to the wall, not sure if Lore would send her out too. Minutes later, the guards and new recruits began to disperse, moving toward the main doors to carry out their orders. She rolled her shoulders and waited.

"Rowen, it's good to have you back," Geoffrey said as he walked by.

Rowen watched him exit the doors, somewhat puzzled. Geoffrey was one of the older guards, but he hadn't talked much to her in the past. Then again, she hadn't let him, either. It felt nice to have him speak to her just now. She tugged at her glove and wondered what he would think when he found out what she really was.

What would any of them think? She knew how quickly acceptance could turn to rejection.

She looked around the room. A couple of the guards still mingled inside the training room. They were gate guards who were due to change shifts in a couple of minutes. Donar stood with them, waiting for his own shift up on the wall. Otherwise everyone else was gone, having already headed out into the city.

Would Lady Astrea's protection actually keep her safe from Ryland's ancient superstition over people with power and edict to eliminate them? Or was there too much hurt and bitterness left over from the Nordic Wars? No wonder her village had treated her like a witch.

Lore made his way toward her. The closer he came, the less confident and more tired he looked. He gave Rowen a quick smile, then frowned, his dark grey eyes darting across her face. He stopped a foot before her and crossed his arms. "You look tired and worried."

"So do you." She gave him a half smile.

"I haven't seen you since you met with Lady Astrea. Is everything . . . all right?"

Had Lore been worried? "Yes. Lady Astrea has promised me her protection."

A genuine smile filled his face. "Oh, that's good! Really good. But then, why the troubled face?"

Rowen sighed and looked away. "I haven't been sleeping well the last two nights."

"Worried?" Lore said.

"About Temanin? Who isn't? But that's not what's keeping me up."

He raised an eyebrow in question.

Rowen sighed again. "I've been having this dream," she began in a low voice, not wishing for those still present to hear her. "And I'm not sure if it means anything, but—"

The floor shook and the muffled sound of thunder rumbled through the training room.

"What was that?" Rowen looked around.

Lore and the other guards were doing the same. "I'm not sure," Lore said cautiously. Another rumble of thunder echoed around the room. Rowen and Lore glanced up. Blue sky filled the dome.

A shadow fell across the glass.

"*Watch out!*"

Lore shoved Rowen up against the wall just as glass shattered above, followed by cries and shouts.

Hot tiny stings dotted her face. Smoke filled her nostrils. A heavy weight pressed against her body. Rowen opened her eyes and found Lore pinning her against the wall, his body covering hers. A shower of glass covered his hair and shoulders.

Slowly he opened his eyes and groaned.

"Captain, are you all ri—" Rowen winced, her face smarting at the movement. Lore stumbled back. She felt her face and found tiny cuts across her cheeks, nose and forehead. Around her she could hear more shouting and one shrill cry.

Lore shook his head and looked dazed.

Rowen glanced around him. She could see a large boulder half wedged into a wall. The shrill scream seemed to be coming from there . . .

She took a step closer, then covered her mouth. *Dear Word.*

Donar and two other men lay crushed beneath the boulder. She could see the legs of the other men, but not their upper bodies or faces. Donar lay with the boulder halfway across his legs and midsection.

Lore turned. "No! Donar!"

Donar's face paled before her eyes, and he stopped screaming. "C-Capt—" he said with a gasp. He focused on Lore. Blood trickled out of the corner of his mouth.

"I'm here." Lore fell to his knees and grabbed Donar's hand. "We're going to get you out." He turned toward Rowen. "Get all the men you can in here. We need to get this rock off of him!"

Rowen nodded numbly and turned. Her mind felt paralyzed. Rumbles continued to shake the room around her. It took her a moment to make her legs work. Staggering around, she left the room, Donar's panted screams filled her ears.

"Oh, Word. Oh, Word. Oh, Word," she whispered and made her way out into the hallway. Down the corridor she spotted someone. Rowen opened her mouth but nothing came out. She swallowed and tried again. "Help!" she cried. "We need help!"

Two servants came running down the hall.

"Quick, the training room." Rowen pointed toward the Guards Quarter. The two men nodded and ran. Rowen continued down the corridor, shouting for more help.

After finding three more, she ran back to the room, only to find everyone standing around. Moving past the servants, she found Lore brushing his hand across Donar's face.

The room began to spin. "No!" Rowen cried. She had to do something. She pulled at her glove and stumbled toward Donar. She fell beside him. "He can't die! He has a wife . . . and a baby—" She ripped off the glove and threw it to the floor. She placed her hand on Donar's neck. The healing came, bursting up from inside her and flowing toward her hand.

Rowen heard Lore speaking to her, but his voice was muffled. She felt his hand trying to pull her own away. She held on. "Please, Lore," she cried. Could he not understand? She had to save Donar if she could.

Rowen could feel something cold moving up her arm now. Fear began to beat inside her chest. She didn't care. She would not let this war take another person. She had power now. And she was going to use it.

"Rowen." Somewhere inside her mind, she could feel Lore's face next to hers, his mouth next to her ear. "You can't save everyone. He's gone. Donar is gone." It was like hearing him through a rush of wind.

He can't be, Rowen thought. She could not see through the haze of her healing. *I can feel his—*

Agony tore into her and blew her away.

Lore heard Rowen shout and looked back. She came tumbling down at his side. Her hand was tugging at something. "He can't die!" she cried. "He has a wife . . . and a baby—"

He saw her pull at her glove and knew instantly what she was going to do. He couldn't let the others see . . .

Lore turned to those gathered. "Go, now! Find others who need help."

It took a moment for the servants and last two guards to move. The servants left first. One guard started toward Lore.

"Find Commander Kelyn. He's on the battlements. Tell him to start launching our catapults." Lore pointed at the door. "Tell him I will be right there."

The guard nodded and left.

Lore turned back toward Rowen. Her hand was already on Donar's neck. "Rowen, he's dead. You can't do anything." She didn't seem to hear him. Life had already faded from Donar's eyes. Fear grabbed Lore by the throat. What would happen to Rowen if she tried to heal a dead man? He grabbed her hand and tried to pull it away from Donar.

Tears streamed down her face. "Please, Lore!"

He couldn't pull her hand away. When had Rowen become so strong? Was this part of her Eldaran power? Lore leaned in next to Rowen and spoke into her ear. "Rowen, you can't save everyone. He's gone. Donar is gone." *Please Word, make her let go—*

Her back arched. An earsplitting scream filled the room, causing the hair on his body to rise. Lore let go of Rowen's hand and sat back. Her legs twitched, then jerked away from her body at odd angles. White bone shoved its way through the black fabric of her pants.

Lore faltered at the sight, shocked. Her healing was nothing like he had imagined: the peaceful laying on of hands. Instead it was a violent affair where Rowen literally took on the injury, shattered bone for shattered bone.

He panicked. He had to get her hand off of Donar before it killed her.

Lore reached over and seized Rowen's hand again. Her strength seemed gone. He pulled her hand away and held it by the wrist, careful not to touch her mark.

Rowen slumped to her side and looked up at him. She didn't seem to recognize him. A small trickle of blood began to flow out of the corner of her mouth.

He placed her hand down. His mind raced on what to do next. He couldn't risk moving her, not with her lower body shattered and who knew what else. But he also needed to get to Lady Astrea. Now that the attack had started and he'd initiated their defensive plan, he needed to see to her safety.

Lore ran a hand through his hair. "What do I do?" He knew the answer. He needed to leave Rowen. He went to stand, shock still tingling along his nerves. He had never seen Rowen heal before. Is this what she had looked like when she had healed him?

Rowen blinked. "Lore?" She moved slightly and tried to sit up.

Lore knelt down and placed his hand on her shoulder. "No, Rowen, stay there." He guided her back down.

"Donar, is he—" She coughed, sending blood flying across his face. Lore lifted a hand and wiped it away. "Is he well?" She looked up at his face.

Lore felt her forehead. Her skin was cold. "No, Rowen." He brushed her hair away from her face. "I'm sorry. Donar is gone."

Her face scrunched up. She covered her face with her hands and sobbed.

Lore felt duty and his heart tearing apart on the inside. Duty said he needed to leave. But Rowen needed him too.

"I couldn't save him. And now . . . his wife . . . and baby . . ." Rowen's voice drifted off. Her hands slowly fell from her face, her eyes shut. Moments later her breathing grew less rattled. Worried, Lore touched her forehead again. The clammy coldness had given way to warmth. He looked over at her legs and found the jagged edge of her bone no longer poking through her clothing.

Once again Rowen had healed herself. She was safe, for now.

Reluctantly Lore stood. *Word, I don't want to leave her like this.* But he needed to go.

"Captain Lore, do you need help?"

309

Lore turned around. A servant stood behind him. He gave an inward sigh. *Thank You, Word.* "Rolph, I need you to get Rowen to Balint." Rolph looked around Lore and gasped. "The others are dead. But Rowen is still alive, and needs to be brought to Balint. I need to get to Lady Astrea."

"Yes, Captain."

Lore took off at a run and didn't look back.

CHAPTER 25

An invisible tether pulled Caleb Tala through the Temanin camp.

The force led him toward the dark forest. He could hear the shouts of soldiers and the heavy twang of taut rope suddenly loosening as nearby catapults launched their projectiles toward the White City. The assualt was fully underway. But the sounds were only a distant echo around him. And in this numb state, he did not care.

A couple of soldiers gave him puzzled looks. Caleb ignored them. All he could feel was steady pressure across his back, guiding him to the woman with the glowing hand—

Caleb lurched to a stop, yanking back with all his might. He cursed loudly and swiftly turned around and headed back toward his tent.

More soldiers looked up as he passed by. He snarled at them, siphoning off some of his anger at his lack of control. This was the second time he had left his tent in what amounted to sleepwalking, following that inner call to find this woman.

I'm stronger than this, Caleb thought, clenching his hands into fists. Whatever forces were out there, he was stronger. He only needed to discipline his mind more to fight whatever was calling him.

Caleb yanked back the flap of his tent and stormed inside. He startled the young red-haired woman tied up nearby. "What are you looking at?" he yelled, pinning her down with his gaze.

She stared back. He could see the faint ember of fury burning beneath fearful eyes. So she had a spark within her, did she? He felt her gaze follow him across the tent, where he sat down with a growl.

I need to do something about this. Caleb drummed the desk with his fingers. Perhaps he could tie himself to the tent post. No, no, too many awkward questions, not to mention loss of respect. Visit the chief healer and demand some herb for these visions? Again, too many questions.

For one moment he wished he knew someone he could confide in, someone who could help him figure out what was happening to him. He glanced over at the young woman, remembering that she was a scribe. She would certainly know a lot, having worked at the Monastery. No, he thought, slamming down that idea. He did not need his prisoner to see how vulnerable he was. Not that she didn't see it every time the vision came upon him.

She probably thought he was insane.

Caleb looked at her from the corner of his eye. She had laid back down on the cushions, her hands and feet still tied. Commander Arpiar had asked him earlier that morning if he had learned anything from her. Caleb had told him the woman was not a spy, just some unfortunate traveler arriving to the White City at the wrong time. After thinking for a couple seconds, Commander Arpiar had told him to place her with the rest of the prisoners of war.

For some reason, Caleb had felt uncomfortable doing that. He knew what would happen to a woman prisoner of war, especially a pretty one like her. So he had chosen to keep her tied up in his tent and wondered where this sudden display of conscience had come from. After a moment longer, he dismissed the idea that it was his conscience keeping her, but rather his fascination with the strange woman.

She was definitely one of the most unique looking women he had ever met, what with that red hair and those dark grey eyes. And her commitment to an order famous for its celibacy and stringent way of life intrigued him. What was it about the Monastery that had made this young woman give up what he considered the best things in life?

Caleb shook his head and turned back to his desk. Now was not the time to dwell on the mystery that lay within his tent. He needed to figure out how to keep from succumbing to—

Wait. He stopped thrumming the table. A thought occurred to him, a thought so foreign that he almost laughed at its simplicity. Yet it was the most dangerous idea of all.

Why not follow the vision?

He had proven he could pull away from the impulse. But instead of turning back, he would follow the vision to its source: the woman with the glowing hand. And there he would find out why she was haunting him, question her until he had his answers. And if she was unwilling . . .

Caleb fingered the dagger he always wore at his side. He knew how to make people talk.

The color of blood tainted the sky. The sun sank in the west, a burning ball of gold and orange behind the smoke. Black smoke belched and swirled above the White City. Fires blazed behind the walls and along the cobblestone streets, consuming wagons, barrels, storefronts.

Shadows spread across the field and surrounding Anwin Forest like long black fingers. Chunks of white stone, broken ladders, and corpses littered the long grass. Small fires burned between the bodies. Long dark streaks of tar stained the once-white walls of the city. Its sickly sweet scent mingled with smoke and blood. Heat blazed across the battlements from the fires and hot summer evening.

Lore stood on the archway right above the gates. Sweat poured down his back and chest, soaking into his undershirt. The chainmail he wore felt like a heavy mantle across his body. His hair was plastered to his head. He wiped his eyes and held the spyglass up.

He could see the Temanin Army teeming within the trees. They were growing bolder, drawing closer to the tree line. As if they sensed the impending death of the White City.

Well, they weren't dead yet.

Lore lowered his spyglass and turned. The battlements stretched across the top of the city's outer walls. The walkway was about twelve feet wide and broken in a couple places where the catapults had found their mark. Archers and soldiers stood behind the merlons, ready for whatever assault came their way. The sky grew darker by the minute. Lore pointed to one of the soldiers behind him. "You, we need the torches lit."

"Yes, sir."

"And you," Lore pointed to another man. "I need you to tell the men at the catapults to prepare another assault." Whatever the Temanins were planning, Lore wanted to be ready. "Archers, watch the fields. Hit anything that moves."

His command flew along the battlements. Sergeants shouted orders. Archers moved along the wall, grabbing more arrows.

A messenger came running from the east side of the battlements. "Here to report, Captain," the young man said, panting.

"What's the message?"

A shout went up. Bows began to twang nearby. Lore ducked and placed a hand on the messenger's head, pushing the young man down with him. Seconds later a shower of arrows hit the wall with flurry of clattering. A few made it past the merlons and hit whatever stood out. Lore looked up, but it was too dark to see the arrows.

A muffled whomp sounded nearby. A soldier stumbled past Lore with a look of surprise and an arrow protruding from his neck.

The messenger watched the man. His eyes grew big, and his face paled. The soldier fell onto the walkway with a gurgle.

"Don't watch." Lore placed his hand on the messenger's shoulder and turned the young man away from the soldier.

The shower of arrows stopped seconds later.

Lore cautiously stood. No more arrows came flying. "We have someone injured here," he called out. His words were passed along. There were other groans of pain in the dark.

"Follow me," Lore said to the messenger. They passed two men slumped against the wall with a healer attending their wounds. Another healer went running by, dark stains across his white robes.

Soldiers were placing torches inside the iron brackets along the wall. The sky rumbled up above. Lore stopped and looked up. Looked like a storm was moving in off the mountaintop.

That was going to complicate things.

Lore entered the gatehouse and hurried down the steps, the

messenger following. At the bottom was a small round room lit by a torch that hung from one of the brackets. It smelled strongly of wet fur and smoke. Weapons hung on racks on one side of the room. Deer and cow skins were piled in another. Barrels surrounded the rest of the room.

A large, robust man turned around. "Captain Lore, what can I do for you?"

"I need water."

The man nodded and went to one of the barrels.

Lore turned back toward the young man. "What is the message?"

"I . . . um . . ." Shock filled the young man's face.

"Concentrate on me," Lore said. "Look at my face. Now, breathe."

The young man took a couple of deep breaths. Slowly, color seeped back into his face.

The large man handed Lore a ladle with water. Lore held it out toward the messenger. "Take a drink."

The young man nodded and took the ladle. He drank deeply. Water trickled from the corners of his mouth.

"Feeling better?" Lore asked.

"Yes."

Lore took the ladle and handed it back to the other man. "Now what is the message?"

"Commander Eirik wanted to let you know the western gate is holding, but there was a surprise attack on the eastern gate. A ram was used. It was a simple one, but it did some damage."

"And?"

"The gate held, barely. He and his men were able to shoot down the Temanins shielding the ram and set the ram on fire."

"When did this occur?"

"About a half hour ago."

Frustration and fear clawed its way up Lore's middle. The Temanins were like ants, millions of them. Every time he thought they would live through the day, the Temanin Army would swarm up to the gates and almost break through. How much longer could they take the pounding?

Lore let none of his emotions show on his face. "Go back to Commander Eirik. Tell him to let me know if he needs back up."

The messenger clapped his heels together. "Yes, Captain."

After the young man left, Lore went to the barrel and dipped the ladle inside for a quick drink of his own. The water felt wonderful on his parched tongue and throat. But he had no time to linger. The battle didn't stop for him, or anyone else. Lore wiped his mouth and left the ladle by the side. He went back up the stairs.

His body felt like it had been dragged across hot coals and ached with deep exhaustion. He hadn't stopped since they had first traveled to Avonai. How long ago had that been?

Lore left the gatehouse and walked along the wall toward the archway over the gates. Two healers passed him carrying a man between them. Light from the torches bathed the battlements in orange light. Lightning arced across the black sky. Seconds later, thunder rumbled.

Lore stopped above the gates and looked through his spyglass again. He could see hundreds of torches among the trees now. What were the Temanins up to? They had not sent another volley of arrows, and it had been hours since the last catapult bombardment.

Commander Kelyn walked over from the west side. He came to stand beside Lore. A fine white powder from crushed rock mixed with the soot across his face. He glanced over the battlements. "A lot of torches out there," he said a moment later. "What are they doing?"

"I don't know," Lore answered. He hated not knowing.

"Captain Lore, if I may speak."

"Go ahead, Commander."

"I think it is time to use fire. Two of the gates have multiple fractures, especially the main one. And for every catapult we take out, they have two more." Commander Kelyn turned to look at Lore. "I know you've seen this as a last resort, but I believe the time has come to burn the Temanins to the ground."

Lore wiped his face and sighed. He looked back over the battlements toward the forest. He had done everything he could, short of this. What kind of conflagration would he create? The entire forest was as dry as kindling this time of year. Then again, what choice did he have? What good would it do to save the forest and countryside if there were no people left to live in it? The people mattered more.

"You're right, Commander. But with this storm coming, I don't know how effective that would be tonight." As if to answer him, the sky lit up again followed by a loud boom. "On the other hand, lightning might start the fire for us."

"Just consider it, Captain."

"I will—"

"Incoming!" came the shout along the wall.

Lore and Commander Kelyn ducked behind the merlons and hunkered down.

Boulders flew into the city. One crashed a few feet from Lore. Rocks cracked around him. Men shouted and screamed. Another projectile flew overhead. He felt the wall shake beneath him. The hammering continued. White powder rose into the air.

Lore coughed and waited. The wooden gates groaned loudly below.

A loud roar of voices came from the forest. Now what was going on? Lore cautiously crawled to one of the openings between the merlons. He waited a moment, and looked out—

His heart froze inside his chest.

A huge dark structure came rolling between the trees. It was at least two stories tall with ropes and cables dangling around it. Temanin soldiers cheered around it and waved torches in the air. The orange torches lit up the dark trees and structure. Lore didn't need to hold his spyglass up to see what the mechanical monstrosity was. It was the largest catapult he had ever seen.

"Dear Word, save us!" Commander Kelyn whispered next to him. "One shot from that thing will break any wall."

Lore knew he needed to move, to shout some instruction to his men. Instead he stood there paralyzed. Death stood before the city. And deep inside he knew he could do nothing about it.

Something snapped inside Lore. But he would try.

He forced himself to turn around. Fearful faces looked at him. His men needed him. He drew from his last dregs of courage. Lore stood straight and tall. "Get ready!" he shouted. "Archers, when the catapult comes close enough, shoot its operators with everything we have. The rest of you, brace for impact and be ready to put out the flames." Lore leaned over the walkway and shouted down to the street below. "Reinforce the gates!"

Voices began to shout along the wall. Lore turned and looked through one of the openings.

A ball of fire the size of a bear blazed behind the catapult now. The Temanins shouted with exaltation. Their voices carried up to the battlements. They were about to launch their first volley.

That's what they had been waiting for, Lore realized. That's why the Temanin Army had gathered at the tree line. The catapult would blast open the wall, and the infantry would rush the White City.

The sight of it shook him to his very core.

Lightning lit up the sky.

The ball of flame pulled back. A hearbeat later it leaped into the air. Lore watched it arc. It flew toward the White City with a fiery tail behind it. Lore wanted to move but couldn't. The sight of death held him transfixed. Thunder rolled over the city. No one spoke on the battlements.

It was going to hit the main gates.

Lore tried to speak. "Brace—brace for impact!" he finally shouted. "Archers, get ready—"

Boom.

A deafening explosion echoed across the wall. Lore was thrown to his knees. The walkway beneath him cracked. Men yelled all around him. Smoke came pouring up from the gates.

His whole body shook with fear and adrenaline. Lore pushed himself up. Panic spread across the walls.

"The gates are on fire!"

"They're coming!"

"Archers, fire!" Lore shouted over the bedlam. "The rest of you, *put out those fires!*"

Only a few seemed to hear him. The rest of the defenders had been thrown into chaos.

"Captain, the Temanins are coming!"

Lore moved to the merlon and looked around. His breathing stopped.

Out of the forest poured thousands of Temanins, dressed in red and black. A huge battering ram led the charge. Torches waved in the air. Battle cries filled the night.

"Take out that ram!" Lore cried. "Shoot the men around it!"

The soldiers along the wall finally began to run to position. Archers fired down on the field.

Lore watched. Where one Temanin soldier fell, three more ran by. The ram stalled slightly when two of the men carrying it were shot, but immediately others took up the load. Temanins ran across the field like a black wave of death. And Lore knew that once they hit, the gates would fall.

Word, help us.

They had to fall back. If they waited until the enemy hit the wall, they wouldn't be able to withdraw.

"Retreat!" Lore yelled. He ran along the wall. "Retreat to the inner gate!"

Men scrambled along the walls.

Lore looked over the battlements. The ram was almost to the smoldering gates. "Now!"

The command to withdraw was shouted along the wall. Soldiers ran down the steps. Archers let loose one more volley before following.

Lore hurried behind them. He'd reached the top of the steps when the ram hit.

Wham.

The wall shook. His knees buckled from the impact. Lore steadied himself and finished the steps, two at a time. At the bottom, he took off in a run. The muffled booms of the ram echoed across the city.

He dodged a burning wagon and raced along the cobblestone street. Broken glass crunched beneath his boots. Other soldiers ran beside him, the sound of their metal armor echoing off the stone homes and stores like a thousand clashing chains.

Lore could barely see through the darkness and smoke. A flash of lightning filled the sky, its jagged edge tearing through the night sky.

In that one bright moment, he saw the streets filled with soldiers running toward the second gates. Then all was swept back into shadow and night.

The sky rumbled overhead. Behind him, he could barely hear the boom of the ram.

Lore slowed and looked behind him. "Move it!" he shouted, motioning with his hand. Soldiers ran past him. He glanced toward the gates. How much longer would it hold? Lore turned and ran. He panted, and his heart thudded hard inside his chest.

More lightning flashed across the sky. Thunder drowned out every other noise.

Sweat poured down Lore's face and back. His legs burned with each step.

As the thunder grumbled away, he heard a new noise. Adrenaline swept across his body at the sound, and Lore turned back. What he saw confirmed his worst fear.

Temanin had broken through the gates.

Men poured through the shattered opening with torches and swords drawn like a legion from hell. Their battle cry made his hair stand on end.

"Run!"

Lore ran as he never had, with every bit of strength he possessed. He had to make it to the second gates. He had to protect these people, his men, Lady Astrea. Rowen.

His fellow soldiers yelled and scrambled around him. Lore passed them, his focus solely on the gates ahead. White rubble lay scattered across the street. He dodged a couple of broken pieces, but tripped over a railing in the dark, and fell to his knee.

The sound of hand-to-hand combat grew behind him. Swords clanked and shouts filled the air. Men screamed.

Lore pushed himself up. Just one more block.

Torches were already lit along the second battlement. The gates were still open.

Flash after flash of lightning scattered across the sky. Thunder rolled across the city in waves.

Twenty feet . . . Ten feet—

"Behind you!"

Lore twisted around and drew his sword. One of his men behind him cried out and toppled to the ground. In the orange torchlight and flashes of lightning he saw a soldier in black pass the man on the ground and advance on Lore.

Lore dropped into defense position.

The man yelled and swung his sword. Lore parried the move and returned one of his own.

The man swung again.

Lore parried, his body acting on instinct and years of training. His eyes studied his opponent. Clad in black and red, the man was a Temanin soldier.

How had the Temanins moved this fast?

Lore moved his sword into a guard position. He barely registered others running past him.

The Temanin thrust to his left. Lore dropped his sword and caught the man's blade, gave a hard twist, and sent the Temanin's sword flying to the right.

Before the man could react, Lore thrust his own sword low, catching the man in the leg. With no armor there, his blade slid deeply into the man's leg.

The man screamed.

Lore pulled his blade free. The Temanin fell to the cobblestone.

Glancing up, Lore saw more men running toward him and the second gates. In the torchlight he could not tell whether the ones running were his own men retreating or Temanins advancing.

A sick feeling twisted through his chest.

Lore strained against the darkness, hoping to see some color or insignia. His mind raced for any other option.

He could see neither.

Lore knew then the moment had finally arrived. The one he had trained for all his life but hoped he would never live to see. The impossible choice.

He could not allow any Temanins to pass through the second gates. Not if he wanted to protect those inside the castle. But closing the gates would leave many of his men on the outside.

With a sick heart, Lore turned and ran. "Shut the gates," he yelled. "Shut those gates!"

"*What?*" he heard someone shout above. He passed beneath the archway. "If we shut the gates, our soldiers can't—"

"I know!" Lore shouted back. Emotion slammed his insides: anger, fear, and grief. If he was wrong, then he was condemning his men to death.

He held his sword and watched the gates pull shut. A couple of friendly soldiers made it through. Many more almost did. They held their hands through the gap, but pulled them quickly back.

Lore looked away. He knew deep inside he was making the right choice, the only choice.

He could not allow the Temanins to make it through the second gates.

The gates slammed shut with a reverberating bang.

Shouts and pounding began to echo from the other side of the wooden barrier. Screams and the clash of metal quickly followed.

The sounds tore at Lore. Each cry carved itself upon his heart.

He looked back at the gates. A sudden desire to open them and rush out and aid his countrymen filled him. Lore clenched his sword and turned.

His duty as captain dictated he protect those inside the castle first.

"How could you *do* that!" someone shouted at him.

Lore barely heard. He staggered away from the gates and collapsed to his knees. He held his sword to his chest. Tears streamed down his soot and blood covered face. All his strength was gone. He felt so . . . helpless.

They couldn't hold much longer. Not with that catapult behind them. And the myriad of Temanin soldiers. Unless something changed, they wouldn't last the night, not to mention the couple of days until help arrived. The White City would fall tonight.

Overhead, the sky lit up with lightning, then boomed as thunder washed over the city.

Lore looked up at the tempestuous storm-filled sky. Unless . . .

"Word," he shouted. "Please, if You're going to help us, we need You now!"

Chapter
26

Nierne watched beneath half-lidded eyes as Lord Tala walked toward the tent flap. His eyes were distant and unfocused, like they'd been the last two times he had left the tent. And, like the times before, he would most likely return full of dark rage.

I need to get out of here, she thought. She watched him walk by the small sitting area where she lay, hands tied behind her back and feet bound by thick cords. The man acted like he was mind-possessed. Perhaps he was going crazy. She didn't want to be here when he finally went over the edge.

Lord Tala lifted the tent flaps and disappeared into the night.

Nierne waited and listened. She could hear nothing other than the muffled sounds of men moving around somewhere outside the tent. The silhouettes of Lord Tala's two guards stood right by the tent entrance. She waited a few more heartbeats, then lowered herself onto the brightly colored rug.

Time to go.

Nierne knew she was taking a risk as she began to inch her way along the colorful rugs. If Lord Tala caught her . . .

Well, eventually he would tire of her, and she'd be dead anyway. Might as well leave now. She was lucky that all he had done was kept her tied up. He could have done a lot worse.

No time for thoughts like that. She needed to pay attention to now. Even so, moving around would be a lot easier if her hands weren't tied behind her back. Nierne shoved her knees into her chest and pushed off toward the next rug. Ahead she could see the side of Lord Tala's dark, wooden chest. She had seen him pull a dagger out of it yesterday, and she wondered if there might be more inside.

After a couple more shoves, she bumped up against the chest. Using the side, she sidled her way upwards until she sat beside her target. Sweat beaded her forehead and she panted from the effort. Nierne eyed the lid. There was a small hole where a key could be inserted.

Her shoulders slumped. Was it locked? She eyed the chest again. One way to find out. Gritting her teeth, Nierne turned away from the chest and sat up on her knees so she could shove her bound hands into the gap between chest and lid.

She tugged with all her might. The lid barely budged. She sat back down on her legs and took a couple of breaths. Then she shoved her fingers back in and pulled again. With a loud creak, the lid slowly opened.

Nierne tensed, her eyes staring at the tent flaps. Had the guards heard the sound? She watched their shadows, but neither of them moved.

She sighed softly and turned around on her knees. She leaned over the chest and looked inside. The candle nearby barely lit the interior of the wooden box. She could see clothing, bits of metal and leather, and . . .

A sheathed dagger.

Hope soared across her heart. Nierne awkwardly turned around and sat down on the lip of the chest, then she leaned backwards, hoping to snag the dagger with her bound hands. After three attempts, she finally fingered the loop on the sheath and pulled it up.

Nierne stood and hopped away from the chest. She dropped the dagger on the rug. Turning around, she fell to her knees beside it and studied the dagger. An intricate pattern was etched across the dark leather sheath. But the dagger itself was not bound to the sheath. It would easily slip out.

"Thank the Word," Nierne whispered with a sigh. She turned around and leaned back, feeling for the handle. Once she had it, she pulled the blade loose, then imagined the dagger's edge and maneuvered the sharp end toward herself. After two sharp pricks to her wrist and one to her back, she finally found her rhythm and began to carefully saw away at the rope that held her hands together.

Rowen felt . . . peace.

Opening her eyes, she gazed up at a star-studded sky, the stars like tiny white flecks against a backdrop of the deepest black. Small blades of grass waved gently in evening breeze, bending down to kiss her cheeks.

Had she reached the Celestial Halls? Rowen moved her hands and pressed against the cold, damp ground.

She sat up and glanced around her. No, Rowen thought she recognized the stone ruins nearby, illuminated by the faint light of the crescent moon that hung overhead. The ruins were the Eldaran Sanctuary that lay just outside the White City.

So how had she ended up here? Hadn't she just been in the Guards Quarter? She stood, and a faint light caught her eye. Looking down, Rowen found her hand pulsing with light. Lifting her palm, she stared as the light grew brighter and brighter until her entire hand lit up. Rowen blinked and looked away. She turned her palm face down and glanced back. Her hand lit up the entire field. Every blade of grass, every flower reflected the bright light from her mark.

What is happening to me? Rowen took a step back. *What is wrong with my hand? Has my power gone mad?* She felt her chest with her other hand. She could only feel a faint heat burning inside of her. *But then why is my hand so bright?*

Rowen kept her hand facing away from her and backed away. Images began to filter through her mind. Standing in the training room. The glass dome shattering. Lore covering her. The boulder slamming into the wall. Cries and shouts. Donar's body . . .

Rowen lifted her left hand and covered her mouth. She had been unable to save him. The grief of that knowledge tore through her. *I can't do it. I can't save everyone. I'm weak.*

No, you're not weak. Somewhere in her mind, she could hear Lore's voice chastising her.

Rowen took another step back. Perhaps Lore was right. Perhaps she wasn't weak. Even as an Eldaran, she couldn't save everyone, as much as she wanted to. Wasn't that what Balint had said the first time he'd told her she could heal?

But how did I end up in Anwin Forest? Rowen looked around again. *Why have I been brought here? Why am I not in the castle? This doesn't make any sense. Wait, the Temanin Army—*

She whirled around, half expecting to see enemy soldiers lined up between the trees. She held her marked hand out like a lantern and searched past where her light reached. Rowen felt for her sword with her other hand, wondering how she would see if she had to begin wielding her sword with her marked hand. She patted her side and felt . . . nothing.

Shocked, Rowen looked down. Her sword was gone. As were her cloak and boots. She stood barefoot in the grass with just a white shirt and pants on.

Movement near the trees drew her attention. A man walked out of the trees. Tall with dark hair. He looked up. Even from a hundred feet away, she could see small pins of light reflecting from the darkest eyes she had ever seen. Rowen sucked in her breath.

The man from her dreams.

She took a step back and watched him slowly walk across the field. Was that what this was? Another dream? And yet this one was so different than the others. It felt so . . . real.

It is time, Daughter of Light.

Rowen spun around, but found no one there.

Time to show him the truth.

She spun the other way, only to find the field empty. Out of the corner of her eye she could see the man draw closer. Fifty feet . . . Twenty feet . . .

Heat began to fill her, boiling up from deep inside her chest. *I can't*, she screamed in her mind, remembering the first time she had used her truthsaying power, seeing the darkness inside Cleon. But the heat continued to burn through her, racing toward her palm.

Do not fear, Rowen, the voice whispered inside her mind. *I will be with you. But you must hurry. Your entire city is at stake . . .*

Rowen sat up with a gasp.

She looked around. There was no field. No trees, no grass, no Eldaran ruins. And no man walking toward her. She was not outside at all. She was in some sort of chamber, and—she looked down—she was covered by a sheet.

Candles burned in sconces along the stone walls, barely lighting the chamber. There were three rows of five beds that filled the room. Each bed held an occupant covered with a white sheet. She could hear the soft breathing of those around her. The subtle scent of lavender filled the air.

Rowen sat in the last bed in the corner near a lead-lined window. Looking through the glass, she could see the night sky, looking exactly as it had in her dream.

But she was here, and not out there.

Rowen took a deep breath and placed a hand across her chest. She could still feel the heat of her power, ebbing and flowing inside, though not as strong as it had been moments ago. It had seemed so real.

You must go, Daughter of Light.

Her heart quickened again. The dream . . . it *was* real? Rowen looked down at her hand. It glowed with a faint light. She looked up. Fear twisted inside her middle until her chest hurt. She knew what the dream was now. It was a summons to finally meet this man, a real man . . . and to show him the truth.

Her hand began to tremble in her lap. Her stomach tightened into a knot and her mouth went dry with fear. The heat inside her chest flared. Rowen touched her chest as if to calm it. The heat slowly cooled. She dropped her hand and squeezed her eyes shut.

She never wanted to use that power again.

"Please, Word," Rowen whispered. "Please don't. Please don't make me do this . . ." Her thoughts conjured up images of what she might see. "I can't—"

I will be with you.

Rowen covered her face with her hands and pressed her palms into her eyes. Hazy light filtered red through her lids from the mark on her hand. She heard the rustle of sheets. A soft snore replaced the noise. A faint metallic smell mixed with the lavender scent in the room.

Rowen knew she had a choice to make. Did she believe the Word? Would she do what He was asking her to do? There was no more time to debate. She could feel time ticking away with each heartbeat. She had to make her decision now.

A woman in the bed next to hers moaned. Rowen brought her hands away from her face and looked over. In the candlelight she could see the woman's face wrapped in white linen. In another bed over, a man with both arms bandaged lay sleeping. A young man dressed in a healer's robe sat in a chair in the opposite corner from her bed, his arms folded across his chest, his head tilted to the side in sleep.

Rowen looked across the room and took a closer look at the people who lay in the beds around her. Each one was hurt by this bloody, senseless war. She balled her hands up in her lap. How could her going outside the city gates do anything to stop it? She should stay here and heal these people. How could touching one man save the people around her?

Trust me.

Rowen opened her palm and watched the mark pulse with faint light. Then she looked around the room again. If there was a chance that touching this man could save all the people in this city . . .

She let her breath out sharply and threw back the sheet. She eased her way off the bed, and found her boots on the floor. Rowen picked one up, shoved her foot in, then picked up the other.

A faint rumble filled the room. She stopped and looked up. For one panicked heartbeat, she waited for boulders to come crashing through the walls. A flash of light dashed across the window. Rowen watched the brilliant light explode then fade immediately into darkness. Her shoulders sagged with relief. It was only thunder, not catapults.

As Rowen pulled on her other boot, she realized a summer storm could work to the White City's advantage. Summer storms in these mountains were wild and unpredictable, filled with tempests of rain and destructive lightning. Such a storm could slow down or even halt the Temanin's assault. Unfortunately, it would not be stopping her tonight.

Rowen stood. Her head swam for a moment. She held onto the wall until her body steadied. She took two deep breaths and looked around. The healer in the corner didn't seem to hear her. The others in the room kept sleeping. She turned and made her way between the beds toward the door ahead.

Torches lined an empty and quiet corridor. Rowen paused and looked up and down the hallway. She could see the set of double doors that led into the Healers Quarter. She was in the northwest corner of the castle. She leaned against the doorway and closed her eyes. In her mind she could see the ruins that lay on the edge of that small field she had found weeks ago. That was where the Word was leading her. But how could she get there? The entire Temanin Army lay between her and that field . . .

Rowen opened her eyes and stared off down the corridor. A memory filled her mind. A memory of Lore and a door outlined in blue. The Gateway of the Mountain. The secret passageway through the mountains. And it was right down this hall.

Rowen turned and hurried down the hall. Silence filled the dark passageway, broken only by the crash of thunder outside and the soft patter of her leather boots. The air grew cooler the closer she drew to the mountainside. Rowen gripped her shirt closer to herself, wishing for one moment that she had brought her cloak with her. But there was no time to go back.

A small door lay at the end of the corridor. Rowen stopped before it, looked behind her, then pressed down on the long metal latch. The door opened silently. She stepped inside and closed the door behind her.

The light from her palm lit up the tiny room. She could see the jagged wall of mountain on the far side of the room. Cobwebs and dust filled the corners. Rowen held her palm out like a light and made her way to the jagged wall.

It took a moment to locate the small indent that activated the hidden door. She pressed her finger inside the indent. A thin blue light appeared, moving across the mountain face, accompanied by a quiet clicking noise.

Rowen placed both her hands inside the blue silhouette, then stopped. *This is it.* She stared at the wall. *Once you go down this tunnel, there is no turning back. No turning back . . . No turning . . .*

Rowen pushed past the words and opened the door. Stale cool air filled her nostrils. Blue fre stones twinkled along the stone passageway. The air grew even chillier. She rubbed her arms as she stepped inside the narrow passageway. *No turning back . . . no tur*—The door slammed shut behind her.

Rowen jumped and turned. Eerie blue light danced along the solid wall. She slowly pulled out her hand and held out her palm. The soft white light from her palm replaced the blue light from the stones. *No turning back . . .*

She turned and flew down the corridor. Suddenly Rowen felt fear settle across her chest. It began to prod her heart, looking for a weak spot within her. What would she see inside this man? What darkness did he hide? Anger? Hatred? Or worse?

Rowen ran passed the fre stones that lined the tunnel. Fear reached up toward her mind. *Remember,* it whispered. Remember the man from the inn at Mostyn?

She stumbled to a stop and leaned against the wall. Visions of lust filled her mind. The man's touch, his breath, his mind in hers . . .

The women, the little girl . . .

No, *no!* Rowen shook her head. The visions dimmed into darkness.

Rowen pushed away from the wall and staggered down the tunnel. She could see the door at the end. She reached it and grasped the handle. *Remember, remember,* fear whispered. The door disappeared, and in its place stood Cleon. His face twisted up in hatred. "You're nothing but a witch. You should be burned!"

Rowen let go of the handle and cowered down. "It's not real, it's not real," she whispered.

But it is. You've seen it.

"No!" Rowen shouted, the word bouncing off the tunnel walls. She stood up and grabbed the handle with trembling hands. The door swung open. She stumbled out into the cold dark night, the phantom feelings from those touchings washing over her.

Rowen turned and pushed the door shut with all her might. The lines sealed until the door resembled only a couple of cracks along the surface of stone.

The tall dark trees of Anwin loomed over her. Behind her stood the sheer rock face of the mountain. Rowen held her hand against her thigh to hide the light and peered into the darkness. She could see no one amongst the trees. But that didn't mean the enemy wasn't nearby.

So she waited and listened, her breath a whisper. The wind stirred in the trees, and an owl hooted nearby.

Fear settled back inside her chest. Do you really want to see inside the man from your dreams? What kind of darkness does *he* hide? Fear slid a frigid finger across her heart, causing shivers to run up and down her spine. Do you really want to see?

Rowen wrapped her arms across her middle and staggered toward the trees. Her own mind started turning against her. No, she did not want to see inside the man. She wanted to go back and be safe. Fear felt heavier with each step. But she kept walking, placing one foot in front of the other.

Fear grew angry, its voice rising with insistency.

Something snapped inside her. Heat began to burn inside her breast. It filled her, spreading across her limbs. She felt consumed by its blaze, feeling its warmth burn away the coldness that had filled her veins moments before.

Fear dropped from her chest and back. Its lingering scream faded behind her. Rowen straightened and felt strength return to her body. The truth she carried inside would not be extinguished by fear.

She ran through the trees, the power inside growing stronger. Minutes later, she stepped out onto a meadow. Nearby she could hear the sound of rushing water. Rowen looked around and realized it was the same meadow from her dream. With that realization came the same deep sense of peace she had felt in her dream. The light from her palm now shone as brightly as if she were holding a sliver of sunshine.

I am with you, Daughter of Light.

Rowen felt the presence of the Word. She looked directly at a spot in the distant tree line, and out from the woods beyond stepped the man with the dark eyes.

Show him the truth.

Caleb saw light streaming between the trees and knew he was almost there. He moved past the brush and he stepped out into the lit meadow. It was as bright as noon. Ahead he saw the woman, the same woman from the city. She was beautiful and young, her hair looking especially blond in the dark. But it was her hand that caught his attention. It burned with white brilliance, illuminating the woman and her surroundings.

He took a few steps forward then stopped. She lifted her eyes and looked straight at him. For one second he wavered, the thought of turning back pressing heavily against his mind. But he knew that, if he did, he would always wonder what he had let pass. This wasn't the sort of thing he encountered all the time. So he began walking again.

"Who are you?" he said and drew near. His hand rested on the dagger at his side. Somewhere in the dark he could hear the sound of falling water.

"My name is Rowen," she said.

His eyes traveled over her body, noting the simple white shirt and dark pants. Nothing about her appeared threatening, but he knew more than most people how deceiving appearances could be.

He stopped a couple of feet in front of her. "Why did you bring me here?"

Lightning lit up the sky behind her.

"The Word brought you here."

A resounding boom filled the air, then faded away with a grumble. Caleb glanced up at the sky, his mood growing foul at the thought of being caught in some rainstorm. He looked back at her. "Then why did the *Word* bring me here?" He should have known all of this would have something to do with the Word. Ever since Delshad's death, the Word seemed to plague his every footstep.

"I have a gift." Rowen raised her hand and took a step toward him. "A power that shows the truth inside a person. And the Word has brought us together so that I might show you what is—"

"Forget it," Caleb said. "I'm not interested."

Her hand fell. "Then why did you come?"

It was the same question he was asking himself. Why did he come? He could turn back now. Last chance . . . "I wanted to see if the dreams were real," Caleb answered. He was going to stay and put an end this. "Most of what I dream is not real . . . but apparently you are." He slowly pulled his dagger out. "And now that I know you are real, I want you to stop whatever it is you are doing to me."

"Doing to you?" Rowen gave him a puzzled look.

Caleb scowled. "I want the dreams to stop, the compulsions to stop, and any other mind twisting games you're playing with me."

She shook her head. "I'm afraid I can't. I have no control over you or your dreams. I'm having dreams of my own. And I myself was brought here by the Word too. He wants me to . . . to show you the truth."

At her words, the light around her hand increased.

Caleb stared at her hand. "What *are* you?"

"Apparently I am an Eldaran."

The hair on the back of his neck rose. The word triggered some distant memory, something his mother had said a long time ago. Another flash of lightning brightened the sky, followed by a loud boom. The storm was almost here.

Rowen held out her hand again. "The only way to stop whatever it is that is happening to you is to allow me to touch you."

Caleb stared at her palm, both eager to be rid of the constant dreams and terrified of what she might do. After all, if she really was an Eldaran, whatever that was, it meant she wasn't human. For all he knew, she might possess his mind and make him do whatever she desired. And as one of the highest-ranking officials in Temanin, that would not be good.

"Do you want peace?" Rowen asked, looking at him.

Peace. What a foreign word. Had he ever known peace? Absence of war, perhaps, but real peace? Yes, he desired true peace, a peace of mind where his victims no longer haunted him. Peace of heart where guilt no longer held him in its grasp.

"Yes," Caleb found himself saying. "But just how can you give me peace?"

"The Word said to show you the truth." Rowen took a step toward him. She was close enough now that she could to lift her hand and touch him. "Only after you confront the darkness inside yourself and allow the Word to heal you will you find peace."

Caleb looked closer at her face. He could see something now, something he saw on his victim's face the moment before he killed. Fear. There was only a hint of it, but it was there. She was afraid to touch him. Why?

Before he could reply or even step back, she placed her hand upon his cheek. It trembled against his skin. Her touch felt warm, almost burning. She closed her eyes and took a deep, shuddering breath.

Caleb's intincts were to bat her hand away and plunge his dagger into her chest. No one touched him without his permission. Instead, he stood there under the storm clouds with her warm hand pressed against his cheek. He could see light escaping from the palm out of the corner of his eye. He felt himself begin to relax, the tightened muscles beneath his shoulders loosening. Was she doing this to him? But he felt no magic flowing from the hand. Caleb sighed inwardly. There had been nothing to fear. This woman had no real power—

Suddenly the air around them began to churn. Light flared from her palm.

"Aaaaih!" Caleb cried, jerking back. White light filled his eyes and burned through his entire body. Another scream tore from his lips. He felt the light begin to search every corner of his mind, his heart, his soul . . .

He sunk to his knees, holding his hands over his chest. Unbidden, images began to step forward into this probing light. He watched helplessly as his darkest deeds were exposed. He saw the faces of women he had used for his pleasure, the lies he had uttered to cover his indiscretions, the disgust he had felt for those beneath him. *No!* he shouted. She mustn't see—

But it was too late.

The ghosts of those he had murdered danced across his vision, their pale and distorted faces taunting him. Somewhere along their connection he could feel Rowen's revulsion at his acts.

But he had only been following orders. None of this was his—

The light tore away the scant excuses and deceptive thoughts he used to clothe himself. No, he had taken these lives *willingly*, for power and gold. And for the pure pleasure of it.

Caleb moaned and tried to turn his face away. But he could not escape. With each pulse of light he felt himself stripped of everything, until he lay in cold darkness, blinded by the single beam of truth shining over him. He could not run from it. He could not hide from it. Instead, he lay crouched beneath it, naked and exposed.

And, for the first time in his life, Caleb saw himself for what he was.

Rowen felt as if she were drowning. Her power poured into the man kneeling before her. The depravity of his heart, the darkness in which he had covered himself, overwhelmed her until she felt as dirty and revolting as she saw him.

Images of women flashed through her mind, along with the acts the man before her had committed with them. The feelings of rage and hatred he carried swirled inside her chest. And the blood . . .

Rowen sank to her knees, her hand still firmly planted upon his cheek. This man had murdered so many, the blood of his victims covering his hands and soaking into hers.

"Oh, Word, I don't want to see any more." Rowen tried to pull her hand away, but it would not let go. Her hair now whipped around her face in a sudden wind, and somewhere beyond her power, she could the feel rain falling on them.

You must go deeper, a voice whispered.

Everything inside her said no, to pull away *now*. But instead, Rowen obeyed. Closing her eyes, she fell deeper inside the man's heart, pushing her powers as far as she could. From far away, it seemed, she could hear the man cry out. More blood filled her vision, followed by faces twisted with fear.

Then everything disappeared.

Looking around, she found herself in darkness, save for a single beam of light shining over the quivering form of a man, alone and bare. It was him, the same man in whom she had witnessed such darkness moments ago.

He looked up at her with a face so stricken it pierced her heart. "Help me," he pleaded. His dark eyes no longer looked cold and hostile, but scared. He lifted toward her a hand covered in blood.

She stared at his hand. "I-I can't," she whispered, torn between revulsion and pity.

He returned his hand to the ground and lay crouched in a ball, naked and shivering.

"You see," said a voice beside her, "even this man, so dark and vile on the outside, yearns for healing and forgiveness on the inside." Rowen found a man beside her clothed in brilliant white and covered with scars. It was the man from the Eldaran temple. "But you would never have known that if you had not been willing to see past his darkness to the man hurting deep within."

"My Lord." Rowen fell to her knees and bowed her head. Her heart beat so loudly it echoed inside her ears.

The Word placed a hand upon her shoulder. "You have done well, Daughter of Light. Now it is my turn to do what only I can do." As the Word walked past her, she felt herself being drawn from the dark and lonely plain upon which the man lay.

The man looked up, stared at the Word, then collapsed to the ground like a dead man.

Rowen pulled farther away, and everything began to disappear. But in the darkness she heard the Word speak.

"Awaken, Son of Truth."

CHAPTER 27

Snap.

Nierne pulled her hands around front. Her bindings dropped from her wrists. She rubbed at the skin, careful to avoid the burns left by the coarse rope. A tingling sense of elation filled her. She was almost free.

A shadow moved along the tent wall.

Panic doused her joy. Nierne hurried back to the cushions, her flight hampered by her feet, which were still bound. Frustration and fear swelled inside her chest. She stared at the tent flaps. Was Lord Tala back already?

The two guards that stood outside the tent flaps moved, then walked away. They were replaced by two new shadows. Nierne let out the breath she had been holding. It was only the guard change.

She dragged herself back to the dagger and began to saw away at the thicker cords around her feet. What would she do once she was free? The next guard change would not occur for at least a couple of hours . . . and Lord Tala would probably be back by then.

Perhaps I had made a mistake, Nierne thought with a pang. She began to saw on the rope with renewed vigor, her brows drawn close in stubborn thought. If he came in, she could hide her hands and feet beneath the cushions. After all, Lord Tala never came near her. He wouldn't know she had broken free until—

A shout went up outside the tent.

Nierne lurched at the sound and the tip of the blade bit into her ankle. "Ouch!" She quickly rubbed the small cut. She grabbed the dagger and crawled back to the cushions. Outside, she could hear more shouts rising. Shadows ran past the tent.

She turned over into a sitting position and sawed with a renewed effort. Something was going on outside. Had the White City decided to bring the battle outside the walls? Or were the Temanins winning? Either way, fighting in the dark seemed foolish to her, but then again, what did she know of war?

Nierne pulled her ankles apart to put more pressure on the cords around her feet. She sawed a couple of seconds more before the rope snapped. Elation once again filled her, stronger this time. She was free!

She scrambled to her feet and hurried across the tent. She picked up the sheath, and placed the dagger back inside. Then she moved toward the chest to place the dagger inside. For one moment, she hesitated, holding the dagger just above the opening. The dagger could be helpful in her escape.

No, Nierne thought and dropped the dagger. It landed with a soft thud across dark-colored clothing. It wasn't hers to keep. She would just have to make do without.

Outside the tent, more shadows passed. Men shouted as they ran by. Nierne watched in alarm. Memories of her flight from Thyra filled her mind. Would she be caught in the battle if she tried to leave? Or worse, would she be killed before she could prove she wasn't a Temanin?

Nierne looked toward the front of the tent and realized the two tall shadows that had stood before the tent flaps were gone. She tiptoed across the rugs toward the entrance and carefully peeked between the flaps.

Everything outside was dark, save for the few fires that burned between the tents. Nierne looked right. No one. She looked left. No one there either. The two guards were gone.

A couple soldiers ran by. "There, the light is coming from there," she heard one of them shout. Nierne shifted the flaps to look. A surprised gasp escaped her lips. Nierne leaned past the flaps, consumed by the sight before her.

A pillar of light swirled and spun as it flowed up past dark trees. Jagged white fissures of lightning danced around the pillar, followed by muffled booms.

What in all the Lands was *that?*

She stared at the strange phenomenon, racking her mind for anything she had ever read to compare to what she now saw. Only one thing came to mind. Her heart beat faster.

Could it be an Eldaran?

Suddenly Nierne began to shake. Had she really found one? She could not remember ever reading of Eldarans forming pillars of light, but that did not mean they couldn't. And often the old scrolls spoke of Eldarans brokering peace in times of war . . .

"Word," Nierne whispered. Tears pricked the edge of her eyes. Her journey was almost done. If only Father Reth had lived to see it!

Her head sunk down. Father Reth gave his life so that she could find the Eldarans and bring them back to Thyra. Well, she had. Nierne looked back up with determination. And now she needed only to escape.

She ducked her head back inside the flaps. Nierne took a deep breath and closed her eyes. *Think, Nierne, think.*

She fought past thoughts of pillars of light, Lord Tala, and her fear of being caught. Instead, she concentrated on the night she'd been captured and brought here. Tents flew past her mind. She had counted them, both to calm herself and to keep track of where she was going.

Eleven. Nierne pictured the layout of the Temanin camp in her mind. She hadn't been able to see everything, so there was a chance she could wind up lost. But it was worth a shot. She opened her eyes. She would need to count her way out of here.

Nierne went over her route one more time in her mind, then crept back toward the tent flaps. She peeked outside. Nothing, save the pillar of light. The camp was deserted. Everyone had run to the commotion.

Nierne took a quick breath and slipped between the tent flaps. It felt odd to be outside after living inside that tent for the last week. She walked across the open space toward the next tent. The column of light continued to flow toward the sky. Thunder boomed nearby.

She fought the desire to stare at the pillar of light. She had never seen anything like it. But the part of her that wanted to live forced her to move swiftly past the tents. Nierne turned left after passing three. Eight more to go.

Abandoned fires burned low between the tents. Nierne carefully made her way past six more. She met no one. Ahead she could barely make out the tall, dark trees of Anwin. She passed the last tent and broke out into a run toward the treeline. Large ferns and bushes greeted her.

Nierne went a couple feet into the forest and fell against a tree. She panted with fear and relief. Tiny drops of rain fell across her face. Nierne looked up. No moonlight tonight. She squinted past the treeline. None of the light from the campfires reached past the first couple of trees. Everything beyond lay in darkness.

Nierne carefully made her way into the forest. After a couple feet, she put her hands out in front of her and felt around. The wind moaned between the trees. Leaves shuffled beneath her feet, and twigs snapped. Nierne turned back every couple of steps to see if anyone had noticed her escape. The camp remained empty.

After passing the first layer of trees, the light disappeared altogether. She could feel the ferns and made her way around them. Her foot snagged on a root. Branches clawed at her clothes. Still she pressed on through the darkness.

More rain fell. Nierne wiped her wet hair from her face. Her clothes grew damp. She had no idea where she was going or even if she had gotten turned around. All she could see was darkness.

A bright arc of light appeared ahead. Nierne stopped and stared. What in all the Lands? The light seemed to be moving—more like *racing*—through the trees.

Straight at her.

Nierne sucked in her breath. She looked frantically around. The arc sped toward her. In its light, she could see some low branches, Nierne ran to the tree, grabbed the branches, and pulled herself up. The arc drew closer. She reached for a higher branch. The air began to fill with the sound of rushing wind. Nierne scrambled for the next branch. "Dear Word, help me, help me!"

The arc hit her. Nierne screamed. Waves of light plucked her from the tree like a rag doll. The light tossed her high into the sky, suspended her for a moment, then hurled her back down. She screamed again. The ground came rushing toward her. The light washed past her, leaving a wake of darkness.

Her head smacked the ground, and everything went black.

Men pounded on the second gates. Lore sat on his knees and held his sword to his chest, tears trailing down his soot and blood covered face.

He had condemned them, his own men.

The sky lit up with lightning followed by a boom. Thunder roared over the city.

Lore looked up. "Word," he shouted. "Please, if You're going to help us, we need You now!"

As if in answer to his prayer, a stream of light tore out of Anwin Forest to the west, churning its way toward the sky, white against the dark storm and the coming night.

"What *is* that?" a voice nearby shouted.

Lore lurched to his feet. He gazed at the strange phenomenon. A shiver tore down his spine, causing the hairs across his arms and neck to stand on end.

Had the Word answered his cry for help?

Without waiting for a reply, Lore sprinted across the castle lawn toward the staircase that led to the battlements along the second wall, passing men who stood stunned, staring at the pillar of light as it licked the heavens. He ran up the stairs and leaned over the stone edge, peering into the forest in hopes of seeing what was causing the light.

"Captain." Geoffrey ran up beside Lore. "What *is* that?"

More men joined them on the battlements.

"I-I don't know," Lore said. He had never seen anything like it before. It was a blaze of white light, churning like water toward the sky.

"I heard you shout to the Word. Do you think . . . Do you think He is actually saving us?"

Lore didn't answer. Instead he stared at the tower of moving light and felt another shiver run down his back. For years he had followed the Word, acknowledging His existence and power, but the moment Lore had fallen to the ground and cried out to the Word, he had cried from desperation, not faith.

"Dear Word," Lore whispered, "forgive me. I did not believe . . ."

"Captain!" another man shouted. "The fighting . . . it's stopped."

Lore moved away from the ledge and ran toward the wall that separated the castle from the city. A mixture of wonder and shame filled his soul. Glancing around one of the merlons, he saw faces far below turned toward the sky, lit faintly by the beam of white light surging toward the sky.

Lightning split the black clouds overhead, followed by a loud boom. At the same moment, the light changed.

The men below him raised hands, pointing toward the light. Some began to shout. Lore looked back toward the beam of light . . .

The topmost edge of the surging tower of light, which moments before had been licking the sky, came pouring down like waves of white water.

Lore watched in disbelief, his position on the wall giving him full view of the tidal wave of light as it came crashing down. The light hit the ground, then changed direction and began rushing through the trees.

Shouts of fear filled the air. Lore looked back down and watched as men ran in a panicked stampede.

The light hit the outer city wall, but instead of passing through it, the light turned and flowed like water toward the Temanin camp in the forest. Lore stood rooted on the wall, unable to move, his eyes following the river of light.

A heartbeat later, the faint sound of screams filled the air. Arcs of white light filled Anwin Forest, illuminating the trees as if it were day.

Lore watched the light move toward the front of the White City and pass through the main gates. The river of light rushed between buildings and broken walls like eager fingers searching out every crevice. As the light moved toward the castle, the radiant wave picked up anyone in its path. It tossed men into the air as it hurried toward the wall he stood upon.

Lore gripped the ledge. He watched the luminous tidal wave draw closer and closer.

Two blocks away, one block away . . .

Light slammed the wall, each arc hammering the stone beneath his feet, shaking him until his teeth chattered.

Lore closed his eyes, waiting for the light to come pouring over the wall and sweep him away. Terrified shouts filled the air below him. His grip loosened with each hit.

Then, slowly, the shaking subsided.

Lore cautiously opened one eye, then the other. He looked over the city wall—

And saw nothing.

The light was gone. All light. Not one ray remained, not even the twinkle of a distant campfire. It was as if someone had blown out every light, leaving the world in the darkness.

Faint drops of rain splattered across his face and shoulders. The sky grumbled and another peal of thunder echoed across the city. Unable to see, Lore listened.

Below the wall, he could hear sobbing, punctuated by sudden terrified screams that died like the lingering death cry of an animal. The sound made the hair on his body stand on end.

A hand gripped his arm. Lore went for his sword.

"Captain, it's me: Geoffrey."

Lore let out a gasp of air. Turning, he saw the faint lights from torches flickering up near the castle.

Geoffrey's face stared at him, barely visible in the orange light. "Your Word . . . did He just save us?" Geoffrey asked in an awed and frightened voice.

Lore looked back over the battlements toward the far end of the city, where the Temanin camp had stood minutes before. He could not see or hear anything, save the mournful cries of those nearby, down where the light had flowed.

"Captain?"

"I . . ." Lore felt too shocked to think. Had the Word saved them? *Yes*, he thought with sudden conviction. He believed the Word had. It was the *how* that eluded him. That light, where had it come from? What had it done to the Temanins—or to the White City's own soldiers, for that matter?

Realizing that Geoffrey was still waiting for an answer, Lore turned. "Yes," he said, noticing more men gathering. "I don't know how, but yes. The Word—" His throat suddenly felt tight. They were saved, the people whom he had sworn to protect. Lore closed his eyes and felt relief finally pour through his heart. *Thank You, Word.*

"And our men?" Geoffrey asked. "Are they safe?"

Lore opened his eyes. "Let's find out." He directed his gaze toward the men nearby. "Bring more torches. We need to find out what happened out there before the rain starts." As if in warning, the sky grumbled above them again.

"Yes, Captain," several voices shouted at once.

Minutes later, Lore and a handful of guards stood before the gates. In one hand, he held his sword, in the other he held a torch. Lore looked up. "Open the gates," he shouted.

The gates began to slowly creak open. Lore felt adrenaline flood his body. What would they find on the other side? He gripped his sword tighter.

More raindrops fell. They sizzled on the hot tip of his torch. The gates widened further. Lore took a deep breath. This was it. He let out his breath and stepped between the wooden barriers.

The entire city lay in darkness, save for the small orange flames emanating from Lore's and the other men's torches. He held out the burning brand and ventured away from the gate. He squinted into the darkness, relying on his sense of hearing to alert him to any movement.

Moments later he was able to discern a body, lying face-downward on the cobblestone street.

Lore knelt and felt along the man's neck. A heart beat faintly beneath the skin. Pulling his hand back, Lore moved his torch along the man's body, searching for any injury. Nothing.

Out of the corner of his eye, he saw his men, armed with torches, moving along the street. No one said anything. No one *needed* to say anything—the silence itself was deafening.

Lore stood, his mind whirring. What should they do with the men they found? He quickly counted the torches making their way along the street. There were not nearly enough guards to carry back to the castle every northern soldier they found. Not to mention—

Someone moaned nearby.

Lore swung his torch around and spotted a Temanin soldier lying a couple of feet away, dressed in black and red. He moved cautiously toward the Temanin and knelt down.

A bloody face looked up into his. "The light," the Temanin whispered. He shuddered and held a hand to his face. "The light . . ."

The muscles along Lore's neck and shoulders stiffened. Ten minutes ago, he would've killed this man and not thought anything of it. What now? Lore placed a hand on the Temanin's shoulder. This soldier was the enemy . . . and yet he was still a man.

"Captain," Geoffrey said nearby. Lore glanced over his shoulder. "We're finding both Temanin and northerners soldiers scattered across the streets." Geoffrey knelt down near Lore, his torch lighting up his tired face. "What should we do?"

Lore looked back around. The Temanin whose shoulder his hand lay upon had crouched into a trembling ball.

Geoffrey watched the quivering Temanin soldier. "Captain, what happened to these men?"

What indeed? Suddenly Lore stared at the Temanin, his mind dredging up a memory of another man crouched down, clutching his face, and shouting about light . . .

The man Lore had found in Rowen's room way back at the Mostyn inn. Lore's mouth went dry. Rowen, a Truthsayer. Rowen, a Daughter of Light—

Lightning flashed above him, followed moments later by a deafening boom.

"Geoffrey," Lore turned to look at the guard, his heart pounding now, "I need you to run back to the castle, to the infirmary, and have Balint check on Rowen. She should be there."

"Rowen?" Geoffrey's eyebrows drew together in confusion. "What does she have to do with—"

"No time to explain. *I need you to do it now.*"

"Yes, Captain." Geoffrey stood and darted back toward the castle gates.

The Temanin soldier continued to shiver beneath Lore's hand.

Had Rowen done this? But how?

The Word.

Glancing west where he had seen the surging beam of light, Lore felt an invisible fist punch his midsection. If that light had truly come from Rowen, then she was somewhere out there in Anwin Forest. Everything inside him exploded, demanding he rise to his feet and race to the forest and find her. Had the Temanins caught her? Was she all right? But most importantly, *where was she now?*

Another jagged flash of light ripped across the sky. This time the bolt tore open the dark clouds that for an hour had hung heavily across the White City. A loud boom filled his ears. Torrential rain came pouring down and snuffed out his torch in an instant.

Lore found himself in complete darkness with the rain pelting across his head and back. He dropped his torch and held out his hand, feeling in the darkness. He could feel the uneven ridges of the cobblestone beneath his boots.

He could do nothing now, he realized. Not without light. His only option was to find his way to the castle and regroup with his men. Then, using covered lanterns, they would scour the city.

The fierce staccato of rain drowned out all noise. He could not see his guards, nor could he hear them. He hoped his men found their way back to the castle through the storm. The darkness and rain made it hard to see or do anything.

Lore held out his hands and felt his way in the dark. Fear and impatience began to twist inside his chest. He hated feeling helpless, hated being delayed by the rain when the men scattered around him needed him, hated knowing Rowen could be out there, in this storm, and potentially in danger—

Wait. The word flowed like cool water across his mind. *Wait and trust.*

Lore's heart slowly returned to its normal beat. He knew that prodding. He let out a sigh. He had no choice: He would have to wait.

His hand bumped up against rough, wet stone. Lore felt along its surface and realized it was the inner wall that surrounded the castle. Moving more quickly now, he felt his way toward the gates. His clothing clung to his body, and his hair hung across his face in long wet strands. The rain continued to pound down on him, intent on crushing him to the ground.

A minute later, his hand left the wall. Careful to keep his right hand on the stone, Lore leaned to his left. Orange torchlight flickered in the distance. It was the castle. He left the wall and hurried toward the lights ahead.

Impatience began to build inside him again, but this time Lore held it in check. He could do nothing more now, no matter how much he desired otherwise. He had to find lanterns and wait for the others. But once he could leave, he would be the first one out. He would find his men.

And he would find Rowen.

CHAPTER
28

Bright light filled Rowen's eyes.

She opened them with a groan. Clear blue sky shone overhead. Birds twittered to her right and somewhere behind her she could hear the roar of water. Twisting her head, she found herself lying in long green grass.

As her mind awakened more, she realized her entire body was damp. A cool breeze brushed along her body. Her skin prickled at the sensation, and she shivered. Rowen sat up and rubbed her arms.

Grass and white flowers waved in the sweet mountain air. The tall dark trees of Anwin Forest stood a hundred feet away. Twisting her neck, she saw the ivy-covered ruins. Mist drifted from the waterfalls to the right. A hint of a rainbow shimmered in the spray. She was in the same meadow. Rowen looked to her left.

The man from last night was gone.

For one heartbeat she wondered if it had all been a dream, a strange dark dream. She stood and looked down around her. Nearby, the grass lay crushed.

No, no dream. She could see where the man had fallen. So where was he now? Rowen glanced around again, but she could neither see nor hear anything other than the waterfalls and a bird singing.

She felt exposed here, out in the open. A Temanin could find her here at any moment. She needed to get back to the tunnel. Rowen took a step toward the tree line and found she could barely move. Her strength felt sapped, and her body ached. She wrapped her arms tighter across her middle and slowly continued. She couldn't stay here, not when the enemy could be around.

Events from last night began to trickle back to her awareness. Touching the man with the dark eyes, seeing—

Her stomach roiled as her mind replayed the darkness she had seen. Lust, lies, greed . . . murder. So much murder. Rowen let go of her arms and wiped her hands. She could still feel the blood he carried. Such an evil, dark man.

But also a lonely and fearful man. A man who wanted peace, forgiveness. Healing. She knew. She had seen it in his eyes when he had reached out to her with his bloody hand.

Rowen shook her head, ashamed of her disgust. On the inside, that man was no different than she was before she had met the Word. Darkness filled all hearts. And every heart needed the touch of the Word. Even one so evil as him.

A soft breeze brushed her face. Rowen watched the small white flowers at her feet bow to the wind. She remembered power flowing through her. At first, it had been her truthsaying power reaching inside the man, tearing away the lies he had wrapped himself in. But from the moment the Word had appeared and moved toward the man, she had become merely a conduit of the Word's power.

Rowen closed her eyes. She had been able to hold on only briefly before sinking into oblivion. But from those few heady moments, she understood why He, and no one else, was the Word. She might be an Eldaran, with a power unlike any other mortal, but she was nothing, *nothing* compared to the Word.

When her power had moved in her, it had felt like a raging river being channeled through her palm. Powerful and wild and heady. As if with a twist of her wrist, she could've done anything to that man. But the Word's power had felt like liquid metal flowing through her body, evaporating her own power until only steam remained.

Yet even within that searing power she had felt the cool, soothing touch of love and peace. For one brief moment Rowen had watched as the One and All had humbled Himself to touch, to heal, to take on the darkness of that evil man.

Rowen opened her eyes and felt a single tear run down her cheek. She still didn't understand why the Word would heal that man—or herself, for that matter. Such darkness did not belong with such light. But the Word had chosen to heal them anyway. And Rowen knew she had a long way to learn to love like that.

Sudden movement amongst the trees tore her mind away from her thoughts. A man stepped out from the trees.

Rowen clutched her chest, paralyzed. The Temanins had found her. She took a step back, ready to run. Then she hesitated. The man, he looked . . . familiar.

Lore?

Her breath came out in one long rush. Lore looked up and saw her. He began to run across the field toward her. Her heart twisted strangely. Rowen hesitated, then took a step forward—

Her legs buckled beneath her. Rowen gasped and threw out her hands. Down she went, knees and palms hitting grass and hard earth. Waves of fatigue washed over her. Trembling, she tried to get back up.

Boots flashed in front of her eyes and strong hands gripped her forearms. Lore lifted her to her feet. "Rowen, are you all right?" His eyes roved across her face, his eyebrows drawn together in concern.

"Captain," Rowen said, overwhelmed by the intense look in his dark grey eyes. She couldn't think. The adrenaline rush was morphing into shock.

"What happened to you? Do you need to sit?" He readjusted his hold on her.

Rowen looked up and opened her mouth to speak. No words came. It felt as though everything had been drained from her. Perhaps everything had. She could hardly stand now. If it weren't for Lore holding her up, she would be lying on the grass.

Lore's frown deepened. He spoke, but his voice faded away.

Heat began to swirl again inside her chest. Her eyes widened at the feeling. Panicked, Rowen looked down, expecting to see her hand glowing again. But the heat, instead of flowing down her arm toward her hand, seemed to radiate out from her, as though her power were reaching outside her body, feeling those around her . . .

Suddenly she could feel Lore's deep concern for her . . . and his relief at finding her. And something else, like a blazing fire inside of him—

Rowen gasped. Had she just used her truthsaying power on Lore . . . without touching him?

A cool hand touched her forehead. Immediately, the heat inside her dissolved. "We need to get you back to the castle." Lore removed his hand. "You're warm and pale . . . and wet," he finished, his eyes taking in the rest of her physique.

Rowen glanced down, seeing herself for the first time. Her blood-splattered uniform clung to her shivering body. "I-" she stuttered, still shaken over the fact that her power had somehow been triggered without her mark. Had her experience from last night somehow amplified her ability? Rowen shuddered at the thought.

"Here." Lore tugged at the clasp around his neck and pulled the dark cloak off of his shoulders.

"How did you find me?" Rowen watched his face as he placed his cloak over her.

"I saw the light last night," Lore said in a strange tone. He clasped the brooch shut.

"Light?" Rowen gripped the cloak close to her body. Lore took a step back. The cloak smelled like rain and leather. Like Lore, she realized. Before Lore could answer, another man emerged from the forest. Blond hair pulled back. Black tattoos across his right cheek.

"Captain!" Aren shouted. Then, "*Rowen?*"

Rowen watched Aren dash across the tall grass.

"Aren!" Lore yelled back.

"Captain." Aren came panting to Lore's side. "I can't believe it! You found her—" he turned to look at Rowen. "But how? Where have you been, Rowen? We've been so worried—"

"There will be time for questions later," Lore said. "I need you to go back to the castle and tell Balint I found Rowen."

"Balint?" Aren said in surprise.

"Yes."

Aren hesitated, a frown on his face. "Yes, Captain. But what about Lady Astrea? She will want to know that Rowen has been found."

"I will tell her myself after I get Rowen back to the Healers Quarter."

Aren nodded. "Yes, Captain." He gave Rowen one more look before turning and heading back toward the forest.

Rowen watched Aren disappear into the trees. "I don't understand." She turned back to Lore. "How are you and Aren getting in and out of the city? I had to come through the tunnel."

"The Temanin Army is gone. Or at least, most of it."

"Gone?" Rowen stared at Lore, speechless. "But-but how?"

"We'll talk about it on the way back. Do you think you can walk?"

Rowen brought enough of her mind back to assess her body. She could stand—but walk? "I don't think so."

Lore moved to her side and held out his arm.

Rowen took it. Her legs trembled. Lore slowly led her across the meadow. The Temanin Army . . . gone? Impossible! But then, how were Lore and Aren here? And Lore wouldn't lie . . .

"A lot happened last night," Lore said. He grew quiet, as if thinking of what to say. "I'm not sure how much you remember of yesterday." He turned and looked at her.

"Not much," Rowen replied. Her mind felt hazy. "I remember . . ." She stopped. She remembered boulders flying. She remembered Donar, and trying to heal him. Rowen swallowed and looked down. She wasn't ready to talk about that yet.

Lore nodded as if understanding. They began to walk again. "The bombardment never stopped yesterday," he said in a quiet voice. "I had a servant take you to the Healers Quarter, and I made sure Lady Astrea was safe. Don't worry, she is," he said when Rowen looked at him.

"Afterward, I headed to the outer walls. I did everything I could think of to keep our city safe. We fought all day and into the night. But nothing we did seemed to stop the tide of the Temanin Army. They outnumbered us. For every Temanin soldier we shot down, three more took his place. Their catapults pounded our walls and gates. But we held on. And when evening came, I thought we might actually live to see the next day. Then the Temanins brought out their greatest weapon. A catapult like none I have ever seen." Lore paused. "It took out most of the main gate with one hit."

"No!" Rowen looked up at Lore.

His eyes were now seeing another time. "I knew the end had come. I called for a retreat. We raced to the second gates. The city burned behind us. Temanin soldiers were storming through the city. And then . . ." Lore's voice hitched.

Rowen felt her stomach clench.

"Then I ordered the castle gates shut." Rowen turned and stared at Lore's face. His lips were now pressed in a grim line. She saw the agony written across his features. "I had to shut the gates on our own soldiers to protect those inside the castle."

Her throat tightened. To condemn your own men . . . "But what happened?" Rowen shuddered inwardly at the scene Lore painted. "How is it you're here?" *And not a prisoner,* she thought. *Or dead.*

"The Word," Lore said quietly. "The Word saved us."

Rowen scrunched up her face. "How?" The word fell from her lips.

"All hope had left me, Rowen," Lore said. They reached the trees and stopped. He turned to look at her. "I did not believe we would live to see morning. I could hear the battle raging on the other side of the gates. And I stood there, knowing I had shut the gates on our own men.

"I fell to my knees and cried out to the Word. But deep in my heart, I did not believe we would be saved." He gave her a small laugh. "I forgot that the Word could do *anything.* And He did. As I knelt there beside the gate, yelling at the sky, suddenly this pillar of light shot out of Anwin."

"Light?" Rowen remembered Lore had said something about that earlier. Something about how that was how he had found her . . .

"It soared toward the sky, lighting up the entire area. All the fighting stopped. Everyone stared at the light. Then the surge of light . . ." Lore seemed to search for a word . . . "collapsed. The light flowed through the trees, tossing men like a flood as it swept across

Anwin Forest and into the city. Men screamed like I'd never heard before."

Light. Anwin Forest. Men screaming. Rowen had heard men scream before, when she had used her mark on them . . .

Suddenly Rowen felt lightheaded. She could barely breathe, barely believe what her mind was now telling her. It all made sense. And yet the truth of it terrified her. That pillar of light Lore spoke of . . . It had come from . . .

Her.

"It was me," Rowen whispered, scarcely realizing that Lore had stopped talking. "The light came from me."

He turned to face her directly. "I know."

Rowen looked up in surprise. "You know?"

"After the light disappeared, a handful of guards and I went out into the city. I spoke to one of the Temanin soldiers, and all he could say was 'The light.' I remembered that night in Mostyn when I found that man in your room—you remember?"

Rowen nodded slowly. She did not like to think about that night.

"He had said the same thing. 'The light!' Then, when I discovered you were gone from the Healers Quarter, I knew it was you—that some way, somehow, your truthsaying power had caused that light. And that light terrified everyone it touched. I believe it caused each person to see the darkness inside themselves, incapacitating those we found outside the walls."

Rowen remembered what the Word had told her last night: *You must hurry. Your entire city is at stake . . .* She had gone to that meadow thinking she would be touching only that evil man. But the Word had used the power inside her to do far more. He had saved the White City . . . through her.

Rowen felt horrified and awed at the same moment. What was this thing inside her that could do such things? She began to shake again. What other things could she do? And should anyone have such power?

Trust me.

The words drifted softly inside her mind.

Trust Me, Daughter of Light. You have been gifted to help those who cannot help themselves. And under My guidance, you have nothing to fear. But the road will not be easy . . .

The vision she had seen of her life as a dark road came back to her: a long dark road that led toward light. To trust the Word would be to have His hand in hers, a companion along that dark path. To not trust would be loneliness and fear. And to possibly fall away from that path into total darkness.

Rowen shivered at the thought. *Oh, Word, I will trust you,* she cried inside her mind, mentally reaching for Him . . .

Peace rushed over her. She would hold the Word's hand and walk the path wherever it took her. And let *Him* use her gift as He saw fit.

"Rowen, are you all right?"

Lore held her arm and looked at her with concern. "Did what I say scare you?"

"Yes and no," Rowen said. She could still feel the Word's peace washing over her. "I cannot change who I am, *what* I am. But I can place my power in the Word's hands, to do as He likes." She took a deep breath. "I must choose to trust Him."

The corners of Lore's mouth moved upward, and his face relaxed. He gave her arm a squeeze. "I will not say I understand what it must be like to be an Eldaran," he said. They began to walk through the trees again. "But I do know what it means to trust the Word. And *that* is not easy."

No, Rowen thought, it is not. But it was a choice she would be making for the rest of her life.

CHAPTER 29

Valin tugged at his black glove. He could still hear the prisoners' whispers: *Shadonae*. And feel the fear the word invoked.

He remembered the first time he had been called that, back when he'd first chosen this path. He had been young then. Young, naïve. He'd still thought of the world in black and white. But now he knew better. He knew the power inside of him was his, to do with as *he* wanted. And what he wanted was . . . the world.

Valin placed his hand on the ledge of the balcony. The city of Thyra spread out before him like a rich banquet. Hills were topped with beautiful white buildings and carefully chiseled columns. Winding streets made their way through the city, lined with oak trees, their full green branches covering the city in a ceiling of green. The sea sparkled beyond the walls as the sun set. The city of knowledge and wisdom.

And it was all his.

Valin turned away from the ledge and walked back inside the Senate Hall. Bright white walls surrounded the round, domed hall. Windows were strategically placed around the room so that every part of Thyra could be viewed from the circle of high-back chairs that sat around the inner perimeter, an area marked off by dark tiles on the floor. Once upon a time, the finest intellects of Thyra had sat upon those chairs. Now the room lay empty, save for Malchus and himself.

As if sensing his thoughts, Malchus glanced up from his perch near one of the windows. His pale hair hung around a beautifully chiseled face. His eyes, though, looked haunted. Valin knew Malchus had split the curtain again to bring more shadows over.

The pull always left him drained and spooked. Sometimes Valin wondered what Malchus saw on the other side.

Valin looked out one of the windows. He inspected his reflection in the glass and brushed back his dark hair. At least his own power never left any signs on his face.

His eyes slowly drifted away from the glass to the pictures hanging between the windows. Each one depicted a man or woman exquisitely dressed and painted in both bright and somber colors. Thick, ornately carved golden frames surrounded each picture. These were famous senators dating back hundreds of years into Thyra's past, hung here in the Senate Hall as a memorial.

As Valin studied each picture, he couldn't help but laugh at how easily mankind could be seduced. These men and women had no idea how their greed, their selfishness and jealousies, their darkest fears, had given him power over them. Even if they realized that and desired to escape, they could not. No human could escape the darkness within.

Out of the corner of his eye, Valin saw the far doors open. He dropped his hand and turned.

Two soldiers walked in with a man held between them.

Valin started. He knew that man. Regessus. Out of the corner of his eye he saw Malchus stand, a hungry look on his beautiful face. "Where did you find this man?" Valin asked, crossing the room.

The soldiers turned their heads as one his direction. "Outside Cragsmoor," the first soldier replied. His eyes never moved, never blinked, as he answered.

Valin stopped a few feet away and stroked his chin. "I wonder why he returned," he murmured. He studied the man before him. Cuts and bruises covered Regessus's gaunt face.

Regessus's eyes began to flutter. "Wha-what?" he muttered. His head slowly came up. He blinked and shook his head. "Where am I?"

Valin did not answer. He continued to stare at the man. Meanwhile, Malchus moved in like a ravaged wolf for the kill.

Regessus looked up at Valin. His features hardened immediately.

"You!" he cried and strained against the soldiers on either side of him. "*You!*"

Malchus came to a stop beside Valin. Out of the corner of his eye, Valin saw Malchus begin to tug at his black glove. Regessus saw it too and renewed his fight with grunts and shouts.

Valin held his hand out in front of Malchus. "No, wait. He might be more useful alive."

Regessus stopped. He stared at Valin with a look of loathing. "Never! I will never become one of your twisted servants."

Malchus leaned toward Valin. "I need him," Malchus said under his breath. "This last pull took a lot out of me. We don't want the shadows to see me weak."

"I know," Valin replied, his eyes back on Regessus. "We'll find you someone else. But this man is important."

"How?" Malchus looked back at the man with a frown. "I do not recognize him."

"He is Regessus Vondran."

Malchus lifted one perfect eyebrow. "That name means nothing to me."

"The one senator who escaped."

Malchus hissed between his teeth.

Valin went back to stroking his chin. "My question, though, is why did he return?" Regessus stopped struggling and looked up. "You heard me. Why did you return here? You escaped. Why didn't you run off to some other country? Of course, we would have caught up to you sooner or later."

Regessus tightened his lips and said nothing.

"Who cares why he came back?" Malchus said with an edge to his tone. "Just let me have him."

Valin studied the tall, gaunt senator. "You know I will eventually find out. Even now, my people are looking for your hiding places."

"We can tell those who have been twisted," Regessus said with a sneer.

Laughter bubbled up inside Valin's throat, bursting out in a low, hearty guffaw. He smiled one long smile, enjoying the look of confusion that spread across Regessus's face. "You don't really think everyone who works for me is twisted, do you?"

Confusion turned into a frown.

Valin had him. "My dear senator, you should know that people can be bought with promises. And there were those here in Thyra who were willing to pay for mine."

Regessus's face turned to stone. He stared up at Valin.

"But you are a man of principle." Valin began to walk around Regessus and the two soldiers. "The only one I found, I might add. So you leave me two choices: let Malchus here have your life . . ."

The senator's face paled.

" . . . or let me twist you."

Valin came to a stop in front of Regessus.

Malchus came up beside him. "You're like a cat with a mouse," Malchus whispered. "Just let me have him, and be done with it."

"No." Valin eyed Regessus. "He wants that. He wants to die." A smile crept back across his face. "He is afraid to be twisted."

"Twisting him won't get you any information."

"I know."

"Then why not let me have him?"

Valin began to pull at his glove. "Simple. Demoralization. And fear."

"That is not enough of a reason, Valin. Stop playing around, and let me have the man. The senator is more useful to me." Malchus finished pulling off his glove.

Valin stepped in front of Malchus and extended his hand toward the senator.

Regessus pulled back from the two soldiers holding him, his eyes growing white as he watched Valin's outstretched hand draw near.

Valin could feel rage and fear emanate from Regessus. He breathed it in as if it were a fragrance. Closer, closer . . .

From far away inside his mind came an unfamiliar blast of wind, heat, and light. Valin stopped. His vision faded from the room.

The torrent around him grew until Valin felt like a lone tree against a storm of light. Somehow his hands found their way to his face. He covered his eyes, but still he saw the red glow behind his eyelids. Then the light faded. The redness grew faint. Slowly, Valin pulled his hands away. He found himself back in the Senate Hall.

"Did you feel that?" Malchus said in a hoarse whisper.

Valin looked back at Malchus. His face looked even paler than usual. "Yes."

"It's not possible. They're all dead."

"Not all of them," Valin said, shaken by the vision. "Mercia escaped."

"You let her go!" Malchus glared at Valin. "I told you to not let your emotions interfere. And now all that we have accomplished might be undone because of you."

Valin shook his head. "No, the wolves would have found her and killed her, eventually. Besides, it doesn't matter. Mercia never had the gift."

"So we thought. But what else can explain that light? Perhaps she *did* survive—"

"Enough!" Valin turned away. Malchus was starting to get on his nerves. His eyes wandered back to Regessus. "Take him away," Valin said with a fling of his hand.

"Wait, you're letting me go?" Regessus said, shocked.

The two soldiers lifted him to his feet.

"No, I'm simply delaying for now."

Regessus began to shout in protest.

Valin turned toward one of the soldiers. "Take him to Cragsmoor and lock him up."

The two men nodded. They dragged Regessus from the room, his long legs sliding along the tiled floor. Valin watched.

Malchus moved past him and closed the door. The shouts and screams muffled instantly. "I know what you're thinking," Malchus said.

"I don't want to talk about it."

"It's not her. Can't be. Only a powerful Eldaran could have done that. So even if she did survive, Mercia did not have the gift."

"Neither did Anwar. Or any of the others. No one did." Valin folded his arms across his chest and stared down at the tiled floor. He let out his breath. "But that raises the question: Then who just shook us? Who else was left?"

Malchus shook his head. "I don't know. But whoever it was is far away. The shaking barely reached us."

"True. But reach us it did." Valin lifted his head. "Should this Eldaran ever come to us, he or she could jeopardize our plans." He looked over at Malchus. "Alert your shadows, especially the one down south. Tell them to watch and listen. Impress upon them all the danger of this person and to let us know the moment they hear anything."

"It will be done. But I must say something," Malchus looked at Valin, his eyes turning an icy blue. "If it *is* Mercia—if somehow she survived all these years and the wolves never found her—you cannot let her live this time. She must die."

Valin turned and stared at the door Regessus had been dragged through minutes before.

"I know."

CHAPTER
30

Awaken, Son of Truth.

The words bounced around inside his mind. Caleb slowly drifted toward consciousness. *Son of Truth . . . Son of Truth . . .*

"Ugh." Caleb blinked a couple times. Cold, hard ground pressed against the side of his face. Slowly he lifted his head and looked around.

Darkness. Nothing but darkness. Except for a beam of light that seemed to shine right above him.

Caleb looked around again. It was a strange darkness—not the type found on a moonless night or deep inside a cave. It felt cold . . . and empty. He shivered and pushed himself up off the ground. A jolt of shock raced across his body. He looked down.

And found he had nothing on.

Caleb stood up. "What in all the Lands?" he cried. He looked around for his clothing. Nothing. Not even a bit of silk. "Where in all the sands—"

Suddenly everything came rushing back: the woman with the glowing hand, the blinding light, the truth . . . A sick feeling rose up inside of him. He lifted his hands and rubbed his chilled arms. She had seen it all, that woman with the glowing hand. Everything he had ever done. Every lie, every defilement, every act of greed, every murder—

Caleb stopped and held out his hands in horror. Bright red liquid covered his palms and fingers. The smell of blood filled his nostrils, making his stomach turn. Sickened, he realized the red film was blood.

Caleb flung his hands out as far away as he could from his body.

Turning this way and that, he looked around for anything to wipe his hands on.

Nothing but darkness surrounded him, except for that beam of light shining from above . . .

Caleb glanced up, but looked away immediately. The light was too bright to see its source.

He caught sight of his hands again. He fell to the ground and began to wipe his hands against the hard black surface. Back and forth, around and around. But the blood would not come off.

Desperate now, he sat back on his knees and began to wipe his hands on his thighs, sickened at the thought of blood still on him, but better on his legs than on his hands. Anything to get the blood off his hands . . .

Caleb wiped vigorously for a minute and then raised his hands. The blood remained. He rubbed them against his thighs until both his hands and legs hurt. But the blood remained. He stared at his hands and began to shake. Why could he not clean his hands?

He stopped. Cocking his head toward his right, he thought he heard . . . water. But how? Looking out toward the darkness, he realized he could now see the faint silhouette of trees. Could there be a stream nearby? Sweet relief poured through his soul. He could wash away the blood. Caleb shot to his feet and listened a moment longer, then took off toward the sound.

The light overhead seemed to expand, flashing above him as he moved in and out of shadows cast by unseen branches above. He kept his face forward and moved steadily through the dark trees. The sound of water was his only guide. Moments later, he found the source.

A small stream wove its way through the trees, rushing over black rocks. Caleb fell to his knees and sank his hands into the cold, clear water. He waited for the blood to rinse off his hands, to float away in the trickling waters.

But nothing happened.

He shook his hands beneath the water, then rubbed them together. Nothing, not even a slight change in the water's color. Fear rose in his throat. What was happening to him? Why wouldn't the blood wash away?

A shadow fell across the clear water. Caleb looked up—

A man covered in scars looked back. Long, jagged wounds marred the man's face, distorting his cheeks and brow. White smaller scars were scattered across the rest of his face. Further down, two ugly red lines ran down his neck until they disappeared into his white gown.

Caleb staggered back. Was this another one of his nightmares? But he didn't recognize the man. His eyes darted to the scarred man's hands, but he saw no dagger. Caleb looked back at his face. Yes, he would definitely have remembered this repulsively wounded man.

However, he wasn't going to stick around and find out if the scarred man wanted to murder him. Caleb went to turn around, but some unseen force held his face. He could not twist his head.

The man raised his hand and looked at Caleb with dark, fathomless eyes.

"It is time, Son of Truth. The Lands need a Guardian once again."

ABOUT THE AUTHOR

Morgan L. Busse is a writer by day and a mother by night. She is the author of the Follower of the Word series and the award-winning steampunk series, The Soul Chronicles. Her debut novel, *Daughter of Light*, was a Christy and Carol Award finalist. During her spare time she enjoys playing games, taking long walks, and dreaming about her next novel.

Find out more about Morgan and sign up for her newsletter at: *www.morganlbusse.com*.

Facebook: *facebook.com/MorganLBusseAuthor*
Twitter: *twitter.com/MorganLBusse*

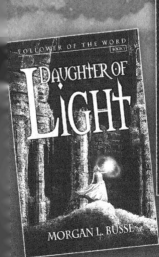